I WAS STARING INTO THE FACE OF THE LAST PERSON ON EARTH I WANTED TO SEE.

"I have a gun in my pocket," the killer informed me in a low, even voice. "And I want you to stand here quietly; don't even move a muscle. If you do exactly what I tell you, you'll be fine."

Yeah right! I am in a whole lot of trouble, I thought, even as I dutifully obeyed the instructions. The perp was right beside me now, jamming something into my ribs. I didn't have to look down to know the gun was no longer in anybody's pocket. My own thirty-two, of course, was exactly where it would do me no good at all. In my bedroom, at the bottom of a drawer....

MURDER CAN RUIN YOUR LOOKS

by

Selma Eichler

A SIGNET BOOK

SIGNET
Published by the Penguin Group
Penguin Books USA Inc., 375 Hudson Street,
New York, New York 10014, U.S.A.
Penguin Books Ltd, 27 Wrights Lane,
London W8 5TZ, England
Penguin Books Australia Ltd, Ringwood,
Victoria, Australia
Penguin Books Canada Ltd, 10 Alcorn Avenue,
Toronto, Ontario, Canada M4V 3B2
Penguin Books (N.Z.) Ltd, 182–190 Wairau Road,
Auckland 10, New Zealand

Penguin Books Ltd, Registered Offices:
Harmondsworth, Middlesex, England

First published by Signet, an imprint of Dutton Signet,
a division of Penguin Books USA Inc.

First Printing, April, 1995
10 9 8 7 6 5 4 3

 REGISTERED TRADEMARK—MARCA REGISTRADA

Printed in the United States of America

PUBLISHER'S NOTE
This is a work of fiction. Names, characters, places, and incidents either are the
product of the author's imagination or are used fictitiously, and any resemblance
to actual persons, living or dead, events, or locales is entirely coincidental.

BOOKS ARE AVAILABLE AT QUANTITY DISCOUNTS WHEN USED TO PROMOTE PROD-
UCTS OR SERVICES. FOR INFORMATION PLEASE WRITE TO PREMIUM MARKETING DIVI-
SION, PENGUIN BOOKS USA INC., 375 HUDSON STREET, NEW YORK, NEW YORK 10014.

For Lloyd Eichler,
known to his friends and relatives
(of which I am both) as Puck—

my husband, sounding board, dictionary,
thesaurus, ground-floor-level editor,
and constant source of ideas,
encouragement, and love.

ACKNOWLEDGMENTS

My special thanks to David Gruber of Lehman, Lehman & Gruber, who supplied the legal information so necessary to the development of the story line for this book. He showed remarkable patience in providing pertinent sets of laws and regulations every time (and there were quite a few of them) I had a change of heart—and plot.

Invaluable assistance in the medical area came from Martin Turkish, M.D., who answered the thousand and one questions I put to him on death, comas, and other cheerful matters. Extremely helpful, too, were Michael W. Grzelak, D.M.D., who traced the course of my bullets for me; Dr. Joseph O'Connell of Personal Diagnostics, who presented the facts and cleared up my misconceptions on AIDS; and June Smith, Assistant Director of Emergency Services at St. Vincent's Hospital, who spared the time to educate me on hospital procedure.

I am also grateful to my agent, Luna Carne-Ross, for guiding and prodding me throughout the process and whose critiques were always on target (well, 99% of the time, anyway)—even when they weren't what I wanted to hear. My thanks, too, to my editor, Danielle Perez, for pointing the way for me to correct my mistakes, clarify my ambiguities, and hone and polish what was left.

And I can't overlook my friends Rudy Valentini, who helped me shop for my Mac, and Joe Todaro, who taught me how to use it. Without their kind services, I'd probably still be in the manuscript stage. And then there's Julian Scott, who so willingly pitched in to assist me in my fact finding.

Finally, there are two other very dear friends who contributed to this book who are no longer here: Bea Langerman, ACSW, who—whenever I asked a question outside her field of expertise—always said, "I don't know, but I'll find out and get back to you soon." And no matter how busy she was, Bea always did. And Joan Seidman, who served as a prototype for Desiree and whose wit, humor, and warm-heartedness I attempted to impart to my heroine. Without Bea and Joan, it's quite possible there wouldn't have been any Desiree or any book, for that matter. I miss them both.

No more grisly murders. No more desperate killers. No more life-threatening encounters. I'd had a taste of the heavy stuff, thank you. And I'd made myself a promise: There was no way I'd take on any case likely to cause me any injury more serious than a paper cut. Not ever again. . . .

Up until a year and a half ago, being a private investigator was—for me, anyway—a really benign way to earn a living. I always managed to pay the rent and some pretty sizable food bills, thanks to a small but fairly steady share of New York's unfaithful wives, philandering husbands, and phony insurance claims—along with some missing animals here and there.

Okay. Maybe they weren't the kind of cases you could really sink your teeth into. But they weren't the kind of cases that were likely to land you in the morgue, either.

Then my niece Ellen got me involved in this double homicide that almost evolved into a triple—with my own amply proportioned five-foot-two inch frame coming *that close* to occupying a third slab in the city morgue. (And I'd prefer that slab to revealing how really ample these proportions of mine are.) Anyway, while I eventually solved the murders, even now I get crazy just thinking about that whole fiasco. Which is why I swore off the kind of cases that could in any way endanger either my physical or mental well-being.

And while I admit that my one and only murder case turned me into a coward, the truth is, I hadn't been all that brave to begin with.

Chapter 1

I suppose I have a nurturing thing when it comes to men. It's the only way I can explain being totally unsusceptible to the good-looking ones and having this penchant, instead, for the little skinny guys. You know, the ones who look truly *needy*. I guess my maternal bent stems, at least in part, from the fact that Ed and I never had any children— Ed being my late husband, Ed Shapiro, who was also a P.I. Anyway, when it came to the man who walked into my office that Wednesday afternoon, I was prepared to make an exception.

He was over six feet tall and well built, with dark hair, light eyes, and the most beautiful cleft chin. He was, in fact, good-looking enough for me to consider losing thirty— maybe even forty—pounds for. But when he drew closer, I noticed, with just a tinge of relief, that the sacrifice would not be necessary after all. This guy was definitely not a candidate for romance. His eyes—I could see now they were blue—were red-rimmed and dead-looking, and there was a bleak expression on that handsome face. Besides, he was a couple of years younger than I am. (All right. More than a couple.)

"I'm sorry I didn't make an appointment," he apologized in the sort of hushed tone most people reserve for church or, at the very least, the public library.

"That's okay," I said, motioning for him to take the seat alongside my desk. "There's no line outside my door today."

"The thing is, I just found out about a half hour ago that you were a private detective here in New York, and I didn't want to waste any time in coming to see you."

"Do I *know* you?"

"You *did*. I'm Peter Winters."

It took a moment for that to register. "Peter Winters . . ." Came the dawn. "*Little Petey* Winters?"

My visitor managed something close to a smile. "Guilty."

"My God!" I could hardly believe it.

I jumped up and rushed over to him, and we hugged for a minute. "I wouldn't have recognized you in a million years," I said.

"I would never have recognized you, either. You're a redhead now." Then, apparently concerned that I might be offended by this reminder of the humble roots of my most striking attribute, he added hastily, "Looks good on you."

What a nice, sensitive person Petey'd become, I decided, as I self-consciously patted my gloriously hennaed hair. I hadn't always been so kindly disposed to him though. . . .

Little Petey Winters and I had grown up next door to each other in Ohio—with me, I confess, doing the growing up a long time before Petey did. Nevertheless, because his sister Maureen and I, born just three days apart, were practically joined at the hip since kindergarten, I saw a lot of him back then. Actually, a lot more than I wanted to.

I can't even count the number of days and nights I kept Maureen company when she had to baby-sit her little brother; it was really as if he were my little brother, too. I guess that's why I often resented him like hell just for *being*. (As you can gather, this nurturing nature of mine did not have its beginnings in the teen years.)

But, anyway, Petey abruptly stopped being much of a factor in my life at the beginning of my senior year in high school. Because that's when Maureen formed an even stronger attachment than the one she had to me. His name was Roy Lindstrom. And right after graduation, he and Maureen got married and moved to California.

At first there were letters and snapshots and, of course, an exchange of birthday and Christmas cards. But gradually it all stopped.

As for me, I went on to college and, from there, to New York—and a career, marriage, and eventual widowhood.

But right now, for a minute or two, I was in Ashtabula, Ohio, again with my very best friend.

I could picture with absolute clarity (although probably not complete accuracy) the long, straight brown hair; the tall, angular frame; and the tiny dimples hovering at the corners of those Kewpie doll lips. But what I remembered best about Maureen were her wide, deep-set blue eyes. They were the same color and shape as the blue eyes that were filled with so much anguish right now.

"How *is* Maureen?" I asked.

"She's doing okay. She moved back to Ashtabula about six years ago, you know. These days, she's got five kids—three of them still at home—and an ex she can't even find. But Maureen's a strong lady. She opened her own travel agency last fall, and it seems to be going pretty well. She's the one who suggested I get in touch with you."

"I didn't think she even knew my married name or that I was living in New York."

"She said an old friend from Ashtabula, Amy somebody-or-other, had heard where you were and what you were doing and that you were Desiree Shapiro now." He didn't smile when he said the name; didn't even look like he was *suppressing* a smile. So I knew that Petey Winters (I'd have to stop thinking of him as Petey) had a whole lot on his mind. That was verified a second or two later.

"I need your help, Desiree," he said, leaning toward me. "*Really* need it."

"What's wrong?"

"The woman I was engaged to marry may have been murdered."

"*May* have been?"

"Well, no one's sure if she's the one who's dead or the one who's in the hospital damned *near* dead. And I *have* to know." Then slowly, haltingly, he began to tell me this horrifying story.

It seems that two days earlier his fiancée and her twin sister had been shot in their Chelsea apartment. And now one was in the morgue, and the other lay in a coma in St. Catherine's Hospital. "And nobody can tell which is which," Peter said, his voice cracking. "Because whoever did this shot them in the face. Both of them."

"God! I'm so sorry," I murmured. I rummaged around in my suddenly vacant head for some comforting words and came up empty. So I just told the truth. "I wish I knew what to say to you," I admitted weakly.

"I know; it's okay."

"Do you have any idea who might have wanted to harm them?"

"None." It came out in a whisper.

"Let me put you in touch with an investigator who—"

"But I was hoping *you'd* take the case."

"I can't, Peter. I don't take murder cases."

His voice, no doubt bolstered by desperation, was suddenly stronger. "You don't understand. Finding out who committed this . . . this . . . finding out who *did* it is the last thing on my mind right now. All I'm interested in is whether Mary Ann is dead or alive."

"Why not wait just a little while? Let's hope the woman in the hospital regains consciousness soon."

"They—the doctors—have no idea when that will be. Or even *if* it will be. Please, Desiree."

I shuddered at the thought of getting embroiled in another murder investigation. But here was Peter, who was once almost like family to me and who was now in one of the most terrible situations I could imagine. I just couldn't bring myself to turn him down. (It also didn't hurt that those gorgeous blue eyes were looking at me so pleadingly.)

So, in the end, I agreed to handle the investigation. After first warning myself I'd have to keep some emotional distance from the proceedings and then stipulating to Peter that my sole purpose would be to establish the identities of the victims. "I won't take it any further than that," I said firmly.

"That's all I'm interested in," my new client assured me.

Chapter 2

It was a little after five, and I was full of questions—and very little else. (I'd had a really *tiny* lunch, and that was hours ago.) I took a good look at Peter. His cheeks were definitely hollow; there was no question about that. I was willing to bet he hadn't had a proper meal since the tragedy. Or at least what I'd consider proper. (Which has nothing whatever to do with a nutritionist's definition of the word. Or the dictionary's, either, for that matter.)

Very reluctantly, Peter agreed to join me for an early supper at this new deli which had just opened two blocks from my office and which I'd been promising myself to try.

Now, from the time my late Jewish New York husband introduced me to delicatessen food when we first started going out, I've been addicted to the stuff. In fact, after all these years, I consider myself to be something of an authority on the subject. So I was disappointed when, as soon as we sat down, Peter let me know that all he could manage was a little cup of mushroom and barley soup.

Could I allow him to deny himself this ambrosia?

It took work, but I finally coaxed him into following up the soup with a sandwich. We both ordered the pastrami—overstuffed portions and very tasty, but a little too fatty as far as I was concerned. Along with it, we had cole slaw, french fries, sour tomatoes, and a generous portion of kishka—good, but not nearly as good as the Second Avenue Deli's. All in all, though, the meal wasn't half bad, and when the waiter came to remove our plates, Peter's looked like it had just walked out of the dishwasher.

"I guess I was hungry, after all," he admitted sheepishly.

It was time to get down to business. And since the restaurant wasn't too crowded, it seemed as good a place as any. "Tell me about the twins," I said. And, over coffee and three or four refills, Peter obliged.

Mary Ann and Meredith Foster, he told me, had moved to this country from London about six months ago, soon after Meredith's husband died. "Meredith still uses her maiden name because she's an actress and her husband had this long Italian name," Peter explained. "It began with a *C*, I think. Or maybe it was an *R*."

They were only here a short while, he went on, when Mary Ann—his fiancée—opened a gift shop in the East Village. Meredith, meanwhile, began getting some work in little theater and off-Broadway productions. Most of them *way* off Broadway. But her future looked promising. In fact, in December she got a terrific break: She landed the second lead in a new off-Broadway comedy/drama that, according to Meredith, was with a really professional company. The play was in rehearsal now.

I asked Peter how he and Mary Ann had met.

"Through Meredith, actually. I don't know if I mentioned it, but I'm a casting director—I work for an advertising agency down in Soho. Anyway, one afternoon just a couple of weeks after she arrived in New York, Meredith came in to try out for this radio commercial we were casting. We needed a woman with a British accent, but the account guy decided Meredith's sounded phony." Peter shook his head in disgust. "Can you believe it?" he demanded of no one in particular. Then, to me: "I guess it's because she mentioned she was American by birth; her father relocated the family when he took this job with the London office of Merrill Lynch or maybe it was Smith Barney. Well, one of them. But that was when Meredith and Mary Ann were little kids, for God's sake! Meredith sounded as British as ... as the Queen!" He paused for a couple of seconds to give me a chance to let the idiocy of his co-worker sink in.

"Well, thanks to that pea-brain," he continued, "Meredith didn't get the part. But I wound up asking her out to dinner. I don't usually do that—date the talent, I mean. But there was something about her."

They went out a couple of other times after that first evening, Peter informed me, but, while he genuinely liked Meredith, it wasn't long before he concluded that the chemistry just wasn't there. Then she invited him to the opening of this new play she was in. By that time, he had pretty much made up his mind not to call her again. But she caught him off guard. And besides, he didn't want to hurt her feelings. So he went.

And that's how he met Mary Ann.

"I was just sitting there in the theater, waiting for the curtain to go up," Peter said softly, a little smile flitting across his lips for a moment as he played back the scene he'd stored in his memory. "All of a sudden the woman in front of me turned sideways, sort of in a three-quarter profile. I've gotta tell you, I was floored. She looked exactly— and I mean *exactly*—like the woman I was expecting to see onstage. Or at least I thought she did at the time. I really couldn't get over it."

"You didn't know Meredith had a twin sister?"

"All I knew was that Meredith had a sister and that they were very close; she mentioned it to me when we were out together. But she never said it was a *twin* sister."

"Anyway, during intermission, Mary Ann and I started talking. Mostly about how lousy the show was—it closed a couple of days later—and about how Meredith was making the most of what was a pretty small part. She—Mary Ann— was genuinely *agonizing* about her sister's being in such a turkey. I was impressed right away by what a compassionate person she was.

"Then, later, when the show was over, the three of us went out for something to eat. We couldn't have been in that restaurant for even an hour. But it was long enough for me to realize that Mary Ann had all the qualities that had initially attracted me to Meredith—plus so many more."

"Like?"

"Well, she was softer than Meredith—and don't ask me to explain what I mean by that; I can't."

"Less ambitious?" I suggested.

"I guess that's part of it, but only part of it," Peter replied. He thought for a moment. "I really can't put my finger on it," he finished lamely.

"I shouldn't have interrupted. Go on."

"Mary Ann laughed more, too," he said, his voice taking on a dreamy quality and his eyes seeming to focus on something far away. "And she was a terrific listener. And we found out we had a lot in common. We both love westerns and stand-up comedy and spy novels and country music. We both enjoy spending Sundays at museums. And we're both crazy about the beach. And neither of us can stand Madonna or Andrew Dice Clay. Silly things like that," he acknowledged, smiling shyly. "But that night we thought we'd made the greatest discovery in the world. You know, by the time we left the restaurant, I was convinced Mary Ann and Meredith didn't even *look* that much alike."

"That's love, I guess."

Peter actually broke into a broad grin. "Of course, they *did* look alike. Very *much* alike. But after a while it was easy to spot the differences, too. Mary Ann's features aren't as perfect as Meredith's; she even has this little bump on her nose. And their expressions aren't the same. Mary Ann looks *softer*. Uh-oh," he put in almost apologetically, "there goes that word again."

"The two of you got serious right away?"

"*Right* away. We knew immediately this was it. For both of us. The next day I called Mary Ann at her shop. I don't think Meredith minded; I'm sure she wasn't romantically interested in me, either. But whether it was an honorable thing for me to do or not didn't even cross my mind. And it wouldn't have mattered if it did. I was completely gone."

"How soon did you plan on being married?"

"Well, we hadn't set a date, but neither of us saw any point in waiting very long. We were officially engaged a few weeks ago, although I didn't get around to giving her a ring. Or, I guess I *should* say, Mary Ann didn't get around to picking one out. I kept after her to go shopping with me—I wanted her to choose something she really liked—but every time we made arrangements to meet at the jeweler's, she'd get busy in the shop or something and we had to cancel. I hoped she'd at least have the ring for her birthday on February first, but that came and went, too. And now some bastard's shot her; maybe even *killed* her." Peter covered his face with his hands then, and when he took them away a few seconds later, his eyes were moist. But he seemed in control. "Would you like to see the face that scum destroyed?" he asked evenly, reaching into his pants pocket and producing a worn brown leather wallet. Then he carefully removed a photograph from the wallet and placed it on the table in front of me.

I picked it up. It was a snapshot of Peter hand-in-hand with a tall, willowy blonde about twenty-five years old. She was wearing jeans and a T-shirt and a New York Yankees baseball cap. And, if the photograph was telling the truth, she was really extremely pretty.

"That was at the Central Park Zoo."

"She's lovely."

"You should see her now! She—the woman in the hospital, and I'm *praying* it's Mary Ann—had to have her jaw wired together. And her whole head is covered with bandages. She looks like some Egyptian mummy, for chrissakes!" Then Peter's voice became so low I had to strain to hear him. "That bastard! That . . ." He pressed his lips together and kept the rest of the thought to himself.

We sat quietly for a moment, and Peter's eyes began to fill up. Brushing a tear from the corner, he swallowed hard. "The thing is," he said wretchedly, "May Ann wasn't even supposed to be home that night. She was supposed to go out to dinner with a friend of hers, only the friend canceled at the last minute." He paused, and when he spoke again, it was to say just one word. "God," he whispered.

That "God" held more grief and pain and despair than I've ever heard packed into a single word before. In spite of my very sensible resolution about emotional involvement, I felt my own eyes beginning to well up, too.

Suddenly Peter broke the mood. "You might want to see this," he said in a normal tone as he extracted a second photograph from his wallet and handed it to me. "Mary Ann and Meredith."

I examined the head shot closely. The sisters *were* remarkably alike.

"Mary Ann's on the left," he informed me, anticipating my question.

"Do you know if the police have checked out the twins' dental records?" I asked, returning the photos to him. "That should tell us something."

Peter shook his head. "The detective in charge of the case, this Sergeant Fielding, asked me if I knew the name of their dentist, but I don't know if they even *saw* a dentist after they came to New York. In fact, I kind of doubt it. Mary Ann said one time that she really should get a checkup, and she wanted to know who I went to. I gave her his name, but she never brought it up again."

"Maybe she *did* go and just forgot to mention it," I offered hopefully.

"Uh-uh. I told the police about it, and they checked with

Dr. Fischel—that's my dentist. But he told Fielding she wasn't his patient. I guess she never got around to calling him."

"There's always their London dentist. Is there someone in the family who could give us *his* name?"

"I'm afraid not. Both parents were killed in an automobile accident a few years ago, so there's just the one brother. He's in town right now, in fact. On a business trip. We talked on the phone last night about this dentist thing—he said the police had asked him about it—but he has no idea who they went to over there."

"Are there any other relatives? An aunt, maybe? Or an uncle?"

"I don't think so. Not that I know of."

At this point, I made up my mind to get to the question that had been running around in my head almost from the moment Peter first began telling me about the crime back in my office. It's the kind of thing I'm very uncomfortable talking about, and I could feel myself blushing all the way from my chin to my henna-red hair. "Listen, when you were, um . . . together—you and Mary Ann, I mean—did you notice anything, anything at all, on her . . . on her body? A mole? A birthmark? *Anything* that might help with the identification?"

It was Peter's turn to blush. "Mary Ann's very shy. We always made love in the dark."

Leave it to a client of mine to wind up with maybe the only girl in New York who had a problem with taking her clothes off!

I quickly changed the subject. For both our sakes. "What do the police suspect? Do they think it might have been a burglary?"

"They seem pretty sure it wasn't. They said there was no sign of a break-in."

"You told me before that you didn't know of anyone who might have wanted to harm them; but the sad fact is, someone *did* harm those two girls." (Now, I realize that some women might not be too pleased with me right at this moment. But I can't help it; I consider any member of the female sex who's under thirty a girl.) "Think hard," I instructed. "Is there anyone who might have had a grudge against either of them? Somebody who caused some trouble in the past? Or who had been a problem to one of them—or to both of them, for that matter?"

"Well, I don't know if you'd call it a problem. . . ."

"What?"

"Meredith and her brother were on the outs. But that goes back years. It was something to do with her marriage. I don't think her brother approved of the guy."

"Mary Ann and the brother got along okay?"

"Mary Ann's a very family-oriented person. She was always hoping Meredith and Eric would bury the hatchet. I imagine one of the reasons it was so important to her was that her parents were both gone."

"You said Mary Ann had a shop of some kind. Any business disagreements you know of?"

"None. Not that she mentioned to me, anyway. And I think she would have if there'd been something."

"And Meredith?" I prodded. "Acting can be a pretty cutthroat profession."

"There *were* some bad feelings at first. Mary Ann talked about it once; it just kind of came up in conversation. But I didn't get the impression it was really serious."

"What did Mary Ann tell you?"

"She said that some actress in Meredith's show resented her. She—this actress—had been promised the part that Meredith got. So the other woman—I can't remember her name—had to settle for a minor role in the show."

"You don't happen to know the name of the show, do you?"

"Sure. It's called *Love and Stuff*. It's rehearsing at the Berkeley over in the West Village."

"And Mary Ann never talked about anyone resenting *her*?"

Peter shook his head. "Everyone liked . . . *likes* Mary Ann. She's just so thoughtful, so easy to get along with."

Nobody could be that perfect. "She *never* had a disagreement with *anyone*?"

"Well . . ."

I pounced. "Who?" I demanded. (You'd be surprised at how often I feel vindicated for being a pain in the ass.)

"This ex-fiancé of hers. But they broke off right after she came to New York. I can't see him waiting all this time." And then Peter went on to explain.

Mary Ann, he said, had been engaged to a man from

New Jersey—Hillside, Peter thought it was. The man's name was Roger somebody-or-other, and he was in real estate or maybe it was insurance. "That's about all I can tell you about him," Peter said, embarrassed. "I'm afraid I'm pretty terrible at names," he added unnecessarily. "And I don't know all that much about the relationship, either. I *do* know they met at Harrods—the department store. Mary Ann was working there, and this Roger was in London on vacation. I guess he was pretty well off, because he extended his vacation to be with her, and after that he flew back and forth a lot."

"When was all this?"

"I think they started going together about six or eight months before Mary Ann moved to New York, which is where the family was from originally."

"Meredith came here at the same time as her sister?"

Peter nodded. "When Mary Ann first started making the arrangements, Meredith's husband was still alive, although he was already pretty sick. Mary Ann felt really guilty about leaving her like that, but Meredith insisted. Mary Ann was engaged by then, see, so she pretty much *had* to make the move." If Peter felt any jealousy about his fiancée's previous involvement with another man, you couldn't tell by his voice. He was relating the information calmly and impersonally, as though it had all happened in another lifetime. And I suppose, in a way, it had.

"But then Meredith's husband died," he continued. "Right before Mary Ann was scheduled to leave. So Meredith got it all together in a hurry and came with her."

"Okay, so Mary Ann comes to this country intending to marry Roger, but . . . ?"

"But almost as soon as she got here, she found out the guy had had two previous wives he never considered worth mentioning."

"So she broke it off."

"So she broke it off," Peter echoed.

"I don't suppose the breakup was very amicable."

"No. I have a pretty good idea this Roger got a little nasty, although Mary Ann never said much about it. I guess the only reason she brought the whole thing up at all was because she thought she should. But I could see she wasn't anxious to go into detail, so I didn't pursue it." Peter glanced at his watch then, so quickly that I could tell he didn't mean for me to notice.

"Do you have an appointment somewhere else?"

"It's not that. It's just that I'm anxious to get back to the hospital. But if there's anything else you need to know . . ."

"No, you get going." I was pretty much questioned out. Besides, the place was beginning to fill up, so any minute now we could expect the manager to start giving us the fish-eye. "I'll talk to you soon," I promised.

Looking back, I realize something that at the time I wasn't ready to acknowledge: The questions I put to Peter that day were at least as much about uncovering the killer as they were about discovering the identities of the victims.

Chapter 3

I waited until after nine that night to call my niece Ellen. (Ellen's an assistant buyer at Macy's and she works until eight-thirty some nights, but I can never remember which ones.)

The phone rang six times before she picked up, and when she did, she was breathing hard. "Hello?" she said, making it sound like a question.

"What's the matter? Did you just get in?"

"Aunt Dez?" she asked, still trying to catch her breath. "I heard the phone just as I was putting my key in the lock. I was sure whoever it was would hang up before I could get to it."

"I was ready to. Listen, I'd like to talk to you about something; it's kind of important. Do you want to call me back after you've had a chance to take off your coat? Or, if you want to grab a bite first, call me when you're through."

"No, no. I can get out of my coat while we talk, and I ate earlier. What's up?" I was trying to decide how to put things, so this was followed by a worrisome pause. Worrisome for Ellen, that is, who happens to be the world's champion worrywart. "There's something wrong, isn't there?" she demanded. God only knows what she was beginning to conjure up.

"Everything's fine, Ellen, really," I assured her hurriedly. "I just want to tell you about this very attractive man I—"

It was as far as I got. "Ohhh, Aunt Dez!" she shrieked. "You met someone!" Her voice was so piercing I had to hold the receiver away from my ear. Ellen is nothing if not enthusiastic. When she can't find anything to stew about, that is.

"Well, there *is* someone. But not for me. For you. He's a young lawyer who started at the office about three weeks ago."

I guess I should explain. By "the office," I was referring to the law offices of Gilbert and Sullivan (that's right, Gilbert and Sullivan), where I rent space. And Elliot Gilbert and Pat Sullivan not only make it possible for me to conduct my business in a decent section of the city, but these two very sweet guys also throw work my way whenever they can. *Plus,* under my arrangement with them, I am able to avail myself of the services of the best secretary in Manhattan. But back to Ellen . . .

She wasn't quite as pleased with my news as I'd hoped she'd be. "You didn't!" she accused so shrilly that I had to remove the receiver from my ear again. A moment later, she said more calmly, "I *know* you have my interests at heart, Aunt Dez, but it is *so* embarrassing to—"

"Just hold on!" I commanded. "I did *not* do what you're thinking I did. Will Fitzgerald approached *me* about introducing him to someone. He hasn't been in New York very long, and he's busy studying for the New York bar most of the time, so he hasn't been able to develop much of a social life. We got into a conversation this morning, and he asked if I knew any nice girls, and I said no. The only one I know jumps to all kinds of conclusions and has her poor old aunt on a Maalox diet."

Ellen giggled for a second, then stopped abruptly. "I'm sorry. Really," she said, chastened. "I guess I'm overly sensitive sometimes. Tell me, what's he like?"

"Well, this was the first time we actually talked—I mean, besides our usual 'good mornings' and 'good nights'—but he's very personable. And Elliot Gilbert was telling me last week how bright he is. And he's really nice-looking, too. Not very tall, but taller than you—five-nine or -ten, I'd say—with curly brown hair, a good build, and a dynamite smile." It was time to close the sale. "Look, what have you got to lose? I thought maybe the two of you could come over for dinner Sunday night. I don't think Will has much money; besides, I figured if it didn't click, you could excuse yourself right after the meal and cut out."

She agreed that the dinner was a pretty good idea. "You know how nervous I get when I don't know someone, so your being there should make it a little easier. But I hate to see you go to any bother."

Now, I love to cook—as Ellen is very well aware. (She's eaten at my place often enough, for heaven's sake.) But, at any rate, I assured her I'd be happy to do it, and she thanked me and said great and that she'd come.

Then I told her about my new case.

"Oh, my God!" she exclaimed. "I read about that in the papers. It was just awful! They were really beautiful, too, weren't they? And even younger than I am!" She mulled the whole thing over for a moment, then said excitedly, "You know this case could make you famous, don't you, Aunt Dez?" Those last words were barely out of her mouth when she gave me another "Oh, my God." But this time it came out in a whisper.

"What's the matter?"

"You could get yourself killed; don't you realize that? You said you'd never accept another murder case as long as you lived. And you had a good reason for saying it, too. Don't you remember what happened the last time?"

I explained that a condition of my taking the case was that my involvement would be limited. "My client just wants to know whether his fiancée is dead or alive. He doesn't even *care* who the perpetrator is—or at least that's how he feels now. Anyhow, I made it clear that once I find out what happened to his fiancée, my job's over."

Ellen was not the least bit mollified. "I don't see how that's possible—restricting your investigation like that."

"I think *I* know better what's possible," I retorted in this withering tone I usually reserve for people in the supermarket who try to get on the ten-item express line with twenty items. I can only blame my reaction on an unwillingness to admit—particularly to myself—that Ellen was right. And, of course, I felt like a real bitch a second later. Ellen spoke before I had a chance to say how sorry I was.

"Well, I *still* don't like it," she grumbled. "Just be very, very careful. Promise me."

I promised her.

She got the last word, though. "And by the way, you're a fine one to talk about Maalox; you should have *you* for an aunt."

When we hung up, I was shaking my head and smiling to myself. Ellen's twenty-eight, but there are times I could swear they screwed up on her birth certificate. She's usually so naive and open, so basically *young,* that it's hard to believe she's been around that long. And in New York, too. But then, at other times she'll come up with something remarkably perceptive or intuitive, putting her finger on a truth I hadn't considered. Or, as in this instance, hadn't wanted to.

Later that night, right before I drifted off to sleep, I thought about Ellen and Will Fitzgerald. He really *did* seem nice. I fervently hoped it would work out between them. Poor Ellen was due. Her last relationship had been with a guy who turned out to be raw sewage.

I began building a few castles in the air. Wouldn't it be something if this turned out to be *it* for her. I was even wondering if they'd be able to find a priest and a rabbi willing to perform a joint ceremony. (I don't know if I mentioned it, but Ellen is actually Ed's niece. She's Jewish, while—with a name like Will Fitzgerald—it was fairly safe to assume that the prospective bridegroom was not.) It didn't matter, though; the deliriously happy couple could always be married by a judge or a justice of the peace or somebody.

Suddenly my mouth felt like it was stuffed with cotton batting. What would my sister-in-law, Margot, Ellen's mother, have to say about all this? She'd kill me, that's what she'd do, for finding her only daughter an Irish Catholic fiancé.

Worse yet, she might not invite me to the wedding.

Chapter 4

First thing in the morning, I called the homicide detective Peter had mentioned as being in charge of the case.

It happens that Tim Fielding and I have a kind of special relationship. He and my husband, Ed, had been pretty tight when they were on the force together years ago—before Ed left and became a P.I. Before Ed and I even met, in fact. And, quite apart from their friendship (which for the longest time I was completely unaware of), I got to know Tim myself, crossing paths with him on any number of occasions during my investigations. He wasn't working homicide back then, of course. And in my younger, smarter days, I wasn't, either.

Fielding sounded pleased to hear from me. Until I told him why I wanted to talk to him.

"That's the only thing this lousy case was missing," he groused. "You."

Now, you have to understand something about Tim Fielding. He's one of the nicest, most good-natured people you'd ever want to meet. From my point of view, if there was one lucky thing about this tragedy it was the fact that it had taken place in Fielding's precinct. But you'd never be able to tell all this by listening to us rag each other. Which is something we do a lot of. I think it's because, for some dumb reason, we're determined to make sure our feelings for one another—which, I assure you, are as platonic as they can get—don't show. I guess it's become almost a game with us by now.

It was my turn with the needle. "It'll be nice working with *you* again, too," I told him. "You have *such* a gracious manner."

"What's this 'working with you' crap? Since when did *you* become a member of the force? And in case you forgot, I already have a partner, thank you."

Fortunately, I hadn't eaten much of a breakfast. Even so much as thinking about Walter Corcoran turned my stomach. As Fielding very well knew. "I realize that," I retorted sweetly, "and you sound like he's been giving you some sensitivity training lately."

We spent another minute or two on more inane banter before I got around to asking Fielding to meet with me. He gave me a little bit of a hard time, which figured. And then he gave in. As I knew he would.

He suggested a twelve-thirty lunch at this coffee shop not far from the precinct.

I was almost a block away from the place when I spotted Tim going in. Even from the back, you couldn't miss that short, muscular, fireplug body of his, the close-cropped salt and pepper hair. And nobody else has a walk like that. Actually, *walk* is probably a misnomer. It's more like a strut.

"I thought you were through with homicides," he said when we were seated, making it sound like a challenge.

"I am. I'm looking into something else entirely. Let's eat first; then I'll explain."

"You better start explaining as soon as we give the order. I have to be back in an hour."

So right after the waiter took our sandwich orders, I told Fielding about Peter and Ashtabula, making it very clear that my only interest was in helping my client establish whether his fiancée was dead or alive.

"That's all you're interested in, huh?"

"Honestly, Tim, it's what I was hired for, and it's the only thing on my mind. Don't you believe me?"

"I believe *you* believe it; let's put it that way. Or, I should say, that you'd *like* to believe it. But you're not even as smart as *I* thought you were if you really think it's possible to separate things out like that." *Swell. Just what I needed to hear. Again.* "But we'll leave that discussion for another time," he went on. "So just what is it you want from me? You want to know how it went down, right?"

"Right."

"Let's see," he ruminated, screwing up his face as he combed his memory for the details. "One of the twins, Mary Ann—I'll tell you later how we know it was her— was found on the living room floor, a few feet from the sofa. There was no sign of a struggle, nothing to indicate forcible entry. So we have to assume she was acquainted with the perp. Anyway, the other sister ... what was her name?"

"Meredith."

"Yeah, Meredith. She was shot at the end of this long entry foyer, right where you turn the corner into the living room. The doorman's pretty sure the first sister to come home that night—that would be Mary Ann—got in around seven-thirty, maybe a few minutes before. He told us she came in at the same time as one of the other tenants; he remembers because the two of 'em were joking around together. We checked with the man—a Mr. Milano—and he verified the doorman's information. He says he walked into his apartment at exactly seven-thirty. Says he was aware of the time because he was so disappointed at not being able to catch even the last few minutes of *Jeopardy!*"

"Milano knew it was Mary Ann he'd been talking to?"

"As a matter of fact, he didn't. It was a casual conversation. But that's okay. I told you; *we* know it was."

"What about Meredith? When did she get home?"

"We can't pin that down as closely. Doorman *thinks* the second sister got in around an hour later. But he admits that's just a guess. And we haven't been able to find anyone else who can nail down the time for us. But it's very unlikely Meredith came home before eight, at the earliest. We can be reasonably certain of that from the facts we already have."

"Which are?"

"Hold your horses, will you? I'm getting there. Now, the way we piece it together, the perp was in the living room with Mary Ann. Could be they even sat around and talked for a while. Maybe waiting for Meredith."

"Then you think Meredith was actually the intended victim?"

"That's certainly one possibility. Did you know Mary Ann was supposed to be going out to dinner straight from work that night?"

"Peter told me." Just then, our sandwiches arrived. The minute the waiter walked away, I said, "You know, it also could have happened the other way around. I mean, who's to say the killer knew about Mary Ann's dinner plans? Maybe *she* was the target. And then Meredith walked in right after the shooting and, thanks to her lousy timing, got *her* face practically blown off, too."

"Sure. It *could* have gone down like that," Fielding conceded. "The only trouble is, by ten of eight at the outside, the perp was already in the apartment." I opened my mouth, but Fielding anticipated me. "And don't ask me how we know that. I'll—"

This time, *I* anticipated *him*. "I'll explain later, so hold your horses," I cut in, mimicking his tone.

He touched his hand to his forehead and presented me with a mock salute before going on. "The point is, if Mary Ann *was* the target, why not make the hit and get the hell out of there? Why hang around until Meredith came home? Unless *she* was the intended victim or unless it was supposed to be a doubleheader all along. Right?"

He didn't expect an answer. And he didn't get one. I started to ask about something else. "Say, what do you—"

"Why don't you cool it for a couple of minutes and start eating? Your sandwich is getting cold."

"It's tuna fish, Tim," I reminded him, picking up the sandwich anyway.

"Well, then let *me* eat," he said, taking a large bite of his grilled Taylor ham. "And by the way," he informed me after a couple of minutes, "Meredith wasn't just shot in the face; neither of them were. They both sustained body wounds first; one of them in the thorax—that's the chest area—and—"

"I *know* where the thorax is," I put in, slightly miffed.

"—And the other," Fielding continued, ignoring the interruption, "in the abdomen. Only we don't know which one was shot where," he said, rolling his eyes back in his head, "because EMS screwed up. What we got with this case, Dez," he grumbled, "is a really beautiful example of Murphy's law: 'Anything that *can* go wrong *will* go wrong'; isn't that how it goes?"

A few seconds and another bite of Taylor ham later, he added characteristically, "Not that I can really blame those guys." (I *told* you how nice he is.) "Both women were a bloody mess but they were both alive at that point—although barely—and the Emergency people were in a helluva hurry to get them to a hospital. So I guess what happened is understandable. But, damn it, it would certainly make it easier on everyone if we knew who was lying in St. Catherine's right now."

"What *did* happen, anyway?"

"EMS didn't discover the body wounds until the women were in the ambulance; *that's* what happened."

I have to confess that, for a moment at least, I had no idea what Fielding was getting at. And I must have been wearing my stupidity on my face, because he went ahead and cleared things up for me. "Look," he explained patiently, "I told you we're sure Mary Ann was shot near the living room sofa and that Meredith bought it at the end of the foyer. So if the EMS guys had been able to tell us where the woman who had the chest wound was lying—she happens to be the survivor, incidentally—we'd know if it was Meredith or Mary Ann who made it."

Of course! I should have picked that up right away!

"Don't feel so bad," Fielding consoled, aware of my embarrassment. "This case is such a ball-buster it has me biting my nails up to the elbow. A few more days like the ones we've had, and I'll probably wind up talking to myself."

"I suppose you checked to see if anyone in the building knows anything," I said, anxious to move on.

"No, we didn't," Fielding replied in this deceptively pleasant voice. "That's why I agreed to have lunch with you. I was hoping to get some tips on how to conduct a proper homicide investigation."

"I'm sorry. Naturally you checked; I know that. It's just that sometimes my brain can't catch up with my mouth."

"Sometimes *nothing* can catch up with that mouth," Fielding muttered. But I could see that he was trying to smother a grin. "For your information, we started talking to the other tenants on Tuesday morning, and we're still talking to them on the chance that we'll find someone who saw something. We're *sure* no one *heard* anything; that's one of the few new luxury buildings around that's really soundproof. Figures, doesn't it?"

"What did the doorman say? About visitors, I mean," I asked then.

"Just what you could predict he'd say, with the way things are shaking out. That the twins didn't have any visitors that night—at least while he was on duty. He insists no one could have gotten past *him*."

"Incidentally, how could you tell it was the second shot that was the one in the face?"

"Because, from the position of the bullets, we know the perp was standing over his victims when the facial wounds were inflicted. Both women were already *flat on their backs* when he let them have it in the face."

I shuddered and hoped Fielding—hardened homicide detective that he was—hadn't noticed. But he had. "If you think it *sounds* grisly, you should have seen those two."

"What did he use?"

"A thirty-eight. And we're still looking for it."

"It's amazing that one of those girls is still with us."

"More than amazing. This doctor I was talking to yesterday morning called it a miracle. The bullet missed the surviving victim's heart by *that much*." He held up his thumb and forefinger, positioning them so there was barely an inch of space between them. "And then the second bullet—the one in the face—ricocheted off the jaw and up into her brain. That woman must have some constitution! All I can say is, it's gotta be the genes, because the other sister lasted until she got on the operating table. And with the damage *she* sustained, the doctors consider that an even bigger miracle. But listen, I need for you to promise me something."

"What?"

"That business about the twin with the chest wound being the one who's hanging on? That's not for publication. In fact, I'd be in big trouble if it got out I told you. We don't want the perp to know which of his victims is still around. The hospital personnel's under strict orders not to discuss her condition with anyone, and there's a twenty-four-hour guard in the room to make sure no one gets a close enough look at her to find out."

"I won't tell a soul; you have my word."

"That includes your client, you know. We've even had the hospital put her in a special gown to conceal the chest wound."

"Peter won't find out about it from me. Hey, you don't think—"

"No, I don't. Otherwise we wouldn't let him camp out in the room like that, even *with* a man stationed there. Although, to be honest, I'm not too comfortable about letting anyone at all in to see her."

"But you *are* allowing it."

"The doctors tell us that, comatose or not, if the patient is Mary Ann, Winters's presence could do her a world of good. And if it's Meredith, his being there might still help some. At any rate, it won't do any harm. Unless, of course, he's our killer."

I was about to protest when Fielding smiled. "Look, if I considered that to be a serious possibility, there's no way I'd let him within a hundred feet of her," he said.

I suppose I must have been frowning then without even realizing it, because Fielding broke into my thoughts. "What?" he wanted to know.

"This business about their both being shot in the face like that. What do you make of it?"

"I wish I knew. All I can say is that there's something personal in an act like that. Something *very* personal."

"I think so, too."

"That's another reason I can't buy this thing as a burglary. Although I gotta admit the pickings in that apartment would probably not be too shabby. You should see the place."

"I'd like to," I told him pointedly.

Fielding ignored the remark, commenting instead that the death of their parents must have left the twins extremely well off.

I tried again. "I'd really like to have a look at the apartment."

"I'll think about it—after we're through with it. But I don't know why you're so anxious. I'm *telling* you everything you could learn by going up there, aren't I?"

I decided to drop it—for a while. "Who discovered them, anyway?"

A neighbor. Man named Charles Springer. He rang their doorbell around ten of eight. When no one answered, he couldn't understand it. Seems he called ten minutes earlier and told Mary Ann he'd be by in a few minutes."

Well, we'd finally gotten around to it! So *that's* why Fielding was so sure Mary Ann was the twin in the living room! "Ohhh, now I get it," I said, mostly to myself.

He grinned. "See? Didn't I tell you to be patient and I'd explain? Anyway, from Springer's statement we know it was Mary Ann who came in at seven-thirty. She even said something to Springer on the phone about her sister not being home yet. By the way, Meredith left the theater a little before seven, and she mentioned to this other woman in the cast who happened to be leaving the theater at the same time that she was going to run up to Macy's and return a blouse. So I can't see how she could possibly have made it home earlier than eight o'clock. And that would be cutting it pretty damn close.

"At any rate, at some time after eight, Meredith opened the door to the apartment, hung up her coat in the foyer closet, and started to walk into her own living room. She never made it."

Something about the sad, simple way Fielding said that made my stomach constrict and then drop straight down to my toes. I could picture Meredith lying there, with Mary Ann only a few yards away, both of them covered with blood, their beautiful faces all smashed up. . . .

"Anything wrong, Dez?" Fielding asked anxiously. "You don't look too hot."

"It's nothing. I'm fine. Tell me about Springer."

"Yeah. Well, after a while he tried calling the apartment on the phone. No answer. Then, around nine o'clock, for some reason, he went back there again. The door was open about six or eight inches. He started to walk in and saw Meredith at the end of the foyer. He rushed back to his own place and dialed nine-one-one."

"So Mary Ann could have been shot any time between seven-forty and nine," I said, more or less replaying what Fielding had just laid out for me. "And Meredith had to have been hit sometime after eight."

"You got it."

"Which means that when Springer rang the bell at ten of eight," I murmured, thinking aloud, "either Mary Ann was being restrained at gunpoint or she'd already been shot."

"Right," Fielding concurred. Then, abruptly: "Okay, now you know what I know, and, according to that clock in back of you, it's twenty after one already. So let's get the check and get the hell out of here."

I decided, in view of Tim's being so forthcoming with me, that I had to share what I'd learned from Peter. "Hold on just a few more minutes. I am about to give *you* some leads," I informed him, trying to sound like Lady Bountiful.

"Did you know," I asked, "that one of the other women

in Meredith's show was jealous of her? Seems the other woman was promised the part that went to Meredith."

"That would be Lucille Collins," Fielding said, a little smugly, I thought.

I tried again. "Did you also know Meredith and her brother didn't get along?"

"Yup. Foster contacted us the day after the murder. He had a lunch date with Mary Ann set up for Tuesday, and she was supposed to call him in the morning to confirm. When he didn't hear from her, he telephoned her store, but no one answered. He finally went to lunch by himself, and after he left the restaurant he stopped at a newsstand. And there were these pictures of his sisters plastered on the front page of the *Post.* I can't even figure out how they got ahold of them."

"So he called the police?"

"As soon as he saw the paper. Anyhow, that's what he claims."

"What did he say about the feud with Meredith?"

"The man *volunteered* that he and his sister hadn't spoken in years because he tried to interfere when she was going to marry this drug addict—the guy she eventually married anyway. He—Foster—is taking this thing pretty badly; seems to be really busted up over it."

"You haven't let him see his sister in the hospital?"

"Just the one time. When we were through questioning him, he pleaded with us to let him go up there. So Walt and I went over with him."

"Apparently, he couldn't help with the identification."

"C'mon, Dez. The woman's face—what's left of it, anyway—is all bandaged up."

"I wasn't thinking about his *recognizing* her," I countered. "I was thinking maybe he could give you some family-type information. Like one sister's having a birthmark or a mole or something." As soon as I said it, I was reminded of the question I'd had so much trouble putting to Peter. It must have showed.

"We asked him about that. But he didn't know a thing. And what's with you, anyhow? You're red as a beet."

I didn't care to explain. "Any problem with Foster about wanting to leave the country?"

"None. In fact, he voluntarily turned over his passport.

Says he has no intention of going home until he finds out what's what with his sisters."

I could see from the direction of his gaze that Fielding was checking the wall clock behind me again. "Jeez, it's one-thirty," he announced, confirming my thoughts. "*Some* of us gotta get back to work—even if you high-priced P.I.s can keep your own hours."

He was unsuccessfully attempting to signal the waiter when I gave it one last shot. "I suppose you're aware that Mary Ann was engaged once—before Peter, I mean—and that it ended very badly."

"Now, *that* I didn't know."

I relayed the meager information my client had given me, and when I was through, Fielding said, "Looks like we've got another suspect, doesn't it? Or we will once we can pin a name on this guy."

I left Tim that day feeling somewhat gratified. While I'd been on the receiving end through most of our lunch, I'd finally been able to come up with a piece of information for him. Maybe it wasn't all that much, but, as I learned a long time ago, it's important to have *something* on the credit side of the ledger.

Chapter 5

From the coffee shop, I took a cab to Greenwich Village. Finding the Berkeley Theater was an adventure in itself. I don't know if you're familiar with that area, but it's like a maze. It's not unusual to find a street breaking off at an intersection and then turning up a few blocks north or south of where it was before. Compounding the problem was the fact that my young driver, who was Indian or Pakistani or some Middle Eastern nationality, spoke almost no English. I guess the really amazing thing is that we made it to the Village at all.

We must have circled the same five or six blocks for fifteen minutes, with me instructing Ahmed (that's what the license said) to stop and ask directions at least half a dozen times and him saying "Sure, lady," every time and then tossing a quick, beatific smile over his shoulders as he continued to zip up and down the same damned streets. Finally, just as I'd more or less made up my mind to get out and see if I could find the place on foot, we stopped for a traffic light alongside another taxi.

Well, it was worth a try.

I rolled down my window, sticking my head out so far that most of the rest of me was hanging outside the cab, too. "Do you know where the Berkeley Theater is?" I yelled.

The light was changing. And it's a rare New York taxi driver who, sans passengers, will waste much time being helpful. "Two blocks *mmft*," he shouted before zooming off in a cloud of gas fumes. I wasn't sure whether that last word was "up," "down," "north," "south," or what. But the finger he dangled out of the window *had* been pointing left when he said whatever it was he said.

"Did you hear that?" I asked Ahmed.

"Sure, lady," he said, smiling. Just before turning right.

I told him to pull over. He gave me another of those beaming smiles of his, said, "Sure, lady" again, made one more turn, and—astonishingly—we were right in front of the Berkeley Theater.

I paid the outrageous amount on the meter (and resented it like hell, expense account or no expense account). I even added what I thought was a generous tip—under the circumstances, that is. Just as I was leaving the cab, Smiley gave me one last, blinding smile. "It was a true pleasure driving you, lady," he said in flawless English. "And please to have a lovely day."

The Berkeley was a small theater—I don't think there were more than a hundred seats—and rehearsal was in full swing when I got there. I spotted a man seated in the middle of about the tenth row, so I tiptoed down the aisle and entered the row behind him. I leaned over, tapped him on the shoulder, and very quietly explained who I was. He responded with a long, loud snore.

"Hey, you shouldn't be in here!" someone shouted at me from the stage, as everyone else up there stopped in their tracks and turned to stare. "I'm going to have to ask you to leave."

Now, you might think that, being a P.I. for so long, I'd be used to getting thrown out of places by this time. Well, I don't think I'll *ever* get used to it. I was feeling pretty uncomfortable right about then. Nevertheless, I marched purposefully up to the stage and even managed to speak with all the authority and composure you'd expect from a confident, in-control, Sam Spade type of investigator. "I'd like to talk to the cast about Meredith Foster; my name's Desiree Shapiro," I said, addressing the large, sandy-haired man who had so unequivocally requested my departure. "It won't take long," I assured him, waving my license at him. He bent down and reached over the footlights to accept it, then quickly returned it to me.

"The police have already questioned the entire company," he informed me, not unkindly, "and I'm sure we've all told them everything we know. Which I'm afraid isn't much."

"I'm sure you have, too, but I've got some additional questions." I could see a look of apology begin to form on the well-lived-in, fortyish face, so I quickly intercepted it.

"It's very important. And we're all interested in the same thing, aren't we? Making sure this murderous slime is caught."

"All right," the man agreed with a sigh. "C'mon in back. You can use my office."

"I guess I should introduce myself," he said when he was leading me backstage. "I'm Larry Shields; I'm directing this play." He showed me into a room so tiny it could barely contain its sparse furnishings. Sharing the extremely cramped quarters were a smallish, badly scarred desk, which was piled unbelievably high with papers of every sort, and a pair of identical and extremely rickety straight-backed chairs. "Have a seat," Shields said, indicating the chair nearer the door. Then he lifted the other chair from behind the desk, placing it a couple of feet from where I now sat nervously shifting my buns and praying that my own chair would not let me down. (And I'm talking *literally*.) "I'll have the company come in one at a time; I assume that's what you want," Shields told me.

"Thanks. I'd appreciate it."

From the first five people to enter what I now regarded as my interrogation room, I discovered that *everyone* liked Meredith Foster. Of course, she didn't really socialize much with the other cast members, I was told. But that was because she was so committed to her craft. She was always sitting there studying her lines whenever she had even a few minutes' free time, her fellow thespians said admiringly.

As for Lucille Collins originally having been promised Meredith's role, no one seemed to know a thing about *that*.

Okay. So who took over the part after the shootings? I wanted to know.

We-e-ll, it was reluctantly conceded, Lucille *was* playing Hope *now*. However, a suggestion from me that there was some ill-feeling between the two actresses, that even Meredith thought Collins resented her, was met with firm denials, a couple of them pretty impassioned. *Everyone,* I was informed again and again, liked Meredith Foster.

Then Tara Wilde walked in. Small and dark, with huge brown eyes and a totally ingenuous manner, she couldn't have been more than nineteen years old. I immediately pegged the young actress as my best hope.

"Someone mentioned that Lucille Collins was all set for

the part of Hope before Meredith came along," I said, not even bothering with foreplay.

"I never heard that," the girl responded, eyeing me warily.

"From what I understand, it was a pretty good part, so it would—"

"*Pretty* good? Are you kidding? Any actress would *kill* for a part like that!" Tara's hand flew to her mouth. "Oh! I didn't mean it like that! I would *never* ... Lucille would never—"

I interrupted quickly. "Oh, I don't think either of you would, either. Still, if what I heard about Lucille's losing out is true, it would be understandable if she'd been a little jealous of Meredith, don't you agree?"

"Lucille liked Meredith just fine," Tara retorted. And then she added, almost as if she were parroting the words, "*Everyone* liked Meredith."

I can't tell you how fed up I was with that tune. Also, I decided that a little shock therapy could conceivably do some good here. "Not *everyone*," I reminded her in a voice dripping with irony. "Someone disliked Meredith Foster enough to shoot off her face. So if there's anything you can tell me—"

"But there isn't!" Tara protested, her improbably large eyes growing even larger and her voice rising sharply. "If there *was,* don't you think I *would*?"

When she rushed out of the office moments later, she was almost in tears. And I was furious with myself, convinced that if I'd just pushed the right buttons, I could have gotten her to open up. But as it was, the only thing I learned from my meeting with Tara Wilde was how it must feel to kick a puppy.

Two other people came and left after that, including the show's snoring producer, who was still no more than semiconscious. Then Lucille Collins put in an appearance.

I hadn't exactly formed a mental picture of the woman—not that I was aware of, anyway. Still, what I saw surprised me.

She was well into her thirties, tall and very thin and almost plain-looking. Except for her long, thick hair, which was this incredible shade of auburn. (And, I realized with a twinge of jealousy, the color was natural, too.) But it was when Collins began to speak that she seemed totally transformed. Her voice was low and husky. And she had this way of turning her complete attention to you and fixing you with these piercing hazel eyes of hers—eyes that an instant earlier you probably wouldn't even have noticed.

I didn't waste much time before asking how she felt about the part of Hope going to Meredith Foster. She said she was disappointed; maybe, for the first week or so, anyway, even angry about it. "But I didn't blame Meredith for what happened. How could I blame *her* for someone else's decision?" she pointed out. Quite rationally, I thought.

Still, that didn't let her off the hook. "Would you mind telling me where you were on Monday night between quarter to eight and nine o'clock?"

"Home alone with a book. And it was a lousy one, too."

Collins stayed a couple of minutes more without saying much of anything else. And soon afterward Larry Shields poked his head in.

"That wraps it up," he informed me. "That was the last one—except for me." He came in and set his meaty six-foot-two- or -three-inch body down opposite me. (And it was with some kind of perverse satisfaction that I noted that, with his oversized frame, Shields's little chair was as imperiled as mine was.)

I opened with, "How well did you know Meredith Foster?"

"Very well," he said gravely. "We were going together."

It took a few seconds to digest what—to me, at least—was very interesting news. Then I said, "How did Lucille Collins feel about the part she'd been promised going to Meredith?"

"First off, *promised* isn't exactly the right word. I'd planned on doing this play for some time, and I mentioned the part of Hope to Lucille quite a while ago. I knew she'd do a fine job." And then with a trace of irony: "In fact, she *is* doing a fine job. But at any rate, once I saw Merry, I realized I needed someone younger—someone more like Merry—although I wasn't thinking of Merry herself at that point. Not consciously, anyway. All I knew was that if I put Lucille in the role, I'd be settling."

"You said *once you saw Merry*. When was that?"

"It was the end of September. I attended an opening night production of *Show Boat*. It was at one of those little theaters on the Lower East Side that's so small and dilapidated, it makes this place look like the Shubert." His voice grew animated as he warmed to his subject. "It was really like amateur night there, too. The actors tried hard, but most of them were very young, and they just weren't up to their parts. All except Merry."

Shields looked down at his hands then. I looked, too. He was slowly, almost rhythmically, clenching and unclenching his fists. Without stopping, he said quietly, "I'd give anything for five minutes alone with the bastard who did this. Five minutes with him, that's all I'd need." A moment later, he very deliberately folded his hands in his lap, lifted his head, and told me sheepishly, "Sorry. I guess I got carried away." Unexpectedly, he forced a grin. And, forced or not, for an instant his ordinary face wasn't so ordinary after all.

"Don't apologize. Please. This must be very difficult for you."

"It's hell," he replied simply.

"You said you first saw Meredith in *Show Boat*," I prodded.

"Right. She was playing Julie, the second female lead. Merry's voice wasn't great, but she really knew how to read a lyric. Mostly, though, I was impressed with the way she delivered her lines—her speaking lines. She even had the dialect down pat; you'd never know she'd been living in England most of her life. In fact, she was *so* good that I went to see the show again just before it closed."

"So you and Meredith met in September?"

"No. We didn't even meet that second time—which was at the beginning of November. After the performance, I was on my way backstage when I ran into an old friend, and by the time I broke away, Merry had left the theater. I was disappointed, but I decided it was probably just as well; I was seeing someone else at the time, and I had a feeling Merry could complicate things for me."

"And then?"

"And then, less than a week after that, I went to a cocktail party. And there was Merry. I broke off with the other woman a couple of days later."

"This other woman—would you mind telling me who she was?"

Shields hesitated. "Lucille Collins," he muttered, flushing.

Somehow, I wasn't at all surprised. Well, it now seemed

that Ms. Collins had a *couple* of reasons for not being overly fond of Meredith Foster. I said as much to Shields.

"You're wrong. Lucille isn't like that. Besides, by the time I met Merry, things had already started to cool between us."

"On your part or hers?"

The flush deepened. "Both. We probably would have split up soon even if Merry hadn't come into the picture."

I wondered, briefly, if that was true. But I realized it was something I'd never know. And, for that matter, Shields and Collins probably wouldn't, either. Right now, though, it was time for me to wrestle with *that question* again.

It was not easy spitting it out. "Did you ever notice ... uh, I mean, does she—Meredith ... uh, Merry—have any distinguishing marks on her body?" (Believe me, practice does not always make perfect.)

"The police asked me the same thing. They asked if I remembered seeing a small mole right next to her navel. But if Merry *was* the one they spotted that mole on, it must have been *very* small, because I never noticed it." Then his voice broke as he added huskily, "God, I wish there *was* something. At least I'd *know*."

I shook my head, commiserating. Larry Shields truly appeared to be suffering, just as Peter was. I reminded myself he was a suspect. In fact, as far as I was concerned, *everyone* was a suspect—at least for the time being. My client excepted, of course.

"They won't even let me into the hospital room," Shields fumed. "I keep trying to change their minds, but a lot of good it does talking to *those* assholes." Suddenly he stood up. "I'd better snap out of it," he said. "I have a rehearsal to direct. So if you'll excuse me ..."

"One more question. How did Collins feel about the part she wanted going to Meredith? You never *did* say."

"She wasn't thrilled about it—naturally. But she understood. And she certainly didn't hold it against Merry. Lucille's a pro."

"One thing more," I put in hastily. "Where were you on Monday night between quarter to eight and nine o'clock?"

"In Brooklyn, having dinner with my mother."

"Can anyone verify that?" I asked.

"Does my mother count?" Shields asked back, almost playfully.

"I'm afraid not."

I walked out of the theater a few minutes later, marveling at how tight-lipped that little group had been. I mean, no one, other than Shields himself, had said a thing about the director's previous relationship with Lucille Collins (and I had no doubt everyone was aware there'd been one—theater gossip being what it is).

And wasn't it strange that nobody had mentioned Meredith's involvement with Shields? Or that—in a profession rampant with egos—not one single person had speculated as to this being the real reason she'd wound up with the plum role of Hope?

Chapter 6

All in all, it had been a very tiring day. So at a little after eight-thirty, I took off my makeup, put on my pajamas, and got into my rattiest-looking, most comfortable bathrobe. (That's one advantage of living alone; there's no one to care if you look like the wrath of God. As long as you stay away from mirrors, that is.)

I confess that around then I was feeling pretty depressed about what I'd learned from Fielding earlier. (I could forget about that solemn vow I'd made myself to keep my feelings in check this time. I should have known, given my track record, that that wasn't even a remote possibility.)

The truth was, I had to admit, that there was a damned good chance—better than even, I figured—that Mary Ann had been shot before her sister got home. Maybe more than an hour before. And that meant she could have been lying there bleeding on the living room floor for a hell of a long time before EMS rushed her to St. Catherine's. Which didn't exactly put the odds of being the survivor in her favor.

But, hey, what did odds mean, anyway? Didn't I play the lottery? And what were the odds on *that*? And how about Publisher's Clearing House? And that other one, the one Ed McMahon was always hawking? I wouldn't be plunking down all that money for tickets and postage if I didn't believe you could beat the odds. So I was not going to think terrible thoughts. In fact, right now I was not going to think at all.

What I *was* going to do was plant myself in front of the TV for the entire evening. *Cheers* would be on soon. And, later, there was *L.A. Law*. Not a bad night at all to put your brains on hold. But first I thought it might be a good idea to set something up with this Charles Springer—the neighbor who'd discovered the victims. Maybe I could get

him to see me sometime tomorrow. I checked the telephone book, and there was a listing for a C. Springer at
the twins' address.

The man who answered the phone sounded hyper. He
spoke in a nasal, high-pitched voice, and the words tumbled
out one after the other so quickly I wondered that he had
time to breathe. When I told him I was a private investigator and that I was working for Peter Winters, Mary Ann
Foster's fiancé, he said I could come over in about an hour.

Now, I'd really been counting on a reprieve that night,
but what could I do? P.I.s aren't exactly on everyone's "A"
list. So if he was willing to meet with me, I wasn't about
to quibble.

I got dressed in record time (for me, anyway), practically
jumping into my clothes and then slapping on some
makeup and plopping on this wig I have that looks exactly
like my own hair only it's usually a lot easier to reason
with. In less than three-quarters of an hour, I was in a taxi
heading for West Fifteenth Street.

The twins' apartment building, with its brand-new hunter
green canopy, white-gloved doorman, and huge, mirrored
lobby, looked like it had been transplanted from Sutton
Place. The elderly doorman instructed me to go right up;
Mr. Springer was expecting me.

"Listen, I'm a private investigator," I told him before
heading for the elevator. "Could we have a little talk when
I come down? You *were* on duty Monday night, weren't
you?"

"That's right. You want to know about the shootings?"

"I just want to check a couple of things with you."

"Terrible what happened, wasn't it? And the two of them
such pretty young girls. And always so pleasant, too. It's a
sorry mess this world of ours has come to, isn't it?"

"It sure is," I clucked. "I should be through upstairs in
about half an hour. Okay?"

"No problem. I'm on till eleven."

Charles Springer was a short, thin man in his early thirties with a bad complexion, a friendly, if agitated, manner,
and just a few strands of hair remaining on his dome-
shaped little head. He led me from a small foyer, papered
in an interesting pink and silver geometric, into a large,
elegant living room, which was eclectically furnished with

striking contemporary pieces and handsome antiques (or very good reproductions; I'm not sure which). The room was done almost entirely in off-white, the major exception being a small turquoise velvet sofa accented with off-white and pink throw pillows. The pink was repeated in most of the soft pastel prints decorating the walls and in a stunning arrangement of silk flowers that was displayed in a contemporary crystal vase standing atop an antique cherry sideboard.

"What a beautiful room!" I exclaimed. I was seated on the turquoise sofa, with Springer sitting on the off-white bergère at right angles to it.

"Thank you so much," he said, his face lighting up with pleasure. Then he confided, in that rapid-fire way he had, "I love to decorate. I just wish I could afford more than a studio. A little more space to work with, and I'd *really* be able to let loose. I wouldn't need a place anything like the twins', of course—" He broke off abruptly, and the glow was gone. "How is she? Do you know?" he demanded. "I just called St. Catherine's a few minutes before you got here, but they said her condition was still critical."

"I'm sorry, but I haven't heard anything."

"I don't suppose they've figured out if it's Mary Ann or Meredith who . . . who's in the hospital?"

"No. It looks like that'll take a while. I understand you were the one who found them."

"Yes. And it was just awful," Springer whispered. "I haven't been able to get a night's sleep since."

"I don't think I'd be able to, either," I told him honestly. "The police say that the first time you called the apartment it was twenty to eight."

"That's right."

"You're sure of the time?"

"Oh, yes. I had something in the oven, and it had ten minutes to go." Then he added the clincher: "You don't make a mistake with the time when you're baking a soufflé."

I couldn't argue with that. I realize this may sound immodest, but two of the extremely few blemishes on my own outstanding culinary record were soufflé-induced. So I accepted Springer's declaration as gospel.

"There's no doubt, Mr. Springer, that it was Mary Ann who answered the phone?"

"No. She told me it was. And, please, call me Chuck."

"All right. And I'm Desiree. Did Mary Ann give you any indication there might have been somebody with her when you called?"

"Oh, no. Just the opposite, really. I said I'd just whipped up a strawberry soufflé and it would be ready in ten minutes, and I asked if she and Meredith would volunteer to be my guinea pigs. You see," he explained, "I'm expecting company next week, and it's a new recipe, so I wanted to try it out beforehand."

"What did she say?"

"She told me Meredith wasn't home yet but that she could be walking in any minute. Then she laughed and she said, 'And if Merry doesn't get here on time, the hell with her. I'll eat *her* portion, too.' Those were practically her exact words. She *didn't* say, 'So-and-so is here, and maybe he'll volunteer, too.' Well, that certainly didn't sound to me like there was anybody else in the apartment."

It didn't sound that way to me, either. "What happened next?"

"At ten minutes to eight, I rang the doorbell, soufflé in hand. But nobody answered. I really didn't know what to make of it, but what could I do? You have to understand that I had no reason to think anything *dire* had happened." Springer was looking at me as though begging for reassurance.

"No, of course you didn't," I obliged.

"Anyway, I went back to my own apartment and had some of the soufflé myself. Naturally, it was flat as a pancake by then, but I wasn't concerned about that; I'd *seen* that it could rise to magnificent heights. I just wanted to find out how it *tasted*."

"What made you call the Foster apartment again?" I asked, trying to move him along.

"I can't even tell you. It just kept bugging me—Mary Ann's not answering. I couldn't understand it, you know? So after I had the soufflé and a cup of coffee to go with it, I picked up the phone."

"It never crossed your mind that something might have suddenly come up and Mary Ann had to run out at the last minute?"

"Of course. That was the first thing I thought of. But she was expecting me. And, knowing Mary Ann, she wouldn't have gone out without calling me first. Not unless it was a real emergency, anyway."

"So you were worried."

"Not exactly. At least, not then. I think curious would be more like it. I was just wondering what could have happened. I never *dreamed* . . ." He seemed to shrink from putting the rest of the thought into words.

"You had no reason to suspect anything. None at all," I told him firmly.

Springer gave me a grateful little smile before going on. "Anyway, after the phone call, I sat down to do some work that I'd brought home from the office, but I just couldn't concentrate. Who knows? Maybe by then I *was* getting a little worried. Maybe it was some sort of premonition."

"So you went back over. The door was open that time?"

"Just partially. Six inches maybe. I stood there in the doorway and called out. But nothing. Not a sound. So, without even thinking about what I was doing, I started to walk in. That's when I saw her—Meredith, the cops say it was. God! She was all covered with blood. . . ." He sat there for a moment, recalling the horror. Then he asked softly, almost fearfully, "Do they have any idea yet who did it?"

"Not yet."

"How's Peter holding up?"

"He's in a lot of pain. But he *is* holding up. You know Peter?"

"Oh, yes. I've met him a number of times."

"You were very friendly with the twins, I gather."

"They were dear, dear friends of mine."

"Can you think of anyone who might have wanted to harm either of them?"

"Good grief, no! They were both wonderful ladies."

"Think. Please. Is there anything you can tell me about their relationships with other people that might help? Anything at all?"

Springer's high forehead wrinkled up like an accordion. Then, closing his eyes and pursing his lips, he seemed to retreat into an almost trancelike state. But when he spoke a few moments later, it was to tell me what I already knew: that, years ago, Meredith had had a falling out with her brother over her future husband and that Mary Ann had been engaged to some lowlife whose name he couldn't remember. (In fact, he had serious doubts it had ever even been mentioned.)

I wasn't ready to give up yet. "Mary Ann never had problems with anyone else?"

"If she *did,* she never told *me* about it."

"And Meredith?"

"Meredith was very closemouthed. I didn't even hear about this thing with Eric—that's the brother—from her. Mary Ann brought it up after one of Eric's trips to New York; she said how bad she felt that there was this rift in the family."

"Mary Ann used to confide in you?"

"No, not really. As a matter of fact, she didn't talk much more about personal things than Meredith did. And neither of them liked to dish, either. It was very disappointing sometimes," Springer declared, grinning mischievously, "but I guess that's one of the things that made them so nice." In an instant, he turned serious again. "I'm sorry I can't be more helpful," he said sadly.

Well, that was that. I might as well have stayed home and watched *Cheers* for all I'd found out here tonight.

Then, just as I was getting to my feet, Springer stopped me cold. "Wait!" he commanded excitedly. "I just thought of something! I don't see how it could have slipped my mind! It was only about a month ago, too!"

"What is it?" My heart was starting to thump like crazy.

"Well, one night I went over there to see if I could store this casserole in their freezer; mine was packed, and theirs is always practically empty. Meredith answered the door— she was home alone—and she said sure, no problem. But once I got inside, I realized she'd been crying. I didn't know whether to mention anything or let it pass. But I didn't want her to think I didn't give a damn, you know? So I just asked if there was something wrong."

"What did she say?"

"She said no, but the minute she said it, she burst into tears. I stood there patting her shoulder like a useless turd—I couldn't think of what else to do; I'm terrible when it comes to things like that. And after a couple of minutes she pulled herself together and told me she'd just broken up with this guy she started going with recently. I've never met the man, but his name is Larry Shields and he was directing this new show she was in. Anyway, she said it was all her fault, that she'd done this terrible, unforgivable thing—I remember her using that word: 'unforgivable.' And then she said she wouldn't blame him if he wanted to kick her out of the show. She said that even if he didn't, though, he'd probably never come near her again.''

"Did she tell you what it was she'd done?"

"No. That was all she said."

"Did she ever mention it after that?"

"Well . . . no. The thing is, I was really busy with work right around then, so I didn't see her for maybe five or six days. But I *was* concerned," he put in quickly. It was obvious the poor man's overactive guilt mechanism was at it again. "Besides," he rationalized, "she didn't seem to want to talk about it, and I didn't want to come off like some kind of a Nosy Parker, you know?"

He waited for my nod before going on. "And then when I *did* see her, she seemed happy enough. So I figured it had just been a little lover's spat that she'd blown out of proportion—the way we all do, you know?—and that they probably got back together again. Which, I later found out, is exactly what *did* happen." He looked at me anxiously. "You can see why it didn't occur to me right away, can't you? About the breakup, that is. I mean, it all worked out fine."

Well, it seems I'd finally learned something that made giving up my nine P.M. rendezvous with Ted Danson a lot easier to take. (He's really too good-looking for my taste, anyway.)

I stood up then. We'd covered everything I could think of; also, I was anxious to talk to the doorman. But getting out of there wasn't easy. I had to call upon all of my really pathetic willpower to decline a piece of the chocolate torte that, Chuck Springer pronounced, was one of his best recipes.

The doorman's name was Harris. I don't know if it was his first name or his last, because he just said, "Call me Harris."

"I understand, Harris," I put to him, "that you told the police the twins didn't have any visitors Monday night."

"That's *not* what I said," he responded emphatically.

"What did you say?"

"I said that nobody could have got up to that apartment while *I* was on duty. Not without my calling upstairs first."

"Is there another way into the building?"

"Around the side, but you should get a load of the locks on that door. Anyhow, the police checked to make sure no one broke in, and no one did."

"Then how could this have happened? Do you think the killer may be someone living in the building?"

"Oh, I *hope* not!"

"Well, what *do* you think?"

"I think whoever it was did this snuck in during the shift before mine. Diaz—he's on seven a.m. to three—walks around in a fog these days. I guess it's because his wife's expecting a baby, and it's their first. Don't get me wrong, Diaz is a good kid. But lately his body may be on West Fifteenth, but, most times, his head's up on Mars."

I was skeptical. "If the murderer entered the building on Diaz's shift, that would mean he had to hang around for hours."

"That's right. But he coulda hid out in the basement. Or a utility room, maybe. There are plenty of places to hide," Harris said obstinately.

"Was there anyone you saw *leaving* the building Monday night that you recognized as having visited the twins before?"

"Those two detectives already asked me that, and I told them no."

"Isn't it possible someone got by you?" I persisted. "After all, I don't suppose it's really crucial to screen people once they've already been upstairs. And if you're busy with someone who's on the way in . . ."

Harris chewed that over for a couple of seconds before conceding reluctantly, "Well, I guess *that's* possible. I don't have eyes in the back of my head, so there's a *chance* I might've missed someone when they were leaving. Especially if I was busy on the intercom or something. But one thing I'll tell you for sure: Nobody got *in* without being announced; not on *my* shift."

I had this strong conviction that Harris was having a pretty hard time accepting the fact that the tragedy had occurred when he was on duty. Maybe he even felt that his job was on the line. At any rate, he'd managed to convince himself that poor Diaz was responsible for the killer's having gained access to the building. Well, he hadn't convinced me.

"What if someone had had a lot of packages that night?" I asked. "Wouldn't you have lent a hand?"

"Sure. But nobody did. Besides, I always take care to lock the doors if I'm going to help someone over to the elevator, even though it doesn't take more than a minute or two." Then, with a look that can best be described as a glare, he defined his position on the matter again. "Listen," he said irritably," I keep telling you that when Diaz is on duty, he *isn't* on duty, if you get my meaning."

For the life of me, I couldn't see the perpetrator sitting on his hands—or any other part of his anatomy, for that matter—from three o'clock or even earlier until almost eight. And I hate loose ends. I *had* to find out how he was able to slip past Harris. "Look," I said in this nice, even tone, "if something demanded your attention for only a few seconds, that's all the killer would have needed to—"

"How many times do I have to tell you?" Harris interrupted angrily. "No one got past me. No one!"

"Sorry. Just one last question, okay?"

"What is it?" he said, his manner making it clear that one was all I'd get.

"Did you have to provide any special assistance of *any* kind that night? To an older person? Or someone in a wheelchair? Or—"

I could see that he was about to break in with another denial when suddenly he froze, his mouth hanging open and his skin rapidly losing its color.

"What is it?"

Just then, a young couple entered the building, and Harris held the door for them. When he turned back to me, the elderly doorman's face was gray. "God help me," he said softly, "I guess it could have happened when Mrs. Garvin came home."

"When was that?" I asked gently. At that moment, I was not too pleased with myself for doing my job.

"Around seven-thirty. I think it could have been a few minutes after the first Foster twin came in; only don't hold me to it. But I *do* remember thinking how late it was for Mrs. Garvin; she usually gets in around six. Well," he went on, nervously licking his lips, "Monday night, she pulled up in this big stretch limo—she never came home by limo before—and the driver started unloading these two huge cartons from the trunk. I found out later her office was moving, and the cartons were filled with papers she was storing in her apartment for the time being. But that's not here or there, is it? Anyway, what happened was one of the cartons got stuck in the trunk, and the driver started yanking at it. All of a sudden-like, the carton came loose and it caught the guy off balance. I thought for sure he was going to drop it, so I ran over to give him a hand. But by the time I got to the curb, everything was okay; he had a good grip on it."

Harris paused for a second or two, then looked at me pleadingly. "All I did," he said shakily, "was to run over to the limo—just a few yards away—and then turn right around and come back. So how long could I have been away from the door?"

And then, in a strangled voice, he answered the question himself: "Just long enough."

Chapter 7

Getting in touch with Peter wasn't easy. First thing in the morning, I tried reaching him at the office number he'd given me. His secretary—or whoever it was who answered his phone—informed me that he'd taken a leave of absence. So I called him at home. I got the answering machine and left a message. Then I waited. And waited . . .

At noon, I went out to keep an appointment in connection with one of the two other cases I was working on. And when I returned to the office an hour and a half later, I waited some more.

It was close to four when Peter finally got back to me. "I'm sorry," he said. "I've been at the hospital all day, and I just now called home for my messages."

"How is she?"

"About the same," he answered. But there was a little lift in his voice that hadn't been there before. "I was speaking to her neurosurgeon today, though. And he says that every day she's still alive, her chances go up. It's Friday now—that's *four days* since she was shot. And they didn't even expect her to last through the first night."

I wanted to respond with something positive to keep his spirits up, but I couldn't ignore the possibility that at any moment the victim might take a turn for the worse. "She's a real fighter," I told him brightly, if a little cautiously.

"She is, isn't she?" Peter said with something like awe. And then he went on to talk about the one thing I'd been reluctant to even *think* about. "You know, the doctors say it's still too early to determine the amount of brain damage. But the way I look at it, first, I want to know that it's Mary Ann. And second, I want to see her out of that coma. After that, I can deal with whatever I have to when the time comes."

I was very touched by Peter's love and courage and that

almost childlike faith he seemed to have. Besides, who was I to break those rose-colored glasses of his? "Maybe there won't be much damage," I offered encouragingly.

"That's what I'm hoping." A moment later, his tone changed. "Anyway, what did you want to grill me about today?" he asked, and I could hear the smile.

"Look, suppose I meet you over by St. Catherine's and we grab some dinner? We can talk then."

I was certain Peter would expire of malnutrition if I didn't see to it that he got some nourishment once in a while. But I was prepared for an uphill battle. I figured he'd try to beg off with the excuse that he didn't want to leave the hospital or maybe that he just plain wasn't hungry, so I was both surprised and pleased when he said, "Sounds good. What time do you want to make it?"

I guess keeping a vigil can get pretty lonely.

My taxi pulled up to the hospital's main building at six on the button. Peter was waiting for me outside.

The weather had turned bitter cold in the last hour or so, and the wind was howling shrilly. I conservatively put the wind-chill factor at minus fifty, at best. It was the kind of night I'd have loved to spend at home in my own apartment, just sitting in front of the fireplace with a good book. If I had a fireplace, that is.

My teeth were already beginning to chatter in the brief minute or two since I'd left the warmth of the cab. "It's f-freezing out!" I told Peter. "Why didn't you wait inside?"

"Didn't anyone ever tell you that fresh air's healthy for you?" he responded, grinning.

He wasn't even wearing a hat or gloves, and it was an effort to restrain myself from lecturing him about it. But I recognized that the last thing Peter needed at this stage of his life was for me to play big sister again.

"What kind of food would you like?" he asked.

"You choose."

"There's this little Italian restaurant I keep passing. I've never eaten there, but it looks pretty nice. And it's close."

"C-c-close is good," I said, my teeth clicking together like castanets.

Laughing, Peter took my arm. It was the first time I'd heard him laugh since Ashtabula. "I can't believe you! How can you possibly be cold?" he demanded. "Just look at you! A coat almost all the way to the ground, a hat pulled way down over your ears and a scarf that's up past your nose. It's a wonder you're getting any oxygen."

He laughed again, and it was almost worth freezing my buns off to hear him like that. I said "almost."

He was steering me around the corner. "It's just a couple of doors down," he let me know. "We'll be there in three minutes."

And we were.

We walked into a lively and very noisy bar area; "happy hour" was obviously in full swing here. Adjacent to that room was the dining room, which was already pretty crowded even at such an early dinner hour. Fortunately, there was an empty table toward the back, where the people were less happy and we'd actually be able to hear what each other had to say.

As soon as our waiter came over, I ordered a glass of red wine to help me defrost. Peter ordered a beer. I could barely stand it: a *cold beer* on a night like this!

After the waiter hurried away, Peter looked at me with this little smile. "Go!" he said.

Well, I hate to have business interfere with a good meal. But this was definitely not the kind of place where you could put your agenda on hold until coffee and then, over three or four refills, sit around and discuss all the things you were here to discuss. Every table was occupied now, and a waiting line for dinner was already forming in the barroom. So I didn't waste any time. "You knew that Meredith and Larry Shields—her director—were going together, didn't you?"

"Yeah, sure."

"Well, did you also know they'd split up recently?"

"Didn't I . . . you mean I didn't tell you about that?" Peter asked, blushing.

"No, you didn't."

"I don't know what's the matter with me," he said, slapping his forehead with the palm of his hand. It's a wonder I can remember my own name."

"It's understandable with all you're going through," I assured him. "Tell me what you know about the argument."

"Actually, I don't know *anything* about it. All Mary Ann ever said was that Meredith and Larry had split up and that Meredith was in pretty bad shape over it. But Meredith made her swear not to tell anyone *why* they split—not even me. I think she—Meredith, that is—felt guilty about something, but I'm not sure now if Mary Ann actually said that or I just had that impression. Anyway, they got back together again very soon, so I guess whatever it was couldn't have been that serious. Matter of fact, we all went out to dinner not too long after the fight, and they really seemed crazy about each other."

"Maybe that's why you didn't say anything to me about it," I offered.

"Nice of you to give me an alibi," Peter said, a sheepish grin on his handsome face. "Listen, do you mind if we order now? I'd like to go back to the hospital for a little while tonight."

We picked up the menus that were sitting in front of us on the table and quickly made our choices. Once we'd passed them on to the waiter, I was unable to contain the urge to make like big sister at least one more time. "Peter, I hope you won't mind my saying this," I began, realizing that, chances were, he would. "But do you think it's wise spending all your time at the hospital this way? It's got to be a terrible strain, and there's really not much you can do there at this point. Going back to work might help take your mind off things."

"*Nothing* could take my mind off things," Peter retorted sharply. Then he went on more evenly. "Look," he said slowly, struggling to convey his feelings, "I *have* to be there; I just can't stand being anywhere else. I'm even worried about something happening when I go home to sleep. Or when I take some time to go out and eat—like now. Do you understand what I'm saying?"

"Of course," I muttered contritely. "I've got a big mouth; so forget what I said, huh? But you *do* have to eat, you know."

"And I intend to," Peter promised lightly.

"There's something else I wanted to ask you about."

"What?"

"Did you by any chance see Mary Ann sometime on Monday?"

"No." I guess he read the disappointment on my face. "Why? Is it important?"

"It might be. But don't sweat it. There shouldn't be any

problem coming up with someone who saw her that day. Or, if not, someone who saw Meredith."

"What's this all about?"

"You're aware that the twins were both shot twice, aren't you? The first time in the torso?"

"Sure. I thought I told *you* that, but I probably didn't," Peter admitted ruefully.

"As a matter of fact, it was Sergeant Fielding who told me. But anyway, it occurred to me last night that if we could find out what at least one of them was wearing on Monday and if we could get ahold of the clothing, we'd be able to determine from the position of the bullet hole who was wounded where. And then, of course, we'd know the identity of the woman in the hospital."

"You're terrific, Desiree! You really are," Peter said admiringly. "Why didn't the police think of that?"

"Whoa. Don't give me so much credit. We're not sure they didn't. They just may not have been able to get their hands on the clothes for some reason. Anyway, when we finish eating, I want to see what I can find out over in the emergency room. Then, if it comes down to it, I can always check at the theater to see if anyone remembers how Meredith was dressed that—"

"Say, it just came to me! I know what Mary Ann was wearing!" Peter broke in excitedly. "I talked to her on the phone Monday morning, and she mentioned she had on this yellow cashmere sweater. I'd given it to her for her birthday, see—that was on the first—and she wanted me to know she was wearing it."

"Good," I said. "That is, it's good if she didn't change her clothes once she got home that night. But listen, Peter. Do me a favor, huh? Try not to count on something coming of this," I cautioned. "Sergeant Fielding's a good friend of mine, and I know him to be a very competent investigator. So in all likelihood the police have already explored this area. I just don't want to overlook anything, that's all."

"Don't worry, Desiree, I take your point. Now I have a question for you."

"Okay, go on."

"Did Fielding by any chance happen to mention what kind of injury she has? The woman in St. Catherine's, I mean."

I wasn't about to go back on my promise to Tim. Not

just yet, at any rate. "No he didn't," I answered. "But I'm sure he will if I can come up with the evidence to help us identify her. Any special reason you're asking?"

"It's only that I'd like to know all there is to know about her condition. And everyone's being so damned secretive about it."

He'd barely said the words when the waiter returned with our food, and for a while both Peter and I tried to forget the reason we were having dinner together that evening. Over our entrées (in deference to Peter's time concerns I'd skipped the appetizer), we talked about our lives and our work and even told each other some funny anecdotes. Dessert, however, was cappucino, cheesecake, and questions.

"Can you give me the names of some of the twins' friends?" I asked. "Anyone you can think of. And I also need to know how I can get in touch with the brother."

"Well, Eric's staying at the Grand Hyatt on East Forty-second Street. Fielding asked me about their friends, too, by the way—just last night, in fact. And I managed to come up with four. Meredith may have had other friends I'm not aware of, but I think those are the people they were closest to."

He ticked off the four names, and I jotted three of them down in my notebook. I didn't bother with the fourth; it was Chuck Springer.

"I don't have any of the phone numbers," Peter apologized, "but they all live in Manhattan, and I'm sure they're in the book. Anyway, I hope so."

"Don't worry. I'll get the numbers."

When we left the restaurant about five minutes later, the wind seemed to be biting even harder than before, and I couldn't wait to get indoors again. But on the way back to St. Catherine's, we passed one of those little fruit and vegetable stands—you know, the kind that carry a million and one other things, too—and Peter suddenly stopped. "Wait here," he ordered. "I'll be right back."

I stood there obediently, shivering like crazy, while he ran inside. He returned in a couple of minutes with two little bouquets of roses: one pink and the other yellow. "I meant to get to a florist this morning and pick up some flowers to take to the hospital," he said. "But you know me; I forgot all about it. They didn't have much of a selection left in this place, but anyway, here." He held out the pink flowers. "These are for you," he told me. "Happy Valentine's Day."

I don't suppose I even have to mention that, right then, it was all I could do to keep from bawling like a baby.

St. Catherine's emergency occupies its own building. When I walked in, the entrance room was practically empty. There was a guard over to my left, but fortunately he had his hands full at the moment. A very large middle-aged woman was standing practically nose-to-nose with him, yelling unpleasant things (I'm sure) in Spanish, a sobbing little girl in tow.

I marched straight ahead and through the double doors marked NO ADMITTANCE, PATIENTS ONLY. I stopped for a second to slip off my coat and drape it over my arm to conceal the roses in my hand. (There's something just a little unprofessional, I think, about conducting an investigation while you're standing there clutching a bunch of flowers to your bosom.) Then I hurried to the end of the short corridor, where I came to another set of doors that I also had no business going through. So I pushed them open—and found myself in the heart of the bustling emergency room.

Just on the other side of the doors were two patients on stretchers, one of them moaning pitifully. Over to my right were the small, curtained-off sections where doctors and nurses provided whatever immediate relief was possible for an almost infinite variety of illnesses and injuries. Behind one of the curtains, a woman was screaming intermittently, and in the spaces between her screams I could hear someone else crying softly. Five or six hospital personnel were rushing around, scurrying in and out of the curtained areas, one of them shouting instructions. They were all too frazzled to give a damn—or even notice—that I was there.

I spotted a large nurse's desk off to my left. Three women were seated at the desk, two of them talking on the phone. I approached the third member of the trio, a buxom blond Hispanic-looking woman who was poring intently over a ledger. "Excuse me," I said. My license was already in the palm of my hand in its little leather case, and when the woman looked up, I opened the case and passed it quickly in front of her. Then I started to stuff it back in my handbag. "I just have a few questions; it won't take—"

"Hold it a minute there, kiddo. Let me see that thing again."

I gave her the license.

"Private eye," she sniffed. "You're not supposed to be in here, you know. I'm afraid I'm gonna have to ask you to leave."

"Listen, this is very important," I said. "And it won't take long."

"It's against hospital policy. You have to get permission to come back here."

"Can't you even spare me a minute or two?" I coaxed.

She didn't respond one way or the other, but I noticed that some strange things were happening with her eyes. I turned around to see what was going on. It only took a split second for it to register that the woman was attempting to signal this guard across the room, a skinny, mean-looking creep who was standing there scowling, arms folded across his chest. He got her message almost immediately. Dropping his arms to his sides, he began striding purposefully toward us.

I talked fast. "It has to do with the Foster twins," I told her, "those poor girls who were shot in the face Monday night."

"Problem, Carmen?" asked a thin, raspy voice behind me.

Looking around, I saw the guard glaring down at me with an expression that most people reserve for multilegged little crawling creatures.

I quickly turned back to Carmen. "I'm trying to get some information on those twins; it's really vital."

She hesitated. "Well ..." And then, while I held my breath: "It's okay, Mike."

"You sure?"

"Yeah."

As soon as the guard made his reluctant departure, I said, "I'd like to speak to the nurse who took care of the twins that night."

"What do you want to talk to me about?"

"You're her?"

"Yeah. One of the 'hers,' anyway. But I'm too busy for any chitchat right now. Look, you go have a seat around the corner out of the way," she ordered, indicating with a toss of her head the general direction of the area to which she was exiling me. "I'll get to you as soon as I can."

I followed the head toss to a short, walk-through aisle lined on either side with a row of uncomfortable-looking black and chrome chairs. Taking a seat in the middle of the row, I placed the roses on the chair to my right, carefully adjusting my coat on the back of the chair so it would cover the flowers without crushing them. I'd been sitting there for only two or three seconds when this heavy hospital cart came zigzagging down the narrow aisle, headed straight for my feet. I pulled my legs back just in time to avoid having all my toes squashed. The attendant maneuvering the cart thoughtfully alerted me to the danger. "Coming through! Watch those feet!" he yelled. But not until he'd already flown past.

You take your life in your hands coming to a place like this, I decided.

I glanced idly over at the only other person around, a man or a woman seated diagonally across the aisle from me. I have no idea of the gender because this person was wearing pants and lace-up shoes, and all the time I was sitting there his/her head was buried in his/her hands. The only thing I could see was the top of a dark brown head of hair.

Just to give myself something to do, I decided to prepare a shopping list for Sunday night's dinner with Ellen and her maybe future husband. I'd already made out a list in my office that morning; in fact, it was in my handbag at that very moment. Still, I usually manage to forget *something,* so it wouldn't hurt to write out another one and double-check myself. Besides, it beat staring across the way at his/her dandruff.

I was almost through with my little chore when someone sat down heavily alongside me. I looked up, surprised to see Carmen.

"I didn't expect you to be able to get to me this soon," I told her.

"Well, there's nothing crucial waiting for me at the moment. But I don't have much time; I *am* busy. So let's get down to it."

I got down to it. "What happened to the clothes the

Foster twins were wearing when they were brought in here?"

There was a moment's hesitation before the nurse responded. "We *did* try to follow procedure," she informed me, sounding defensive. "But it was like a zoo in this place that night—I'm talking even worse than usual—and—"

"Procedure?" I cut in.

She eyed me suspiciously. "You *do* know what the procedure is in a case of violence like this, don't you?"

"Of course; the word *procedure* threw me for a second, that's all," I retorted indignantly, not having the slightest idea what she was talking about and not having any intention of betraying my ignorance, either. After all, was it my fault none of the straying spouse types I usually investigate ever got blasted for their sins? "So just what happened this time?" I asked, hoping things would become clearer to me as we went along.

"Well ..." Carmen replied carefully, "I told you how hectic it was here Monday night. There was a bus accident—a really bad one—at eighty-thirty or so, and we all had our hands full; we were running around like cockroaches. And when things are that frantic, you gotta realize it's possible to make a mistake." She took a deep breath, exhaling slowly before going on. "Anyhow, there were these two young cops hanging around over by the desk waiting for the clothes—"

"The police have the clothes, then?" So much for the smarts Peter had so kindly credited me with. Checking the victim's effects was *standard police policy,* for God's sake!

"No. That's what I'm trying to tell you," Carmen groused, looking none too happy. "In all the excitement, we wound up giving them *someone else's* property. By the time the cops realized it and came back a couple of hours later, it was too late. We'd already tossed the twins' stuff—or what was left of it, anyway. We had to cut their clothes away so's we'd be able to work on them," she explained, "and everything was in shreds, so ..." Her voice trailed off, and she shrugged her shoulders.

Fielding was right. I mean, talk about Murphy's law!

"You didn't by chance notice what either of the girls had on?"

"You gotta be outta your *bird*! They were a real mess, the two of them, all covered with blood. Besides, who had time to look? We had to get them out of those clothes fast."

"There's a good chance one of them was wearing a yellow cashmere sweater," I said in a forlorn attempt to prod her memory.

"Look, kiddo, I keep telling you it was mayhem here; I wasn't paying any attention to fashion. The only thing I was interested in—the only thing we were *all* interested in—was getting to as many people as we could in as short a time as possible." She eyed me curiously then. "What's with this yellow cashmere, anyhow?"

"Well, I don't know if you're aware of this, but one of the twins died on the operating table and the other one's still in a coma."

"Yeah, I know. I was just asking one of the floor nurses today how she is," Carmen responded, her tone softening. "I understand they were very pretty, too, although there was no way you could tell. Not after what that son of a bitch—whoever he is—did to those faces."

"That's why it's so important to find out what they were wearing. Because of what was done to them, no one knows which twin survived and which one died. One of those girls was my client's fiancée. And you can't even imagine what he's going through."

"Poor man. That's rough, really rough," she murmured, shaking her head sympathetically.

"But we're almost certain the one twin—Mary Ann—had on a yellow cashmere sweater."

Carmen caught on fast. "I see. You want to know where the woman in the yellow sweater was wounded, is that it?" Making this little clucking sound, she said quietly, "I wish I could help you. Honest." Then, obviously thinking—or hoping—I was finished with my questions, she lifted one cheek off the chair.

"Listen Carmen, I'd really appreciate the names of any of the other emergency personnel who might have worked on the twins that night."

"It won't do you any good, kiddo. That sergeant what's-'is-name already quizzed everyone in E.R. who was on duty then, even those who didn't go near those women. Believe me, if they knew anything, they would have told him."

"I realize that. But I'd feel better if I could speak to them myself. I just think I owe it to my client."

"I guess I can understand that. All right. Lemme see, the other R.N. was Kirsten Anderssen. She's off tonight, and I haven't got time to look up her phone number right this minute; I've really gotta get back to work. But I *will* get it for you," she promised, lifting that same cheek off the chair again.

"And the doctor?"

"There were two doctors taking care of them, but I can't remember for sure who they were. I'll find out, though. Tell you what. You leave me your number, and I'll ask the three of them to get in touch with you. Don't worry; I'll explain how important it is." This time, Carmen lifted both cheeks.

I stood up, too. "Let me give you a few of my cards," I told her. Propping myself against the wall, I started fishing around for my wallet in the overstuffed, suitcase-sized accessory I call a handbag.

Apparently Carmen wasn't too optimistic about my prospects for any immediate success. "Just drop them off at the desk for me," she instructed. "I gotta take off." Before I could say anything, she was walking briskly away.

The second she disappeared around the corner, I came up with the wallet.

"Wait!" I called out, running after her while I attempted to extricate some of my business cards. "You didn't even give me a chance to thank you," I said, catching up with her and handing her five or six cards. "You've been great, and I really appreciate all your help."

"That's okay; no problem," Carmen assured me, shoving the cards in her pocket. "I just wish I'd been able to tell you more. Anyway, I hope you catch the son of a bitch."

She began moving away again, and then she stopped. "Oh, I just remembered," she said, spinning around, a mischievous grin on her face. "Happy Valentine's Day." The grin widened. "And listen," she cautioned, "don't forget your flowers."

Chapter 8

In a way, I was relieved. It's true that I hadn't really learned anything at St. Catherine's. But that also meant I hadn't learned anything *bad*.

I went to bed Friday night grateful that I wouldn't have to carry any heartbreaking news to Peter—at least, not yet.

The next morning—Saturday—I was at it again.

Just before ten, I called the Hyatt. There was no answer in Eric Foster's room, and I didn't want to leave a message. I'd try him later.

I took a look at the names I'd gotten from Peter. The name at the top of the list was Lydia Brodsky. Her number was in the phone book, and, fortunately, she was home. I explained who I was and asked when it would be possible to talk to her. I figured she'd probably put me off until Monday.

"Where are you calling from?" she wanted to know.

"My apartment—on East Eighty-second Street."

"Let's see," she mused, "I don't have any appointments until later this afternoon, but there's this errand I've *got* to run up on East Eighty-sixth. That's right near you, though, isn't it? All right," she said slowly, still turning things over in her mind, "it'll take me a couple of hours to throw on some clothes, go up to Eighty-sixth Street, and then do what I have to do. But I should be able to get over to Eighty-second by twelve-thirty. No," she concluded firmly. "Make that one. Would that be okay for you?"

"Perfect." I gave her the address and we hung up.

If I didn't dawdle too much, there would be time to straighten up the apartment for a few minutes, shower, dress, and then run out and shop for Ellen's dinner tomorrow night.

I managed to fit everything in, getting back from D'Agostino's around quarter of one, five minutes before Lydia Brodsky showed up.

When I opened the door, I got the weirdest feeling. It was almost like looking in the mirror. The woman standing there was close to my own age—which, of course, I have no intention of letting you in on. And she was as short as I am. And as wide. She was dressed in a full, floor-sweeping coat (even longer than mine), a scarf that was pulled up to her nose, and a hat that came down over her ears.

The similarities, however, stopped when she took off the coat.

Lydia Brodsky had on yellow sweatpants with a matching top, which is something I absolutely forbid myself to do— wear pants, I mean. From the rear—and in that yellow outfit—she bore a strong resemblance to the back end of a taxi. Then, when she removed the hat, I noted that her hair was much too short for her very full face and much too blond to go *that* long without a touch-up. You couldn't even compare this woman's hair with my own gloriously hennaed head.

Nevertheless, her physique was enough like mine to make me swear to myself I'd go on a diet as of Monday. But I was lying, and I knew it. It's tough to diet when eating is almost like a religion to you; but it's damned near impossible if you happen to be crazy about cooking, too. Besides, my one or two successful attempts at losing weight had not altered my life in any meaningful way. What I'm trying to say is, Prince Charming didn't appear and carry me off into the sunset somewhere. And if he wasn't going to do any carrying, why bother staying thin?

Lydia waddled over to the sofa (I guess we both did a little waddling) and sat down. She passed on my offer of coffee, tea, or soda and immediately began speaking tearfully about the twins. "Mary Ann and I were supposed to get together Monday night. Did Peter tell you that? If only I hadn't gotten sick, Mary Ann, at least, would still be alive."

"She still *may* be," I reminded her.

"Yes, you're right," she mumbled, a little disconcerted. "I meant that she wouldn't have been shot. I hear ... I hear they were both horribly mutilated." With that, the tears started trickling down her cheeks, and she reached into her shirt pocket. Coming up empty, she began rummaging around in her spacious and overpacked handbag. I knew the feeling. I got up and went into the bathroom, returning with a large box of tissues. She took a few, smiling gratefully. "Thanks," she said, wiping her cheeks and returning the box to me. "I can never find anything in this damned bag when I need it."

I put the tissue box on the cocktail table in front of her. I had a very strong premonition that Lydia would be going to it again and again before our little talk was over.

"You weren't feeling well Monday; that's why you had to cancel your plans with Mary Ann?" I put it like a question to get her started again.

"Yes. We were supposed to go out to eat and then take in a movie. But when I woke up that morning, I knew I was coming down with *something*. I kept hoping until the last minute that I'd start feeling better and be able to make it, but I just kept on getting worse. At seven, I finally threw in the towel and gave her a call at the shop. You know, by the time I got home that night I had a temperature of a hundred and two. Oh, I just *wish* she'd listened to me!"

"About what?"

"Well, since I couldn't keep our date, I suggested to Mary Ann that she call Peter; I said maybe she could still get together with him. I felt really bad about waiting so long to cancel."

"She didn't want to call?"

"She told me Peter was meeting this old college friend of his for dinner and that it was probably too late to get in touch with him. I said that it wouldn't hurt to try, and she said that maybe I was right. But two seconds later, she changed her mind. She told me that, on second thought, she was kind of tired, and besides, she could use the time to take care of bills and things. I think maybe she also figured that Peter and his friend might have some catching up to do, although he *had* invited her to join them—before he knew she'd made plans with me, that is. But Mary Ann was ... is ... oh, I don't know ... she's like that. Really thoughtful."

Lydia reached for the tissues again. Scooping up a handful, she dabbed at her eyes, brushed the newest accumulation of tears from her cheeks, and then noisily blew her nose a few times. "Damn!" she said when she was through.

"If only she'd called Peter. If only she'd called *someone*! Why'd I have to pick *that* night to come down with the flu, anyway? I'm usually healthy as a horse." She forced a smile and helped herself to another handful of tissues.

"Listen, did you mention to anyone else that you were going out with Mary Ann Monday night?"

"Not that I can recall. . . . No. As a matter of fact, I'm sure that I didn't."

"And Mary Ann—would you know if *she* said anything to anyone besides Peter?"

"I wouldn't have any idea about that," Lydia answered regretfully.

"How did you happen to meet the twins in the first place?" I asked then.

"Didn't Peter tell you? They bought their condo through me. We got to be really good friends, too. There's a little difference in age, of course," she quickly put in, sounding a bit defensive, "but it didn't matter. I seem to have more in common with younger women."

"Ohhh, you were their real estate agent," I concluded with that remarkably keen mind of mine. "I understand it's quite a place, that apartment of theirs."

Lydia nodded her agreement. "I wish *I* could afford it."

"Just how much was it, anyway?"

"Oh, I don't think I should—"

"Please," I said. "I'm not asking to be nosy. It could be important."

She thought it over for a couple of seconds. "All right," she conceded, "it was one and a half."

"Million?" Any number with six zeros after it really throws me.

"Million," an amused Lydia echoed.

"Who actually purchased the apartment—Mary Ann or Meredith?"

"They both did; it was in both names. Although Meredith was the one who took most of the initiative when it came to the decision making."

"The twins were quite different, I'm told."

"Definitely. Mary Ann was more . . . laid back, I guess you'd say. While Meredith was a take-charge kind of person. Maybe it was because she was a month older."

I did a sort of double-take, which must have been the kind of response Lydia was after, because then she grinned and said, "They were born four minutes apart, you know. Even though they both celebrated their birthday on February 1, Meredith was actually born on January 31—just before midnight. And then Mary Ann came along right *after* midnight. Meredith used to refer to Mary Ann as her kid sister."

She didn't say anything more for a few moments, but I watched the brief lightheartedness evaporate. And when she spoke again, it was to speculate sadly, "I think maybe the real reason Meredith was more dominant has to do with all she went through. I don't know if you're aware of it, but she lost her husband just this past year, and a tragedy like that can make you grow up pretty damned fast."

"I heard about that."

"He was very ill for a while, too, before he died. And Meredith *devoted* herself to his care. Not that she ever complained; she never even mentioned it. But Mary Ann told me how rough things had been for Meredith right before they came to New York."

I got around to my standard question then: "Can you think of any reason someone might have wanted to harm either of them?"

"God, no! Is there any chance it could have been a plain ordinary robbery?" Lydia asked hopefully.

"The police more or less ruled out that possibility."

"This is all so ... so ... *unbelievable*," she said, sniffling. "I still can't believe it happened." That called for another bunch of tissues.

I gave her a little time to blow her nose before I asked, "Would you happen to know if either of them had any other close friends?"

"Well, there's Peter, of course. Poor guy. I've been talking to him regularly to find out how ... uh ... *she's* doing in the hospital. He doesn't even sound like the same person anymore."

"Anyone else?"

"That director boyfriend of Meredith's—Larry somebody; I met him once at the apartment. They were also pretty friendly with a couple of people in the building. Some guy down the hall—I'm *positive* he's gay—and a woman who lives upstairs. I don't remember *his* name, but hers is Claire. Now, let me think, what was the last name?"

"I was able to supply it, courtesy of Peter's list. Josephs. Claire Josephs."

"That's it."

"What about Roger, Mary Ann's ex-fiancé?"

Lydia's eyes flew open. "This is the first I've heard that there *was* an ex-fiancé."

She left a few minutes—and a few more tissues—later. I got one last view of the Brodsky rear end before she put on her coat.

The sight, a living reminder of my own ample dimensions, really unnerved me. As soon as she walked out, I headed straight for the freezer. I wasn't myself again until my second portion of Häagen-Dazs Macadamia Brittle.

Peter called around eight, just as I was finishing dinner. "How did you make out at the emergency room last night?" he asked.

"Nothing," I said, briefly explaining what had happened to the girls' clothing.

"I've been putting off this call all day," he confessed. "Even though I kept checking my machine and telling myself that if you had any news, good *or* bad, you'd have left a message."

"You *know* I'd have gotten in touch with you if I had anything to report," I verified.

"Have you spoken to Eric yet?"

"Not yet. I tried him this morning and again around six, but he wasn't in his room."

"I don't suppose you've had a chance to reach any of the friends."

"As a matter of fact, Lydia Brodsky was here this afternoon."

"Did you find out anything?"

"I can't really tell *what* I found out at this point. Certainly nothing dramatic. She mentioned, though, that you'd asked Mary Ann to join you and a friend for dinner that night."

"Uh-huh. My old college roommate was in from Maine. But Mary Ann had already made these arrangements with Lydia." Then he added poignantly, "You know, when the police told me about her being shot in her apartment like that, I thought at first that they'd made a mistake, that it wasn't Mary Ann at all. I was *sure* she wasn't even home when it . . . happened."

"So you and your friend had dinner, just the two of you?" I asked quickly, unwilling to let him dwell on that ultimately tragic change of plans.

"Right." There was a pause before he whispered: "Unfortunately."

"Peter, do you have any idea if Mary Ann told anyone—besides you, I mean—about making that date with Lydia?"

"Just Eric, I think. He wanted to get together with her that night, too. But when she couldn't make it, they decided to have lunch on Tuesday."

Now, *that* was interesting. . . .

"Listen, Desiree," Peter was saying, "I haven't had anything to eat all day. And if I don't grab a bite soon, I'm going to start chewing on the telephone wire."

"Oh, then I won't keep you." But, of course, he didn't get away that easily. "Are you calling from the hospital?" I wanted to know.

"No, I just got home."

"How was she today?"

"Holding her own, the doctor says."

"Well, that's something to be thankful for," I told him. "Now go eat, and I'll talk to you soon."

We hung up, and I spent a few minutes bracing myself for the exciting event I'd planned for the remainder of the evening: tearing my apartment apart. The necessity for this had evolved because Charmaine, my every-other-week cleaning woman, had failed to show up for so many weeks that I'd lost track of which week she was due. And while I'd been filling in for her myself on a fairly regular basis, I'm afraid I wasn't exactly committed to my work. That night, however, I made up my mind to devote myself body and soul to dispelling the dust, mopping the floors, and scrubbing the toilet.

After all, it wouldn't do to have Will think that Ellen came from a dirty family.

I got up early on Sunday morning to prepare my do-ahead dishes. By a little past one, I was out of the kitchen and just getting ready to set up the folding table in the living room. That's when Ellen called.

"I need your help, Aunt Dez."

"Sure. What's up?"

"I can't decide what to wear tonight. I've narrowed it down to the blue wool or my black ribbed turtleneck with the black leather skirt."

"Gee, I don't know. You look good in both."

"You're a big help."

I made up my mind. "The blue, I think; it's a great color for you."

"I was kind of leaning that way myself. Thanks."

Ellen showed up at seven-fifteen that night—in the black leather outfit. But that was okay. She looked really cute.

Will Fitzgerald was at my door at seven-thirty, right on schedule. He was carrying a large bouquet of flowers which, I have to admit, really impressed me. But the minute I introduced him to Ellen, I could see from his expression that they would not be heading for the altar.

Now, as I said, Ellen looked very cute. But then, Ellen *is* cute: tall (from where I stand, five-six is tall) and boyishly slim, with large dark eyes, silky brown hair, and a lovely smile. I think she resembles Audrey Hepburn. Maybe not a *lot,* but a little, anyway. Besides, all Will had said was that he was interested in meeting a nice girl; he didn't list any physical requirements.

At that moment, though, I was pretty positive that Will's idea of "nice" was 38-24-36.

I served the hors d'oeuvres—a wonderful baked clam dish and these tiny mushroom tarts for which just about *everyone* requests the recipe. Then I left it to Ellen to see to the drinks while I went to check on dinner. From the kitchen, I could hear Ellen trying to make conversation and Will responding in monosyllables.

I basted the rib roast, gritting my teeth. I'd decided on prime ribs because I knew Will was a meat eater—he was always scarfing down hamburgers at his desk. With the meat, we'd be having Yorkshire pudding with horseradish sauce, a potato and cheese casserole, and a large salad with a tasty vinaigrette dressing. A really nice menu, I thought. *Too* nice for Will Fitzgerald.

When I returned to the living room, Will was devoting himself entirely to the hors d'oeuvres, and Ellen was sitting there with this tiny, pathetic smile plastered on her face, bravely trying to cover her feelings of rejection.

Things got even worse at dinner when Will made an at-

tempt at humor. "You should have another helping of pota-
toes," he told Ellen. "The way you are now, if a man
jumped your bones, that's what he'd get: bones." (Did I
say *humor*?) His accompanying laugh was almost as offen-
sive as the remark.

Ellen turned crimson. *Oh, God,* I thought, *how can she
ever forgive me for Will. How can* I *ever forgive me for
Will?*

Did I want to tell that bastard off! But that would have
made things even worse for Ellen than they already were.
So I restrained myself with what, let me assure you, was a
superhuman effort.

The meal seemed interminable. The one break we had
was that there was no need to even attempt polite conversation. Will, you see, was interested only in the food, shovel-
ing down almost mind-boggling quantities.

Finally, the end was in sight.

My delightful dinner guest was just finishing his second
helping of cold lemon soufflé—which is my *most* special
dessert and which I was sincerely hoping he would choke
on (and there's *no way* I'd have rendered the Heimlich
maneuver, either). Ellen was on her third cup of coffee.
And I was seriously contemplating pouring a fourth for
myself. Suddenly there was this loud beep, which, in a room
so heavy with silence, sounded more like a siren. Ellen
spilled her coffee, and I, steel-nerved soul that I am,
damned near suffered a coronary.

"My beeper!" Will exclaimed, removing same from his
pants pocket. "Do you mind if I use your phone?" he
asked politely.

I directed him to the one in the bedroom, more to get
him out of my sight for a few minutes than to afford him
any privacy. But he insisted on making the call from the
living room.

"What's up?" he said into the receiver. This was followed
about two minutes later by a disbelieving "You're kidding!" and then, in rapid succession, by a shouted "Of
course not!" a strangled "Christ!" and an authoritative
"Call the cops!" He concluded with a brusque "I'll be right
home," slamming down the phone.

Now, somewhere between the "You're kidding!" and the
"I'll be right home," it dawned on me that this crisis of
Fitzgerald's was a little something he'd cooked up in ad-

vance. You know, to use as an escape hatch if it should turn out he wanted one. I sneaked a look at Ellen, and I could tell that, unfortunately, she'd caught on, too.

"That was my next-door neighbor," Fitzgerald was saying. "Apparently someone's broken into my apartment. Jules—my neighbor—heard a lot of noise coming from the place, and he knew I wasn't home. He wanted to check and see if I had someone staying there before he called the police." It wasn't a bad performance, really. He was even managing to sound a little breathless, almost like he was hyperventilating. A pretty nice touch.

Without commenting, I quickly got him his coat.

"As much as I'd like to stay," he told us as he hurriedly put it on, "I'm afraid I don't have any choice." A rueful smile flitted across his troubled, lying face.

I glanced anxiously over at Ellen again, hoping she'd be able to control her tears until that S.O.B. got the hell out of the apartment. I needn't have worried. My niece rose to the occasion magnificently, handling her humiliation in a manner that I'd have sworn was not even in her nature. (But, as I said before, with Ellen, you just never know.)

Jumping up from the table, she rushed over to Will and held out her hand. As soon as he took it, she looked directly into his eyes. "I just thought I should tell you," she said, sounding cool and sophisticated and totally sincere, "how interesting it was to meet you. I hope you won't be offended, though, if I ask a favor of you."

"No, no, of course not," a thoroughly confused Will Fitzgerald assured her.

"I'd appreciate it if you wouldn't attempt to pursue this relationship. I know it's very shallow of me, but I really *do* prefer taller men."

Chapter 9

Miraculously, Ellen managed to contain herself until Will was not only out of the apartment but probably in the elevator on his way downstairs. Then came the deluge.

"He c-certainly was anxious to g-get away from me," she gulped between sobs. "And what does a lawyer need with a b-b-beeper, anyway?"

"It's for dire emergencies like tonight," I said tartly. "And I bet they come up all the time." Then I hugged her awkwardly and added "The guy's a pig" before running into the bathroom for what was left of the tissues.

For the next fifteen minutes, I was busy telling Ellen what scum Will was and how attractive *she* was. "Any man whose measure of a woman is her bustline has got to be the world's foremost jerk," I summed up.

Ellen's comment was drowned out by her snuffles, so I went with an all-purpose response. "Okay. Maybe you're not a forty-D. But then," I reminded her, "neither is Audrey Hepburn."

I think that made her feel better. Anyway, she pulled herself together a short time later and, at my insistence, spent the night on my sofa.

I went to bed as soon as I got Ellen settled, but it took me a long time to fall asleep. I was too busy making plans.

I was going to hire myself a hit man. Of course, I'd have to find out first where to get one and then make a few inquiries about the going rate. Wait a minute. . . . On second thought, I'd have Fitzgerald's kneecaps broken instead. (Would I still need a hit man for that, I wondered, or were kneecaps a specialty field?) But that idea eventually went by the boards, too, in favor of a scheme in which I personally did the slime in. The last thing I remember before dropping off was this mental picture of me behind the wheel of a sleek, black car, smiling gleefully as I ran Fitzgerald down and then slowly backed up over his lifeless body.

I woke up at seven, and the little scenarios I'd conjured up at midnight seemed a lot more improbable and a little less appealing in the light of day. (Although, to be honest, the idea of *one* broken kneecap still held a very strong attraction for me.) Anyway, after a large breakfast, which a much improved—even if far from cheerful—Ellen insisted on preparing, I headed for the office.

Jackie, my secretary, was on the phone when I walked in. "This is for you," she said, putting the call on hold, "a Dr. Gail Schoenfeld."

Dr. Schoenfeld, it turned out, was one of the emergency room doctors who had tended to the twins the night they were shot. But, as Carmen had predicted, she had nothing to add to what ridiculously little I already knew.

I devoted most of that morning to making phone calls, which is something I'm very unfond of (an unfortunate aversion for a P.I.). But I didn't have much choice if I wanted to make contact with the outside world.

First, I tried the Hyatt. Again, Eric Foster was out. This time, though, I figured I'd better leave word. It was awkward going through the operator, so I limited the message to saying that I was a private investigator working for Peter Winters and that it was urgent Mr. Foster call me back as soon as he could. "You'll see that he gets this?" I asked the operator harmlessly—if unnecessarily.

"Yes, of course," she retorted in a tone that made it clear that what she was *really* saying was: "What do you think I'm here for, stupid?"

After that, it was time to take a crack at the other two friends on Peter's list. I got out the telephone directory and found phone numbers—or, at least, *probable* numbers—for both of them.

The name I'd written down directly below Lydia Brodsky's was Charlotte Bromley. There was a C. Bromley on West 20th Street, and Peter had told me Charlotte lived downtown somewhere.

The answering machine let me know I'd come to the right place.

"Hello, this is Charlotte," a breathy, little-girl voice informed me. "I'm taking a well-deserved vacation, but I'll be home on March sixteenth. Please leave a message, and I promise I'll return your call when I get back. And don't forget to wait for the beep."

The hell with the beep! March sixteenth? That was a month away! "Damn!" I grumbled, clicking off.

Dialing Claire Josephs, who lived in the twins' building, I was primed for another conversation with a machine. It took a couple of seconds for it to register that there was a real live person on the other end of the line.

The woman sounded totally frazzled. And who could blame her? A baby was shrieking in the background, and the sound was so piercing that, even as removed from it as I was, it jangled every nerve in my body.

When I asked about meeting with her, Josephs informed me that her son was suffering from a slight ear infection. The pediatrician who had seen him first thing that morning assured her it was nothing serious, but try telling Greggie that, she said. Then, apparently inspired by having some-one—*anyone*—over age three to talk to, she rattled on about how she was quite used to Greggie's doing more than his fair share of squalling—he was colicky right from the start—but these last two days, he was really driving her over the edge. She did want to get together with me, though, she put in quickly. "Why don't you come over later in the week?" she suggested. Then she added almost prayerfully, "I'm *sure* he'll be better by that time."

"Whenever you say," I told her.

"How's Thursday?"

Thursday was good.

"Could you be here in the afternoon? Around two?" She was practically yelling now in an attempt to be heard over the screeches, which seemed to get louder by the second. "That's when the baby has his nap," she shouted at top volume, "so it's the best time to come."

I hurriedly agreed, only too anxious to get out of earshot of little whatever-his-name-was.

I left both my phone numbers in case there was any change in plans, and we hung up. For a couple of minutes, I did absolutely nothing but luxuriate in the comparative quiet of my moderately noisy surroundings.

It was about quarter of eleven, when I was on my way to the water fountain, that I came face-to-face with Will Fitzgerald.

He spoke in the most sincere voice imaginable. "Hi, Desiree. I was just coming in to see you. That dinner last night was absolutely terrific—one of the best I've ever had. I'm only sorry I had to run out like that. I found a real mess when I got home, too."

I gazed at him stone-faced as he went on. "Those guys sure cleaned me out. They got away with my TV, the new six-hundred-buck stereo system I bought when I moved to New York, and the Omega watch my grandfather gave me when I graduated from law school. And God knows what else they boosted that I'm not even aware of yet!"

I suppressed the urge to tell him to drop dead; that would hardly have been ladylike.

"Immolate yourself, huh, Will?" I suggested instead before turning my back and walking briskly away.

Right before noon, I heard from the other emergency room doctor. He was very nice but as uninformative as his colleague had been. "We were terribly busy that night," he said regretfully. "Besides, those women spent hardly any time in emergency; we had to rush them right into O.R."

Well, it was what I'd expected, wasn't it? Nevertheless, the morning had left me so thoroughly drained that I decided to treat myself to pizza for lunch. But when I was sitting there at the counter at Little Angie's, nibbling away at the absolutely thinnest, crispiest crust in the city, the back end of Lydia Brodsky suddenly flashed before my eyes.

And I limited myself to two slices.

Chapter 10

I got home a little after six, and the red light on my answering machine was flashing.

The first message was from Kirsten Anderssen. "Carmen Velez asked me to call you," she said. "I'm the other E.R. nurse who took care of those twins you wanted to know about. But I couldn't possibly tell you what they were wearing." Then she went into all these details about how frenzied things were in emergency that night, prattling on and on until the machine, mercifully, cut her off in midword.

The second message was from Eric Foster. "I'm on my way to a business dinner with an associate just now," he said, sounding veddy British. "I'll ring you when I get back to my hotel if it isn't too late. Otherwise, you'll hear from me in the morning."

Peter was next. "Everything's status quo at this end," he reported. "I'm calling because I spoke to Maureen the other day, and she made me promise not to forget to send you her love. But, well, I forgot."

I was shaking my head in exasperation and grinning at the same time. That was *so* Peter.

I ate very well that evening on the leftovers from Sunday's disastrous little get-together—or whatever you want to call it. Then I turned on the television. I soon found out that my tolerance level for Monday evening's sitcoms was practically at ground zero that night, and I kept on playing with the remote until I succeeded in getting myself nuts. I finally shut off the set, went to the bookshelf, and took down an Agatha Christie. *Sad Cypress*. That was one I'd only read twice—three times, tops—so it would be practically like a new experience for me.

At ten, I dragged myself away from Hercule to call Ellen. But she beat me to it. The phone rang just as I was about to lift the receiver.

I wanted to ask if she was okay, but if she *was,* the question might remind her that she had reason not to be. So I clamped a lid on myself and went to something innocuous. "When did you get in?"

"About a half hour ago. And I put your care package to good use. I had a big slice or roast beef, some Yorkshire pudding, and a *huge* portion of the potato casserole, *and* I polished off the lemon soufflé. I made such a pig of myself that I am now ready to barf."

"Gee, Ellen, thanks so much for sharing that with me."

We both laughed (although Ellen doesn't really *laugh;* she giggles), and I decided that she certainly *seemed* to have recovered from her lovely evening at Aunt Dez's.

"How's the case coming?" she asked.

"Damned if *I* know," I grumbled.

I hadn't exactly made any monumental inroads in the investigation so far, and I was beginning to feel a little discouraged. (Patience may be a virtue, but it's never been one of mine.) So it didn't bother me to hear Ellen—who is president and sole member of my fan club—swear that I would definitely solve the case and that I was the *only one* who'd be able to do it because I was so much more clever and resourceful than the police or *anyone.* (I mentioned how exceptionally wise Ellen is in some ways, didn't I?)

Anyway, our conversation boosted my confidence a little, and I went back to my mystery, certain I could even keep pace with the indomitable Poirot. Especially the second time around.

When I walked into the office in the morning, there was a message waiting on my desk. It was from Eric Foster, and he'd provided a number where he could be reached. I didn't waste any time in returning the call.

"Foster here," said last night's clipped British accent.

"This is Desiree Shapiro."

"Oh, yes, Ms. Shapiro." His tone grew solemn. "You phoned me yesterday. About my sisters, I would guess."

"That's right. I wonder if I could come over and see you—as soon as possible."

"Well, my firm just made a furnished flat available to me for as long as I'm here in New York, and I'll be moving in later this afternoon. But it shouldn't take very long to get myself settled. You could stop by this evening, if you'd like."

"Thanks, I'd appreciate it. Just say when and where."

"Eight o'clock, if that's agreeable to you. Three fifty-four East Forty-ninth Street."

"I'll be there."

I considered calling Larry Shields before heading over to the theater but decided that would give him the option of telling me he couldn't see me that day—an option I was not willing to make available to him. So I occupied myself with some paperwork, then took a cab to the Berkeley around eleven-fifteen. Maybe I'd catch him right before a lunch break.

They were rehearsing when I got there. I looked around for Shields, but he was nowhere in sight. Then I heard a familiar voice bark some instructions at the actors. I was trying to figure out where the voice had come from when there was another bark. This time, I got a fix on the general direction. I walked toward the front of the theater, and there was Shields in the audience, seated off to the side some six or seven rows back. No wonder I hadn't spotted him! He was slumped so far down in his chair that only about an inch or two of his head was visible over the back.

I tiptoed over, then bent down and very softly said his name.

He damned near shot out of his seat. "Jesus!" he bellowed, everything sort of froze.

"I'm sorry," I told him, "I didn't mean to startle you."

"You're here again, huh?" he said, now sitting ramrod-straight. "You could scare the crap out of someone like that, you know?" Then, to the cast: "Okay, gang, let's break for lunch. A half hour. And I *mean* a half hour, got it?" He looked up at me. (But not very far up, since Shields was almost as tall sitting down as I am when I'm standing.) "You got any news for me?"

"I wish. Look, can we talk for a few minutes?"

"Let's go back to my office."

Remembering that office—and, most particularly, those tottering chairs of his—I was quick to offer an alternative. "How about if I buy you lunch instead?"

"There's nothing I like more than having a woman spring for a meal for me, but I don't have much of an appetite lately. In fact, I haven't even been *eating* lunch. Thanks, anyway, though." He stood up. "But, hey, it's not *all* bad; I lost almost ten pounds this past week." With that, he turned around, making this pretense of letting me admire him. Then we headed backstage.

"I didn't see Lucille Collins up there," I commented as we were walking.

"She's home nursing a bad cold," he informed me.

When we got to his office, I saw that, since my last visit, Shields had managed to accomplish the impossible: almost doubling the clutter in that incredibly cramped little space. He even had to dump a huge stack of papers from one of the two killer chairs so we'd both have room to sit down.

"What did you want to see me about?" he asked immediately after I'd perched *very carefully* on the cleared-off chair. I had one cheek on the seat and the other sort of hanging out there in space, and Larry Shields was looking at me and trying very hard not to smile.

"Why didn't you mention that you and Meredith had broken up for a while not too long ago?" It was supposed to be a question, but somehow it came out sounding more like a challenge.

It put the director on the defensive. "I don't know who fed you that garbage," he countered testily, "but it's not true."

"I have it on good authority that—"

"I don't care if your authority's the pope," he broke in. "Merry and I never split up." A moment later, he was calmer. "Listen," he said with exaggerated patience, "when we first started rehearsals, I was so wrapped up in getting the play under way that things may have cooled off a little between Merry and me. I just didn't allow myself time for anything but my work. But it was only temporary."

"Meredith told someone you'd broken it off because she'd done something unforgivable. She didn't say what it was, but she did use the word *unforgivable*."

Shields's forehead wrinkled up and his eyebrows came together, forming two deep lines just above his nose. But very quickly his brow cleared. "Oh, for God's sake! I know what it was!" he announced. "Merry was having a little difficulty with her part in the beginning. She was great with the more dramatic demands of the role, but the part also called for her to be something of a comedienne, and Merry wasn't that comfortable with comedy yet. She hadn't done much of it, so her timing was slightly off, that's all. I kept telling her that that's what rehearsals are for." His tone softened perceptibly. "But the thing is, Merry was . . . *is* . . . such a . . . such a damned perfectionist."

I hated poking away at him like this, but it *was* what I'd come here for. "I don't quite follow you," I told him. "What does that have to do with her feeling that she'd done something unforgivable?"

"You didn't let me finish. I knew she'd be just wonderful by the time we were ready to open, but Merry was really worried about letting me down. And she told me she felt guilty because, unconsciously, she might have used our personal relationship to get me to offer her the role. Which, incidentally, I gave her for only one reason: She was absolutely right for it. Anyway, that's what she was talking about; it had to be," Shields insisted, his eyes fastened on mine.

I must have looked skeptical. (I sure as hell *was* skeptical.)

"Look, Merry has a flair for the dramatic—all actors do. What you'd maybe consider a *problem,* an actor blows up into a *catastrophe.* That's what she was referring to—this business about our relationship influencing my professional decision. Believe me, there's never been any trouble between Merry and me."

Well, he certainly *sounded* convincing enough. And I had to admit it was a nice try. Still, the only thing Larry Shields made me believe that day was that he was a pretty good actor himself.

Chapter 11

I came back to the office with a crumpled sheet of paper on which Shields had reluctantly scrawled the home telephone numbers of the cast.

Lucille Collins answered the phone with what sounded like a death rattle. She was not what you'd call anxious for a visit from me. But with a little determination and a lot of nagging, I persuaded her to let me drop by her apartment for lunch the next day. First, however, I had to promise—twice—that I'd be accompanied by a container of homemade chicken soup.

It wasn't until after five, just as I was about to leave work, that I remembered I'd intended to call Stuart Mason that afternoon.

I should probably explain about Stuart, just so you understand what's going on. I'll make it brief, because it's really kind of awkward for me—discussing my sex life, I mean (even though there's pathetically little *to* discuss, especially lately). But anyway, here goes. . . .

Stuart Mason's my accountant. He's also my friend-turned-lover-turned-back-to-friend. I've know him about a hundred years, since before there was even an Ed in my life. And I liked him (I'm talking platonically) from the first day he started poking his nose in my books, although in the beginning our contact was pretty much relegated to business hours. That changed soon after Ed and I got married. That's when the four of us started having dinner together pretty regularly—with the fourth party being Stuart's beautiful wife, Lynne. Then, quite suddenly, beautiful wife Lynne took off (I have no idea where or why), and we became a threesome. Until Ed died.

It was more than a year after Ed's death—and I won't go into the details—when, somehow, my friendship with Stuart took on the added dimension of *physical* closeness.

I guess it happened because we'd both suffered a loss that hurt us deeply and we were lonely and we liked and trusted each other. What I'm trying to say is that there was never a real romance or anything like that between us. Just a lot of pleasant moments shared by two very good friends.

Anyhow, whatever started it, things went on that way for a long time. But then these circumstances occurred that I'd rather not even think about, and I got to feeling guilty about the physical aspect of my relationship with Stuart. And so we reverted to being platonic friends again. Which is where we were now. Whether I liked it or not.

But about the phone call . . .

Wednesday was Stuart's birthday, and I was taking him out to dinner. We'd made our plans so long ago, though, that I thought I'd better confirm.

I was a little surprised to find him at his office. "I was *hoping* you'd still be there," I said.

"Are you kidding? I've got a long night ahead of me here. April fifteenth is practically around the corner."

"I won't keep you. I just wanted to be sure we're still on for tomorrow night."

"That's okay, I can talk for a couple of minutes. And yes, we are *definitely* still on. Tell me, how's everything going?"

I screwed up my face, then realized that wouldn't communicate too well over the phone. "So-so," I answered.

"Is anything wrong?"

Now, I don't like to complain—not more than two or three times an hour, anyway. Besides, I'd already gotten some bolstering from Ellen just the night before. So I merely said, "No, nothing's wrong. It's only that I've taken on a new case—one that's a real challenge. And once in a while I get a little concerned about being up to it, that's all. I'll tell you about it when I see you." Then, in an attempt to put the topic to bed, I added lightly, "Whether you want to hear it or not."

"I definitely *do*," Stuart responded, chuckling, after which he immediately turned serious. "Look, Dez, you're an extremely competent investigator. The way you solved those murders in your niece's building should have proved that to you, if nothing else ever did." There was the briefest pause before he tagged on, to ensure that I was sufficiently encouraged, "I have no doubt you'll do the job this time, too; you'll see."

I was really touched. But not surprised. Stuart's a very sensitive, caring person. It's just too bad he's so good-looking (and you know how I feel about *that*!); otherwise, we might have had a future together.

I gave him the address of the restaurant, which had been highly recommended by Ellen, and told him I'd see him there on Wednesday at seven. Then we hung up, and I went downstairs to fortify myself with a sandwich for my eight o'clock meeting with Eric Foster.

I didn't have the trouble I usually run into in getting a cab at that hour, so I arrived at Foster's building—an older, but well-kept high-rise—ten minutes early.

Now, I, personally, am not too thrilled when people show up at my place before they're expected. Invariably, it's while I'm in the middle of doing battle with this unbelievably perverse hair of mine. Or when I'm trying to clean up the mess under my eyes that I seem to make more often than not when I'm applying mascara and which leaves me looking like I play outfield for the Mets. So I decided to take a nice, slow walk around the block. After all, I didn't want to start off on the wrong foot with Foster.

When I finally gave myself permission to go upstairs, it was just eight o'clock.

Eric Foster was a tall man, lean and trim, and, like his sisters, he was fair. Although at first glance he appeared to be quite young, when I looked again I noticed the sharp lines that ran from his nose to his mouth, and I saw that his light brown hair was liberally flecked with gray. I put him in his late thirties somewhere, maybe twelve or thirteen years older than the twins.

He showed me into a small, almost totally beige living room, and I sat down on this ugly modern sofa, which was obviously not built for anyone under six-foot-three. It was so deep I had to move all the way to the edge so my feet would touch the floor. Foster settled into the matching club chair opposite me, and as soon as I was through squirming around, he apologized at length for not having anything but Diet Pepsi and instant coffee to offer me. I really wouldn't have minded the coffee, but I decided to wait until I got home so I could pair the last cup I was allotting myself that day with what I had left of the lemon soufflé. I did think he had perfectly lovely manners, though. (But then, the English always appear to be so much more polite than we are. Probably because with *that* accent even something like "You bastard, you" sounds like a pleasantry.) It was hard to believe the man was actually an American. Or at least he was when he started out in life.

"You must have been very young when you moved to London," I commented.

"I was close to fifteen. But the twins weren't even a year old yet," he replied, smiling cordially.

I figured I'd get the heavy question out of the way first. "Would you mind telling me where you were last Monday night—when your sisters were shot? Let's say between seven-forty-five and nine o'clock."

End of cordial smile. "I've already given the police a statement about that."

"Yes, I know. This is just for my records."

"And because I'm considered a suspect. That *is* the case, isn't it?"

"At this point, I consider everyone who even said hello to your sisters a suspect."

"Apparently the New York City Police Department does, too," Foster observed dryly. "Don't misunderstand me. I appreciate the need to be thorough; I really do. But your police here take it to an extreme. Did you know I'm not allowed into the hospital room—even with a twenty-four-hour guard stationed there?" He shook his head in disgust. Then, looking at me through narrowed eyes, he threw down the gauntlet. "Tell me, Ms. Shapiro," he said in this low, even voice, "if I shot my sisters, what the hell was my motive supposed to be?"

"Well, you and Meredith weren't exactly on the best of terms, and—"

"God! Do y'know how long that's been going on?" Foster cut in. "And Merry's the one who was furious with *me;* I've been trying for years to make things right between us." He sat there in silence for a moment or two, caught up in thought. Then he challenged me again. "But let's put *that* aside. Why would I want to harm Mary Ann?"

"There's evidently a lot of money involved here. And you *are* the closest living relative."

"For all I know, the money might have been left to the boyfriends. Or to some society for the preservation of one-legged orangutans."

"I gather, then, there was a will."

"Actually, I haven't the vaguest notion whether there was or not; I said as much to your Sergeant Fielding. But it's a moot point, since I've quite enough money in my own right, thank you. Plus, for those records of yours, I have an excellent position—vice president of New Delhi Imports, which is a large and very solid company with offices round the world."

"I'm not—"

"But what matters most, Ms. Shapiro," Foster concluded almost fiercely, overriding my words, "is that I loved my sisters very much. *Both* of them."

"Listen," I told him quietly, "I'm not asking you these questions to trap you. I'm just looking for information—information that could conceivably even *remove* you from suspicion."

"I doubt I can provide anything like that," Foster responded with a wry smile. "At least, it didn't work that way with the police. But if I can help you to find out who shot Mary Ann and Merry—although I honestly can't think *how* ..." He broke off. Then, straightening his spine, he said decisively, "Well, let's have at it anyway. You wanted to know where I was that night.

"We had an office meeting until almost seven. My employers are very kindly allowing me to work out of the New York office until things are ... resolved," he explained. "It's certainly preferable to sitting around and thinking for twenty-four hours a day." He paused before adding grimly, "About what some *fiend* did to my sisters."

"And where did you go after you left work?" I asked gently.

"I went for a bite of supper. This little hamburger place on Fifty-third, right off Park. It's two or three blocks from the office."

"Do you think anyone there might remember you?"

Foster shook his head. "The police already checked; showed them a photo, but absolutely no one recognized me. It hurt my feelings, too, that this face—which my mother had always told me was one in a million—left no impression whatsoever." Then, more seriously: "It's not surprising, really. I'm not known there—it was only the second or third time I'd been in the place. And before you ask, I paid cash. The Heavenly Burger," he informed me, smiling, "is not the sort of establishment to accept American Express."

"What time did you finish eating?"

"I'm not too certain. I would say about twenty before eight."

"And then?"

"I returned to the hotel—the Grand Hyatt over on Forty-second Street. I'd had a rather tiring day, and I decided I'd do a bit of reading and go to bed."

"You got to the hotel a little before eight, then?"

"I would guess it was close to eight-fifteen. I walked over, and I'm an awful dawdler; I stopped and looked in every shop window I passed."

"Did anyone at the hotel see you when you came in?"

"It appears not. Or so the police say."

"You had asked Mary Ann to have dinner with you that night. Is that right?"

"That's right. But she'd made previous arrangements. My fault. I hadn't let her know what date I'd be here."

"Were you angry that she didn't cancel her plans? After all, you're not in town that often."

"She offered to. But I insisted she go ahead and meet with her friend, and we made it lunch on Tuesday instead. To be honest, I wasn't *too* disappointed she couldn't come out with me on Monday. I was a bit under the weather when I got here Sunday—that's when I called her, Sunday evening—and the way I felt then, I wasn't at all sure I'd be able to manage food the next day."

I was about to say something when Foster made a point. "Incidentally," he said, "if I intended to do in both my sisters, as you suggested, I wouldn't have chosen that night, when I had every reason to expect that Mary Ann would be at dinner with a friend."

I'd have to think about that. But at the moment I couldn't come up with a response. So I moved on to something else. "Could you tell me about your feud with Meredith? You objected to her marriage; was that it?"

"I objected strenuously. Merry was just twenty when she began seeing this Garibaldi punk—that was his name: Gene Garibaldi." *That figured; according to Peter, the guy's name began with a C or an R.* "He was well in his thirties," Foster was explaining, "and heavily into drugs. At the time they met, Merry was studying theater and she'd already been cast in a few small parts on the BBC. Which is quite a coup for a young girl, don't y'think? At any rate, our parents were still alive then, and they begged her to stop seeing him, to concentrate on her career. Well, Merry made it clear she had no intention of giving up either her career *or* this Garibaldi. She was quite taken with him. He was ... uh ... handsome, I guess you'd say," Foster admitted grudgingly, "and he treated her like a little queen. Naturally, he swore he was quitting the drugs, and Merry believed him."

"And did he? Quit, I mean."

"Not at first, anyway. He may have done later on; I can't be certain."

"So you intervened?"

"Yes. But not when I should have—in the beginning, when it might have done some good. I was married and living in Dorking by that time, y'see, so I was pretty removed from things. I was aware of how concerned my father and mother were, of course. As a matter of fact, they kept after me to have a talk with her. The girls had always looked up to me, y'know, my being so much older. But at any rate, I was far too wrapped up in my own life to put myself out that much," he confessed, his voice filled with self-loathing. "So I convinced myself it wouldn't do any good for *me* to badger her, too. Eventually, though, my mother persuaded me to go and see what I could do. But by then Merry was hopelessly infatuated with the man."

He looked so despondent that this damned bleeding heart of mine went out to him (just as it seemed to be doing with practically everyone I talked to in this case). "How did Meredith react?" I made myself ask.

"Not surprisingly, she deeply resented my meddling. And then, a short while after our talk, she and Garibaldi became engaged, and she cut off all contact between us."

I don't know what I'd expected—probably that the split between brother and sister would have had a more dramatic origin. I found that I was almost disappointed. "And that's why she hasn't spoken to you in all these years?"

"Not quite," Foster admitted, flushing. "Because of Garibaldi's drug habit, I was terribly afraid for Merry." He looked at me intently. "Please understand," he said softly, "I know that I was out of line. But what I did, I did for *her* sake. I was desperate for her to be rid of the man."

He hesitated for a few seconds, while I sat there waiting anxiously. I think I may even have been holding my breath. "So I went to see him," Foster finished, seeming to cringe at his own words, "and offered him money if he would get out of Merry's life."

Well, that certainly made Meredith's hatred of her brother a little easier to understand! "And?"

"And he told me to go to hell."

"Garibaldi, I suppose, reported back to Meredith?"

Foster nodded. "And she rang me up and said she would never again have anything to do with me." There was a catch in his voice when he added somberly, "And she never did."

"I'm sorry." It was all I could manage with that lump in my throat.

"It's the biggest regret of my life," he murmured, "what happened between Merry and me. My sisters are my only family, y'know. I'm divorced—close to two years now, it's been—and Zoe and I never had any children." And then he just sat there for the better part of a minute, staring at nothing, saying nothing. Finally, he seemed to work his way out of the mood. Shifting around in his chair, he glanced over at me. I got the idea he might be getting impatient.

"Just one more question," I said before he had a chance to maybe suggest (very politely, of course) that it was time for me to leave. "How long ago did Meredith and Garibaldi get married?"

"It was that same year; just a couple of months after I went to him about the money—1988, I think it was."

"His death—was it drug related?"

Foster shook his head. "A short while before he died, I had lunch with Mary Ann. I asked her how Merry was doing—as I always did—and she told me that Garibaldi was gravely ill. An inoperable brain tumor. It was a matter of months at most, she said. And a few months later, he was gone.

"You know, this is only the second time I've been to New York since my sisters moved here," he informed me. "And the last time I was in town, back in October, I didn't see as much of Mary Ann as I would have liked. I was taking an extra three days this trip just so we could have a decent visit and so there'd be a chance to meet her fiancé. We planned on having dinner later that week—Mary Ann and Peter and I. And now ..." Turning away from me, Foster reached into his pocket for a handkerchief and took a furtive swipe at his eyes.

"Peter and I did have a late supper together one night last week," he continued, facing me again. "But, of course, it was only the two of us." He swallowed hard. "Nice chap, that Peter, very nice. We talk every day, y'know. He keeps me advised on how things ... uh ... on how things are."

I nodded before saying "Just one more question" one more time. "What do you know about the man Mary Ann was engaged to?" I asked. "Before Peter, I mean."

"Roger Hyer?"

At last! "How do you spell that?" I pounced.

Foster spelled the name for me. "I only met Hyer once," he went on to say. "The three of us had tea at the Savoy."

"What did you think of him?"

"Not very much, I'm afraid. Hyer's a weasel. He'd been married twice but never mentioned a word about it to Mary Ann. He's also disgustingly full of himself. I guess I didn't approve of either of my sisters' choices." Then he put in hastily, "Former choices, I should say."

"What else can you tell me about this Hyer?"

"Only that he has money—he's an investment counselor and a very successful one, apparently. And I can tell you that he considers himself something of a Don Juan and that he doesn't look you straight in the eye when he talks to you."

"You wouldn't happen to know where he lives, would you?" This past week had taught me I couldn't exactly rely on Peter's recollection of things.

"Let me think for a moment. . . ."

"Was it Hillside, New Jersey?"

"That sounds right."

I silently begged my client's pardon. But I was premature.

"No, that wasn't it," Foster amended a couple of seconds later. "It wasn't Hillside; it was *Hillsdale.* Hillsdale, New Jersey."

"Thank you, Mr. Foster; thank you very much. You've been very helpful." I struggled to my feet. "I've just about run out of questions, you'll be happy to hear." He started to protest, but I cut off his gallant effort, quickly covering myself with: "For now, anyway."

He got the idea. "Well, if any other questions *should* occur to you," he said, rising, "you can ring me either here or at the office." He took a business card from his wallet and wrote down the phone numbers.

"You'll be around for a while, I suppose," I remarked when he held the card out to me. It was an offhand comment, but Foster's face darkened and something frightening suddenly appeared in his eyes. When he spoke, however, it was in his normal tone of voice.

"That's something you can depend on, Ms. Shapiro," he said. "Even if the police should allow me to leave—which I very much doubt—I have no intention of going home until I find out which of my sisters is lying in that hospital. And just who the bastard is who put them *both* where they are today."

Chapter 12

About two minutes after I walked in the door that night, I called New Jersey information for Roger Hyer's number. It was a little before nine-thirty.

The first time I dialed, Hyer's line was busy. So I figured it might be a good time to touch base with Peter. The conversation was brief. I found out there was no news at the hospital, and *he* found out there was no news at my end, either.

Then I tried Hyer again. And got a busy signal again. I kept trying him on and off for the next forty-five minutes. Finally I had the bright idea of checking with the operator—something that would have occurred to anyone with at least a normal amount of intelligence a good half hour earlier—and was informed that the receiver was off the hook.

Okay. If that was the case, I might as well relax for a while. I decided to do my relaxing at the kitchen table with that cup of coffee I'd promised myself earlier, accompanied, of course, by what was left of the lemon soufflé—which, by the way, was still so sensational I came close to going into mourning when it was gone.

At about ten of eleven, I took one last stab at Hyer.

"Hello," said a deep, resonant male voice. You can't imagine how sexy he made that word sound.

"Is this Roger Hyer?"

"It is."

I told him who I was and apologized for calling so late, explaining that I'd been trying to reach him for over an hour but that his phone had been off the hook.

"I know; sometimes I find that necessary," Hyer responded with this salacious little chuckle that left no doubt as to his meaning.

"Uh, I . . . um . . . suppose you've heard about Mary Ann

and Meredith Foster being shot," I began. (I *hate* it when anyone goes out of their way to get me flustered—and succeeds.)

"I read about it in the papers," he said matter-of-factly. "Look, let me save you some trouble. I haven't seen either of them since we—since Mary Ann—called off our engagement."

"I'd still like to come out and talk to you. Maybe—"

"There's really no point in it," he interrupted. "There's absolutely nothing I can tell you."

"That's what everyone always thinks, but you'd be surprised at what you know that you don't—"

"The answer is no," Hyer said decisively. And quite rudely, too.

I tried appealing to the man's sense of morality. "I'm aware that you and Mary Ann didn't part on the best of terms," I told him, "but I'm sure you wouldn't want the person who shot her—maybe even *killed* her—to get off scot-free."

"I'd rather that didn't happen, of course. But to be brutally honest, catching whoever it was who attacked my ex-fiancée and her sister isn't really a top priority of mine. In other words, Miz . . . ?"

"Shapiro. Desiree Shapiro."

"In other words, Miz Desiree Shapiro, since I can't help you—and you'll just have to take my word that that's true—I'm not about to waste my time and yours on a meeting that will, believe me, prove fruitless."

"Look, Mr. Hyer, since I'm a *private* investigator, you don't *have* to meet with me. But the police are anxious to talk to you, too; in fact, they'll be getting in touch with you soon." (I had my fingers crossed that they hadn't already tracked him down and questioned him.) "And I'm working very closely with the homicide detective who's in charge of this case," I said in this quasi-confidential tone. "If I'm satisfied you had nothing to do with the shootings, it could make a difference in the way the police view you."

I steeled myself for an explosion, but, unexpectedly, Hyer laughed. "Well, well," he said, "it seems that the lady P.I. isn't above a little blackmail, now, is she?"

"Wait just a—"

"It's okay," he assured me pleasantly. "I like your spunk. I happen to have a dinner date in Manhattan Friday evening. Suppose I meet you for a drink beforehand. Around seven." He wasn't *asking.* "Let's make it the Plaza. The Oak Room. I'll be wearing a navy suit with a navy and red polka dot tie." Before I had a chance to mention *my* wardrobe, he concluded with, "And be on time." Then the phone went dead.

On Wednesday morning, I called New Delhi Imports and, after being transferred four times, was finally put through to a Mr. Selby in personnel who had an annoyingly unctuous manner and talked through his nose. I told Selby I was with Cosgrove, Ltd. (a classy name, I thought), and that I was verifying the employment of a Mr. Eric Foster in connection with a purchase he intended making at our store. I was informed that not only was Mr. Foster a vice president of the firm, but an extremely valued employee who had been with New Delhi for almost fifteen years.

"Uh, just what did you say was the nature of the purchase that Mr. Foster is contemplating?" Selby asked nosily in his oil-slick voice.

I was sorely tempted to say "A Concorde jet" but settled for "I'm sorry, but I'm not at liberty to give out that information" and clicked off.

Actually, I could have predicted what I'd find out from New Delhi. Eric Foster was too smart to lie about a thing like his employment. Still, it was something I couldn't *not* follow up on, if you know what I mean.

At about twenty after eleven, I left the office and stopped in at this little grocery store on the next street, which is famous in at least a two-block radius for its homemade chicken soup. (I never promised Collins I'd be the one at home doing the making, did I?) I picked up two quarts of the soup, a quarter of a pound each of roast beef and sliced turkey, half a pound of potato salad, a rye bread with caraway seeds, and a half dozen pieces of the most *unbelievable* apple strudel. After all, even if Collins turned out to be too sick for dessert, there was nothing wrong with *my* health.

I arrived at the actress's Soho loft at ten of twelve, but that day my being early worked out just fine. Collins lived on the fourth floor, and I had only one way of reaching her: on foot (although by the time I made it up those four long, *long* flights to her apartment, I was practically on my hands and knees). And I don't have to tell you that I didn't break any speed records negotiating all those stairs, do I? Especially since I had to sit down and rest three times between the third and fourth landings.

As soon as she opened the door, you could tell the woman was not exactly in the pink—except for her nose, that is, which was closer to crimson. Her skin was chalky, her eyes vacant and watery. Even the beautiful auburn hair I'd so shamelessly coveted during our last meeting was stringy and disheveled. And, to add to this lovely picture, she had on a soiled gray flannel robe that was just begging for a spin in the washing machine. All in all, just then, Lucille Collins was not a beautiful thing to behold.

"Come on in," she said. This was punctuated by a hacking cough that absolutely ruined the impact of her wonderfully husky voice. I quickly accepted the invitation, literally falling into a chair.

"I dropped off to sleep again," she explained. "I think I'd better go and repair the damage." With that, she retreated to the bathroom.

While I was struggling to catch my breath, I glanced around the huge space that served as Collins's living room, bedroom, and kitchen. The white brick walls were covered with photographs—many of them of the actress herself— along with playbills and other theater memorabilia. I would have liked a closer look, but that would have required lifting myself out of the chair, which I was definitely not up to at the moment. I contented myself with taking an inventory of the rest of the loft.

The scarred wooden floor was bare (and in dire need of a sweeping, too). And there was surprisingly little furniture, a fact made even more apparent by the room's impressive dimensions.

Hugging one wall was a dark blue sofa bed, now open and covered with rumpled white sheets topped with a dingy yellow blanket that was strewn with crumpled tissues. There was a large wicker wastebasket in front of the sofa, a sizable portion of its contents—mostly used tissues, from what I could see—overflowing onto the floor. Adjacent to the sofa was a battered wooden end table which hosted a tall, chipped, blue china lamp—and still *more* tissues. Completing this unattractive grouping was a single Queen Anne–style chair—which I was extremely grateful to at present—upholstered in a grungy tweed that might have originally been beige but whose color was now anybody's guess.

On the long wall opposite the sofa, there was only a small chrome and Formica kitchen table that stood in the corner along with two chrome chairs that had torn vinyl seats. A tiny Pullman kitchen with grimy, discolored fixtures was recessed into the short wall next to the table and chairs.

I took a look behind me at the only other items in the place. In front of a large triple window at the far end of the loft was a shiny new exercise bike surrounded by five or six bulging cartons. The cartons had me wondering whether Ms. Collins was coming or going.

The sound of footsteps interrupted my speculations, and I turned back around to face a much more presentable Lucille Collins.

She had changed to a fresh, clean robe, and her long hair was pulled neatly back and tied with a ribbon. Her eyes seemed clearer, too. She'd even applied some lipstick and, if I wasn't mistaken, a little something to her cheeks. Only the scarlet nose remained to attest to her debilitated state.

Obviously, Collins had noticed I'd been staring at the cartons. Either that or she always felt that an explanation was necessary for new visitors. "I haven't gotten around to unpacking yet," she said.

"Oh, did you just move in?"

"About eight months ago," she answered without even blushing.

There was no resistance when I suggested she relax while I got our lunch ready. "Thanks, I'd appreciate it; I feel like shit." A loud honk into a crinkled tissue followed by a prolonged and wracking cough attested to the words. "I don't know when I've had a worse cold," she complained, crawling back into bed.

From her horizontal position, she provided instructions on where everything could be found, and I went about heating the soup, putting up the teakettle, and setting the table. Then, while I was waiting for the water to boil, I attacked—over the mildest of protests from my hostess— what looked like a week's worth of dirty dishes in the sink. But don't give me credit for being a good Samaritan or anything. I only did it because, frankly, that greasy, food-encrusted mess had the potential to ruin my appetite. (And if you saw *my* apartment, you'd know that I'm not exactly a fanatic about cleanliness, either.)

We sat down to lunch a few minutes later, and Collins managed to do justice to everything—including the strudel. (Anyone who could pack in food the way she did, I decided, could have found the strength to rinse off a few dishes.)

Anyway, I let the woman eat in peace, but after I'd poured us both a second cup of tea, her immunity was over.

"Let's talk about the night the twins were shot," I said.

Collins nodded.

"What time did you get home?"

"After seven sometime. I can't tell you just when." With that, she began to cough. And cough. It was so intense and went on for so long that I started to get nervous.

"Would you like some water?"

Shaking her head, she continued hacking away. By the time the cough subsided, the color of Collins's face matched her nose to a T.

"Have you seen a doctor?" I asked. I mean, it was possible the woman had TB or something.

"Oh, no. I don't need a doctor. I'm a *lot* better than I was," she assured me. "But I hope I don't give *you* anything."

Amen, I thought fervently.

"What else did you want to know?" Collins was saying, apparently attempting to get things moving again.

I was happy to oblige. "You stayed in all evening?"

"Uh-huh. With a book. Just as I told you before."

"Can anyone verify that?"

"Well, a friend called me a few minutes after ten. But I guess that's too late to provide me with an alibi, isn't it?" Then, looking at me earnestly: "I had no reason to kill Meredith—much less her sister. Can't you see that? After all, Meredith didn't give *herself* that part." Even when not in top mesmerizing form, those eyes of Collins's were compelling enough to swear to her sincerity.

It was time I let her know that *I* knew. "I understand you and Larry Shields had been going together before he met Meredith," I said meaningfully.

"Yes, but it had actually been over for quite a while by that time. We just hadn't bothered making it official."

"Were you surprised that Shields and Meredith got back together again after *their* breakup?"

"I have no idea what you're talking about," Collins answered flatly.

"You don't know that they split up for about a week?"

"No. And I'm sure I *would* have known about it if they *had*. Listen, Larry gets tied up in knots when one of his plays first goes into rehearsal. So maybe they didn't see each other for a few days. Or a week. It's the way he is." Then she added with this wistful little smile, "I should know, shouldn't I?"

At that point, she began to cough again, even more violently than she had earlier. We sat at the table until the coughing stopped and she was able to swallow a couple of spoonfuls of cough medicine. After that, she went back to bed. I stayed around just long enough to clean up our lunch dishes.

Walking down those four flights of stairs, I had plenty of time to think. And the first thing that occurred to me was that I hadn't said anything about Shields and Meredith Foster breaking up when the play *first went into rehearsal*. It sounded very much to me as though Lucille Collins had been coached.

You know, the woman was really something. I mean, for her to be so protective of the man who dumped her. *Unless,* of course, she was hoping to get him back.

But what *really* got to me was that she actually expected me to believe she didn't resent Meredith Foster one little bit for walking off with the part—and the guy—she wanted. (I didn't give any credence to that junk about the relationship with Shields having cooled before Meredith came into the picture—at least, not as far as Collins was concerned.)

Hey, if I accepted what Lucille Collins was trying to sell me, I'd have to regard her as some kind of saint. And I just couldn't picture a saint living in such a dirty apartment.

Chapter 13

By the time I made it down to street level, I was bone tired. No doubt due to all that enforced exercise. So even though it wasn't much after two-thirty, I figured I'd forget about going back to the office and knock off work early, for a change.

There was no trouble at all getting a cab. It was an off hour; besides, the day was sunny and not too cold, unseasonably warm for February, in fact. I was home by three and in bed ten minutes later, determined to take a nap before my seven o'clock dinner with Stuart. The alarm was set for four-thirty, which would give me plenty of time to get ready.

I woke up with a start to the insistent ringing of the telephone.

"Yo, sweet li'l baby," a young male voice said.

Unfortunately, I had not been anyone's sweet li'l baby for quite a while, and I politely told Romeo as much. After we said our good-byes—or, at least, after I'd said mine—I looked over at the clock. It was five forty-five. God bless Romeo, whoever he was!

I bolted out of bed, cursing myself for forgetting to pull out that little plug on the alarm clock.

Well, there'd be no leisurely bubble bath tonight. I settled for a quick shower and then set some kind of speed record for applying my makeup. Naturally, I wound up with even more smudges than usual under my eyes, and it took me longer to get through with my face than if I'd taken the time to do it right in the first place.

I devoted the next fifteen minutes to fussing with my hair. But, for me, fifteen minutes wasn't that terrible; I've been known to wrestle with this hair of mine—which definitely has a mind of its own—for close to an hour. Anyway, when I was satisfied that the results weren't god-awful, I let loose with half a dozen extremely liberal spritzes of extra-extra-hold. By the time I was finished, even a tornado couldn't have coaxed a single strand out of place.

Now I was ready to get dressed.

I was planning on wearing this almost-new royal blue silk that the saleslady had insisted made me look practically sylphlike. Of course, I didn't believe *that* for a minute. Still, I did love the dress.

I stepped into it carefully, buttoned a couple of buttons, and checked myself out in the full-length mirror. As I stood there admiring my reflection, I saw it: a spot just below my left breast!

It was only a small spot, really; I doubt that anyone would have noticed it. The trouble was, though, that *I* knew it was there. You see, I've got this *thing* about neatness—when it comes to personal grooming, that is. I guess it's because of my weight. I mean, there's nothing I can do about someone referring to me as fat (although I much prefer "full figured" or "well rounded" or even "amply proportioned"). But I refuse to give anyone a reason for calling me fat and *sloppy*.

Well, I did have another choice—the pale gray wool. Which was really very pretty and very appropriate. *But* which went on over my head.

I can't tell you how slowly and painstakingly I eased myself into that dress. And when I was through, there wasn't a wisp of hair out of place. There was an entire section standing straight on end! And, what was worse, I couldn't even run a comb through that sticky mess!

By then it was ten of seven, so I knew Stuart—who's ridiculously prompt—would already have left the office. I called the restaurant with the message for him that I'd be a *little* late. Which was definitely a case of optimism triumphing over experience.

After that, I got out my wig and was relieved to find that it was actually quite presentable. I only had to expend ten minutes or so of really concerted effort to make it look almost as good as it had when I'd taken it out of the closet.

When I finally left the apartment, it was past seven-thirty. And I was in so much of a hurry I forgot to put on the new gold-plated earrings with the faux pearl stones that I'd bought especially for the occasion.

*   *   *

Ennio and Michael's, Ellen's excellent recommendation, is all the way downtown in Greenwich Village, so I showed up more than an hour late. Which really unnerved me. But in spite of that, it turned out to be a really lovely evening.

The restaurant itself was attractive and comfortable. And I can say the same about Stuart. Not only is he tall and blond and good-looking and one of the most considerate people you'd ever want to meet, he's also great company. I'm really amazed that no one's snapped him up in all this time since his divorce. (But don't get me wrong, I'm not complaining.)

We started off by toasting his birthday with a very nice burgundy. (Stuart rarely indulges in anything alcoholic, but he finally gave in to my completely spurious argument that no one over eighteen has any business celebrating a birthday without a good bottle of wine.) With the wine, we ordered some fried zucchini, and it was as crispy and delicious as Ellen had assured me it would be. My entrée was the veal Sorrentino, which Ellen had just about insisted I try, while Stuart had the veal parmigiana, and we were both extremely pleased with our choices.

As always with Stuart, conversation was easy and animated. He didn't even mention my getting my papers together so he could start on my taxes, something he'd been after me about practically since the first of the year. (Maybe he figured it was unsportsmanlike to badger someone who's picking up the tab for your birthday dinner.) Anyway, we were having this heated argument about a best-selling mystery we'd both read recently. I was going on and on about how much I'd enjoyed it, while Stuart was contending that it was highly overrated. That discussion ended abruptly when he proclaimed, not too softly and with a straight face, "You know, it doesn't make you an authority on murder just because you've got one or two of your own under your belt."

The woman at the next table, who had been listening intently to our conversation (and don't ask me why; it wasn't all that interesting), stared at me with an expression I can't possibly describe but which sent Stuart and me into prolonged spasms of laughter.

When we'd both sufficiently recovered, Stuart said, "That reminds me. You haven't told me about this new case of yours."

I filled him in, very briefly, and when I was through, he

whistled softly under his breath. "You've sure got yourself a weird one this time," he remarked.

Since I really needed a break from things, even if it was only for a few hours, I wasn't anxious to get into any big discussions just then. So when he started to comment further, I quickly asked—because I couldn't think of anything else to say—"Have you been to any good movies lately?" The minute it was out of my mouth, I couldn't believe I'd said it. I mean, talk about inane—to say nothing of obvious—remarks!

I began to apologize, but Stuart cut me off. "Listen, I know how you feel. You don't hear me talking about Schedule Cs tonight, do you? But I *would* like to say one thing, if it's okay." He was looking at me for permission, and I felt like a prize jackass.

"Please. Go ahead."

"I was just wondering if you ever checked out your client's alibi."

Peter's? If Stuart had spent just two minutes talking to Peter, he couldn't possibly have even *thought* of anything like that! And I was about to say as much, but just then an acquaintance of Stuart's walked in and came over to the table to say hello. And right after that, we got busy with a couple of very generous portions of tartuffo.

When we'd done justice to the desserts, I suggested we stop off somewhere for a drink. We found a quiet little bar a couple of blocks from the restaurant, where I had a B&B and I could not dissuade Stuart—birthday or no birthday—from reverting back to his designer water.

We spent almost an hour in the place, doing a lot more talking than drinking. But the subject of Peter's alibi didn't come up again. Before too much time would pass, however, I'd remember my friend's words. And wish I'd taken them seriously.

Going home, Stuart and I shared a cab uptown. And all the way over to my apartment, I kept wondering if I should invite him in, what I'd say if he turned me down, and whether it would even be wise to try to get things back to the way they used to be. . . .

Suddenly we were in front of my building, and Stuart was telling me he'd see me upstairs. Then, with his hand on the door handle, he turned back to the driver. "Wait for me," he instructed. "I'll be right down."

And *that* was the end of that.

Chapter 14

Claire Josephs's two-bedroom condo was on the sixth floor, two floors above the twins'. The apartment had very little furniture—not much more, in fact, than Lucille Collins's loft. But the few items that were here looked attractive and appeared—to me, anyway—to be of really good quality. Claire, a pretty, obviously harried blonde in her twenties, had been anxious to explain the austere surroundings. "We spent so much on the place—it was much more than we could afford, actually—that we had practically nothing left for furniture. So we're filling in one or two pieces at a time."

We were sitting at the kitchen table, and Claire had just poured us some coffee when she warned me that her napping son might wake up at any moment. "He usually sleeps for an hour at least, but these last couple of days . . ." Looking a lot like someone condemned to purgatory, she shrugged her shoulders.

"Still that infection?" I asked, trying to sound sympathetic but cringing inwardly at the remembrance of the last earful I'd had of little whatever-his-name-was.

"I don't think so," Claire replied, looking anxious nevertheless. "At least I hope not. I had him to the doctor's this morning, and the doctor tells me the infection's pretty much cleared up." She made a try for optimism. "Well, let's wait and see. Maybe he'll sleep right through until three today."

Then, without any prompting from me—probably because she figured she might be on borrowed time—the young mother started to talk about her long friendship with the victims. She spoke quietly, often nervously licking her lips and occasionally fighting back tears.

"I met them when I was only ten years old," she said. "My father had just been transferred to the American Embassy over there, and we went to the same school, the twins and I. We got to be really close; we were best friends practically from the first day we met. Maybe because we had a common bond, you know, being American."

"How long did you live in London?"

"Until I was fourteen. But we still kept in touch after I moved back here. We wrote each other regularly, and once in a while, like on a special occasion, we'd even spring for a phone call. And then, when I was seventeen, my parents gave me a trip to London as a graduation present. I stayed with some friends of the family's for a month, and I saw Mary Ann and Merry practically every day. It's funny. Everyone's always saying you can never pick up where you left off, but we didn't have any trouble at all."

"I've been told the twins were very different. I mean, as far as personality."

"Oh, yes. Mary Ann was very warm and, well, gentle, I guess you'd say. She had a great sense of humor, too. And she was friendly to everyone. Merry was more reserved. Not that she was standoffish," Claire hastily clarified. "It's just that she wasn't quite as outgoing. Merry was the one with the guts and the backbone, though; she's the one you'd go to if you needed someone on your side. And she was very goal-oriented, too." Claire paused then and smiled sadly, remembering. "Even as a little girl, Merry wanted to be an actress. And she was really caught up in it. More than caught up, *dedicated*. Like when she played the lead in *Annie* at school. I suppose you know the play." She looked at me questioningly.

"Oh, sure."

"Then you know that Annie had a headful of these little red curls. Well, at the school, they expected Merry to wear this wig. She tried it on without saying a word. But the next day she went out and got one of those home perm kits and some hair dye, and Mary Ann and I did her hair for her." Claire had a smile now that seemed to cover her entire face. "The things you do when you're kids," she remarked, shaking her head wonderingly from side to side.

"Anyway, we—Mary Ann and I—cut off all of Merry's beautiful long hair, and then we gave her this perm—the worst perm you ever saw! It looked like she'd stuck her finger into an electric socket! And that was our *best* work. The *color* was what was really not to be believed. It came out bright orange! I got so scared when I took a look that I was out of their house like a shot. I was terrified for days that Mrs. Foster would call and tell my mother what we'd done."

"And did she?" I asked, laughing.

"No. But do you want to hear the funniest part? Merry couldn't have been happier. That's what I mean about her being dedicated. She never cared one bit about how she looked—as long as she looked right for the part. She still doesn't. Just a couple of years ago, she was playing Joan of Arc, and off went the hair again. She wrote me that a lot of people even mistook her for a boy that time. But that didn't bother Merry! Anyway," Claire informed me, "one good thing came out of the *Annie* business."

"What was that?"

"They used to play these tricks on me once in a while. I'd think I was with Merry, and it would turn out to be Mary Ann. Or the other way around. They thought that was hilarious, but after a while I didn't find it so funny. But, of course, with Merry's hair so different, they couldn't pull that on me anymore. And by the time her hair grew out, they seemed to have forgotten all about that little game."

"They were pretty much identical, I gather."

"Pretty much, but not exactly. Mary Ann's nose had this tiny bump in it. And Merry had a stronger chin, I thought. And there was something different about their eyes, too. But I think the differences were more pronounced once they grew up. Or maybe I just got a little smarter—more perceptive—when I got older. But they were—" Suddenly, Claire broke off. "Oh," she whispered, looking stricken.

"What's wrong?"

"Do you realize that all this time I've been talking in the past tense . . . about my two closest friends in the world? And *one* of them, at least, is still alive."

"It's only natural under the circumstances," I assured her. "Besides, mostly you've been telling me about what happened in your childhood, and that *is* the past tense." I saw that the girl's eyes were moist now. *Uh-oh,* I thought, bracing for a good, long cry. But she surprised me. "I promised myself I'd control myself today," she said with an obvious effort. "So where were we?"

"I was about to ask what you could tell me about their brother."

"Eric? I hardly knew him. He was a lot older than we were; he was already out of the house by the time I moved to London. So I didn't see very much of him while I was living over there. And I haven't seen him at all since the twins came back to New York."

"You do know that there was some trouble between him and Meredith."

"Oh, sure. They had this colossal fight because Merry's future husband was on drugs."

"Just what did Meredith say about the fight?"

"Only that Eric tried to break them up and that she was never going to speak to him again. I wasn't around when it was all going on, of course, so that's all I know." Then Claire had a thought. "Listen, have you spoken to Helen Ward?"

Now, *there* was a name I hadn't even heard yet. "Who's Helen Ward?"

"Another friend of Merry's. An actress. They were in a play together when Merry first moved back here. The play didn't last very long, but they hit it off right away and I know they kept in contact. Merry wasn't much of a talker, though, so I wouldn't count on anything. But it's always *possible* she mentioned something to Helen."

"Do you know how I can get in touch with Helen?"

"I'm pretty sure she lives on the Upper West Side somewhere. In the nineties, I think."

"Just one more thing," I said—not altogether truthfully. "Have you ever met Larry Shields?"

"Only once, when Merry brought him up here for coffee. He seemed like a really nice guy; Merry was pretty crazy about him, too."

"So I've heard. Were you aware they split up for a while?"

"Yes. But I don't think it lasted a week."

"You wouldn't happen to know the reason for the split?"

Claire shook her head. "Merry said she couldn't talk about it, so I didn't ask any questions."

"How about Roger Hyer? What can you tell me about him?"

Our peaceful little talk was interrupted at that moment by the most ungodly, high-pitched shriek. Claire leaped up as if someone had just put a tack on her chair. "Excuse me," she called over her shoulder as she ran from the room.

In a couple of minutes she was back, carrying this fat, pajama-clad Buddha who was maybe six months old (but then again, maybe not even—my experience with babies being what it is). As young as he was, though, this kid had the smuggest expression on his face.

"I'm really not supposed to do this—pick him up when he cries," Claire confessed. She sat down at the table again, wiping away the one or two tears she'd allowed to accumulate on her son's puffy little cheeks. "But all I can say," she continued defiantly, "is let Dr. Fink see what Greggie's lungs do to *his* nerves." She scowled malevolently at her firstborn. "Now where were we?" she asked as she began to bounce him up and down on her lap while keeping up a dialogue of widely spaced little clucking sounds.

"Roger Hyer," I reminded her.

"Right." Then, between bounces and clucks, Claire pretty much restated what I'd already heard from the others.

"Did you ever meet Hyer personally?"

"A couple of times. I thought he was a real slimeball, too, but, of course, I never said anything to Mary Ann. Do you think Roger might have had something to do with this?"

"I haven't got the vaguest idea yet *who* was responsible. I was hoping that you might."

"*Me?* Oh, no! I still keep expecting to wake up and find that it's just some terrible nightmare!" Giving herself over to the horror of it all, for a brief moment Claire neglected to jiggle the Buddha, and he immediately made himself heard.

It seemed like a good time for an exit.

Chapter 15

Since she was an actress, there was a better than even chance that Helen Ward (the girl Claire Josephs had suggested I talk to) wasn't working. Also, that I'd be able to reach her at home in the morning. So as soon as I got to the office on Friday, I looked up Ward's phone number. Then I waited until ten-thirty to call, figuring it was a reasonable hour even for someone in the theater to be up. I figured wrong.

"Yes? Hello?" said a sleepy female voice, following which there was this terrible racket in my ear signifying a monumental catastrophe at the other end of the receiver.

In a moment the girl was back on the line. "I'm sorry. I dropped the phone," she explained, yawning.

"No, *I'm* sorry. I woke you, didn't I?"

"That's okay. I had to get up early today anyway," she said graciously.

I told her who I was and why I was so anxious to meet with her. When I was through, she asked groggily, "Uh, just who did you say it was that got shot?"

"Your *friend,* Meredith Foster, along with her twin sister." I'm afraid my tone was a little sharp, but, after all, we were talking life and death here.

"Meredith Foster?"

That's when it finally dawned on me, quick study that I am. "This *is* Helen Ward, isn't it?"

"No. It's her roommate."

I soon learned that Ward was on location shooting a movie in the middle of the jungle somewhere and that there was absolutely no way I could get in touch with her. (Considering how my luck was running, it was probably the first job she'd had in months, too.) She'd already been gone five weeks, and, according to the roommate, my guess was as good as any as to when she'd be back. "To tell you the

truth," the girl said, "I thought she'd be back by *now*."
After which she confided cattily, "She doesn't have much
of a part."

"Well, if you should happen to hear from her, please ask
her to call me—any time of the day or night." I provided
both my home and office numbers, then added, "You won't
forget, will you? It's very, *very* important."

"Oh, I won't forget," she replied pleasantly. "I wrote
down the numbers in Helen's message book. But don't
count on her calling me from over there. She's been gone
all this time, and she hasn't yet."

"Well, when she comes home, then, have her get in touch
with me right away. Will you do that?"

"Sure."

"It's really *vital*." (As you've no doubt already gathered,
I have this tendency to resort to overkill to make a point.)
"And thanks very much, Ms. . . . ?"

"Shakira. Just Shakira. You know, like Madonna. And
Kenny G."

Kenny G.?

The Plaza Hotel's venerable Oak Room, with its dark
wood paneling and lovely subdued murals, its comfortable
leather armchairs and worn oak plank floors, has a kind of
faded and genteel charm you won't find in any other room
in New York. Or anywhere else I've ever been to, for that
matter. I had to admit I approved of Roger Hyer's choice.

Just from our phone conversation, I swear I could have
picked Hyer out of the crowd. But the navy suit with the
navy and red polka dot tie *did* clinch things.

A dapper, dark-haired man in his late thirties, he was
staring absently at the drink in his hand when I walked
over to his table.

"You're—"

"Roger Hyer," he finished for me. "And you must be
Desiree." Then he flashed these large, even teeth that—
particularly against his George Hamilton suntan—were so
startlingly white I practically had to blink.

Getting to his feet, he came around to hold out my chair
(with what I thought was an exaggerated politeness), and I
realized he was only an inch or two taller than I was in my
heels. Which would put him at five-six or maybe five-seven,
at most. But he was well built, with a slender yet substantial

frame that displayed his expensively cut suit to good advantage.

The waiter appeared at our table the instant we were both seated. "You'll have to drink fast to catch up with me," Hyer told me. "My second," he added, indicating the empty glass in front of him.

I asked for a Perrier with a twist of lime, and Hyer ordered another Chivas—neat. As soon as were alone again, he said, "You wouldn't believe me when I told you I didn't know anything that could help you." His lips curved in a faint, lopsided smile. "But it's your party. Go ahead. What did you want to ask me?" There was something really contemptuous about that smile. Also, I saw now that Eric Foster was absolutely right: The man didn't look you in the eye when he talked to you.

But I had no intention of letting Hyer's manner unnerve me. "You and Mary Ann Foster were engaged for about six months, I hear."

"That's right. And I'm sure you also heard we split up months ago—back in August."

"Yes, I did. But everyone's given me a different reason for the breakup," I lied.

"Then let me enlighten you as to the *real* reason Miz Foster called it off," Hyer snapped. "It's because she was still a child."

I should have known this guy would justify his behavior. "In what way?"

It was at this moment that our drinks arrived, and as soon as the waiter walked away, Hyer took a few deep swallows. Then, looking in my general direction, he said bitterly, "Mary Ann had herself a fit because she found out that I'd been married—never mind that it was years before I even met her!"

"Married *twice*. And hadn't told her," I reminded him.

"All right, *twice*," he conceded, glowering at me. "Where'd you hear about it, anyway, her stuffed-shirt brother? Never mind. Listen, if you can suspend your obvious damn bias for a minute, it's possible you'll even understand *why* I didn't tell her."

"You're right; I apologize. I had no business prejudging you," I admitted.

Hyer nodded. "The fact is," he continued, "when Mary Ann and I first met, there wasn't any reason to bring up anything like that; I had no idea it would ever get serious between us. And later, when things *did* get serious, it didn't make any sense to ruin things by going into ancient history.

"I was married the first time when I was only eighteen years old. Did anyone bother telling you *that*? Eighteen! A baby! We were divorced two years later. The second time was when I was twenty-seven; that lasted less than a year. There were no children from either marriage, so how could it possibly affect my relationship with Mary Ann?"

Hyer stopped talking just long enough to take another healthy swallow of the Chivas. Then he resumed his rationalization. "Well, once we were engaged, I figured, why go into it now? What does it have to do with today, with us—Mary Ann and me? So I put it behind me. I didn't think there was much chance she'd ever find out. But if and when she did, there'd be plenty of time for explanations then."

Suddenly there was something vulnerable in Hyer's face, and the hand reaching for the scotch wasn't any too steady now. Draining the rest of the drink in one large gulp, he signaled for a refill before saying softly, "It seems, though, that I underestimated the spitefulness of some people. And I *overestimated* my fiancée."

I knew it wouldn't help to point out anything about honesty and trust. Besides, I didn't want to rub it in. I'm ashamed to admit this, but, much to my own annoyance—and notwithstanding my less than terrific opinion of the man—I found myself feeling a little sorry for Hyer right then. (Of course, I didn't know if he was suffering because he'd lost the woman he loved or because he was just a guy who hated losing.) Anyway, I moved on. "Someone told Mary Ann about your ex-wives out of *spite*?" I asked.

"Probably. I've made a few enemies in my life."

"Do you know who it was?"

"No. I wish I did," he said in this low quiet voice that made it sound pretty ominous. Even through the tan, I could see the dark flush that was beginning to spread from his neck to his forehead. "But whoever it was made sure she heard about it as soon as she set foot in the States."

"Did you tell her why you hadn't said anything to her before?"

"Put it this way: I tried to. But she let me have it with both barrels. Threw a two-and-a-half-carat ring in my face! No matter what I said, all *she'd* say was that I lied to her.

Which is a lie in itself. I never *lied* about having been married; I just didn't volunteer the information." He picked up his drink and rolled the glass around in his hands. "Mary Ann," he muttered, "was hardly the most understanding woman in the world. *Or* the most forgiving."

"Was that the last time you saw her—when she threw the ring at you?"

"More or less."

"Which means?"

"Well, I called her half a dozen times after that, and she kept hanging up on me. But I still felt I had to give it one last try. So early one morning I drove into New York and parked in front of her building, waiting for her to come out. I sat there for over two hours until she finally showed. But the minute she spotted me, she jumped into a cab and took off." It was time for another swig of the scotch. Then Hyer said, "I ask you, is that any way for a grown woman to act?"

I refrained from telling him no, that that was the action of a naive young girl who expected the man she was planning to marry to play it straight with her.

"Do you know she wouldn't even move in with me when she came to the States?" Hyer demanded, working up steam. "Insisted on living in New York with her sister until we got married. Some crap about not wanting people to talk. Incredible, isn't it, in this day and age! She was such a damn little prig she wouldn't even make love with the lights on, for crying out loud! To tell the truth, when I think about it now, I'm wondering what I ever saw in an immature little kid like that."

"The time you drove into the city to talk to her—when was that?"

"The end of August."

"I gather you were pretty upset when she broke it off."

"I won't deny it. I was crazy about her, and I took it hard—until I realized how infantile she was. And once I realized that . . . well, I haven't exactly been lonesome for company since then. I found out there are plenty of women out there who are a little more grown-up. And, I might add, a *lot* more giving." If there'd been any question as to what Hyer meant by that, his smarmy grin made it clear.

I must be just pure, unadulterated mush, I decided, to have allowed myself to feel any sympathy at all for a sleaze like this. I tried to keep my aversion to the man from creeping into my voice. "When did you learn that Mary Ann had gotten engaged again?"

There was total silence. Then Hyer, looking stunned, said quietly, "She got engaged again?" (Was it my imagination, or did his tan actually fade for a moment or two there?)

I nodded.

"Didn't take her very long, did it? Who's the lucky guy?" he asked sardonically, at the same time signaling the waiter for still another refill.

"A casting director for an advertising agency here in New York."

"When were they engaged?"

"Just a few weeks before she was shot. You didn't know about it?"

"Would I be asking if I did?"

"Look, just for my records, I'd appreciate your telling me where you were the night of the murder."

"I don't have to answer that, you know; you're not the police." But Hyer's tone was a lot less argumentative than his words would indicate. I guess the news (assuming it *was* news) had knocked a little of the attitude out of him.

"That's true," I agreed. "But the police will be contacting you any day now to ask you the same question. And if *I'm* satisfied you—"

"Don't start *that* again," he groused, picking up his fifth glass of scotch—or was it his sixth?—which had just now been unobtrusively placed in front of him. I was amazed at how unaffected he seemed to be by the alcohol he'd been consuming in such impressive quantities. Even his speech was clear. "What night was that, anyway?" he was asking.

"Monday. February tenth."

He screwed up his face and, pressing his left palm against his temple, sat there staring intently into the drink he was holding in his right hand. It was as though he were gazing into a crystal ball for the answer.

Oh, come on, I wanted to say—but didn't. *You knew I was going to ask you this, and you know very well where you were that night.*

"I just remembered," Hyer told me at last, a self-satisfied expression on his face. "That's the weekend I was in Vermont. I didn't get back until almost eleven Monday morning, and I stayed at work a little later than usual that night to catch up. Until a few minutes past seven, I guess it was."

"Was anyone with you?"

"No. Everyone else had left at least a half hour earlier."

"Any phone calls? Anything that can help confirm you were there?"

"No. Not as far as I remember, anyway." Then, impatiently: "But is this necessary? I can't *really* be a suspect. It wouldn't make sense for me to suddenly try and kill Mary Ann after all these months." He came close to actually looking me in the eye. "Use your head. What motive could I possibly have?"

"Could be you'd just heard she was engaged to another man," I speculated.

"I didn't have any idea Mary Ann was seeing anyone else until you told me a few minutes ago," he informed me testily. "Besides, if you think I've been pining away for her all this time, you haven't listened to one damn thing I've been telling you."

I wasn't through with my questions yet, so I wanted to get things back on a friendlier basis. "Look," I responded in the most placating voice I own, "I've been asking everyone who knew the twins the same kind of things I'm asking you. As a matter of fact, between the two of us, I don't even think Mary Ann was the target; I think she just happened to be there when the killer came to pay Meredith a visit. But I have to cover everything anyway, for my rec—"

"Okay, okay. But let's get this over with, huh? I *do* have a date tonight." He checked his watch. "Ten of eight! Christ! I'm supposed to be all the way across town by eight!"

"Why don't you give the lady a call and tell her you'll be a few minutes late?"

"That's not necessary. She won't mind waiting for me."

I refused to let that get to me. "Well, we're almost through here," I informed him pleasantly. "You were just about to say where you went after work."

"Was I?" Another of those nasty smiles of his. Then: "All right. When I left the office, I stopped off for a quick bite at Burger King, or maybe it was McDonald's or Roy Rogers, for all I know. Anyway, it was one of those fast food joints. And don't ask me if anyone there would remember me."

I took his advice. "Where did you go afterward?"

"To this bar in town—the Screaming Red Eagle. Burgers make me thirsty."

"What time was that?"

"Maybe eight. Or even a little before. And I didn't leave until twelve-thirty, when the place closed. Look, why don't you talk to Carl? He's the bartender there. I wouldn't be surprised if he remembers; the guy's got a phenomenal memory. Now, if I'm excused . . ."

With that, Hyer stood up and motioned to the waiter. "The lady would like the check," he announced when the man hurried over. Then he bent down and said slyly in the vicinity of my ear, "I *told* you it was your party."

When he walked away, I was happy to see I'd been wrong; the liquor *had* had an effect on him. He was definitely listing to one side.

This was one night, I thought smugly, that Roger Hyer would not find it necessary to take the phone off the hook.

Chapter 16

I slept until almost ten Saturday morning. Before I even had my coffee, I phoned Peter and left a message on his machine. "I haven't talked to you in a few days, and I was anxious to know how everything is," I informed the machine. "Also, I wanted to give you an update. But don't expect much," I added quickly. "Anyway, call me when you get a chance."

As soon as I hung up, I plugged in the coffee and fixed myself some breakfast. When I was finished, I typed up the notes I'd made the night before. And then I read over *all* my notes on the case—and I had a fairly hefty folder by now. I was pretty discouraged when I was through. I'd learned a few little things, of course. But nothing that really mattered.

The telephone interrupted my thoughts—or, more accurately, my lack of them.

"Desiree? It's Peter. I just called the apartment, and I got your message." The voice was dull, almost a monotone. There wasn't even a trace of his recent optimism.

"What's wrong, Peter?" I asked, a little fearful of what he might be about to tell me.

"Nothing. Not really."

"But?"

"But, well, sometimes it just gets to me."

"Listen, Peter," I said gently, "the doctors told you—"

"Yeah, I know what the doctors *told* me. But there doesn't seem to be any change at all."

"Well, it's—" I began.

"You know what the worst of it is, though?" he went on, caught up in his own thoughts. "Not knowing how to talk to her."

"What do you—"

He wasn't even listening. "The thing is," he said miserably, "I'm hoping that on some level she can hear me. But, as much as I don't want to think about it, I've got to accept the possibility that the woman I'm talking to could be Meredith." His voice grew sharper now, more intense, honed by his pain and frustration. "That even restricts what I can say to her, don't you see? It's not even right to tell her I love her. So most of the time I just sit there holding her hand and telling her that she has to get better, that everyone's praying for her." He choked up before confiding softly, "But if it's Mary Ann, that's not what she wants to hear." A pause. "And, God knows, it isn't what I want to say to her."

Well, what could *I* say to Peter? Fortunately, I didn't get the chance to come up with something entirely meaningless and inappropriate.

"I'm acting like a dumb, self-pitying wimp this morning, aren't I?" he put in with an embarrassed little laugh. "And you called *me* in the first place, didn't you? What did you want to tell me?"

Now I was the one who was embarrassed. "I just wanted to check in with you, that's all. I'm afraid I don't have a whole lot to report, though. I wish I did. Anyway, here's what's been happening...."

I gave him a brief synopsis of what had transpired since our last talk. But it all sounded so flimsy, so *nothing* to my own ears that I just couldn't leave things like that. "I know there still isn't anything we can hang our hats on," I conceded, "but don't worry. I promise you that before too much longer you'll know for sure whether the girl in St. Catherine's is Mary Ann."

"Thanks, Desiree," he murmured. And, a moment later, "Thanks," he said again. "Uh, the police don't have any idea yet who was responsible, do they?"

"No, not yet. Not as far as I know. But whoever it was won't be getting away with it. You have my word on that, too."

I wasn't aware until several minutes after the phone call was over that I'd finally admitted to myself—and out loud—that I was actively hunting for the killer. And, in spite of our agreement to the contrary, even Peter didn't seem surprised.

Maybe, like everyone else, he knew from the beginning that it just wasn't possible to handle things any other way.

*   *   *

Well, that bit of bravado I'd displayed on the phone had resulted in my putting even more pressure on myself. I'd actually *promised* to have some answers soon.

Wishing passionately that I'd ripped my tongue out before Peter's call, I went back over my notes again. And again. But I still wasn't able to make a whole lot out of them. Either there wasn't anything important in there—or I didn't *recognize* that there was anything important in there, which was a lot worse.

And just how frustrated was I by the end of my second reread? So frustrated that I actually decided to engage in a little physical activity to unload some of my angst. And since I consider even a brisk walk a little too exotic for me, I settled on cleaning my apartment. (At least I didn't have to go outside to do *that*.)

Of course, with Charmaine, my phantom cleaning woman, a no-show again that Saturday, there wasn't a soul to stand in the way of my ambition. (And in case you're wondering why I don't just fire her, it's because whenever Charmaine *does* deign to come to work, I'm always so grateful I forget that I ever made up my mind to get rid of her.) Anyway, that day I was actually glad to stand in for her.

I dragged half a dozen assorted cleansers out of the cabinet, after which I got out the broom, the mop, the squeegee, the brushes, the rags and my new vacuum with its four separate—and totally useless—attachments. Then, completely ignoring the fact that I'd turned the apartment inside out the week before, I tore through the place like a dynamo—scrubbing and polishing and dusting and sweeping and mopping and vacuuming. You wouldn't believe how enthusiastically I tackled all those nasty little jobs I usually try not to even think about.

When I was through, I'd surpassed even the previous week's efforts, and I had this tremendous sense of accomplishment. The apartment looked so . . . so *clean*. On the downside, though, I could barely make it over to the sofa to sit down. I had a seven o'clock appointment for dinner and a movie with my neighbor, Barbara Gleason, but that was over three hours away. And I wasn't *so* decrepit that I wouldn't bounce back after I had a couple of minutes to catch my breath. Come to think of it, maybe I'd even throw a few things in the washing machine downstairs later. In the meantime, I'd just sit here and relax for a little while. . . .

The doorbell prodded me into consciousness. I looked around. The room was dark now. For a minute or so, I was fogbound; then I remembered my sudden, draining spurt of domesticity. Switching on the lamp next to the sofa, I went to the door. I had to stand on tiptoe to see out of the peephole. And what I saw was Barbara Gleason all bundled up in her coat, her hand on the buzzer, a very agitated expression on her long, thin face.

"You really had me worried!" she scolded when I let her in. "I've been ringing and ringing. I thought you might be dead or something." She took in my attire—this ugly print *thing* that's at least a hundred years old and that I hate for anyone to see me in even when I'm just going out to the incinerator. "You don't plan on wearing *that* tonight!" she said, which was very perceptive of her.

"Of course not," I told her indignantly. "What time is it, anyway?"

"Five of."

"Five of what?"

"Seven. Five of *seven*."

I couldn't believe it! "God! I'm sorry! I fell asleep on the sofa. I must have slept for hours!"

"Well, we can have dinner and make the late show—it goes on at ten-thirty. That is, if you don't spend forever getting dressed."

"Listen, would it be more convenient for you if we put off the movie till tomorrow night?" I asked hopefully, not exactly loving the idea of going out at that point.

"I told this woman I work with that I couldn't have dinner with *her* tonight because I'd already made plans with *you*."

What could I say?

Barbara went back to her own apartment, and I frantically went about getting ready. It was another fast shower, another slapdash makeup job, and another intense—but, of necessity, brief—battle with my hair. I was at Barbara's door in less than an hour.

"You look like a raccoon," were her first words when she came out in the hall to join me. "Better fix your eye makeup in the cab," she told me in that decisive way she has. (Barbara doesn't really talk to you—she *mandates*.

Which I always put down to an occupational hazard; she teaches third grade.)

We went to a seafood restaurant in midtown, not far from the movie theater. I was really primed for the shrimp scampi, but Barbara was aghast. "For God's sake! Do you have any idea how much cholesterol there is in scampi? And the calories! You know, Dez, I don't like to say anything . . ." She said it anyway. "But you should really do something about your weight. It's a shame you've allowed yourself to get so heavy—especially since you have *such* a pretty face." (Have you ever noticed that all heavy women have one thing in common? I mean, you could look like the Creature from the Black Lagoon, but if you're overweight, everyone else in this skinny world we live in insists that you've got "*such* a pretty face.")

I wanted to clue Barbara in to the fact that there's life after size ten. Still, my cholesterol *was* 286 the last time it was checked. Besides, why get bitchy; I liked the woman. Okay. So sometimes she was a little grating—and that night she was really outdoing herself—but she was also interesting and intelligent. Plus, ever since she moved next door to me a few months back, I'd felt beholden to her. You see, the walls in my building are paper-thin. And the previous tenants in 4A were two no-talent, piano-playing idiots who had been driving me crazy for years. The truth is, I was so delighted when Barbara replaced them, I was practically ready to function as her handmaiden.

Anyway, what I'm trying to say is that I wound up convincing myself to have the poached salmon with dill sauce. And it really wasn't bad. But it wasn't the scampi, either.

We finished our dinner in ample time to make the ten-thirty showing of *Beauty and the Beast,* which was absolutely the most charming movie I'd seen in years. I came out of the theater dabbing at my eyes. Barbara laughed at me.

"Now, that was a nice movie if you're under twelve," she commented dryly when we were going home in the cab. "I have no idea why I wanted to see it."

"I loved it," I countered.

"How old are you, Desiree?" I could feel the flush rapidly coloring my face. Barbara didn't miss it, either. "All right. Never mind, if you're so sensitive about it. *I'm* forty-three, and I outgrew that kind of thing years ago. I find it very surprising that you didn't."

"Don't be such a cynic; it was a beautiful love story," I protested.

"It was a *cartoon,* for Christ's sake!"

Well, I just couldn't understand how anyone could not like *Beauty and the Beast.* But I told Barbara that, of course, she was entitled to her opinion. Which, to be honest, isn't what I thought at all. But maybe a lot of my intolerance had to do with the scampi.

Chapter 17

On Sunday, I met Ellen for brunch at a little restaurant in the forties that's about halfway between her apartment and mine.

I thought she looked very chic in her brown pants, white turtleneck, and Harris tweed jacket. In fact, I thought she was having an exceptionally Hepburnish—as in Audrey—day. She seemed to be in good spirits, too.

We had mimosas and then Ellen ordered the apple crepes, while I chose the eggs Benedict, which is one of my very favorite things (and which, that morning, offered the added satisfaction of defying Barbara Gleason's admonitions).

By tacit agreement, we postponed our discussion of the crime until after we'd eaten. In the meantime, I told Ellen about *Beauty and the Beast,* and then she talked about her job at Macy's, sounding a little more optimistic than usual about her prospects at the store. After that, she provided me with an update on her parents, who'd been living in Florida for the past four or five years. I was more than half expecting that any minute she'd ask if I'd spoken to Will Fitzgerald, but his name never came up. Which was good. I didn't want Ellen to even *think* about that insensitive slob.

It wasn't until we were having coffee that she brought up the case. "Have you made any progress yet?"

"None," I told her glumly. "I have no more idea now which of those girls survived than I did that first day Peter came to see me."

"Oh, you'll find out," she assured me blithely. "It just takes a little time, that's all."

"I hope you're right." I would be one very happy P.I. if I had the same confidence in me that Ellen does.

"I am; you'll see. Not that I'm exactly thrilled that you even got involved in this thing," she reminded me.

I gave her what I intended to be an intimidating look.

"Well, I'm *not*," she grumbled. It took a full two seconds before she asked (and with what seemed to me was a certain amount of eagerness, too), "Anyway, have you got any suspects?"

"Now, that's the one thing I *do* have."

I proceeded to fill her in on Eric Foster's feud with his sister. After that, I told her about Larry Shields and *his* argument with Meredith. "I'm still trying to find out what that one was about," I said. "And then there's Lucille Collins. She had a small part in the new play Meredith was in, but it seems she lost this really *terrific* part in the show to Meredith. And besides that, Collins was Shields's girlfriend before Meredith came along."

"So you think it was Meredith the killer was after?"

"Not necessarily. There's at least one person I know of who had a grudge against Mary Ann—Roger Hyer, her ex-fiancé. She broke off with him not too long before she met Peter."

"When was that?"

"The breakup? In August. But her engagement could have set him off."

"He knew about the engagement?"

"He *says* he didn't."

"It doesn't sound like you believe him."

I hunched my shoulders. "Right now, I don't believe anyone."

"Have you questioned them all yet?"

"I have. And so far I don't see where any one of them looks guiltier than the next one. But I also haven't been able to eliminate anybody, either. Eric—he's the brother—and Lucille Collins don't have an alibi for the time of the murder. Roger Hyer claims to have been in a bar in New Jersey that night—I'll be driving out there to check it out in the next day or two. And Larry Shields says he was in Brooklyn having dinner with his mother."

"What does his mother say?"

"I didn't bother to ask. Let me put it this way: Under those circumstances, what would *your* mother say?"

Ellen giggled. It was a giggle that was vintage Ellen. "The same thing *his* would, I'll bet." Then: "Do you really think their brother would have waited all this time to kill

Meredith? And why would he have wanted to kill Mary Ann, anyway?"

"He more or less put those same questions to me. The answer is: I don't know. But there's another angle to this thing we haven't even talked about yet."

"I know."

I was sure she didn't. "*What* do you know?"

"It's the way they were both . . . ugh . . . *where* they were both . . . ugh . . . shot, isn't it?" she finally managed to get out. They don't come much more squeamish than my niece.

"That wasn't what I was going to say. Although it's the thing that bothers me the most about this case. I mean, why in God's name would anyone want to do a horrendous thing like that? They were both shot in the torso first, you know, and afterward the perp stood over them and deliberately destroyed their faces."

Ellen shivered. "It sounds like someone really had it in for them, doesn't it?" she said softly.

"*Both* of them?"

She pondered that. But only briefly. "Maybe the murderer hated the one sister so much he couldn't even look at the same face on the other sister."

"Maybe," I agreed without much conviction. It was really pretty far-fetched. Still, if what we had here was a crime of passion, it wasn't entirely out of the question. "I hadn't considered that," I admitted.

Ellen looked delighted. "Or," she went on, figuring she was on a roll, "whoever did it might have had two *different* motives, one for killing Meredith and another for killing Mary Ann. And one of those motives is something no one's even come up with." In deference to my sensibilities and also because of that inexplicable faith of hers, she hurriedly added, "Yet."

Now, this theory I wasn't quite ready to buy. But I didn't have to tell Ellen that. "Mmmm," I responded vaguely.

"Oh," Ellen said, suddenly remembering, "I think I interrupted you before, didn't I? You were going to talk about something else, and I kind of sidetracked you."

"I was, wasn't I? But I have no idea what I had in mind."

"You mentioned something about there being another angle to the case."

I drew a blank for a second or two. And then it came back to me. "Money," I told her.

"Money?" Ellen parroted.

"Listen," I said, "judging from the way the twins lived, they weren't exactly paupers. Their parents had been killed in a car crash, and it seems they were left pretty well-fixed. The apartment alone set them back a million and a half."

Ellen made this weird sound, which I realized (since the same sound occasionally comes out of my own mouth) was a truly pathetic attempt at a whistle. "And who gets all that if they die?" she wanted to know.

"Well, if neither of them made a will, the brother, apparently."

"But wouldn't he have inherited from his parents, too?"

"Most likely. But some people *never* have enough money." Ellen is probably the only person living in the twentieth century who would have to have that pointed out to her. "Of course, if there's a will involved, it could change everything. That's something else I've got to find out about."

By that time we were on our third cup of coffee. "You know what I think?" Ellen asked. She looked at me expectantly.

I didn't let her down. "What?"

"I think," she stated with conviction, "that if we could find out why they were shot in the ... you know ... we'd know who shot them."

I couldn't argue with that.

Chapter 18

The instant my head hit the pillow that night, my mind went into overdrive. I kept thinking and thinking about my conversation with Ellen. It's possible there was something in that crime of passion business, I decided. The only trouble was I just couldn't seem to get anywhere with it. Until I suddenly remembered what Claire Josephs told me.

The twins liked to fool around and switch identities when they were kids, she'd said. Well, suppose, for some reason, that Monday evening Mary Ann had pulled that childhood prank of theirs one last, fatal time. Even if the girls didn't look *exactly* alike anymore, there was still a remarkable resemblance. And if Mary Ann had *said* she was Meredith, would the perp have bothered examining her features? And who knows how good the lighting was in that place anyhow? (Which reminded me, I was going to get Fielding to let me into that apartment if it killed me. *Or* him.)

I visualized the story line playing out. . . .

The killer—a faceless, sexless figure—goes to the Foster apartment. Mary Ann, home alone, pretends to the visitor that she's her sister. I could picture the two of them sitting in the living room and talking for a few minutes. Then Mary Ann gets to her feet (maybe because Chuck Springer is ringing the doorbell). And—before she ever has a chance to say, "Ha-ha, fooled you!"—the perp, still under the impression she's Meredith, takes aim and fires at her.

Now I could see her on the floor, her shadowy attacker standing over her. And that's when he (or she) gets a really good look and realizes that it's not Meredith who's lying there but her twin. He makes up his mind that he's not going to leave until he does what he came there for. So he waits around until the *real* Meredith comes home.

So far, so good. But why blast the girls in the face like that?

Well, where Meredith was concerned, I finally had a plausible answer. (Not necessarily correct, you understand, or even probable—but plausible.) Assuming that what we had here *was* a crime of passion, I didn't see it as too off the wall for the murderer to want to destroy his intended victim's face.

I was still stymied, though, as to why he'd deliberately shoot the *wrong victim* in the face.

It took a good fifteen minutes' worth of tossing and turning and a few healthy punches to the pillow before I came up with something that would let me off the hook. And, in the end, my explanation was simplicity itself: The perp could just have been *that furious* at having been deceived.

Of course, I was aware that my theory needed some work. I hadn't even *tried* to apply it to a particular suspect yet. The basic idea, though, seemed to make sense.

But so many things do at one A.M., don't they?

The next morning, before leaving for the office, I called Peter.

"I won't keep you," I informed him. "Just two things. First: What night this week are you coming to dinner?" Anticipating his protest—since it was already the third time I'd extended the invitation—I told him quickly, "And your excuses won't mean beans to me this time. We can make it a late as you want, too."

I guess I'd worn him down. "Thanks," he responded. "That would be great—if you're sure you wouldn't mind eating at around nine."

We set it up for Thursday.

"One thing more," I said then. "Just tell me this: Did Mary Ann have a will?"

"I don't think so, Desiree."

Nothing about this case was easy. Nothing.

I brought my car to work that day, hoping to drive out to the Screaming Red Eagle in the early evening. I started calling the place as soon as I came back from lunch, just to make sure that the bartender I needed to talk to would be there that night. Someone finally picked up at a few minutes of four.

"Screaming Red Eagle," this deep, raspy voice announced.

"What time do you open today?"

"We're open now, lady."

"Is Carl working tonight?"

"You're talkin' to him. Who's this?"

"I'll surprise you," I said.

As soon as I clicked off, I dialed the coffee shop on the next block and ordered a burger and some fries. Then I did a little research on this other case that, like everything else, had been getting pretty short shrift since the day Peter reentered my life. I ate between a brief, gossipy chat with Jackie and phone calls to my gynecologist and ophthalmologist, both of whom had sent me postcards at least three months back notifying me that I was now due for my annual checkup.

At around quarter after five, I left the office to pick up my Chevy at the garage around the corner.

The second I got downstairs, it started to pour. And I mean *pour*. The weatherman on WNBC that morning had predicted cloudy and cold with the chance of a few light, intermittent showers. I would very much have enjoyed seeing that man hang by his nose.

I ran back up to the office for the spare umbrella I keep in my desk and then made for the garage. Even with the umbrella, I was soaked by the time I got there. My hair, which was loaded down with the usual quarter can of hair spray, was plastered flat against my head and looked like red mucilage. (I knew in my heart that I would never be able to run a comb through it again.) My two-week-old suede pumps were filled with so much water I squished when I walked. And what was worst of all, the rain had gone right through my coat and baptized my beautiful turquoise silk blouse.

The drive to Hillsdale was a nightmare. Visibility was so poor, I had to pull over to the side of the road I don't know how many times to wait for the rain to let up a little. Naturally, the minute it did and I'd get back on the highway, there'd be another deluge. Under normal circumstances, the ride shouldn't have taken me more than an hour, tops. That night, it took closer to three. I swear, I could've made it faster if I'd crawled there on my hands and knees.

By the time I walked into the Screaming Red Eagle, I was tired and cold and very, very wet. I had to shake myself vigorously before I could even get out of my coat. I must have looked like something that escaped from a kennel.

I took a seat at one end of the long, circular bar, separated by about ten stools from the only two other customers in the place. Evidently, most people have the good sense to stay home on a night like this.

The bartender was a tall, heavyset man of about fifty with sparse graying hair and fewer teeth. I ordered a blackberry brandy, which was definitely therapeutic in view of the shape I was in. "Are you Carl?" I asked, when he brought the drink over.

"Yeah, that's right."

"I'm your surprise." He stared at me blankly. "You know, the phone call this afternoon, remember?"

He nodded, but he didn't smile. The man didn't seem overly fond of surprises.

I brought out my identification, which he barely glanced at. "So?" he said.

Now, I have no idea what possessed me to tell him this absurd story. It certainly wasn't anything I'd planned on. But all of a sudden there it was, coming out of my mouth. And then I just kept on improvising as I went along.

"I've been engaged by an attorney who's anxious to locate a customer of yours, a Mr. Roger Hyer," I began. "Mr. Hyer's come into some money—not a fortune, but nothing to sneeze at, either—and we haven't been able to reach him."

I want you to know that I realized Carl had almost certainly been prepped for my visit. And all I can say in my own defense is that on the off chance he *wasn't* expecting me, I had a much better shot at getting him to cooperate than if I told him one of his customers was a murder suspect. And after all, what did I have to lose? If he knew I was lying, he'd call me on it.

"I've left half a dozen messages at Mr. Hyer's office and on his answering machine at home," I went on, "but he never got back to me." Carl was staring at me with ice-cold eyes, making it extremely nerve-wracking to continue. But it was too late to stop now. "I even went to his house a few times. I guess he doesn't stay home much, though, huh?" I concluded lamely.

"How come you're lookin' for him here?"

"Well . . . um . . . I had a talk with this cousin of Hyer's—

he's mentioned in the same will that Hyer is—and he told me he came in here with him once. Says Hyer's a regular."

"Drops in maybe twice a week," the bartender said without inflection. Then his eyes narrowed. "And you came out in this kinda weather just in case he showed up?"

"I drove in from New York, and it wasn't even raining when I left my office. Besides, I was hoping that if I didn't catch him, I could leave a message with you explaining what this is all about."

Carl was no dope. "Ever thought of sendin' him a letter?"

"I did—or anyway the attorney did, asking Hyer to get in touch with him. But Hyer never called. Maybe the letter got lost in the mail. So is it okay if I just give you a note for him?"

Carl shrugged. "Suit yourself."

I rummaged around in my attaché for a piece of paper and, with my back to the bar, pretended to write on it. Then I put the blank sheet in an envelope, scribbled Hyer's name on the front, and sealed it.

"Uh, I was just thinking," I said, handing the bartender the envelope. "The last time I was in Hillsdale—on February tenth, it was, sometime in the evening—I was parked in front of Hyer's house for three hours, waiting for him to come home. That was a Monday, by the way. Anyhow, it would be ironic if he was right in here all that while, wouldn't it?" I asked with this insipid little laugh.

Purposefully putting the envelope down on the bar, Carl leaned toward me. His eyes were mere slits now, and his face was so close to mine, I could almost taste his stale breath. "I was wondering when you'd get around to that," he said in an unnaturally quiet voice. For a moment, I felt afraid. Then he straightened up. "Look, lady, I *know* what this is really about," he informed me.

My cheeks felt as if they were catching fire. "What do you mean?" I asked weakly.

"I mean that Roger told me days ago that I should expect to hear from you. He asked me to tell you whatever you wanted to know."

"Well, why didn't you say so in the beginning?" I actually had the nerve to be indignant. (It's really humiliating being on the losing end of a cat-and-mouse game. Even if you did it to yourself.)

"I hated to spoil the fun," was the man's response. But he didn't appear the least bit amused.

"Look, I'm sorry. I just thought it might be easier to get you to level with me if you didn't know I was investigating a crime. Hyer says he was here the night of February tenth and that you might be able to verify it."

"He was here."

"That was two weeks ago. How can you be sure?"

"Because my daughter got married the day before, and it was Roger who recommended the florist. So the night after the wedding—that Monday—he wanted to know if the guy did a good job for me."

"It was definitely the very next night? It couldn't have been two nights later?"

"No, it couldn't."

"What time did he come in? Do you have any idea?"

"Around eight."

"You're sure of the time?"

Carl gave this exasperated sigh. "Listen, Roger always comes in around eight, give or take a few minutes. It woulda registered on me if he came in at a different time."

"All right. But I hope you're being straight with me. Two young girls—one of them Hyer's former fiancée—got their faces blown off that night, and I know you wouldn't want to cover for the person responsible." The bartender's eyes began to narrow again. "Of course you wouldn't," I told him quickly.

I was out of there three minutes later.

Chapter 19

At a little after ten on Tuesday morning, I stopped off at the Twelfth Precinct, hoping to catch Tim Fielding. Fortunately, he was in, sitting at his desk. What's more, he didn't grumble for more than three or four minutes about people who expect you to be at their beck and call whenever it suits them. He wasn't even all that unpleasant when he said, "I don't suppose you thought of picking up the phone to see if I was available before you came bursting in here."

Now, considering how I just about managed to drag myself over there that morning, I definitely did not "burst." However, I appreciated that this was not the time to get involved in semantics.

"I know I should have called," I admitted, "but I was on my way to the office when I decided to drop in here first. If you could spare me just a few minutes—"

"Who are you kiddin'? Remember me? I *know* your few minutes."

I took two containers of coffee and half a dozen donuts from the brown paper bag I was carrying. I had this pleading look on my face when I set them on Fielding's desk.

I can't say for sure whether it was the look or the do-nuts—eight to one it was the donuts—but Fielding muttered, "Okay, sit down." Then he reached for the chocolate donut with the walnut sprinkles. "But don't get too comfortable; you won't be staying long."

I sat on the chair alongside his desk and slipped off my coat—which produced an immediate frown. "Here," I said, handing him the container marked with a *B,* "black, no sugar." I opened my own coffee and picked out a jelly donut, getting in a few quick bites while Fielding was busy doing the same.

"Well?" he said about ten seconds later, drumming his fingers on the desk.

"I just thought it was time we compared notes."

"Which, judging from your past performances, means you're here to find out what *I* know."

"Absolutely untrue," I responded huffily. "I have plenty to tell you this morning; you'll see."

"Fine. I'm waiting."

This was not the way I'd arranged the agenda in my head, but I was on shaky ground. "Well, I thought maybe we could start with the twins' finances."

"Really? And just what information do *you* have on their finances?"

"For one thing, I can tell you they paid over a million for the apartment."

"A million and a half, to be exact. Cash."

"Cash?"

"You heard me. They handed over a certified check for one and a half big ones. What else have you got for me?"

"Peter doesn't think Mary Ann made a will."

"He told me that almost two weeks ago. Anything else?"

"Look, Tim, I *do* have some news for you, I swear, and I'll fill you in in just a couple of minutes. But right now can we talk about who would profit from their deaths? Do you have any idea yet?"

I braced myself for a hard time. Instead, Fielding sounded almost apologetic. "I really wish I had something to tell you, Dez. Besides your client, I've checked with the brother and Meredith's boyfriend—Shields. No one admits to knowing anything about a will."

"Maybe the girls didn't have one; they were pretty young."

"That's certainly possible. But for the time being, I'm going to go under the assumption there *are* a couple of wills out there someplace."

"If they exist, they'd probably be in a safe-deposit box, wouldn't they? Would the police even be able to get into the box? I mean, since neither of the victims can be declared legally dead."

"Not without showing probable cause, most likely. But you're way ahead of yourself. The first thing to find out is if either of them even had a box. We checked with every bank in New York City, and guess what?"

"No box."

"You got it. Not only that—and this is the really strange

part—the only record we could find of a bank account for either of them is a joint checking account with a little over three thousand bucks and a business account of Mary Ann's with a couple hundred in it. Doesn't add up, does it?" Fielding mused. "The way I see it, anyone who can afford one and a half big ones for an apartment should have some other assets, too."

"Maybe the rest of their money is in stocks and bonds," I suggested. "Their father was a broker."

We looked at every piece of paper in that apartment, and we couldn't find a damn thing—no statements, no record of anything like that. Nothing."

"Wait a minute. That certified check for the apartment . . . ?"

"Drawn on a checking account at Chase. They opened it in September, right before they bought the place, and once the sale was completed, they closed the account."

"Maybe they figured the apartment was a great investment, so they sunk every penny they had into it."

"Yeah, could be, I guess. But I dunno, something just doesn't *feel* right." Fielding reached for another donut. "Okay, now before you have to leave, I think there was something you wanted to pass along to me."

"It's about Mary Ann's fiancé. His name's—"

"Roger Hyer," Fielding said before I could. "Foster told us. In fact, Corcoran spoke to Hyer on the phone yesterday. He's going to be in town tomorrow, and he agreed to stop in and talk to us for a few minutes. Oh, and incidentally," he deadpanned, "Walt's off today; I hope you're not too sorry you missed him."

I assured him there was no way Walter Corcoran, his asshole of a partner, would ever be missed. Then I told him about my meeting with Hyer on Friday. "He claims to have been in a bar in New Jersey the night of the shootings. I went out there last night to see the bartender, and it seems to check out."

"Seems to?"

"There's always the chance the bartender's a friend of Hyer's—he calls him Roger, by the way. There's also the possibility that Hyer paid him to confirm the alibi or even that he blackmailed him."

"Okay. We'll see what we can get out of this bartender after we're through with Hyer. Now, what else?"

"Well, I wanted to bounce something off you. I was talk-

ing to my niece Ellen the other day—you remember
Ellen—and she had this idea—"

"Swell. Now I'm gonna get a lesson in police work from
a saleslady at Bloomingdale's."

"Assistant buyer—and it's Macy's," I corrected, scowling
at him. "And you didn't let me finish. Ellen's idea got me
thinking, that's all. Besides," I added, just for his information, "Ellen happens to be very bright. Very."

With that off my chest, I told him how I came to remember the twins' childhood prank and how regarding the
shootings as a crime of passion might very well explain
their bizarre nature.

"Let's start with Larry Shields," I said when I was
through laying the groundwork. "He could have been mad
enough at Meredith to blast her in the face. I mean, who
knows with these lovers' quarrels? And once he realized
that Mary Ann had put one over on him—"

"Hold it right there. What's this about a lover's quarrel?"
Fielding asked, coming to attention.

"You didn't know?"

"Me? I'm only a dumb cop. It's you hotshot P.I.s and your
helpers from Macy's who manage to dig up all the juicy stuff."

I proceeded to impart the next-to-nothing I knew about
Meredith's argument with Shields. "But I haven't finished
nosing around yet. I'll keep you posted," I promised.

Fielding nodded and mumbled something. It might even
have been "Thanks." Then he said, "I guess I can figure
out for myself how this crime of passion thing would apply
to Collins, so spare me. And incidentally, in case you're
not aware of it, Collins not only lost her part, she also lost
her boyfriend to Meredith Foster."

"I heard."

"I should have figured," he responded tartly. "One hitch
occurs to me right away, though. If the idea was to off
Meredith, it would make sense to try and get at her when
she was alone. And neither of those two knew the sister
was supposed to be out that night."

"You're just assuming that. Maybe Meredith said to
Shields at the theater on Monday—you know, casually, in
conversation—'Mary Ann's got these plans with her friend
tonight, so it looks like I'm going to be all by my lonesome.'
Maybe she even said, 'Why don't you come over later and
keep me company?' And maybe Lucille Collins overheard

that little invitation and also overheard Shields saying he couldn't make it, that he was going to his mother's."

"I've never heard so many 'maybes' in my life. But go on. How does this crime of passion/mistaken identity business work with Hyer—or doesn't it?"

"Oh, it does. But in his case it works a little differently."

"I'm listening."

"Okay, suppose Hyer finds out the girl he's been carrying a torch for these past six months just got engaged to someone else. Well, he rushes over there out for blood—in his frame of mind, he wouldn't care *who* else was around—and let's say he gets Mary Ann to open the door by telling her he's a delivery man or a maintenance man or something, and then he forces his way inside. Now, we know Mary Ann would definitely not want to see this guy, right? So what does she do?"

Fielding recognized a cue when he was fed one. "Pretends to be her sister so she can get rid of the guy."

"Exactly. Only Hyer doesn't leave. They go into the living room, and Mary Ann—as Meredith—says something that sets him off; it wouldn't take much. And besides, the man drinks—I mean *really* drinks—which would only have aggravated the situation. At any rate, he lets the real Mary Ann have it, and then he waits for the woman he *thinks* is Mary Ann to come home."

"For argument's sake, I'll go along with you so far," Fielding said, "not wholeheartedly, you understand, but I'll go along. Here's where you lose me, though. Why in hell would he blast them *both* in the face?"

"Well, I'm not really sure, of course—"

"Big of you to admit it," he commented wryly.

"But anyway," I went on, ignoring the remark, "maybe he just couldn't bear looking at that face, so he destroyed it. Twice. Or maybe with all the alcohol he consumed, he just got muddled. Who knows?"

"Well, *I* certainly don't," Fielding responded, shaking his head. "This theory of yours has so many goddamn 'maybes' and 'ifs' and 'possibles' that you gotta forgive me if I don't jump up and down. Anyway, I imagine a crime of passion would let Foster off the hook. Or am I just jumping to conclusions?"

"Don't be so cute. It *would* let him off the hook. I'm inclined to think that if Eric Foster killed his sisters, it was because, as their next of kin, he stood to inherit a minimum of one and a half million dollars—the value of the condo."

"Assuming," Fielding said pointedly, "there's no will around to change all that. Because if there is, we've got ourselves a whole different ball game. But tell me—and I'll probably hate myself for asking—you got any theories to explain those shots in the face if money's the motive?"

"No. At least not yet. But there's also another possibility with Foster. Maybe there was more to his feud with Meredith than anyone's aware of. And maybe *that* had something to do with his blasting them in the face."

Abruptly, Fielding got up. "I can't take any more 'maybes.' Thanks for the donuts, Dez, and let me give you a hand with your coat."

"Just two more minutes; I'm not quite through yet."

"Oh, yes, you are," he informed me, helping me to my feet and draping the coat around my shoulders.

"The gun," I put in quickly, "I don't suppose you found it?"

"We did not."

"And when am I going to be able to see that apartment?"

"I'll let you know. Now go to work, will you? I'm gonna go take a couple of Tylenols. And listen," he called out as I reluctantly walked away, "if you and Ellen come up with any more little theories like that, please, don't feel obligated to share them."

That night, I met a friend of mine for dinner.

Pat Martucci, formerly Altmann formerly Greene formerly Anderson, had just broken off with her most recent significant other, and she was as down in the dumps as I'd ever seen her. (As you can probably gather just from all those surnames she's accumulated, Pat has a big problem functioning without a man in her life.) Well, under the circumstances, I felt it incumbent upon me, her close friend and confidante, to spend a little time with her to try to cheer her up. It didn't work out as well as I'd hoped—for either of us.

The truth is, it had been a long time since I'd had anyone special in my own life. And once in a while I couldn't help letting it get to me. But by and large I handled things pretty well, I thought. That is, until that two-hour dose of a manless Pat Martucci.

By the time we said good night in front of the restaurant,

I was practically suicidal. Pat, however, thanked me for being there for her, assuring me that she felt *so* much better after our talk. I have to tell you, though, that she was wiping away a few tears when she said it.

It wasn't even nine-thirty when I left Pat and, between feeling bad for her and worse for myself, I just couldn't bring myself to go straight home. Which was probably a fortunate thing; it might not have been wise for me to be anyplace I'd have access to sharp knives and/or a gas oven. So, on the spur of the moment, I went to the movies. I don't even recall what picture I saw. But I do remember it was a comedy and that when I got out of there, it was safe for me to go into the kitchen.

As soon as I came home, I checked the answering machine for messages. There was only one. But it was the one we'd all been waiting for.

At first I didn't even realize I was listening to Peter. His voice was about an octave higher than normal and just this side of hysterical. And the words spilled out in quick time.

"Desiree? Peter. Big news! Finally! I stayed at the hospital a little later tonight—I don't know why. Anyway, I was there when it happened! I still can't believe it! She came out of the coma! Isn't that the greatest—the most sensational—news you've ever heard? You can't call me back; I'm not home. I'm at a bar near the hospital, and I was hoping you'd be able to meet me here and celebrate with me. But you're not home, either. But I guess you realize that, don't you?" Then came this silly laugh that was a true soulmate to Ellen's giggle. "Listen, if I sound high to you," he rushed on, "I want you to know this is no cheap drunk; it's champagne. Moët something-or-other. Anyway, wish you were here." Another Ellenish laugh. "I'll speak to you in the morning. Good n—"

Even talking at that rate, he couldn't beat out my impatient little machine. But he'd already told me the only thing that mattered:

She was out of her coma!

Wait a minute. . . . *Who* was out of her coma? I played the message again. Peter hadn't said that it was Mary Ann; he hadn't even mentioned her name. But that was because he was so excited, I told myself. After all, would he be celebrating like that if it was Meredith?

Still, I was a little uneasy.

Chapter 20

On Wednesday I woke up before seven, but, as crazy as I was to talk to Peter, I didn't have the heart to call him that early. From the sound of him on the phone last night, it was no stretch to assume he'd be pretty hungover this morning.

I got out of bed, made myself some coffee, and then sat in the kitchen and stared at the wall clock until seven-thirty. At which point I couldn't restrain myself any longer. Rationalizing that he might be leaving for the hospital any minute now, I dialed Peter's number.

As soon as he picked up, I knew that I'd dragged him out of a sound sleep. "Any news?" he asked when he realized who it was.

"You're the one with the news—the *fantastic* news!" I reminded him.

"Geez, how did you find out so soon?" he asked groggily, attempting, not too successfully, to stifle a yawn.

Welcome to *The Twilight Zone.*

"You called me; don't you remember?"

For a couple of seconds, I thought the line had gone dead. Then Peter admitted sheepishly, "I guess I don't. I did a little celebrating after I left the hospital, and everything's sort of hazy."

"I found a message from you on my machine when I came home last night," I prompted.

"I'll take your word for it," he responded with this diffident little chuckle. Then, abruptly, he seemed to come fully awake, and there was excitement in his voice. "Did the message say that she regained consciousness?"

"Yes! And I can't tell you how thrilled I am! How did it happen?"

"Uhh . . . look, Desiree, is it okay if I call you back in a few minutes? All of a sudden I feel a little queasy."

I didn't hear from Peter for about twenty minutes. In the

meantime, I was so intent on waiting for the phone to ring that I couldn't even muster the concentration to open a box of cornflakes.

When Peter finally got back to me, he insisted he was feeling better, although he still sounded a little funny—like he'd lost his salivary glands.

"Sorry about hanging up on you. I'm not one of the world's great drinkers, I'm afraid. But I just *had* to celebrate."

"So tell me!"

"It was really a miracle, Desiree," he began, eager to talk now. "At a little after seven, I was getting ready to go home. I had this terrible headache, so I decided I'd make an early night of it, maybe grab a quick sandwich and go right to bed after that and see if I could sleep it off.

"Then the strangest thing happened. I put on my coat, even buttoned it. But something just wouldn't let me leave—I can't explain it. So, anyway, I took off the coat and sat down next to the bed again. I was sitting there looking at her when I noticed that her eyes . . . well, they seemed to be open a little. Only a crack, really, and I couldn't be positive—it was hard to tell with all those bandages and everything. Even so, I went a little nuts. I ran outside and dragged this resident in. He took her hand and started talking to her. He kept asking if she could hear him, but with her jaw wired shut like that, it was hard for her to answer. Or maybe she just didn't have the strength. So then he told her that if she could hear him, she should wiggle her finger. And she did!"

"I can't believe it! It's what we've been praying for!" I screeched into the phone. Poor Peter. With that hangover of his, my soothing tone was undoubtedly just what he needed. "So then what?" I demanded.

"Then he had me walk over to the bed, and he said, 'Do you know who this man is?' She looked straight at me, but she didn't seem to show any recognition; her finger didn't move at all."

"It could be she was a little disoriented," I offered. "What happened after that?"

"Well, a couple of seconds later she shut her eyes and drifted off to sleep. And then right away all these doctors started pouring into the room, and they had me wait in the hall for a while. Finally one of the doctors came out and said there was a little problem. She was awake now, but she didn't seem to know who she was."

God! Doesn't it ever end?

"They had me go back in," Peter continued, "and they tried again. Told her to wiggle her finger if she recognized me. But nothing happened. Anyway, the doctors more or less threw me out then and told me to come back this morning. But one of them said not to worry, that at least she was conscious now, which was the big thing."

"It sure is," I agreed, my voice beginning to quiver. Suddenly I seemed to be overwhelmed by so many different emotions at once: joy, relief, thankfulness, and a gnawing fear of what might be in store for Peter next. But somehow I managed to stem the tears that were on the brink of splashing all over the telephone receiver. "Well, that explains one thing, anyway," I murmured, more or less talking to myself out loud.

"Explains what?"

"Why you haven't mentioned Mary Ann's name at all. When I got your message last night, I wondered about that."

Peter was quick to respond. "If I haven't mentioned her name," he asserted, "it's only because I'm afraid I'll jinx things. The truth is, I still can't get over how lucky I am she's recovering. It doesn't even matter to me what *she* knows—things'll come to her in time. All that's important is that since last night, I've known for sure that she's Mary Ann." Then he added, a note of triumph in his voice, "There, I've said it: She's Mary Ann!"

"Oh, I hope so!" I told him softly, succeeding in another brief struggle to turn back the tears.

"She really is; I'm positive of it," Peter insisted fervently. "Look, I don't want to sound mystical or anything, but something *made* me take off my coat last night so that I'd be there when Mary Ann came out of her coma. That wouldn't have happened if it was Meredith; I'm convinced of it." Then, a little hesitantly: "I suppose I sound like a real kook, don't I?"

"Not to me, you don't. How does that line in *Hamlet* go—I think it was *Hamlet*—about there being more things in heaven and earth than we can explain? Well, I believe that's true."

And I really *do* believe it. Oh, maybe I should have told

Peter to go easy, not to count on anything yet. But the way I looked at it, after all these terrible weeks he rated some happiness. Even if it should turn out to be for just a little while.

That afternoon, I began thinking about wills again. I didn't seem to be able to help it, although I was sure that all I was doing was spinning my wheels. I mean, Fielding had been looking into that area pretty intensively. If the damned things *did* exist—and that seemed to be a big "if" at this point—he'd eventually manage to turn them up.

Still, for the hell of it, I found myself approaching the subject as though, like the twins, I'd just arrived here from London. Now, let's say I wanted to make out a will. (Naturally, it was necessary to start with the premise it hadn't already been taken care of over there.) Well, first off, I'd have to get myself a lawyer. Okay, how would I go about finding one?

There were the Yellow Pages, of course, which would certainly make sense if I didn't know anyone in New York. But suppose I did? Suppose that one of my closest childhood friends was living right in this city?

Maybe it was a carryover from my conversation with Peter, but in spite of myself I was actually optimistic when I dialed Claire Josephs's number.

"Yes, as a matter of fact, Merry *did* ask me if I knew a lawyer who could help with a will," Claire said when I put the question to her.

"And did you recommend anybody?" I think my heart stopped pumping for the split second it took her to answer.

"I talked to Rick—my husband—and he suggested this law firm in the building where he works. We've never had occasion to use a lawyer ourselves—although I guess we should make out a will, too, now that we're parents." (I'll bet she shuddered when she said that.) "But anyway," she went on, "Rick said that firm had a pretty good reputation."

"What was the name of the firm?"

"Let me see ... was it Lefkowitz? No, not Lefkowitz, but something close to it. Wait. ..."

Claire's mind search was rudely interrupted by her little Buddha, who, I can report, was in his usual fine, robust voice.

"I'll call you back in a few minutes," she told me hurriedly.

After we hung up, I couldn't sit still. I began pacing back and forth in my office, which, since the room is only about seven-by-nine, had the effect of making me feel like I was walking in place. When I heard from Claire ten minutes later, I was still on my feet.

"I just checked with my husband," she said. "It's Leibowitz, Leibowitz and O'Donnell." She even provided me with the phone number.

I gave her my genuine, heartfelt, enthusiastic thanks for her help and was about to say good-bye when she stopped me. "You know, I was going to call you."

"About what, Claire?"

"Remember when you were here last week, and we were talking about Roger Hyer?"

I told her that of course I remembered.

"It's probably not that important or anything, but I don't think I mentioned that my brother ran into Roger a couple of months ago at Le Cirque. Simon—that's my brother—is a doctor, so he can afford Le Cirque," she put in sourly.

"And?"

"Well, Roger made a point of stopping off at Simon's table. They met this one time at my apartment when the twins first moved to New York," she explained. "Anyhow, Roger said he just wanted to say hello, but right away he asked about Mary Ann. Simon said she was fine. So then Roger asked if she was seeing anyone and Simon said that yes, she was, and that she was getting engaged soon."

I was practically hyperventilating by now. (I don't think I'm constitutionally capable of handling more than one revelation at a time.) "Is that it?" I asked, just to make sure she had nothing more to add.

"That's it," Claire said regretfully. "I told you it wasn't much."

Chapter 21

I quashed the very strong impulse to get in touch with the lawyers myself, deciding that I'd play it smart for once and let Tim do the honors. Partly that was because I realized that, in his official capacity, it would probably be easier for him to get the information we both wanted. But mostly it was because I still didn't have much on the credit side of my Fielding ledger. I've got to admit, though, that I called the precinct reluctantly.

Fielding—wouldn't you know it?—was out. And I practically had to sit on my hands to keep from dialing Leibowitz, Leibowitz and O'Donnell next. A brief visit with Jackie and a lengthy phone call to Ellen made it easier. By the time I was through talking to the two of them, the digital clock on my desk read 5:37. Leibowitz, Leibowitz and O'Donnell were most likely all on their way home now anyway. So temptation was behind me.

But the next morning I didn't take any chances. As soon as I left the apartment, I headed straight for the Twelfth Precinct. The cab deposited me there at a little after nine, and right away I ran into Walter Corcoran—literally. He was coming out of the front door just as I was entering the building. In view of my feelings toward the man, I chose to blame him for our small collision.

"For God's sake, Corcoran! Why don't you watch it! You almost knocked me over!"

"It would take a bulldozer to knock you over," he countered nastily.

Ours is a truly heartwarming relationship.

When I presented myself at Tim's desk, he seemed only marginally happier to see me than his partner had been. "I thought you were going to call before you came over here next time," he grumbled.

I didn't remember telling him anything of the sort (but maybe I *did* allow him to think it). Anyway, I let it pass; I was here to make points, wasn't I? "I believe I have something that just might make you change your attitude," I announced.

"Chocolate or jelly?"

It was a few seconds before I caught on. "Ohhh, you mean donuts. I didn't even want to take the time to stop off. *That's* the kind of information I've got for you."

"Yeah, I can imagine. Okay, sit down. Corcoran just went out for some breakfast. He's bringing me back a Danish, and if you've really got something good, maybe I'll share. Want some coffee in the meantime?"

Having had the pleasure of the precinct coffee, I courteously declined the offer. Besides, now that I was here, I couldn't wait to tell him my news.

"Hold it a minute," Fielding commanded before I had a chance to open my mouth. "This wouldn't have anything to do with the victim coming out of her coma, would it? Because I already know all about that."

I assured him it would not, although, I told him, I'd heard the good news, too.

"It really looks like she's gonna make it, huh?" he said, pleased. And then: "But, of course, it figures, it wouldn't be *all* good news."

"What do you mean?" It was almost reflexive. I *knew* what he meant.

"I'm talking about the amnesia. Your client *did* tell you about it, didn't he? She finally comes out of the damned coma, and she *still* can't tell us who did this to her; the poor girl doesn't even know what world she's in!"

"Look, that could be very temporary. She could get her memory back tomorrow—today, even; I mean, you hear about that sort of thing all the time."

"Yeah, sure," Fielding responded gloomily.

"Now, are you ready for something that *doesn't* follow Murphy's Law?" I put to him then. And, saving my real coup for later, I proceeded to talk about the Roger Hyer business.

When I was through, Fielding tilted back in his chair, his hands locked behind his head, an ironic smile flitting briefly across his lips. "Well, how do you like that guy?" he muttered. "You shoulda heard him—he was in here yesterday, you know. He sat right where you're sitting now, swearing up and down he had no idea his ex was involved with anyone else. Didn't it occur to that idiot there was a strong possibility the truth would come out?"

"I guess not. Like you said, he's an idiot."

"Of course, this doesn't mean Hyer's our perp. Although I admit I wouldn't be sorry if it turned out that way, considering what an obnoxious S.O.B. he is. Could be, though, that the only reason he denied knowing about the engagement was that he's afraid it would give him a motive."

"I've kind of come to the same conclusion myself—that maybe it means something, but on the other hand, it's just as likely it doesn't."

"Yeah. You could say the same for that alibi of his. Corcoran and I drove out to see his bartender buddy last night, and I'm not at all convinced the guy's legit. Well, I'm gonna have to have another talk with Hyer anyway, just to see what he has to say for himself now. Christ, I'd love to nail that little scuzball!"

At the world "little," I broke into a grin. I mean, Tim isn't exactly Michael Jordan himself. But, mindful of those points I was trying to rack up, I grinned on the inside, where it didn't show.

"Well, Dez, I have to apologize for not rolling out the red carpet for you this morning," Fielding was saying. "You really came through this time. Which entitles you to one half of an only slightly stale prune Danish—provided it gets here in this century."

"Oh, that wasn't my news—not my *hot* news, anyway. *That* has to do with the will."

I'd uttered the magic word. Abruptly returning his chair to its upright position, Fielding leaned toward me. "What *about* the will?"

I filled him in on Claire and Leibowitz, Leibowitz and O'Donnell.

"What did they say?"

"I didn't call. I thought that was probably something you should handle."

There was a moment of stunned silence before he responded. "Thanks, Dez. And I mean that." Then he eyed me suspiciously. "And in return for this magnanimous act of yours, you want . . . ?"

"To see the apartment, that's all."

"I don't know how to break this to you, but you'd have gotten to see the place without giving away the store. I was gonna call and tell you you could come up on Saturday if you wanted to."

Oh, Shit! "How come, all of a sudden?"

"Well, the other night something occurred to me—probably out of desperation. When I first questioned Eric Foster, I asked him if he knew of any dentists or doctors his sisters saw over in London. He said he didn't have any idea—he moved out to the suburbs when the girls were pretty young, you know."

"Yes, I'm aware of that."

"Anyhow, I started thinking that maybe if he came across the *name* of a doctor or dentist, he just might recognize it—even if he didn't know whether either of the women had ever been the man's patient. So I asked him if he'd mind going up to the apartment and browsing through some of his sisters' old checkbook stubs—from back when they were living in England."

"You might have something there," I said admiringly.

Fielding actually appeared slightly embarrassed by my almost-compliment. "You should see the records those women kept," he went on quickly. "In most cases, all they included were names and amounts—not even a date. And there's no notation at all about what the checks were for. I have my doubts they'd be bothered writing down 'M.D.' or 'D.D.S.'—or whatever they're called over there. At any rate, there's at least a chance Foster may spot a name that rings a bell." He inhaled deeply, then let out a long, slow sigh. "We could sure use a set of dental records right now. Or maybe a line on some special physical characteristic that only one of 'em had—*anything*!"

"Like a mole next to the navel?" I put in facetiously, grinning.

"Does your client tell you *everything*?"

"As a matter of fact, it was Larry Shields who mentioned it."

"Anyway," Fielding summed up, "we've made arrangements with Foster to meet him at the apartment on Saturday morning at eleven-thirty."

"And I'm invited?"

"Yeah. Now maybe you'll finally get off my ass." He muttered the words, but his eyes were definitely twinkling.

"Okay, Dez," he said, smiling, "how about we give Leibowitz, Leibowitz and whoever a call?"

"O'Donnell," I supplied, handing him the phone number.

He was picking up the receiver when, at that moment, his partner sauntered in.

"Well, well, look who's still here," Corcoran snickered in this high-pitched voice he has which is so totally incongruous coming out of such a large and loathsome person. "I was hoping you'd be gone by now. But this just hasn't been my morning." Before I had a chance to zing one *his* way, he turned to Fielding. "They were out of prune, so I got you a cheese," he said, handing him a stained brown paper bag. "And by the way, our new leader requests our presence in his office; 'chop chop,' was how he put it. Think you can tear yourself away from Miss Chubbette here?"

Fielding tossed his partner an appropriately black look. "I'd better get going," he told me. "The lieutenant isn't particularly crazy about being kept waiting. I'll call the lawyers as soon as I get a chance, and I'll let you know what's what. Oh, and why don't you take the Danish?"

"Thanks, but that's okay," I said, declining with an effort. "I've gotta get going, too."

I stopped at Jackie's desk on the way to my office. One look at her face, and I knew I was in trouble. I knew why, too.

On her strict instructions, I normally call if I'm going to be detained at all. But that morning I was in such a hurry to get to the station house that I didn't take the time to stop and phone her. Besides, I figured I wouldn't be very late. And besides *that,* I guess this was one of those very rare times I was subconsciously trying to show some balls and assert myself with Jackie. I mean, isn't one of the perks of being self-employed not always having to answer to somebody else?

"I was afraid something was really wrong," she informed me in this accusatory tone. "For all I knew, you could have gotten yourself shot." She glanced at her watch. "It's five of eleven; I've been trying to reach you since ten. Another few minutes and I would have put in a call to your super."

"I'm sorry. I had some business to take care of, and it took longer than I thought it would." Then I added truthfully, "I didn't mean to upset you."

"Look, the next time you're going to be late, just pick up the phone and let me know. I don't think that's a lot to ask, do you?"

I conceded that it wasn't. After all, the best secretary in the world—especially since she was also a good and concerned friend—deserved some consideration. And why was it so important to show some damned balls in the office, anyway?

"Um, any messages?" I asked timidly.

"Wouldn't I have *told* you if you had any?"

Wisely, I beat it at that point, giving Jackie a chance to cool off and, I hoped, even forget what a trial I was to her.

I spent most of the balance of the day closeted in my office, waiting to hear from Tim. I must have checked the clock every five minutes until he finally got in touch with me at a little after three.

"You had a damned good hunch there, but unfortunately it didn't pan out," he said dejectedly. "I just got off the phone with that law firm. Meredith and Mary Ann Foster don't happen to be clients of theirs."

And I'd been so sure! "Neither of them?" I asked weakly.

"That's right. But listen, it's not the end of the world," he consoled, sounding a lot more optimistic than I knew he felt. "Could be the Foster woman'll be able to fill us in herself soon," he offered, presenting me with my own contention.

But I no longer believed it. Any more than Fielding did. There was no way it would turn out to be that easy.

Peter came to dinner that night.

While the lasagna finished baking, we sat in the living room, sipping red wine and nibbling zucchini puffs. "I have to apologize for not returning your calls," he said, referring to a couple of messages I'd left that morning and the night before. "I've been so wrapped up in what's been happening with Mary Ann that—"

"I understand," I interrupted. "I was just anxious to know if everything was okay."

"Everything's terrific! The brain damage seems to be minimal! Her left hand is partially paralyzed and the vision in her left eye is blurred, but there's a possibility that with therapy both those things could clear up. And if they don't, well, I'm still pretty grateful. The doctors were telling me how lucky she is a bullet in that part of the brain didn't do a lot more damage to the optic nerve. And they said how pleased they were it didn't impair her motor skills to a lot greater extent than it did. So when I think about how bad things could have been ..." He broke off with a shudder.

Even in my most optimistic moments, I couldn't have hoped for anything better—at least as far as the victim's physical condition was concerned. "Thank God!" I exclaimed. After which I silently prayed, "Just let it be Mary Ann!"

A moment later, Peter said softly, "She still has no idea who she is, though. That first night, I was hoping she was just a little confused with having been in a coma for so long, but now they claim it's more than that."

"What do they think her chances are of regaining her memory—or haven't they said?" I asked gently.

"Dr. Baker, her neurologist, says that with an injury like hers they can't be sure. It could happen anytime now, or ..." A couple of seconds passed before he was able to finish the thought. "Or she may never remember." There was another pause, and then Peter's mood picked up again.

"But let's get to some more of the good stuff," he ordered cheerfully. "Mary Ann's even talking now! It isn't easy for her, all wired up like that—and you can barely understand her—but she manages it. Yesterday, she asked what happened to her, and the doctors told her she was in an accident. And then she asked what her name was. They told her it was Foster. She just accepted that; she didn't ask about her first name or anything. A while later, she wanted to know who I was. The doctors had made me promise that if she asked me, I'd say I was just a good friend. So that's what I did. But it almost killed me."

"I know it did. But—for the time being, anyway—I think you're going to have to leave it at that."

"I guess so," Peter conceded grudgingly. In an instant, though, his voice became animated again. "But listen, this afternoon she took some nourishment through a straw for the first time. How's that for progress?"

And on that happy note, we went into the kitchen for our lasagna.

It wasn't until we were almost finished with dinner that Peter said excitedly, "Hey, I didn't tell you, did I? The doctors were discussing plastic surgery this morning like it's actually for real, like they expect Mary Ann to be around for it! It would be a series of operations—three or four, I think. But of course they'll have to wait awhile, until she's stronger and her jaw heals a little."

"That's a very positive sign," I told him, marveling at how much things had changed in these last forty-eight hours.

Well, no matter which twin was lying there in St. Catherine's and no matter how everything eventually worked out, this had to be better for Peter than all of those long, agonizing weeks in limbo.

But then I reminded myself that—in spite of what he professed—Peter was *still* in limbo, that he'd *be* in limbo until the question of identity was truly resolved.

And, with a sinking feeling in the pit of my stomach, I had to face the realization that might never happen.

Chapter 22

Peter left at a little after midnight—with the extra pan of lasagna I pressed on him.

About five minutes after the door closed, I was ready to flog myself. How could I even consider the *possibility* of never sorting out the identities of the victims? Peter was depending on me, and I had to come through for him—or die trying.

So on Friday I revved myself up to pursue another angle of the case: I was going to find out the truth about that short-lived rift between Meredith and Larry Shields.

I began with Tara Wilde, the *Love and Stuff* cast member I was convinced represented my best chance of getting the facts. In other words, the person it would be easiest to manipulate.

I called her from my apartment at six-thirty. No answer. And, surprisingly for an actress, no answering machine, either. I tried again twenty minutes later. Still no answer. Maybe she had a date. But then again, maybe she just hadn't come home from rehearsal yet. At seven-fifteen, I gave it what I'd determined would be my final try. (I hadn't eaten since a really puny lunch at twelve, and my stomach would not be denied much longer.) This time, Tara picked up on the second ring.

The girl's tone became wary as soon as I mentioned my name—which she recognized instantly. (That's the one advantage of being a Desiree Shapiro: It's way up there on the memorability scale.) Of course, considering our last encounter, I wasn't exactly stunned by the unenthusiastic reception I got.

"Listen," I told her—making sure all my natural warmth and sincerity came through in my voice—"there's this one small point I'd like to check out with you. I'm in your neighborhood now, and I thought, if you haven't eaten yet,

maybe we could grab a bite together while we talked."
(Since Tara lived in the west sixties, I wasn't anywhere *near*
her neighborhood. But I wanted the invitation to sound
casual so she'd drop her guard a little.)

Evidently I didn't come off as likable as I'd hoped, because she was still leery of meeting with me. "I told you all
I know when you questioned me at the theater," she said.

"Oh, I'm sure you did. But this just cropped up, and I
was hoping you could shed some light on it. It won't take
long; I promise. I'm on West Sixty-seventh now with a client, and I should be through here around eight. And then
I have another appointment a few blocks away at ten-
fifteen, which gives me a couple of hours to kill. You'd be
doing me a real favor if you joined me for dinner. Please.
I'm absolutely starved, and I hate to eat alone." *That* part,
at least, was true.

Tara hesitated, weighing the offer carefully, before responding with what I could tell were the first words of a
reluctant turn-down. "Gee, I'm not ..."

Quickly I played my trump card. "We can go to any
restaurant you like," I told her. (Taking into account what
novice actresses earn, there was a good possibility that for
a really special meal, she might even be willing to put up
with *me*.)

"Well ... there's this wonderful seafood restaurant I
heard about. But it *is* kind of expensive."

We arranged to meet at the restaurant at ten after eight.
Which, I calculated, should allow me to get into my coat,
go downstairs, engage in some ugly battles with my neighbors over the few available taxis (it was a Friday night,
remember?) and—by eventually outwitting someone who
lacked my street smarts—make it over to the West Side
in time.

I got to the Sea Scape at quarter after eight. Tara was
standing in front of the place shivering, her slim frame hud-
dled in a coat about two sizes larger than she was, her
cheeks and nose whipped to a bright pink by the strong
end-of-February wind.

"Why didn't you wait inside?" I asked.

"You didn't mention inside, and I was worried you might
not think to look."

Hey, this just might be easier than I thought!

Over our crabmeat cocktail, I was careful to keep the conversation away from the investigation. How was the show going? I asked. Tara said fine but that the opening had to be postponed until the end of March to give Lucille Collins a chance to work into her new role. And how was *her* part coming along? Pretty good, although she only had a few lines, so how bad could she mess up? Then I asked what the play was about. Food must have had a relaxing effect on the girl, because she cheerfully related the plot.

As soon as the waiter removed our naked dishes, Tara wanted to know how I came to be a P.I. And I undoubtedly told her more than she ever hoped to hear.

By the time we were having our scampi (yes, Barbara, *scampi*!), we were chatting away like old friends. Then, as I was spearing my third huge, succulent shrimp, I finally broached the case. "The reason I wanted to talk to you," I said, "is that I heard from another cast member recently—and I don't know how true it is—that Meredith was very depressed the week she died.

Tara's huge eyes opened wide, and she arrested her fork in midair. "Who told you that?"

"I'm afraid I can't say; it was told to me in confidence."

"Well, I didn't notice anything," she assured me before lustily attacking her food again. "Have you asked Larry about it?"

That was the opening I wanted.

"No, not yet. I was hoping I might not have to. I hate bugging him; this thing's hit him really hard."

"Don't I know it!"

"He was just crazy about her, wasn't he? I guess he had to be to take her back after what she pulled on him."

"You *know* about that?" Tara asked disbelievingly.

"Meredith confided in a friend of hers who clued me in on the whole story." I shook my head slowly from side to side. "It was really a terrible thing she did."

"Terrible," Tara agreed, looking up and nodding for a split second before she began to sop up the butter sauce with her generously buttered roll.

"It was very understanding of him to forgive her, don't you think?"

"Larry's like that."

I kept plugging away. "I guess that's what makes what she did all the more ..." I groped for the word Meredith herself had used in unburdening herself to Charles Springer. Then I nailed it. "Unforgivable," I finished.

"That's the way we all feel. Everyone in the cast."

So the whole cast was aware of Meredith's transgression! "How did you find out about it, anyway?" I asked. *Surely now I'd learn something, too.*

"Well, the day after Meredith told him—at least, I think it was the day after—they were rehashing the whole thing at the theater, in Larry's office. Everyone else had already left, so I guess they weren't worried somebody would hear them. But Midge—you remember her, tall redhead?—she forgot her shopping bag. She bought a beautiful beige tweed skirt at Bolton's lunchtime; it was a real buy, too— $59.95. Anyway, she remembered about the skirt when she was just a couple of blocks away from the theater, so she came back for it. Only Larry and Meredith didn't hear her come in. Midge wasn't eavesdropping, honestly, but they weren't exactly whispering. Of course, she knew they'd be mortified if they thought she overheard anything, so she just stood there in the dressing room, not even moving, until Meredith left and Larry went into the men's room. Then she got out of there fast!"

"And Midge went and repeated the story to the entire company?"

Tara immediately sprang to the other actress's defense— immediately after she finished buttering her fourth roll, that is. (I'd gladly sell my soul for that kid's metabolism!) "Oh, no!" she protested. "Midge only told Diane and me. She felt as though she had to tell *someone,* and she knew we'd never breathe a word to anyone else." (*Diane?* I had a vague recollection of a short, plump girl; some kind of production assistant, I thought.)

"But then Carol found out," Tara continued (as I tried, without any success at all, to recall who Carol was). "I really don't know how, either; maybe she heard the three of us talking. And after that . . ." She broke off and shrugged, spreading her arms, her palms turned upwards. The gesture made it plain she considered this Carol solely to blame for the exposure of Meredith and Larry's secret.

"Midge must have been really shocked—I mean, hearing Meredith admit a thing like that."

"She was floored."

"I guess Larry was pretty steamed," I ventured. *Well, let's see where that got me.*

"Wouldn't *you* be?"

"Sure I would." Frustration made me bolder. "Uh, how did Meredith put it, anyway?"

"Well, of course, I wasn't there, but according to Midge, all Meredith kept saying was how sorry she was and that she should have gotten up the courage to tell him sooner. Midge said she must have used the word 'sorry' a dozen times. Sorry! As though that would make everything all right!"

"And what did Larry say to *her*?" I gritted my teeth, anticipating the kind of less-than-illuminating answer I'd get. And I got it.

"He told her she could stay on in the play but that she was poison and that their relationship was over for good."

"But he did forgive her eventually."

"Yes. But after a thing like that, I don't know how, do you?"

By now we were ready to order dessert. And my head was spinning from the strain of attempting to outsmart an unsuspecting Tara who was stonewalling me at every turn. And, what was worse, without even trying!

Well, I'd asked her all the leading questions I could drum up, and short of being direct—which I knew would only succeed in antagonizing her—there was no place left to go.

So, in the interest of enjoying an angst-free dessert, I finally threw in the towel.

Chapter 23

After all of my nagging and whining and wheedling, I was finally about to visit the scene of the crime. I don't know what I actually expected to find in that apartment; I only knew that I wouldn't be satisfied until I had a look at the place.

As soon as I identified myself to the doorman, a young black man with a friendly smile, he said to go right up, that the officers were expecting me. "The English gentleman just got here two minutes before you did," he informed me.

As I turned the corner to the elevator bank, Eric Foster was entering one of the cars. To join him, I'd really have had to hustle. Which didn't appeal to me at all. Anyhow, I didn't have much of a wait for the next elevator; it came along maybe ten seconds later.

When I got out on four, I spotted Foster way down the plushly carpeted hall, walking briskly. Now, in my building you could yell "Hey, wait up!" and nobody would think twice about it. But here, they'd probably have you arrested. So I showed some decorum. In a moment, he was at the end of the hall; then, without pausing, he turned left and disappeared from my sight.

Walking a whole lot less briskly, I followed in his footsteps and arrived at the door to 4C a couple of minutes later.

Fielding answered my ring, and I entered what under ordinary circumstances would have been one of my daydreams.

There was a long, mirrored foyer with a beautiful parquet floor and the most exquisite crystal chandelier. The only jarring note—and it was a doozy—was that when I reached the far end of the foyer, where it curved into the living room, I immediately conjured up a vision of Meredith Foster lying there faceless, covered with blood.

Fielding led the way into the ballroom-sized living room, which had soft Wedgewood blue walls, floor-to-ceiling windows, and—what really sent my heart racing—a wide staircase leading to what was obviously a second floor.

Only one small section of the room contained any furniture at all, the sum total of the pieces consisting of a velvet, loose-backed sofa the exact shade of the walls and a rectangular glass coffee table with brass accents. Plus there were a couple of old folding chairs and a battered floor lamp—makeshift items I'm sure the twins had been looking forward to replacing. All of the furnishings stood on a pale, cream-colored area rug bordered in the Wedgewood. I estimated that if I ever had a rug that color, it would take two weeks tops before the thing was decorated with telltale reminders of some of D'Agostino's most tempting goodies.

And then, when I got closer, I saw the dark stains on *that* rug, stains that had a much more sinister origin. And now there was the image of another prostrate, faceless young girl. And she was wearing a blood-soaked yellow cashmere sweater, and there was more blood slowly oozing onto the carpet, and ... Determinedly, I banished Mary Ann, too, from my mind.

"Hello," Eric Foster was saying, "how are you, Desiree?" We shook hands. "All right if I call you Desiree?"

"Oh, sure. Please do."

"I suppose you've heard about my sister coming out of the coma?" he asked, his voice ringing with excitement. He had draped his coat and gloves across one of the folding chairs alongside the sofa and was now adding his scarf to the small pile.

"Yes, and it's wonderful!"

This conversation between two human beings was interrupted by a sarcastic "It's nice to see you, too, Shapiro."

I turned around to acknowledge Walter Corcoran, who was sprawled in the folding chair on the other side of the sofa, his long legs extending straight out in front of him almost to the chair opposite. "Hi, Walter." I had made up my mind that, no matter what, I was going to be civil to Corcoran today. I did not aspire to friendly or pleasant, which was really too much to ask of myself.

"Hi, Walter," he mimicked.

Fielding, who was returning from the kitchen with a glass of water at that moment, jumped in quickly, apparently anticipating one of my usual tit-for-tat responses. "Your sisters collected shopping bags full of check stubs from their London days," he said, addressing Foster. "It shouldn't take you too long to go through them, though—at least, I hope not. But either a name hits you or it doesn't, right?"

"Right. You said 'check stubs,' didn't you? No canceled checks?"

"None that we could find, and believe me, we looked."

"A pity," Foster commented. "Undoubtedly there'd have been some sort of designation on the checks themselves." Then he shrugged. "Well, it can't be helped. I'm ready to start anytime now."

Corcoran got reluctantly to his feet, and I immediately threw my belongings on the now-empty chair. After which I followed the men through an arched doorway on the far side of the living room, turned right, and proceeded down a short hallway and then into a nice-sized room I presumed was the study. It contained a massive mahogany desk, behind which was a large burgundy leather armchair. Next to the chair were two bulging shopping bags. Poor Foster was liable to be here till dawn, I thought.

Fielding turned to his partner. "I think it might not be a bad idea to bring those folding chairs in here, huh, Walt? Why don't I go get 'em."

In a few moments he was back with the two chairs. As soon as he set them down in front of the desk, he crooked his finger at me. "C'mon with me, Dez."

"You know," he said when we were out in the hall, "I don't see any point in your hanging around for two, three hours while Foster's digging through all that stuff. Why don't you have a look around—although, for the life of me, I can't figure out what you hope to learn—and leave when you're finished. If he comes up with anything at all, I'll let you know."

"Swear?"

"Swear." With a smile.

"Today?"

"Today." With a frown. "Now where do you want to start?"

"You don't have to come with me; I'm not going to touch anything," I protested indignantly.

"I know that. But I'm responsible here; you're not even

supposed to *be* here. So do me a favor and don't give me any grief, huh?"

Of course, when he put it like that . . .

With Fielding lurking in the background, I returned to the entry foyer, noting that, as beautiful as that chandelier was, it cast more shadow than light. Then I went back to the living room. The single lamp behind the sofa did a very poor job of illuminating even the immediate area. Well, if there was anything in that mistaken identity theory of mine, the lighting in this place only served to reinforce it.

Now that I'd established that, I couldn't think of anything else I wanted to check out. It seemed Tim had been right all along: There was nothing to be gained by my visiting the apartment. But I wasn't about to tell *him* that. And as long as I was here anyway . . .

With my friend not too happily in tow, I spent the next fifteen minutes giving myself a' tour. I found myself yearning for the eat-in kitchen with its enormous refrigerator and industrial-sized stove. To say nothing of how I coveted the separate breakfast area, the real live honest-to-goodness pantry, and a dining room that was easily one and a half times the size of my living room. I won't even mention that there were *three* powder rooms on that floor.

Fielding balked when I told him I was ready to go upstairs. "Okay, tell me what you're looking for up there," he challenged.

"I have a couple of ideas," I said, hoping it came off sounding cryptic.

"You've got five minutes."

The first room we came to on the second level was a handsome wood-paneled library with bookshelves everywhere you looked—and only a handful of books to occupy them. Next to the library was—surprise!—another powder room and, to the right of the powder room, what I took to be a guest room with, naturally, a bathroom of its very own. Finally, on the other side of the hall, there were two absolutely immense bedroom *suites,* each with an adjoining bath complete with sunken tub, bidet, mile-long marble vanity, and magnificent, hand-painted fixtures.

The moment I saw those suites, I knew which twin belonged where.

One of them contained a brass queen-sized bed, covered with navy and red sheets and matching comforter in a bold geometric pattern. The vivid color scheme was picked up in the large modern painting that hung over the bed and in a solid red octagonal rug with navy fringe. The only remaining items in the suite were obviously temporary pieces: a badly scarred triple dresser and an equally scarred night table that held a small brass lamp. This room had Meredith written all over it: strong, vibrant, contemporary.

The second bedroom was furnished with a painted white canopy bed, made up with white linens lavishly edged in lace. There were white lace curtains at the windows and, next to the bed, a beautiful black needlepoint rug with pink, yellow, and white flowers. The mood was soft, charming, romantic. Mary Ann, to a T. As I turned to leave, I remember thinking that I'd have to ask Peter which room was which just to prove to myself I was right. And then, on top of one of the two battered chests of drawers here, I saw a snapshot in a gold filigree frame. I recognized that picture. The girl was wearing jeans and a T-shirt and a New York Yankees baseball cap. And the boy, of course, was Peter.

I was glad the apartment was so sparsely furnished. It gave me a chance to decorate it while I was trying to fall asleep that night. But then I was suddenly struck by the ghoulishness of it all, and I quickly relinquished the project. I mean, what I was doing was practically like dancing on somebody's grave, for God's sake!

It was just before I dozed off that this *thing* in the back of my head began nagging at me, trying to push its way to the front of my mind. And I suddenly got this unshakable conviction that something I'd seen or heard that day was eluding me—something that just wasn't right. I didn't have a clue what it was. But I *did* know it was important.

I woke up the next morning still unable to pin it down. And all afternoon, it was gnawing away at me. I kept reminding myself that I was being foolish. After all, Saturday had been so uneventful—disappointing, really, especially when I thought about how long I'd been anticipating it. But still, I couldn't seem to shake off this feeling. . . .

Ellen had invited me to dinner that night. Now, dinner at Ellen's always means the same thing: Chinese takeout. Which is great with me. You see, except for breakfast, which she really manages quite nicely, Ellen's prowess in the kitchen used to be attested to by one practically raw or incinerated dish after another. I can't tell you how grateful my stomach was when she finally abandoned her efforts.

Anyway, I was lousy company that evening. I couldn't seem to concentrate long enough to string two coherent sentences together. (Ellen was concerned I was coming down with something.) I was even too preoccupied to enjoy the meal, although I'm sure, based on my extensive experience with my niece's takeout of choice, that it was very good. (My lack of appetite must have been pretty obvious, too, because at that point Ellen was *sure* I was coming down with something.)

And then it happened.

We'd just finished eating, and I was pushing my chair back from the table, when that *thing* that had been driving me up the wall finally worked its way through to my consciousness:

How did he know which way to go?

Chapter 24

Naturally, I told Ellen about what had just occurred to me. I was too wired to so much as *consider* keeping it to myself. (Even Sherlock Holmes had his Watson, you know.)

"What are you going to do?" she demanded.

"Go and see him."

"Do you think you *should?* What if he's the perp?"

I grinned. It sounded so strange hearing Ellen use a word like "perp."

She misunderstood about the grin. "I don't see what's so funny," she snapped. "He could off you right then and there."

"*Off*" you? That was an expression even I rarely used; Ellen was definitely spending too much time in front of the tube.

"Look, that's not going to happen," I assured her. "How would he explain the presence of this voluptuous body in the middle of his living room floor?"

"We-e-ll ..." she began, obviously trying to think her retort through as she went along. I interrupted before she got anywhere.

"I had the best meal the other night," I said to divert her. "At a place called the Sea Scape. We've really gotta go sometime."

"Don't try to change the subject," she instructed. Then: "What did you have there, anyway?"

I called Eric Foster at his office the next morning. There was no problem getting him to meet with me. "Eight this evening at my apartment convenient for you?" he wanted to know.

I told him that would be fine.

Foster was very cordial when he answered the door that night. "You look frozen," he observed sympathetically.

Actually, it wasn't a particularly cold evening, so, if anything, I had turned a little less blue than usual. "I always look that way," I said. "Except for maybe the third and fourth weeks in July."

He smiled and helped me off with my coat. "So, coffee?" he asked when I was seated in the same impossibly deep sofa that had dwarfed me the last time I was there. "I even have some tea to offer you now, if you'd prefer—a really excellent blend."

"No, nothing, thanks."

"Are you here about the check stubs?"

It hadn't dawned on me he might think that. The fact is, when I didn't hear from Fielding Saturday afternoon, I knew it was because he had nothing to tell me. Still, I figured it might be better to start with the stubs and then work my way around to the real reason I'd come. "Well, I *did* want to know how you made out."

"Absolutely nothing," Foster said dejectedly. "Almost four hours' worth of stubs, and I didn't come across a single name I recognized as belonging to either a dentist or a doctor. Which isn't to say there wasn't one. Just none I was familiar with."

"You tried. I'm sure Sergeant Fielding realized it was a long shot."

"That may be, but it would have meant the world to me if I'd been able to help."

"Uh, there was something else I wanted to talk to you about, too."

"Of course. What's that?"

"I was wondering if you'd ever been to your sisters' apartment before Saturday."

"With the way Merry feels about me?" The implied denial was punctuated with a short, harsh laugh. "What makes you ask?"

"I was walking behind you after you got off the elevator. And when you came to the end of the hall, you didn't even hesitate for a second; it was apparent you knew just which way to turn."

Foster smiled a very tight little smile. "I hate disappointing you, but there is a simple explanation. And it's *not* that I'd been there on the night of February tenth to do away with my sisters."

"I'm sorry," I murmured, "but I have to ask."

He nodded curtly, but he seemed to relax then. "Actually, I was in the *building* before. Only once—the last time I was in New York. But I never even set a toe in the apartment."

"That was in . . . ?"

"Back in October. I'd come to town a few weeks earlier than I'd expected, y'see, and I thought I'd just pop up there and surprise Mary Ann. Merry wasn't supposed to be at home that evening; she was *supposed* to be doing a play. Anyway, when I arrived at the building, there was a large group of people going in at the same time, and I more or less attached myself to them. The doorman didn't even notice me, unfortunately, so I went up unannounced. Sneaked up, actually."

"Why did you say it was *unfortunate* the doorman didn't notice you?"

"I might have spared myself and Merry some trauma if he *had* done."

"She was home?"

"Oh, yes. She was there, all right. And it was she who answered the door."

"Didn't she ask who it was?"

"I said it was Chuck, this neighbor Mary Ann had mentioned in a couple of her letters—I was still thinking it was Mary Ann, of course. And then, when Merry opened the door . . ." Moving forward in his chair, Foster spoke intently now, his eyes fixed on my face. "It's a bit difficult to explain, Desiree, but y'see, while I never had a problem telling my sisters apart, I was *expecting* to see Mary Ann, so I wasn't really *looking* at Merry, if you take my meaning. And they *did* look quite alike, y'know. But in any event, before Merry had a chance to say a word, I went to kiss her. She backed away from me with the most revolted expression on her face! It was as though I were a leper! And, of course, that's when I knew. But the whole incident was terribly distressing for us both."

"What happened then?"

"Merry informed me that Mary Ann wasn't at home and promptly shut the door in my face. But I promise you, I was only too delighted to get the hell away from there."

"Do you have any idea why Meredith wasn't performing that night?"

"She had a sinus infection, Mary Ann told me later, so she had to take a few days off from the play."

Then, leaning back in his chair again, Eric Foster said quietly, "And that was the last time I saw my sister Merry."

Back home a short time later, I reviewed everything I'd just heard. And I had to admit it. Foster's explanation would certainly account for his knowing the way to his sisters' apartment. (Although I usually get lost the first *ten* times I go anywhere. But then, not everyone is as addle-brained as I am.) Still, I wondered if Mary Ann had ever said anything to Peter about her brother's impromptu visit. I was about to try to reach him when the phone rang.

It was Ellen, wanting to verify that I was still alive and anxious for the details of my meeting with Foster. As soon as I could manage to get off the phone with her, I made the call to Peter.

"Mary Ann never said a word to me about any visit from Eric," he told me. "Anyway, I don't think she did."

Okay, so there was no *confirmation* that Foster had gone there that night. But on the other hand, there was absolutely no reason to doubt what he'd told me.

Then it occurred to me to phone Larry Shields.

I got right to the purpose of the call. "I just wanted to know what made you go and see *Showboat* that time—the production Meredith was in, I mean."

"Why do I think this is some kind of a trap?" he demanded, a sharpness in his voice.

"It's not; I swear. In fact, this has nothing to do with you."

He hesitated before answering grudgingly, "All right. I went because this friend of mine was the director."

"I was hoping it might be something like that. Do you think you could find out from him if Meredith missed any performances in October with a sinus infection?"

"I guess I could try," he agreed reluctantly.

It took about twenty minutes for Shields to get back to me. "I spoke to Raphael, the director, and he remembers Merry being out sick for a few days, but he didn't know just when it was. So he called the understudy, and she says Merry was out for three days in October with a sinus problem. And if anyone would know, *she* would."

"I imagine she would. Thanks, Larry; thanks a lot."

"Yeah," he said a little caustically, "glad to help."

Well, that was that. It all seemed to check out, so once again I'd had a promising lead fizzle out on me. (And what was *with* Larry Shields, anyway?)

I can't tell you how depressed I felt for the rest of that evening thinking about all of these recent blind alleys of mine.

And very soon I was going to feel worse. *Much* worse. . . .

Chapter 25

The following morning, I got the news that *really* kicked me in the teeth.

It came in a phone call from Fielding just before ten. "I found out something very interesting your client," he told me evenly.

"What?" I asked the question calmly. I didn't have a clue that anything could actually be wrong.

"You know the dinner he had with that friend of his the night of the shootings?"

"What about it?"

"It never happened."

"Never happened?" I repeated stupidly.

"To put it another way, your client lied."

"I'll be right down."

When I got up from the chair, my knees buckled, and going down in the elevator, my heart began racing wildly. It wasn't until I was in the taxi on my way to the precinct that I calmed down a little.

Even if Peter did lie about that dinner, it didn't mean he had anything to do with the shootings. Peter wouldn't do anything like that. He *couldn't* do anything like that. Of this I was one thousand percent sure.

When I got to the station, Fielding was on the phone. He motioned for me to have a seat next to his desk. Corcoran, happily, was nowhere to be seen.

Fielding's call didn't last more than another couple of minutes. And then he began his destruction of my entire nervous system.

"On Sunday, we finally looked into Winters's alibi," he told me. "Corcoran and I dropped in at that restaurant he *claims* he had dinner at."

"*Claims?* Didn't you check with his ex-roommate? The two of them had dinner *together*."

"Of course we checked," Fielding snapped. "We questioned the roommate weeks ago, and he confirmed your kid's story. That's why we didn't look into it any further. But we should have gone and talked to them over at the restaurant regardless, right at the beginning. Just as a matter of course. Only at that time there were a lot of other things going on, and we didn't really consider the kid a suspect, anyway."

"So why now?" I asked through parched lips.

"Because with the way we've been striking out all over the place, we decided to go back to square one and rethink everything. And I—" He stopped talking abruptly, scowling. "What the hell's the matter with me? What am I going into all these explanations for? The bottom line is, the kid lied. The restaurant he says he and his friend ate in that Monday night is *closed on Mondays*."

"Is *that* all?" I said, momentarily relieved. "You know how spacey Peter can be sometimes." Not liking the sound of that once it came out, I quickly added, "Especially with the kind of stress he's been under." Fielding glared at me stonily. "He probably got the name mi—"

"Save your breath," he broke in. "We talked to the roommate yesterday, kid named Norman Flynt. And after a few potent threats, Flynt admitted he and your client didn't break bread together the night of the shootings, after all."

Suddenly I felt as though aliens had zapped all the strength from my body.

"They planned to," Fielding was saying. "And as a matter of fact, they were talking on the phone at six-fifteen that night, deciding where to eat, when someone rang Winters's doorbell. He went to open the door, and when he got on the phone again, he told Flynt he'd call him back in a few minutes. He called back in a few minutes, all right— to cancel.

"The next day, Flynt went back home to Maine, and then, that night, he got a call from your client. It was to ask him to swear to that phony alibi he'd involved him in."

"Did Flynt tell you where Peter *really* was Monday night?" My heart seemed to be pounding right in my ears, so loudly I could barely hear my own question.

"Uh-uh," Fielding replied. "Swears he doesn't know. According to Flynt, Peter said he couldn't tell *anybody* the truth about where he was. Flynt says he agreed to go along with him anyway, because he's sure Winters is no murderer." Then, after a pause, he put in darkly, "I wish *I* could be that sure."

"Look. If Peter lied—"

"*If?*"

"Okay, okay. *When* Peter lied, he must have had a good reason. He was crazy about Mary Ann. And besides, Peter's no murderer. I know it."

"You sound just like the roommate." I was about to expand and cite my client's virtues when Fielding conceded, "But if you want the truth, I don't think Winters did it, either. Only *not thinking* and *knowing* aren't exactly the same thing."

"Have you talked to Peter yet?"

"Corcoran and I paid him a little visit at seven o'clock this morning. But we couldn't get a damn thing out of him. So I made arrangements to cut off his hospital visits immediately. We can't take the chance of anything happening to the victim, especially not after the poor woman's come this far."

"But you've got a guard stationed right there in the room," I protested.

"That's true. But still, anything goes wrong, I gotta live with myself. No way anyone who's under even the slightest suspicion gets into that room."

"But Peter had no *motive* for shooting those girls."

"No motive we *know of*. Maybe he and the girlfriend had an argument—just like her sister and Shields did. Or maybe it was about money. Your client could stand to inherit a bundle, for all we know." He shook his head slowly from side to side. "God, I'd like to get my hands on that will," he murmured fervently. A pause. "If there *is* a will," he reminded himself just as I was about to do it for him.

"But Peter thought Mary Ann was going to be out with a friend that night, remember?" I pointed out instead.

"Yeah? Who says she didn't call and tell him her plans had changed?"

What could I say to that? I elected to go down fighting, though. "You know, Tim, you're making a terrible mistake not allowing Peter into that hospital room anymore. You know as well as I do he's no killer. And right now he could be doing that girl more good than her doctors. More good than all of them put together, in fact."

"This is not negotiable," Tim stated flatly. And the expression on his face told me he meant it.

"I'll go have a talk with him," I put in hastily.

As soon as I got outside, I started hunting around for a pay phone. Would you believe the one that used to be almost directly in front of the police station had been ripped out? I mean, talk about chutzpah! On my second try, I found a phone with only the receiver removed. I had to go four blocks away before I lucked out and got an entire instrument that was actually in working order.

It wasn't easy making that call, either. Not with the way my hands were trembling.

"I want to see you," I told Peter.

"Oh. You spoke to the police," he said softly.

"All right if I come over?"

"Uh, look, Desiree, I'm really sorry. But there's nothing I can tell you."

"We have to talk."

"Okay," he agreed, sighing.

Peter lived in a narrow six-story building on West Thirty-eighth Street. He buzzed me in before I even had a chance to ring the doorbell.

"I saw you from the window," he explained when he opened the door.

This was the first time I'd ever been to Peter's apartment. Small and neatly—but far from luxuriously—furnished, it was a homey place, comfortable and lived-in. Besides the obligatory sofa, chairs, and tables, there were a pair of bookcases with a whole lot of books in them and a large faux walnut wall unit that held the rest of the essentials: TV, VCR, CD player, and four or five racks jammed with videocassettes and CD albums. Prints and photographs decorated the walls, and a colorful Indian rug covered most of the light wood floor. "This is nice," I remarked, trying to take some of the edge off my visit.

"Nothing fancy, but it suits me fine," Peter responded, reaching for a polite smile.

I sat down in one of the club chairs next to the sofa, and he took the sofa. I didn't waste any time in confronting him. "What's going on, Peter?" I demanded.

"I can't talk about it, Desiree, honestly. But I swear to you I had nothing to do with the shootings. You believe me, don't you?"

"Of course I do. But what *I* believe doesn't matter. You know, I suppose, that until you level with Sergeant Fielding, you won't be allowed anywhere *near* Mary Ann. (I had my fingers crossed when I said the name.)

"I was talking to her neurologist just before you got here, and I think I managed to persuade him to try and get the police to change their minds. Dr. Baker feels my visits could be really important to Mary Ann's recovery."

"Even if he *does* go to bat for you, I wouldn't count on his convincing the police of anything. They figure it's their only way of getting you to cooperate with them."

"Baker's a highly respected neurologist, so it's conceivable they *will* listen to him," he insisted stubbornly.

You can't imagine how frustrated I was at this point. Still, with the thimbleful of patience I had left, I said reasonably, "I don't understand you, Peter. If your visits could make a difference in Mary Ann's recovery, how can you possibly put yourself in a position where you may not be allowed to see her anymore?"

"I'll have to cross that bridge when I come to it," he replied, looking totally miserable.

"Well, whatever you did that night, you can tell *me,* anyway," I pressed. "I'd never repeat anything without your permission."

"It would be easier for me to tell the police than you," was the startling response.

My brief meeting with Peter left me in shock. What could he have meant by its being easier to tell the police than me? Was it because he was so ashamed of what he'd done? What, in heaven's name, could have been *that terrible,* anyway? And did I come across as being so unsympathetic that I was the last person he could confide in? (Wouldn't you know I'd find a way to put at least part of the blame on myself?)

I was so unnerved by the whole thing, I thought it might not be a bad idea to take a little mental health break that evening and go see a movie or something instead of pursuing the agenda I'd mapped out for myself. But in the end

I stuck with my original plan: resuming my talks with the rest of the *Love and Stuff* company.

At seven o'clock, I got in touch with Midge Corso, the actress who, according to little Tara Wilde, had actually overheard an emotional confrontation between Meredith and Larry Shields. It took perseverance, but I eventually persuaded her to meet me for a drink that night.

Midge, it turned out, was about five years older than Tara and about fifteen years more worldly. She was on to me the minute I broached the subject of the breakup. (And I'd sharpened my technique a little, too, so my approach was really much more clever that time. Or so I thought.)

After three drinks, a platter of chicken wings, and too many hastily improvised strategies to count, I wound up getting absolutely nowhere. Just as I had with Tara. And this time the getting there was a lot less friendly, besides.

And—just so you know—I didn't make out any better with whichever remaining members of the company agreed to see me later on during the next week and a half. In fact, I only learned one thing from that entire *Love and Stuff* bunch: Larry Shields inspired amazing loyalty from the people around him. I mean, for all of them to close ranks and safeguard his secret like that ... well, it was really something.

But to get back to what, for a long time, I would think of as Traumatic Tuesday ...

When my disappointing meeting with Midge Corso was over, I came home to find a message on my machine. It was from Peter, and he sounded thoroughly deflated.

"Please call me," he said. "I just spoke to Dr. Baker. Fielding turned him down."

Chapter 26

I returned Peter's call at eight the next morning.

"I was just going to try *you* again," he told me. "You got my message?"

"Yes, but I didn't come home until almost midnight, and I was afraid you might be sleeping by that time."

"It's okay," he said. Then: "I have a favor to ask, Desiree."

"Sure. What?"

"Could you talk to your friend Fielding for me—see if you can get him to change his mind about the hospital? Please."

"I already tried, believe me. He won't even consider it. Listen to me, Peter. I know you had nothing to do with the shootings, so I'm sure that whatever it is you're hiding can't be as terrible as you think. And just look at the consequences of your holding out on the police. Is it worth what it's doing to you *and* to Mary Ann?"

"Maybe not," Peter answered wretchedly, "but I just can't help it."

When I got to the office an hour later, Jackie handed me a message from Fielding asking me to call.

"What did your client have to say?" he demanded as soon as he heard my voice.

"Uh, I haven't had a chance to talk to him yet."

"You expect me to *believe* that?" he fumed.

"It's true," I said—very unconvincingly, I'm afraid. "I'll try reaching him now."

"You do that."

"I will. I'm—"

But he hung up in my ear. *God, I hate that!*

I figured I'd wait a day before talking to Peter again. Maybe by then his banishment from the hospital might soften his resolve. But when I phoned on Thursday, he had a counterproposal for me. "Tell Fielding if he'll let me see Mary Ann for just a few minutes, I'll give him some important information."

"What important information, Peter?" I asked quietly. If he'd been holding out on me, I would gleefully chop off his beautiful neck!

"About the ring."

"*What* ring?"

"You don't know about it?"

"*What* ring, Peter?" I repeated, gnashing my teeth.

"Didn't Fielding say anything to you?"

As you can imagine, by now I was very close to screaming. It was with a supreme effort that I kept my voice even. "Tell me about the ring."

"It came into the possession of the police last week; I don't know any of the details. Anyway, it's got this amethyst stone, and apparently either Mary Ann or Meredith had it on that night. Fielding showed it to me to see if I recognized it."

"And you didn't even *mention* this to me?"

"I was sure Fielding had already told you. Honestly. I know he confides in you a lot."

"Not voluntarily," I remarked dryly. "Okay, so what about the ring? *Did* you recognize it?"

"Not exactly."

"But you know something about it?"

"Well, when I first saw it and Fielding asked if I'd ever noticed Mary Ann wearing a ring like that, I told him I couldn't remember." (*That* I had no trouble believing!) "And then, on Tuesday morning, when he was over here with that other detective—Corcoran—I asked if anybody else had been able to tell them anything about the ring, and they said not so far. But last night I was thinking about it; I really concentrated on trying to remember whether I'd ever seen it on Mary Ann. I thought maybe I had, but for the life of me, I couldn't be sure. Anyway, I was disappointed, because I figured that if I'd been able to identify the ring, it might have gotten me back in Fielding's good graces—enough so it could get me a half hour at the hospital, at least."

"I doubt if that would have helped," I interjected.

"Then it came to me," Peter continued, ignoring my comment, "about Charlotte—Charlotte Bromley. She's this friend of Mary Ann's who's away on vacation—until the middle of this month, I think you told me. Right?"

"That's right," I confirmed. "And?"

"Charlotte's a jewelry designer. In fact, Mary Ann buys a lot of the stuff for the shop from her—that's how they met. She's friendly with Meredith, too, though. Charlotte would know which of them used to wear that ring, wouldn't she? After all, that's her business."

He could be right! A jewelry designer *would* be likely to notice something like that. It was even possible the ring was one of Bromley's own designs, in which case she'd certainly be able to tell us who it belonged to. But a second later this little voice inside me was warning, *Haven't you learned yet not to count on anything with this case, you cretin?* So, tempering my enthusiasm, I said to Peter, "And this occurred to you just last night?"

"Yes. And I was going to tell you about it as soon as I spoke to you. Not that it's really that important, except to maybe help me with Fielding."

"But this woman's information could establish the victims' identities," I pointed out.

"Mary Ann's the one in that hospital room, Desiree."

"But the ring would give us the *proof*!" I insisted, no longer able to contain my excitement. *What did that inner voice of mine know, anyway?*

"I don't need any proof," Peter maintained with quiet conviction. "About Fielding, though. . . . I was afraid if *I* called and tried to bargain with him, it would sound like blackmail, but if *you* called—"

"It would still sound like blackmail."

"See what you can do, anyway, will you, Desiree? Please? I'm really going stir-crazy not being allowed to see Mary Ann."

Under protest, and with a whole lot of misgivings, I finally agreed to act as the middleman for my client.

Fielding wasn't in when I tried him, so I left a message. He didn't get back to me until the following morning.

There was no "Hello." No "How are you?" None of the normal pleasantries you expect to hear when you pick up the telephone. Fielding's opener was "You talk to your client?" It sounded like he was biting off the words.

"Yes, and he's got a proposition for you."

"A *what*?"

"Don't get excited, Tim. It's about that ring—you know, the one you never bothered telling me about."

"I *beg* your pardon, Ms. Shapiro," he said, his voice so soft and polite there was no doubt he was seething. "Forgive me. It occasionally slips my mind that the police are obligated to report to you."

Well, I'd blown it already. Antagonizing him certainly wasn't going to make Fielding more receptive to my client's proposal, which I definitely knew would make him crazy anyway. And which only Peter's desperation coupled with my fondness for him could have induced me to present.

"So what does Winters want to sell me?"

"Oh, I wouldn't say he wants to sell—"

He stopped me in midprotest. "Cool it, huh, Desiree? Just tell me what this is about."

I spoke quickly to get it over with. "Well, Peter believes there's a way you can find out who that ring belongs to. And all he's asking is that if he tells you, you let him go up and see the victim." Before Fielding could respond, I slipped in, "Just once. And only for a few minutes."

The reaction was as bad as I'd expected it to be. Or maybe a little worse. "You tell your client there's no deal. If he wants to get into that hospital room, we've gotta know where he was that night. And furthermore, if he has any information about that ring, it's his duty to give it to the police. And if he doesn't do that, I'll have that butt of his tossed in jail for withholding evidence!"

Now, as little as I know about the law, I did know one thing: There was no withholding of evidence here; all Peter was keeping to himself were his own thoughts. "But Peter doesn't have what you could call *evidence,* Tim; it's just an idea that occurred to him."

"Which you are about to share with me. Unless you, too, would like to see the inside of a jail, with all of those cute little mice and nice, juicy cockroaches to keep you company."

Now, I wouldn't say I'm suggestible, but I already felt as though something was crawling up my leg. Shuddering, I even looked down to check.

"And don't think I won't do it, either," Tim assured me menacingly. "Whoever shot those two women is one perp who's not going to get away with murder—no matter what it takes."

Remember my good friend Tim Fielding—that nice guy I told you about earlier? Well, right now he was sounding a lot like his extremely un-nice partner. He must be under a tremendous amount of pressure with this damn case, I decided, defending him to myself. I mean, this was really so unlike him.

"And don't hand me any of that 'client confidentiality' crap," he put in then. "Because I won't be able to hear you. Get me?"

"Look, Tim, I don't know what's on Peter's mind," I lied through my recently veneered teeth. "I'd tell you if I did."

"I want you to hang up and have another talk with your client. And I want you to inform him there's no deal. And right after that, you make it clear to him—*very* clear—that he'd better get his ass down here and start leveling with us if he knows what's good for him!"

I gathered the conversation was over then, because, once again, I heard that infuriating sound in my ear.

Chapter 27

I was in over my head. What had ever possessed me to accept this case, anyway? I could have recommended a half dozen—no, a dozen—P.I.s to Peter who were better qualified to handle an investigation like this than I was. And every one of them would probably have the whole thing solved by now, too. I even thought briefly about resigning. I'd taken on the case with the provision that all I had to do was establish the identity of the survivor, hadn't I? And if Peter was so sure that girl in the hospital was Mary Ann, then my job was over, wasn't it?

Oh, who was I kidding? No matter what he said and how many times he said it, Peter *had* to have his doubts. And besides, there was no way I could walk away from this mess. Not anymore.

Right then, though, I really wasn't up to reporting back to my client and getting myself involved in another hassle; that little exchange with Fielding had been more than enough to last me at least until tomorrow, thank you. So when Peter called the office that afternoon, I took the coward's way out and had Jackie tell him I wasn't in.

When I got home at a few minutes after six, there was a message from my neighbor Barbara on the machine.

"I haven't seen you for a while," she said when I returned the call. "I thought, if you don't have other plans, maybe we could go out and grab something to eat a little later."

"Oh, I would have liked that, Barbara, but I'm invited over to my niece's for Chinese." I swear that small falsehood was more for Barbara's sake than mine. In my present mood, if that woman had uttered even one syllable about my weight or my cholesterol, she would have been seriously maimed.

I wanted to just stay home and unwind, anyway. I poured

myself a glass of Chianti—and I almost never drink alone—then kicked off my shoes and curled up on the sofa. In the half hour or so that I sat there sipping, the most important thought that crossed my mind was what I would have for dinner.

After I'd really mellowed out, I went into the kitchen to fix myself what Ellen refers to as one of my "refrigerator omelets"—so named because I throw in just about everything I have in my refrigerator at the moment. Tonight's version featured ham, mozzarella cheese, Parmesan cheese, onions, green peas, a small piece of red pepper, and some leftover chicken. Now, I don't exactly know how that sounds, but I can assure you, it tasted a lot better.

I followed the omelet with some Macadamia Brittle ice cream, which I was certainly entitled to after all I'd been through that day. And I was toying with the idea of following *that* with a Snickers bar when the telephone rescued my waistline.

Still avoiding Peter, I waited until the answering machine went on. It was Fielding. And that call I was even less anxious to take.

"I wanted to know what that client of yours had to say," he snarled over the machine. "I'm off this weekend, but I expect to see him in here on Monday—and in a talkative mood."

I got in the last word. Sort of. "And a happy weekend to you, too," I snarled back as soon as he hung up.

I spent Saturday doing as little as possible. I didn't go through my notes. I didn't call Peter. And I didn't pick up the phone when he called me, either. I also didn't clean my apartment, read a book, or stick my nose out of the door. I just sat in front of the television from eleven A.M. until after midnight—with a brief break for meals, snacks, and other necessities—happily watching one boring program after another. (I think I'd even have been satisfied looking at test patterns, if it came to that.) The thing is, it was like sending my malfunctioning brain on a brief—and badly needed—vacation.

On Sunday morning, I finally got back to Peter with some kind of health-related apology for not calling sooner. (It was either plain food poisoning or Legionnaire's disease—I can't remember which.) When I relayed where things stood with Fielding, he didn't seem overly upset that his proposition had been turned down; I guess he was more or less prepared for it. But as soon as I told him about the threats, his voice grew anxious. "It's one thing to put the screws to me, but can he really throw *you* in jail?"

"Don't worry about that," I said, touched by his concern. Then I added hastily, "But he *can* make things pretty uncomfortable for me. And for you, too." After that, I segued into what must have been my hundredth attempt to persuade him to change his mind and talk to the police. But, as usual, he dug in his heels and very apologetically turned me down.

Ellen called in the afternoon. We spent fifteen minutes discussing her friend Gail, who was being married in a few weeks and who hadn't invited her to the wedding. Ellen—who'd (a) gotten this girl a job at Macy's and (b) held her hand every time she threatened suicide when her fiancé dumped her for three months last year so he could "get in touch with his feelings"—was crushed.

"You know," she explained, "it's not a very big affair, so I didn't really mind her not inviting me until I found out one of her co-workers was going—a girl she's only known six months. Gail and *I* have been friends for over seven years."

The next fifteen minutes were devoted to an in-depth analysis of whether or not Ellen should let Gail know how she felt. (In case you're interested, it was decided that she *would* say something—but not until after the wedding.)

Then I got equal time.

I kicked off by whining about still having this big unanswered question with regard to the argument between Meredith and Larry Shields. Following that, I dropped the news that my client had been lying to me.

Ellen was suitably shocked by Peter's deceitfulness. But then I came to the part where he said he'd rather tell the police his alibi than confide in me, and she refused, at first, to accept that at all.

"Are you sure you didn't misunderstand what he said?"

"Positive."

"Isn't it *possible* you didn't hear him right?"

"No, it isn't."

"And there's no way you can convince him to be straight with the police, either?"

"There doesn't seem to be. And believe me, I've tried—and tried some more. I'll give it another shot tomorrow, but only because I don't know when to lay down and die."

"Maybe if you threatened to resign from the case ..." she offered tentatively.

"He'd let me do it."

Ellen wasn't so sure about that.

"Look," I explained, "compared to being barred from the hospital, losing my services wouldn't be that big a deal." And then I cited the amethyst ring and how Peter had even been trying to use it as a bargaining chip.

"How did that ring suddenly happen to turn up after all this time, anyway?"

"Good question. I wish I knew."

"Well, why don't you ask Tim?" she suggested.

"Because right now Tim isn't really Tim," I answered.

Chapter 28

You know how most of the time when something's really bothering you, you can forget about falling asleep, no matter how tired you are? But then, there are other times that you're just as upset and sleep is like an escape; you drop off the second you hit the pillow? Well, anyway, that night I made my getaway as soon as I closed my eyes.

I was in such a deep sleep that when the telephone jolted me awake, I had no idea where I was. Or even if it was night or day. I glanced at the clock at the same time I lifted the receiver: 6:47.

"I hope I didn't wake you," a familiar voice said cautiously.

I sat up in bed instantly. "Is anything wrong, Ellen?"

"Oh, no, not a thing. Please don't be angry at me for calling so early, but I *had* to talk to you. I have an idea about why Peter wouldn't tell you where he was that night."

"Couldn't it have waited a couple of hours?" I growled. I don't remember when I was less kindly disposed toward my favorite and only niece.

"I guess so. It's just that I was so anxious . . ." It was apparent I'd hurt her feelings.

"Okay, shoot," I said a little less harshly. *But this better be good!*

"Well, after I spoke to you yesterday, I kept trying to think of a reason Peter might feel that way. And then, at about three o'clock this morning, it finally came to me."

I counted myself lucky. At least she'd held out till now. "What came to you?"

"That he was afraid you'd be disappointed in him."

"Oh, I don't see—"

"Just listen a minute, okay? So then I thought about what would *make* you disappointed in him. Well, what *would*?" Ellen demanded. She didn't wait for an answer that I didn't have anyway. "A woman!" she announced, her tone suggesting that a flourish of trumpets might have been appropriate.

"A woman?" I said, repeating the words as I usually do when I'm trying to absorb something.

"If he'd been out somewhere cheating on his fiancée, he wouldn't want you to know about it; I'm absolutely positive of that."

I was just about to pooh-pooh her little theory when I recalled that, for all of Ellen's ingenuousness, she often displays this knack for putting her finger on the things the rest of us tend to overlook. "Maybe you're right," I told her. She hung up happy when I concluded with: "I'm certainly going to check into it."

Peter got a call from me at eight o'clock. "Can I come over this morning? Or can you stop by the office? It's important."

"It won't do any good," he answered softly, obviously anticipating another round of badgering.

Well, here goes. "Look, Peter, I already know it was another woman."

Silence.

"Peter?"

Then, in something very close to a whisper: "When do you want me at your office?"

When I got to work an hour later, Peter was already there, just taking a seat alongside my desk. He looked like he was about to be executed.

I confronted him as soon as I sat down myself: "I think it's time you finally laid it all out for me, don't you?"

"Uh ... how much do you know?"

"Enough. But now I'd like to hear it from you."

His face immediately lost what little color it had come in with. "I probably would have said something in a day or two anyway," he told me quietly. "I don't think I could have held out much longer; it's really hell, being cut off from Mary Ann like this." And, after a long pause: "How did you find out—about the woman, I mean?"

I shrugged. "I have my sources." Then I remembered my manners. "Would you like some coffee?"

Peter shook his head. "No, thanks. I might as well get on with it, huh?" And, without meeting my eyes, he began. . . .

"There's this woman in my building," he said, "an older woman—past forty." I winced. "I used to be pretty friendly with her and her husband—not socially or anything but, you know, in a neighborly way. Frankie—that's this woman—is a great cook, and she knows I'm a bachelor, so every once in a while, she'd bring in a piece of cake or pie or some cookies—even zucchini soup one time. And, to reciprocate, I'd give her and her husband theater tickets or movie passes or baseball or hockey tickets—I get a lot of that stuff through the office. But then, about six months ago, Scott—he's her husband—just split. I found out later on from Frankie that he had something going with this young secretary in his office. Anyhow, after that, Frankie pretty much kept to herself, and I didn't see her around for quite a while.

"Then, this one day, we both came home from work at the same time. I couldn't believe how thin she'd gotten! She'd always had a really good figure, but now she looked like one of those pictures you see of the starving people in Africa. You should have seen how drawn her face was." There was a brief time-out here while Peter nervously licked his lips. "Anyhow," he went on, "she told me she'd cooked this pot roast the night before, and she said, if I wasn't busy, she'd really like some company for dinner. Well, I felt very sorry for her, and I didn't have any other plans because Mary Ann was going shopping with Meredith that night, so I accepted."

Licking his lips again, he abruptly halted the narrative. "Uh, is there a water fountain here?" he asked. "I could really use a drink of water."

Poor Peter. He was having an awful time getting through this. *Well,* I thought, *it serves him right!* (Of course, I know I had no business being judgmental, but since when did that stop me?) I directed him down the hall, and in a few minutes he was back, reluctantly picking up exactly where he'd left off.

"I ran down to the store and got a bottle of Beaujolais, and by the time we were through with dinner, we'd polished off almost the whole bottle between us. All of a sudden, when we were having coffee, Frankie said, 'Scott stopped finding me attractive a long time ago, and you have no idea what that does to a woman.' Something like that, anyway." Peter's expression seemed to be growing more miserable by the second. "We were both pretty crocked by then," he explained, his voice so low I had to lean forward to hear him. "Otherwise, what happened would never have happened in a million years."

He took a moment to compose himself before continuing. "Well, I told her that husband of hers was nuts, that she was very attractive. And then she asked if I was just saying that to be kind. And before I even realized it, we were kissing. And then one thing led to another and, well, you know."

Now, all through this recitation, Peter had been looking at his hands, at the floor, at the ceiling—everywhere but at me. But at this point his eyes locked with mine, pleading for some understanding. "I realize the wine was no excuse," he said plaintively, "but—I can't explain it—it made me feel like the whole thing was happening to someone else; like I was outside of myself, just watching, you know?"

I couldn't think of anything to say, so I just nodded.

"When we'd ... afterwards, she cried and told me her husband hadn't made love to her for months before he left her. And then she thanked me—*thanked me*! For a minute there, I even felt less guilty about things. But it didn't last very long."

Peter must have thought I was going to make some kind of comment then (which I wasn't), because he put in quickly, "I know what you're going to say, but Mary Ann and I weren't actually engaged yet." An instant later, he conceded unhappily, "Although I guess, in a way, we were engaged from the night we met."

Suddenly I was confused. "You weren't engaged yet? Then your ... uh ... your dinner with this woman *wasn't* the night of the shootings?"

"Oh, no! It was *months* before that."

"Now you've *really* lost me."

"Please. Bear with me a minute."

"Sorry. Go on."

"Well, except for once or twice just in passing, I didn't see Frankie for months after that. I suppose she wanted to forget what happened as much as I did. And then the night Mary Ann and Meredith were shot, she stopped off at my apartment after work. She told me she'd gone to her gynecologist at lunchtime, and she found out she was pregnant. She said she hadn't been with anybody since me and that it ... uh ... had to be my baby, and she thought I should know about it." Peter took a deep breath. "Well, how could I leave things like that? I called my ex-roommate back—I was on the phone with him when she rang my doorbell—and canceled these plans we had to get together for dinner that night. Then I went to Frankie's place to talk things over."

Another deep breath. "Anyhow, she said she'd more or less made up her mind to get an abortion, but first she wanted to know how I felt about it. I told her it was her decision but that I'd certainly support the baby if she changed her mind and decided to have it. By the time I went back to my own apartment, though, she was definite about the abortion. She just wanted me to go with her when she had it done, and I promised her I would."

Aside from everything else, I was just incredulous at how careless Peter had been. "Didn't you even use a condom?" I all but shouted at him. "With AIDS and everything, you really have to be an *idiot* not to!"

"I *am* an idiot," a thoroughly dejected Peter admitted, "or I'd never have gone to bed with another woman in the first place." And then he mumbled so softly the words were barely audible, "You must really think I'm scum."

"I don't think you're *scum,* but in my book, betraying someone you're supposed to be committed to isn't exactly admirable," I told him self-righteously. To be absolutely honest, though, at that moment, Peter's cheating on Mary Ann wasn't what was bothering me. What was really sticking in my craw was how he could do this to *me*! I mean, I'd known this kid way back when he was *little Petey,* for God's sake! And the only reason I'd taken this lousy case was because he pleaded with me to and because I believed every damn word he told me. In fact, I trusted him so much I hadn't even *considered* checking out his alibi. Which, of course, made me just as big an idiot as he was.

Well, it didn't take long, before I could have kicked myself all the way to China. The world did not revolve around Desiree Shapiro, I reminded myself. Besides, where did I come off acting like such a sanctimonious prig? The poor kid was feeling rotten enough without my help in underlining his transgressions. I tried to lighten things up a little then. "Hey, we all do dumb things sometimes," I said. "It's probably hard to believe, but I've made a mistake or two thousand in my life, too."

Peter looked at me gratefully. "Thanks, Desiree."

"You know what I can't figure out, though? Why you refused to tell the police where you were that night."

"Don't you *see*? My fiancée was shot—almost killed— while I was with another woman, hearing that I was the father of her baby. I can't even bear to think about that, much less talk about it. And now that Mary Ann's finally recovering, I keep worrying about how *she'd* take it if she ever found out where I was."

"You could have just told Fielding you were visiting your neighbor," I pointed out. "Nobody would have had to know what you were there to discuss."

"Yeah," Peter said, and his eyes were moist, "but *I* know."

"How late were you in Frankie's apartment, anyway?" I asked then.

"It was after nine; I'm sure of that. We sent out for pizza around eight, but it didn't get there for close to an hour."

"Look, Peter, I can understand your feeling guilty about being with another woman. But I can't understand your feeling so guilty that you'd leave yourself open to being considered a murder suspect."

"But how could anyone seriously think I'd try to kill Mary Ann? What *reason* would I have?"

"For one thing, Fielding's considering the possibility you and Mary Ann had a lover's quarrel."

"I know. He told me the other day that he heard there was some trouble between us, but I knew he was just testing the water. In other words," Peter summed up, managing a little smile, "he was full of it."

"His other idea is that you might have wanted to murder her for her money."

Peter looked stunned. "But Mary Ann didn't *have* any money. Meredith was the rich one."

"Hold it a sec. You mean the Fosters cut Mary Ann out of their will?"

"The Fosters?" And then a sharp intake of breath. "Ohhh, I see where you're coming from," he said slowly, "but you've got it all wrong. The Fosters weren't wealthy, Desiree. They lost almost everything they had in some real

estate investment thing a few years before they died; there
was barely enough left to cover the funeral expenses. It
was Meredith's husband who had all the money. He was
an inventor; I'm sure I told you that."

"I don't think so," I responded numbly.

"Well, he was," Peter said hastily. "And in spite of the
fact he was a pretty messed-up guy, a very successful one.
He developed this little gadget—something to do with fuel
consumption—and sold it to one of the airlines for three
or four million dollars."

*My God! All these weeks I'd been operating under a to-
tally false assumption!* And what was so hard to accept was
that it was my own damned fault. I'd just *assumed* the twins
had inherited from their parents. What kind of a P.I. was
I, anyway, that I'd never bothered to check it out? The
kind of P.I. that wasn't even qualified to find a missing
cat—much less a killer—*that's* what kind!

"You look a little strange," Peter informed me then. "I
never realized you thought that Mary Ann had money,
too." And, a moment later: "So *that's* why you asked me
that time if she'd made out a will."

I felt like throwing myself down and banging my head
on the floor! (It's tough behaving like a grown-up when
you've just discovered you're the world's biggest incompe-
tent.) But I put my tantrum on hold for a while, because
something had suddenly occurred to me that, while it didn't
excuse my carelessness, might make it a little easier for me
to accept.

"The condo," I said. "I understood it was in both
names."

"Oh, it was," Peter confirmed. "You know, Mary Ann
and Meredith were closer than regular sisters—twins are
special, I guess. Besides," he explained, "ever since they
were kids, Meredith kind of looked after Mary Ann—almost like a second mother. And then when Meredith
bought the apartment, Mary Ann had just broken off her
engagement, and she was pretty down in the dumps. Maybe
that had something to do with it, too. Anyhow, Meredith
insisted on putting the place in both names. Mary Ann
didn't want that, but she couldn't talk Meredith out of it.
She finally agreed, but with the provision that if either of
them got married, she'd sign her interest in the apartment
over to Meredith."

And that's when I said, almost casually, "I don't imagine you have any idea if Meredith made out a will or not."

Considering how it reflected on me, I was almost sorry to hear the reply. "I think she made one out a few weeks after they came over from London. I know she *had* one, anyway."

"Would you know who her lawyer was?"

"Uh-uh. I'm afraid not."

"Do you, by any chance, have any idea what was *in* the will?"

"I suppose I do, more or less. It came up in a conversation I had with Mary Ann one night."

I couldn't believe it! Why hadn't he said anything to me before? The answer, of course, was obvious: *Why hadn't I asked?*

"See, family really matters to Mary Ann," Peter continued. "And she used to talk a lot about how sad it was that Meredith refused to patch things up with Eric. But this one particular time she went on to say how Meredith's will left everything to her, and if she—Mary Ann—died first, then the money would all go to this AIDS foundation. She felt pretty terrible about that."

"At least Meredith picked a good cause," I remarked.

"That was because of her husband."

"What do you mean?"

"I told you he was a drug addict, right?"

"I think so. Someone did, anyway."

"And that he died of AIDS?"

"No, you never mentioned that," I answered, not yet realizing the significance of Peter's words. "I was under the impression he'd died of a brain tumor. That's what Eric Foster said."

"Meredith asked Mary Ann to tell him that. She didn't want people to know about the AIDS—Eric especially, I guess."

I started to say something—I'm not even sure what it was—and then it hit me. "Oh, my God," I murmured.

"What?"

"Meredith . . . she wasn't . . . *she* didn't have AIDS, did she?"

"Mary Ann told me she tested negative," Peter answered a little uncertainly.

"Didn't you believe her?"

"Of course I did."

"But?"

"But, well, they say it could take a long time for anything to show up in the tests. So who knows if she was really out of the woods yet?"

Chapter 29

He didn't say so, but I had the strong impression that Peter was relieved to finally unburden himself to someone. And having broken his silence, he seemed almost anxious to get to the precinct now, too. After all, it would almost certainly lead to the lifting of his hospital ban.

Rejecting my offer to accompany him, Peter called the station to make sure Fielding was in. Then we talked for a few minutes about just how much he'd tell the police. We agreed there was no reason to divulge any more about his whereabouts that night than they needed to know—which was that he'd been in this Frankie's apartment at the time of the shootings. And, if pressed on his refusal to disclose the information earlier (as we were both certain he would be), he intended to say there were personal reasons. Which, no doubt, would provide a little food for Walter Corcoran's dirty little thoughts.

A couple of minutes after Peter left, I graciously decided to forgive Ellen for doing my job better than I did. "You were right," I told her when I reached her on the phone. She was so thrilled you would have thought *I'd* done something for *her.*

When our brief conversation was finished, I got busy making some notes, and then I spent a long time mulling over them.

At four o'clock, I headed for the Berkeley Theater—and a talk with Larry Shields.

The director was up onstage working with a few of the cast members when I walked in. He spotted me before I was even halfway up the aisle, acknowledging my presence just long enough to shout, "We're in the middle of a rehearsal here!"

I approached the stage anyway.

When he looked over at me this time, he held up his

hand to the others for quiet and came toward the footlights. "What is it you want now?" he called down, scowling.

"I just learned something you might be interested in hearing about."

He thought for a moment, then said brusquely, "All right, but I can't talk to you today. Come by tomorrow— say, seven-thirty."

"In the evening?" I asked hopefully.

"A.M. Is that a problem?"

"No, no. No problem at all." What the hell, there *were* some things that took precedence over sleep.

Shields was just opening the door to the theater when I got there.

"How about letting me buy you breakfast?" I offered.

"No, thanks," he said curtly.

As soon as we were seated in his office, I learned the answer to at least one thing that had been puzzling me: why he'd been so hostile to me recently. (Just thinking about last week's phone conversation with him was enough to give me frostbite.) And the thing is, I didn't even have to ask.

"Did you know," he demanded, "that with the help of one of the doctors at St. Catherine's, I had finally persuaded the police to let me into that hospital room?"

"No, I didn't."

"Really? I'm surprised," he remarked archly. "Before I ever made it there, though, they'd changed their minds. It seems someone told Sergeant Fielding this story about Merry and me having some kind of argument. Now, I heard somewhere that you and Fielding are pretty good buddies. It wouldn't have been you who repeated that stupid story, would it?"

I could feel my face growing warm, and I was praying I wouldn't give myself away with one of those awful flushes of mine at the same time that I was certain I was already doing just that. I tried sidestepping the question anyway. "Why would I do a thing like that?" I said, not meeting his eyes.

"Why don't *you* tell *me*. It happens to be a damned lie, you know."

"I don't think so," I responded in this calm, soft voice.

"Look, I just found out that Meredith's husband died of AIDS."

Now it was Shields who flushed deeply. He didn't say anything for quite a while, just stared straight ahead, and I sat there uneasily, fidgeting with my shoulder bag, while I waited for his response.

"Who told you?" he murmured at last.

"That's not really important, is it?"

"No," he answered sadly.

"You were furious, weren't you, because Meredith didn't tell you about the AIDS? Before you became intimately involved, I mean."

"Yes, as a matter of fact, I was. But only at first."

"What changed your mind?"

"Well, for one thing, it wasn't as though Merry was HIV positive; she wasn't. And she swore to me—and I believe her—that she and Garibaldi, her husband, stopped having marital relations in October of 1990, when he was diagnosed with the disease. Merry and I didn't begin seeing each other until November '91—sometime around the middle of November, it was. Which means that according to her best information—according to *anyone's* best information—there was no longer any question of her being a carrier. If you test HIV negative for a year after you've been exposed to the disease, you're not at risk anymore."

"But that was cutting it awfully close, wasn't it?"

"Not really. A year is the *outside* limit. But still, I felt I was at least entitled to know about a thing like that. Once I'd cooled off a little, though, I tried putting myself in Merry's shoes. She'd been given a clean bill of health before we even met, so it wasn't as though there was a danger of her infecting me. And then I wondered what I would have done if the situation had been reversed. I like to think I would have said something to her before we became lovers, but who really knows what they'll do until they're there? Merry's one of the most forthright people I've ever met; she's strong, too. If *she* found it so hard to talk about, what makes me think I'd be any different?" And then Shields smiled, and I saw again what made him so attractive to women. "But, hell," he confided, "the big reason, the *overriding* reason we got back together is because I loved her. And I still do."

"Well, I guess I understand now why you tried to keep the argument quiet."

"It's Merry's secret," Shields said, confirming my thoughts. "It's up to her once she regains her memory whether or not she wants to tell anybody. But as long as it's all come out, at least I'll be able to start going to the hospital. This doctor I mentioned before? Just yesterday he was saying how—if it *is* Merry lying there—seeing me could help jog her memory."

"That could be. But I'm afraid the police might still have some qualms about letting you visit her."

"What now?" he asked tersely.

"They might feel there's a chance—a very *outside* chance—that you only pretended to reconcile with Meredith to avoid suspicion later on."

"If I could plot things out like that," Shields shot back angrily, I wouldn't be a director; I'd be a playwright. Or a goddamned P.I."

That little talk had certainly produced a few answers. And a few more questions, too.

Would a man like Larry Shields really murder his lover for not leveling with him about her husband's AIDS—even though he was apparently in no danger? Well, all I could say—and with zero conviction—was that it *was* possible. And then I got this idea that made it a whole lot *more* possible.

Who knew for a fact when Meredith had last had relations with her husband? Maybe Shields suspected her of lying to him about that. Or maybe Shields was lying to me. For that matter, maybe he'd already had himself tested for AIDS—and learned he was HIV positive!

Wait a minute. . . .

Maybe I should be looking at the same kind of "maybes" with regard to Lucille Collins, too.

Let's say Collins hoped to get back with her ex-boyfriend eventually (the safest bet on the boards). Okay, then just imagine how she might have felt if she thought there was even a remote chance that Meredith—who had appropriated Shields from her in the first place—had now exposed him to AIDS!

You know, I can think of a lot shabbier reasons for committing murder.

Chapter 30

"Hi, Dez. I was just going to try *you*," Fielding said civilly when I called him from the office that morning. He reminded me a lot of the Tim Fielding I used to know.

"Really? What's up?" I asked cautiously.

"For one thing, we checked out the kid's alibi, and the woman confirms he was with her the night of the shootings from sometime after six until almost nine-thirty."

"You'll let him back into the hospital room now, of course."

"He's probably there right this minute. Listen, the real reason I wanted to talk to you is to apologize. I don't know what the hell got into me last week; my wife even threatened to chop me up and stuff me down the garbage disposal."

"The case is a bitch."

"You can say that again. But it's still no excuse. Anyhow, I'm really sorry, and I owe you a nice lunch—that is, if you can stand sitting across the table from me."

"That depends on where you plan on taking me."

Fielding laughed and said that maybe we could make it the end of the week.

Since he was feeling so remorseful, it was a pretty good time to pump him a little. "Listen, Tim, did Peter tell you about Charlotte Bromley?"

"You mean about her being a jewelry designer?" He laughed again. "We already knew all about that. That friend of the twins' who lives in their building—Josephs—happened to mention it weeks ago."

"Where did the ring suddenly come from after all this time, anyway?"

"I have your word you won't repeat this?"

"Of course."

"Okay. It seems the survivor had the ring on when they

brought her into the recovery room that night. But look, we think it's advisable that no one knows which of the women was wearing it," he cautioned, waiting until I murmured my agreement before continuing. "At any rate, one of the nurses who was on duty noticed it and took it off the girl's finger to put in a drawer for safekeeping. But when she looked for it the next day, it was gone. Well, this nurse was new there, and apparently she felt a little responsible and didn't want to get into any trouble. Also, the ring didn't look particularly valuable—not like a diamond or anything—and, of course, she had no idea it could be important to us. So anyhow, she decided not to say anything about it.

"But then last week, she went to take something else out of that same drawer, and there was the ring; it had gotten wedged all the way in the back. This time, she took it in to her supervisor and told her the whole story, and the supervisor turned it over to us."

"The ring, it was an amethyst I think Peter said." When you're dealing with Peter it never hurts to check things out.

"Amethysts are a purplish color?"

"Yes."

"Then it's an amethyst."

"I think there's a good chance Bromley'll know who it belongs to, don't you?"

"That's what I'm hoping. So far, nobody else is too sure. At any rate, Bromley's due back next week, so we'll find out soon."

After Fielding and I had exchanged cordial good-byes—for a change—I spent about a half hour paying some bills. And then I just sat at my desk thinking. And what I thought was that it might be a nice gesture to forgive myself for all the ways I'd screwed up in the investigation so far.

Okay, I conceded, so I'd made some mistakes. But it *was* only my second murder case. If I ever decided to take one on again—which I considered highly doubtful—I was sure to be a lot better at it. (But then, I almost had to be, didn't I?) Besides, I didn't see where Fielding, for all his experience, was doing such a hot job, either. He'd made the same assumption I had about the twins' money, hadn't he? *Unless* he was just letting me *think* that.

Nah! If he—

It was right in the middle of this silent soliloquy that

Jackie buzzed me. "Stuart Mason's out at reception," she informed me.

Now, that was a pleasant surprise! Stuart had practically been in hibernation since the beginning of tax season. I'd only spoken to him a couple of times since he took those few hours off for his birthday dinner—and then very briefly. I really didn't think I'd be setting eyes on him before May.

"I was with a client right across the street," he explained when I walked out to greet him, "and I thought I'd take a chance and see if you were free for a quick lunch."

Lunch turned out to be not quick at all. We went to HSF—a Chinese restaurant not too far from my office that serves the most fantastic dim sum—and stuffed ourselves silly on an almost endless parade of little delicacies. All the while, we chatted incessantly, the way good friends who haven't talked to each other recently are likely to do.

Stuart immediately wanted to know if I'd made any progress with the case yet.

"Some," I said, "but I'm still a long way from solving it." For the briefest of moments, I thought about telling him how right he'd been in advising me to check Peter's alibi. But then I realized I'd prefer being torn apart by wild animals to admitting something like that. I mean, Ellen's showing me up was one thing. But enough was definitely enough. "You look tired," I remarked instead.

"At this point, I'm too numb to be tired. You don't exactly look like you're full of energy yourself."

"What *I* am is frustrated. There's probably something I know that I don't know I know. If you follow me."

"I'm afraid I do," he told me, grinning, "and it's worrying the hell out of me." Then he made the same suggestion he'd made that other time I was wrestling with a murder case. "Why don't you get away for a little while? My brother and sister-in-law still have that cabin upstate, and they never go there this time of year. I'm sure they'd be glad to let you use the place for a few days or a week— as long as you like. Just so you're out of there by July," he joked. "Seriously, it would clear your head, give you a fresh perspective."

"Thanks, but it wouldn't do any good right now." He started to protest, but he didn't get the words out fast enough. "Honestly, Stuart," I put in quickly, "I wouldn't be able to leave it behind me." And then, before I could stop myself—and knowing I was turning as red as my gloriously hennaed hair—I said, "Why don't we wait till my case and the tax season are both over, so you can come up there with me?"

Stuart knew just what I was suggesting—you didn't exactly have to be a Rhodes scholar—and he looked at me levelly. "I'd like that, Dez; I really would."

Since we were headed in opposite directions, I left Stuart at the restaurant and started to walk back to the office. I'd gone just a couple of blocks when it started to rain. (The WNBC forecast that morning had been for sunny skies all day, so I really shouldn't have been surprised.)

Now, while I didn't have far to go, I also didn't have an umbrella, and it was coming down pretty hard. I checked out Second Avenue. There wasn't an empty cab to be seen, so I cut over to Third. No hope for a taxi here, either. But what there *was,* was a video store. And I'm not so dumb that I don't know enough to come in out of the rain.

Well, as long as I was there, I decided that it might not be a bad idea to rent a movie for the night. I went to the section marked DRAMA. A good oldie would be nice. I spotted *The Diary of Anne Frank.* Uh-uh, too sad. *Gallipoli.* I read the blurb on the cover; sounded grim. *Laura.* One of my favorites, but why not try something I hadn't already seen a hundred times? *Raging Bull.* I'd seen that one before, too—only once, but, if I remembered right, I hadn't been all that crazy about it. *The Elephant Man.* Another tearjerker. I'd probably be better off in that section with the new releases. . . .

Oh, the hell with it. The rain had let up by now, so I should be getting back, anyway.

Maybe I'd stop somewhere after work and pick up a pocket book—a murder mystery. Just what I needed, right?

Chapter 31

I was anxious to know how things had gone on Peter's first day back at the hospital. So as soon as I finished dinner Tuesday night, I called and left a message on his machine.

Then I decided to dig out my notes on the case. Whatever it was I was looking for was in there somewhere; I'd swear to it. And, no doubt inspired by the little talk I'd had with myself that morning, I somehow got the idea in my head that tonight I would find it. But even after going over every page three or four times, I didn't know any more when I closed the folder than I did when I'd opened it.

I had really built up my expectations, too. (And you'd think I'd have known better than to trust me, wouldn't you?) In fact, I'd managed to make myself so manic that I just couldn't seem to wind down after that.

I started reading the new Mary Higgins Clark paperback I'd picked up in Woolworth's on the way home, but I didn't make it any further than the third paragraph. So I put it away and rifled through the newspaper; I couldn't concentrate long enough to take in more than two or three sentences. Then I checked the *TV Guide* on the coffee table; there was nothing on television I was even remotely interested in seeing. I really should have rented one of those videos.

If I'd loved *Laura* the first hundred times, why wouldn't I have loved it the hundred and first? Or maybe I should have tried *Raging Bull* again. I might have enjoyed it more this time, now that I was no longer of such tender years. (All right, so they weren't so tender even then.) It was about that fighter . . . what was his name? Rocky Marciano, I think. No, Jake LaMotta. That was it. There was something I remembered hearing about that movie, too. Now, what was it? Something to do with . . .

I slapped myself on the forehead—a lot harder than I meant to. But it was okay; I deserved it. *Robert De Niro!* Of course! How could I have been so dense?

Chapter 32

Hallelujah!

It was three in the morning. I'd just finished checking my notes again and again and then again, and at last it had all come together! The only problem was what to do with the truth now that I'd discovered it. But a couple of hours later, my perseverance—along with the thousands of crappy movies I'd been watching all my life—finally produced an absolutely foolproof scheme for trapping the killer.

I might have gotten a few minutes of sleep after that; I'm not really sure. All I know is that I was out of bed at six, wide awake and waiting impatiently for seven—the very earliest I *dared* call Fielding. I only managed to hold out until six-thirty.

"Christ," he groused, his voice thick with sleep, "I was better off acting like a bastard."

"I would have called you anyhow. I think you'll be glad I did, too." I allowed for a brief, suspenseful interval. And then, straining to get the pitch of my voice down to ground level and slowly enunciating every word, I announced dramatically, "I . . . know . . . who . . . did . . . it."

The significance of this revelation was totally lost on Fielding, who yawned, "You know who did what?"

Talk about a letdown! "I know who shot the twins!"

He still wasn't impressed. "You woulda known who did it an hour from now, too," he remarked grumpily.

"Listen, I have to talk to you. Can you meet me for breakfast?"

"Uh-uh. The lieutenant wants to see me at nine."

"All right, how about ten?"

"Better make it ten-thirty."

I settled.

*   *   *

We met at this luncheonette near the precinct. I was already in the booth, having coffee, when Fielding showed up, about fifteen minutes late.

"Sorry, the damn meeting was—"

"It's okay." Then, before he could even get out of his coat and sit down, I informed him solemnly, "I need your help, Tim."

"Why aren't I surprised?"

"Look, I have this plan to catch the killer that just can't fail. But the thing is, I can't pull it off alone."

"As Yogi Berra would say, 'It's déjà vu all over again.' Let's start at the beginning, though, huh? What is it you think you know?" He slid into the booth. "And just to keep you from spinning your wheels," he warned, not waiting for an answer, "if you think I'm going to participate in one of your little plots again without having the slightest idea who it is I'm supposed to be after, you can forget it."

He was, of course, referring to how I'd handled our previous collaboration of this nature. But I'd already anticipated his reaction and decided to remove the stumbling block. "Don't be silly; I have no intention of keeping you in the dark," I told him magnanimously.

The waitress came for our order then. I could barely wait for her to walk away so I could share my findings.

I opened with: "Every person involved in this case lied at some point or other in the investigation." I offered up my own client as proof. "Even Peter had a phony alibi," I said, quickly adding, "but, of course, he had a good reason."

"Yeah, I'm sure," Fielding put in snidely. "Your kid's a regular Saint Francis of Assisi."

I was so anxious to get on with things, I was barely aware of the interruption. "But anyway," I continued, "one lie was a little different from the others because of its *implication*. Well, once I realized that, I immediately took another look at the case. Only this time I was a lot more focused, because I had a definite suspect in mind. And that's when I spotted it—a fact that just hadn't sunk in before. And when I analyzed *this fact*, I realized that only the person who had told me *that* lie—the one with the implication— had a motive that fit all the circumstances of the crime!"

"I hope I'm not supposed to understand what the hell you're talking about," Fielding muttered.

I had no idea that things would come out in such a jumble. "No, no," I assured him quickly, "let me explain." And then I proceeded to take him step by step through the process that had led me to the killer.

When I was through, he was thoughtful for a few moments, and this feeling of dread swept over me. *What if I'd missed something? Or what if Tim knew something I didn't?*

And then he conceded softly, "Damned if that doesn't actually make some sense to me. You know, Dez, you're not such a piss-poor detective, after all." He caught himself in midgrin. "Wait a minute, lady," he said. "Whatever happened to that pooling of information you're always yapping about? It seems to me you've been flying solo here. That is, you and that associate of yours, the Macy's Flash."

I could feel my cheeks burn. "Honestly, Tim, for a while I didn't know what was important and what wasn't, and then I—"

"Never mind, we'll talk about that another time," Fielding informed me. "You know, of course," he pointed out then, "that what you've given me isn't exactly *evidence*. Which, I realize, is why I'm getting this free breakfast or brunch or whatever you want to call it." He looked down at the plate of bacon and eggs the waitress had just set before him. "You wanna tell me what I have to do for this?"

So I outlined my plan to supply the killer with some bogus information that was certain to provoke another attempt on the victim's life.

Fielding anticipated the rest. "And you want us to get her moved into another room and have a policewoman take her place, is that it?"

"It doesn't have to be a policewoman. It could be a dummy instead. Or just a bunch of pillows covered up to look like there's really a person under the blankets. But anyway, you've got the idea."

"It wasn't that tough. I own a television, too, you know."

"Hey, I'm not saying I came up with an original plot here, but it should still work."

"Why not?" He commented dryly. "It worked on every cop show that's ever been on TV."

"Well, it was the best idea I could come up with. So? What do you think?" I demanded anxiously.

"I think it's worth a shot. But it's not up to me; it has to be the captain's decision."

"Uh, the sooner we do it, the better, too; don't you agree? I was kind of hoping we could set it up for Monday."

"Believe me, Dez, nobody wants to wrap this thing up more than I do. But like I said, it's not my decision. I'll call you one way or the other the minute I know something."

When the phone rang at around nine o'clock that evening, my mouth suddenly went so dry I could barely croak out a "Hello."

But it was Peter, and he sounded exhilarated. "I really think Mary Ann missed me," he enthused. "You know, when I couldn't get up to see her all those days, one of her doctors told her I was home sick, and then when I walked in yesterday she asked how I was feeling, and her eyes seemed to light up."

Considering how much he could see of the girl's eyes, I had to wonder if that might not be wishful thinking, but I said, "That's just great, Peter."

"I think so, too," he responded, almost blissfully.

Right then, I was tempted to tell him I knew the identity of the killer and fill him in on my plan. But I quickly vetoed the idea. Peter had enough to think about right now without that; better to just wait until the whole thing was over. He made the decision easy for me, too, hanging up without even asking how the investigation was coming. I think he'd given up on that weeks ago.

After Peter's call, I occupied myself with rehearsing, once again, what I'd say to the perp to set things in motion.

As soon as I got the green light from Tim, I'd phone on some pretext or other—there were a couple of options I was considering. Then I'd let it drop that pretty soon (Monday, if I had my way) the victim would no longer be getting round-the-clock protection; there'd just be someone stationed in the room from ten p.m. until six a.m., I'd say. Right after that, I'd go into this whole thing about how the precinct captain was claiming they couldn't afford to have someone guarding her all the time anymore and that he felt she'd be safe enough during the day anyway, with all those people running around the place.

According to my script, the murderer would respond with something like: "Isn't that kind of risky?"

"It sure is," I'd answer, "and Sergeant Fielding is as mad

as hell about it, but there's nothing he can do. The captain's carrying on that it could be years before she regains her memory—if she ever does—and that they don't have the budget or the manpower to keep three shifts on indefinitely."

Then I'd slip in the coup de grâce.

"That's pretty ironic, too," I'd remark.

"What do you mean?" the murderer would, of course, want to know.

"Oh, I thought you might have heard about it," I'd reply. "The other day, she seemed to remember something. I don't know just what it was. It wasn't much, I understand; nothing to do with the shootings, anyway. The captain wasn't impressed enough to change his mind, but the doctors feel she could really be on her way."

Now, with the victim possibly on the brink of regaining her memory, the perp would *have* to make a move—and right away. Monday, I'd bet. I had the time nailed down, too—sort of. Even with the victim unprotected, the killer wouldn't be rash enough to try anything during the day. So the attack would probably occur at night between eight-thirty, when visiting hours were over, and ten, when there would supposedly be a man coming on duty. There was, though, an outside chance it would take place early Monday or Tuesday morning, right after the guard presumably ended his shift. But I considered that less likely. With the hospital staff busy with the morning routine, there'd be a lot more activity at that hour.

Of course, I cautioned myself, I'd have to make sure that all this garbage I'd be spewing seemed to come out naturally, in conversation, so the perp would have no inkling this was a setup.

To tell the truth, though, I really wasn't too worried about that. While I wouldn't say that Meryl or Glenn had cause for an anxiety attack, when it came right down to it, I wasn't a bad little actress. I *was* in my high-school drama club, you know.

Besides, even if I didn't come off as absolutely convincing, if there was even the slightest possibility I was telling the truth, could the killer afford to let the surviving twin survive much longer?

Chapter 33

I can't tell you how many times since my meeting with Fielding that I started to dial his number, only to force myself to put down the phone. When he finally called on Friday morning, I literally had one foot out of the door. I ran back and picked up just in time to beat out the answering machine.

"Sorry for the delay," he said. "The lieutenant dragged his ass getting to the captain. Anyway, I got good news and bad news for you."

Uh-oh. "Give me the bad news first," I instructed, my mouth instantly drying up on me again.

"I can't. It won't work that way. The good news is the captain gave us the green light."

"Terrific!" Then, apprehensively: "Okay, so what's the bad news?"

"We'll have to put the operation on hold for a little while, that's all, mostly because we're shorthanded down at the precinct right now. One guy's on vacation, two others are out sick, and a policewoman went to the hospital yesterday with a fractured rib. Besides, everything will have to be coordinated with the hospital administration people and the DA's office, and the captain wants to make sure everyone'll be available so we can finalize things. Figure we'll have the go-ahead by the middle of next week or the following Monday, the latest."

"Damn!"

"Look, hotshot, you wouldn't want anything to go wrong would you? It all has to be worked out so every contingency's covered."

"Yes, but—"

"And anyway, I thought you only took this case to find out if your client's fiancée was dead or alive. And there's a good chance you'll have your answer on Monday when that jewelry woman gets back from wherever the hell she's been for so long. So concentrate on that in the meantime, why don't you? I'll talk to you as soon as I get the word. Okay?"

I managed a grudging okay. What choice did I have?

Being one of the most impatient people I know, I did not take the postponement of my plan in particularly good grace. So I wasn't exactly Little Mary Sunshine around the office that day. In fact, at eleven o'clock or so, Jackie suggested I shut my door so no one else would have to be subjected to me. I went along, since the only person who deserved to come within a hundred feet of me just then was Will Fitzgerald, and he was on vacation. (And speaking of Fitzgerald, did I mention that according to office dish he was definitely on his way out? Something to do with a client's wife and an elevator, I heard. Which is another one of those good news/bad news things. I mean—like any true Scorpio—I would have enjoyed his troubles a whole lot more if I could have contributed a little something to them.)

At any rate, by late afternoon, my mood had improved considerably. After all, it was just over a week, at the outside, until we'd finally have our killer. Besides, as Fielding said, in three days Charlotte Bromley would be back. And I was feeling pretty optimistic about her ability to tell us who that ring belonged to.

Three more days and we'll know, I kept repeating to myself. *Only three more days....*

Chapter 34

I called Ellen late Friday night and somehow performed the almost impossible feat of keeping my mouth shut about solving the case. I was reserving that for when I saw her in person. And not only because I knew she'd be bombarding me with a million questions, either, but—and I admit this was the main reason—because, after all the grief, I felt entitled to do a little showing off at this point. Which, of course, is a lot more effective face-to-face—especially when you've got the world's best audience.

"There are four absolutely gorgeous veal chops in my freezer," I said enticingly. "So if you don't have anything better to do tomorrow night, how about coming over for dinner?"

"Oh, I wish I could, but I already made plans with Ginger—you know, in my building? I'm meeting her after work, and we're going to grab some deli and take in a movie. Why don't you join us?"

I can't tell you how let down I felt. Or how hard I tried not to show it. "Thanks, but I think I may finally keep a promise to myself and do a wash. My laundry doesn't even fit in the hamper anymore; if I ignore it much longer, it could take over the whole apartment."

"I can make it Sunday," Ellen offered.

Well, on Sunday I was the one with the plans. So it was finally decided that Ellen would come over on Monday night after work. And when I thought about it, I realized that—as eager as I was to give her my news—Monday was actually a better idea, anyway. By then, there was a good chance Charlotte Bromley would have helped us unravel the mystery of the twins' identities.

The way things worked out, though, I had more to tell Ellen on Monday than I could possibly have imagined.

And for that, I could thank my friend Pat Martucci's libido.

*   *   *

All of Saturday morning, I was on edge. Due, I'm sure, to anxiety about both my plot for trapping the killer and Bromley's homecoming. At a little after twelve, I forced myself to get out of the apartment.

In spite of attempting to resist the temptation every inch of the way, I managed to wind up on a bus headed in the direction of Bloomingdale's. With my luck, they were having this absolutely wonderful sale on shoes there, and I picked up a beautiful pair of brown leather pumps—which I really *did* need—for a rock-bottom price. Which led to my paying an outrageous amount for the only bag in the whole place that even came close to matching them.

Well, I'd blown so much money already, I might just as well go all the way. So I capped off the day by treating myself to dinner at a French restaurant not far from the store, where I indulged in all of my favorite things: escargot, Caesar salad, duck à l'orange with wild rice, broccoli with hollandaise sauce, and a truly unforgettable chocolate mousse. I left there maybe five pounds heavier and more than sixty dollars lighter.

In bed that night, I kept tossing and turning. I couldn't stop thinking about the meeting with Bromley and what she might be able to tell us about the ring. I finally put on the television around two, but all I could find at that hour were infomercials. I fell asleep a long time afterward in the middle of the one where you're practically guaranteed you'll become a millionaire selling real estate by following a few simple steps. . . .

The next morning, I was really dragged out. But I'd promised my neighbor Harriet I'd go shopping with her on the Lower East Side that day. Her nephew was getting married in only two weeks, and she hadn't been able to find a dress yet. There was really no way I could disappoint her.

Now, Harriet Gould and I have lived across the hall from each other for three years. And I like her a lot. But she's the world's most infuriating shopper. At the second store we walked into, she found a pale turquoise crepe she loved. It was a great fit, and she couldn't get over how *absolutely perfect* it would be for the wedding. "But I can't just grab the very first thing I put on," she decided.

Three and a half hours, a dozen dresses, and four very tired feet later, she came to the realization that she *had* to have the turquoise crepe. So we rushed back to the store, only to find the dress had been sold. They would *try* to special order it on Monday, they told my tearful friend.

It was three-thirty when I finally got home, and by then I was barely ambulatory. Pat Martucci and I were supposed to be having dinner together that night, and I really didn't see how I'd be able to make it. But after an hour's nap followed by a brisk shower (I know I would have dozed off and drowned if I'd attempted a bubble bath), I came more or less alive again.

We were to meet at the restaurant at 6:45. But at 6:15, just as I was buttoning my coat, the phone rang.

"You're going to kill me," Pat said.

"Why? What's up?"

"Ahhh, the thing is, I met the most *interesting* man yesterday—Paul Castle, his name is. He was visiting his sister, who lives in my building, and we started talking in the lobby, and then he asked for my number. Anyway, we just hung up; he phoned to tell me a friend of his called a few minutes ago to offer him these two tickets to *Crazy for You* for tonight. And, well, he asked if I was free, and I said I was."

There was a brief pause for a change of tone before Pat added imploringly, "Don't be angry, Dez. I know it wasn't the right thing to do, but it just popped out. It isn't the show; you *know* that. I'd never break a date with you to go to a show. As a matter of fact, I saw *Crazy for You* with my ex a week after it opened, and I didn't even like it that much. Honestly. But what I *do* like is Paul Castle. And, uh, I can't seem to help it, I'm fuckin' mush when it comes to an attractive man." This was followed by a self-conscious little giggle, and then Pat asked in this cloying, kittenish voice that made me want to gag, "You mad at me?"

Well, considering how down in the dumps she'd been lately, I wouldn't have been much of a friend if I hadn't let her off the hook. I mean, for Pat to be without a man is almost like someone else being without food or water; there's really a serious question about how long she'd manage to survive.

"No, I'm not mad at you," I told her. "Actually, I had a pretty tiring day, so I'm probably better off just staying home and taking it easy."

"That's what I *thought*. I remembered your mentioning you had to go shopping with your friend today, so I figured you were probably exhausted anyway and that—"

I cut her short. Any minute now, she'd convince herself that concern for my well-being was her main reason for canceling. Which was where I got off. "Look, have a wonderful time," I said. "I'll talk to you tomorrow."

The fact is, it was really just as well Pat had made other plans. The thought of getting into my bathrobe and stretching out on the sofa was suddenly very appealing to me. I began unbuttoning my coat. But when I came to the last button, I stood there for a minute, thinking. *I wonder . . .*

A moment later, I walked over to the phone. I had my hand on the receiver, then pulled it away. Suppose I was right and the woman *was* home. If I called, I'd be giving her the opportunity to say she was too tired or too busy or too something else to see me. No, better to just take my chances and hop a cab over there.

I could picture Charlotte Bromley sitting at the kitchen table, sipping coffee, right now. After all, the message on the answering machine said she'd be back on the sixteenth—tomorrow. Well, I usually tell people I'll be home the day after *I'm* due to return, especially if there's a possibility I won't be getting in until late.

On the other hand, though, I was probably kidding myself—projecting my idiosyncrasy onto Bromley because I was so anxious for her to be there tonight. The message did specify the sixteenth, and that's probably just when she'd be coming back. So why schlep all the way downtown—especially when I was this tired? I mean, after waiting all these weeks, what was the big deal about waiting one more day? I undid the last coat button. I even got as far as slipping one arm out of its sleeve before changing my mind again.

It wasn't as if I had anything better to do, I thought with a smidgen of self-pity. And I was really dying to hear what she had to say. So why didn't I just go down there and see whether she was in or not? What did I have to lose? Determinedly, I put the arm back in the sleeve and redid the buttons.

Suddenly I was sure I'd find Bromley home and that she'd know about the ring.

I could feel it in my bones.

Chapter 35

The taxi dropped me off in front of a faded yellow brick apartment house. It was an old building and quite shabby. But the architecture, with its rounded corners, high double and triple windows, and imposing recessed entranceway, suggested that years back this must have been a pretty good address.

The night was unusually cold—more like February than mid-March—and I was shivering even more than usual when I entered the good-sized vestibule. For some reason, it popped into my head then that today was March fifteenth—the Ides of March. I shivered again. But this time it had nothing to do with the weather.

Just to the left of the door was the tenant listing. Bromley's entry was in black block letters engraved on a silver metal plate. It read c. BROMLEY, JEWELRY AS ART. I pushed the buzzer next to the nameplate and waited nervously. Nothing. I tried again. Still nothing. I was about to give up and leave when the door opened behind me and a chill wind rushed in, whipping my coat around my legs.

Turning around, I found myself staring into the face of the last person on earth I wanted to see.

"I have a gun in my pocket," the killer informed me in a low, even voice. "And I want you to stand here quietly; don't even move a muscle. If you do exactly what I tell you, you'll be fine."

Bullshit! I am in a whole lot of trouble, I thought, even as I dutifully obeyed the instructions. The perp was right beside me now, jamming something into my ribs. I didn't have to look down to know the gun was no longer in any pocket. (My own thirty-two, of course, was exactly where it would do me no good at all: in my bedroom at the bottom of a drawer.)

"Not a sound," I was told as the killer pressed one of the buzzers.

A man's hoarse voice came over the intercom. "Who is it?"

Another buzzer was pressed. This time, someone buzzed back.

Reaching in front of me, my captor opened the door to the once-grand lobby and shoved me inside. "Walk," was the softly spoken command. Now the fingers of one hand tightly gripped my arm, while the other hand pressed the gun—carefully concealed in the folds of my coat—firmly into my side.

I was steered around a corner. Down the hall, a middle-aged couple was just getting off the elevator. "Careful—and smile," the killer warned, jiggling the weapon for emphasis.

The couple was almost parallel with us now, smiling perfunctorily at me and my deadly companion. A jab of the gun was a reminder that I was expected to return the smile.

Putting all the fear in my heart into that one forced expression, I willed those two people to look at me—*really* look at me. But in a moment they had passed, and I heard the front door close firmly after them.

"Keep going," I was ordered. Now we were alone in the long, dimly lit hall, the only other signs of life a muted chorus of TVs and stereos emanating from behind the cold gray doors that lined the corridor on either side.

We came to the elevators, and I thought briefly that the killer—under the impression Bromley might be home—could be planning for the two of us to pay her a surprise visit. But, jerking the gun up and down again, the murderer nudged me forward.

I realized then that we were heading for the stairs. And I knew that once we reached the seclusion of the stairwell, I wouldn't have a worry in the world. Not in *this* world, anyway.

Suddenly, without even knowing I was going to do it, I stopped short. Picking up my foot, I brought the thin spiked heel—fortified by the not inconsiderable poundage behind it—crashing down on my captor's instep. The killer jumped back in pain, and I broke free, reversing direction and running toward the front door.

"Help!" I screeched in a voice that might have been heard on the moon.

Not one gray door opened—a sad testimony to the quality of big-city life in the nineties.

It's amazing how much ground even the most out-of-condition body can cover when fueled by terror. But the murderer had something to fear now, too—along with a body in much better shape than my own.

And then, when there was no more than a foot or so between us, I got my inspiration.

"Fire!" I screamed.

Immediately, a door flew open. And another. With the third, a large, heavyset man in an undershirt rushed out of his apartment, crashing into the two of us and knocking the gun to the floor.

There is something to be said for having a low center of gravity. I instantly regained my balance, and as my assailant bent down to retrieve the weapon, I aimed my foot at the obvious target. The well-placed kick sent the killer sprawling.

It was pandemonium by then, with more and more tenants pouring into the hall by the second. The killer was frantically scrambling for the gun now, amid cries of "What's going on?" and "Is there a fire or isn't there?" and "Is this some kind of a joke?"

Surrounded by people and with the weapon completely obscured from sight, there was really no alternative.

Springing to his feet and shoving everyone aside in a decidedly ungentlemanly, un-British manner, Eric Foster raced from the building.

Chapter 36

I was *that close* to fainting, but I couldn't spare the time. Quickly reaching into my handbag, I got out a handkerchief and, in the same motion, went down on all fours to take up the search Foster had been forced to abort.

I spotted the gun almost at once, but a high-heeled red slipper, a pair of running shoes, and the most beautiful black calf pumps (no doubt Italian) stood between the weapon and me. I rapped a few ankles with my knuckles, and, to the accompaniment of some indignant yelps, the obstacles were removed. Scooping up the gun in my handkerchief, I placed it carefully in my bag.

Now I could spare the time. So, heroine that I am, I promptly passed out cold.

Sputtering, I opened my eyes to a very earnest face just inches from my own. A man in his late twenties—thirty, at most—was kneeling beside me, waving a cotton pad doused with something pungent under my nostrils. He wore a bright-colored plaid scarf around his neck, and there was a stethoscope over the scarf. His face had the pinched look people get when they've just been out in the cold for a long time.

"How do you feel?" he asked anxiously.

"Okay," I coughed, pushing his hand with that lethal cotton pad away from my nose and struggling to sit up. He helped me into a seated position, while I tugged at my skirt, which had crawled up to somewhere in the vicinity of my most private parts. Embarrassed, I looked around. Only a few stragglers were left in the hall now, and they were gathered just a couple of feet away from me, staring curiously and speaking in hushed tones.

"Go back to your apartments, everybody, please," the

young man entreated. "There's no fire, and the lady's all right."

As soon as the small assemblage had dispersed, he said, "My neighbor told me he thought you were mugged."

"Not mugged, exactly. I'm a private investigator, and I ran into a suspect here who pulled a gun on me. And then, once it was all over," I admitted sheepishly, "I guess I fainted."

"I understand someone yelled 'fire' right before I came in. You?"

"Me."

"Good thinking," he remarked admiringly. And a moment later: "I wonder if anyone bothered to call the police."

"I'll take care of it." I was struggling to hoist myself up, but my caregiver cautioned me.

"Sit there for a minute until I get back; I just want to drop this off in my apartment." With that, he picked up the medical bag alongside me and shoved the stethoscope inside it. Then he retrieved the down jacket he'd evidently placed under my head and went loping down the hall.

He returned before I could even think about ignoring his decree. "Does anything hurt?" he asked.

"Uh-uh."

"Okay, then, easy now." Placing a firm hand under my elbow and an arm around my waist, he assisted me in— shakily—reaching my full five-foot-two-inch stature. "Would you like to come in and lie down for a while?" He was addressing me from an altitude of well over six feet, and it made me dizzy just looking up at him. "I'm a doctor," he added hastily.

I smiled to myself. I was tempted to say *So that's why you walk around with a stethoscope dangling from your neck,* but I censored the smart-ass remark. "Thanks, but I really *do* feel better now," I assured him. "Although I'd appreciate it if I could use your phone to report this."

"Of course." He practically bent himself in half to steady me as we walked down the hall to his apartment. And I was grateful. The truth was, I was still a little light-headed. Plus the side of my head was kind of sore (although I suppose it would have been a lot sorer if I hadn't passed out when it was only about nine inches off the floor).

As soon as we were in his apartment, the doctor steered

me over to a chair and brought me a portable phone. Then he retreated to the kitchen.

I dialed the precinct, but Fielding wasn't on duty, so I tried him at home. "Is Tim there, Jo Ann?" I asked when his wife answered. "It's Desiree Shapiro, and I'm sorry to have to bother him now, but it's urgent."

"What's urgent?" Tim asked genially less than a minute later. He always assumes I'm exaggerating.

I began filling him in on what had transpired that evening, skipping the details so I could get to the crucial point as quickly as possible: ". . . and when everyone rushed into the hall, Foster bolted. I knew you'd want to have him picked up right away." Only then did I pause for breath.

"Hold it a minute. Are *you* okay?" But once he was convinced I'd live, Fielding sounded very much as if he wanted to kill me. "Do you really think that limey hump's hanging around the city waiting for the police to come calling on him? Not on your life! Not after you went hotfooting it down there and got him to attack you in front of a building full of witnesses."

(I like *that;* I *got* him to attack me.) "Look, I—"

"Why'd you have to go running over there, anyway? Even if Bromley *had* come back a day earlier, what was so urgent you couldn't have held out until tomorrow?"

"It's just that I—"

"You can bet the son of a bitch is on his way to God knows where right this minute, thanks to you!"

"But he turned in his passport," I protested, finally managing to break in.

"You ever heard of California? Or *New Jersey*?"

With those words, our conversation was abruptly concluded.

A moment later, the doctor returned to the living room. "I just put up a pot of coffee. How about it?" he offered. Which is when—now that I was feeling a little more like myself again—I took note for the first time of how pleasant-looking he was.

"Thanks, but I really have to be getting home. You've been very nice." *Very, very* nice. I sneaked a glance at that crucial finger on his left hand. No ring! "I wouldn't object to a glass of water, though," I told him.

I insisted on accompanying him to the kitchen, which was absolutely spotless. Either the doctor here was a real Mr.

Clean or nobody ever cooked in this place. And he didn't look like an obsessive to me. Then, when he opened the refrigerator for the ice water, I took a quick peek inside. A carton of milk, a couple of cans of Coke, a six-pack of beer, a plate of fruit, and, next to it, something that was probably a wedge of cheese. And that was about all. Not a single container of yogurt or cottage cheese. There was no cohabitating in *this* refrigerator, I decided happily. What I had standing in front of me at that very moment was one of the rarest creatures not yet in captivity: a young, single male who was considerate, attractive, and a doctor, to boot! My sister-in-law, Margot, was going to bless me for this— maybe even if he didn't turn out to be Jewish.

A few minutes later, the doctor and I were standing outside the building. He'd offered to see me home, and when I convinced him it wasn't necessary, he insisted on putting me in a taxi. I extended my hand. "I want to thank you for everything, Dr. . . . ?"

"Lynton, Mike Lynton," he said, taking the hand. "I'm sorry; I should have introduced myself before. But you were out cold when we first met," he reminded me with a grin. "And then I seem to have forgotten about it."

"Is that L-i-n-t-o-n?"

"L-y-n-t-o-n," he corrected.

"Are you in the phone book?"

He misunderstood the reason for the question. "Yes, but I'm not in private practice yet; I have another year of residency."

"That's okay; I already have a pretty good doctor."

Just then, a taxi came barreling around the corner, screeching to a stop in front of us.

Mike Lynton helped me inside. As the cab shot away from the curb, I realized I'd forgotten the same thing he had. I stuck my head out of the open window and yelled, "Mine's Desiree Shapiro!"

Chapter 37

The aftershock occurred when I was sitting in that taxi. All of a sudden, I began to tremble. And by the time I got out of the cab, I was shaking so hard my legs almost gave out before I reached the elevator.

That night, I went to bed without even taking off my makeup, which is something I never—*ever*—do, no matter how tired I am. (What's more, I didn't even give a thought to how the stuff was clogging my pores.) I was so exhausted that I expected to fall right to sleep, but I lay there for hours, too keyed up to close my eyes. When I finally did drop off, sometime in the not-so-early morning, I had this awful nightmare. . . .

I was a little red fox, and I was playing all alone in this beautiful, tranquil meadow. And then, off in the distance, I saw a man. He was handsomely decked out in a red riding coat, black jodhpurs, and black riding boots, a black bowler sitting on top of his head. He began walking toward me, and when he drew near, I saw that the man was Eric Foster. Something in his slow, purposeful approach made me afraid, and I started to run through the grass. But *he* began running, too. And no matter how fast I went, he kept getting closer and closer.

Abruptly, everything changed, and I was in New York City. I can't tell you why I was so sure it was New York, because it was a strange, desolate place. There wasn't another soul around except for me (the little red fox) and—so far away I could barely make him out—Eric Foster.

Now Foster was chasing me up and down the deserted city streets. And before long he was gaining on me. I was terrified! My little paws began to sweat, and my heart was thumping like crazy. And then I felt an icy breath on the back of my neck, and I knew that I couldn't escape.

Suddenly a drainpipe materialized in front of me, and I

scurried inside. At last I was safe! But a moment later I heard this loud, rushing sound. I looked up in horror as an avalanche of water came pouring down the drainpipe, carrying me right along with it into the street and the clutches of my pursuer—who now wore the face of Tim Fielding!

Fielding's hands went around my throat, his strong fingers constricting my windpipe. I opened my mouth, gasping for breath. . . .

The jangling of the telephone released me from my misery. But I was having so much difficulty breathing, I could barely get out the hello.

"Desiree?"

"Yes," I wheezed.

"What's wrong?" Jackie asked sharply.

"Wrong?" I repeated densely. Then I realized where—and who—I was. I turned my head to look at the clock. It was almost ten-thirty. "I'm sorry, Jackie," I said, regaining my voice. "I had a pretty close call last night, and I didn't bother setting the alarm."

"What happened? Are you all right?" she demanded.

"I'm still a little shaky, that's all. I'll tell you everything tomorrow. I don't think I can make it in today."

"Are you *positive* you're all right?"

I had to assure her three times that I was not at death's door before she finally let me off the phone.

I got out of bed then, too fearful of winding up in the same dream again to consider going back to sleep. I was completely drenched and desperately in need of a shower. And I could use a couple of Tylenols, too; my head was even more achy now than it had been the night before.

As soon as I'd attended to these minor matters, I called Peter. "I have some news for you," I told his machine. "Call me as soon as you can."

It took two cups of coffee and a toasted English before I was ready to even think about facing Tim Fielding. And I only hoped he didn't shoot me on sight.

When I arrived at the precinct, Walter Corcoran was sitting on the edge of Fielding's desk, talking softly. He heard the click of my heels and looked up. "Well, well," he sneered, "if it isn't mother's little helper."

I pretended he was invisible. "Can I talk to you privately for a few minutes, Tim?" I asked.

Fielding lifted his head from the folder he'd started to busy himself with the moment Corcoran "greeted" me. His expression was so forbidding, I got this immediate mental replay of him choking the life out of the poor little red fox. "It's important," I put in quickly.

He gestured to the chair alongside his desk, then turned to his partner. "See you later, okay, Walt?" he said pointedly.

Corcoran shrugged. As he was walking away, he mumbled something (no doubt obscene) under his breath, which I was fortunate enough not to hear.

Fielding closed the folder. "Okay, what's on your mind?" He was scowling, and this little blue vein at his temple was jumping up and down. Now, although he *had* blown up at me once or twice before, it takes a lot to make Fielding genuinely angry. (I don't count that business with Peter, which was really an aberration.) But, anyway, I could see that right then he was livid. And I couldn't blame him.

"Anything happen with Foster?" I asked. A big mistake.

"I thought you were here to tell *me* something," he snapped, and the blue vein started jumping in double time.

"Right. I am," I assured him hastily. "I wanted you to—"

"Do you know where we caught up with that S.O.B.? At J.F.K.! With a ticket to Salt Lake City in his hand! Seven minutes more, and we would have been too late."

"Uh, did he confess?" I found the courage to ask.

"Oh, sure, the nice man told us everything," he responded in this soft, pleasant voice. Then, almost shouting: "Listen, the only thing that slimeball had to say when we collared him was five words: "I want to call my lawyer." I didn't dare point out that that was six words.

"There's a real good possibility we can't even tie in what happened last night with the attack on his sisters," he ranted on. "Chances are, all we can hang on him is this thing with you. Did anyone actually see him holding the gun on you?"

"I don't think so. The —"

"So when it comes right down to it, we may not be able to get him on anything more than simple assault!" Fielding shook his head in disgust before spitting out his conclusion. "And all because you couldn't wait a few lousy hours to find out what that Bromley woman had to say!"

"I'm sorry, Tim. It's just that—"

"I suppose you thought you'd do a better job of questioning her than we would."

"It's not that; it's just—"

"Well, from here on in, don't expect any help on your lousy cases from *this* department." He wasn't through yet. "I don't get you; you know that? Your plan was in the works, and we had a good shot—a *damned* good shot—at catching that rotten scumbag red-handed. Now we may never be able to nail him for what he did to those poor women."

He seemed to have wound down, so I opened my handbag. "I think maybe you can," I said, removing a handkerchief-wrapped item and placing it reverently on the desk.

Fielding let out a long, low whistle. "I'll be damned," he murmured, flipping back a corner of the handkerchief with a pencil and staring down at my peace offering.

"In all the excitement last night, Foster had to leave this behind. You hung up before I had a chance to tell you about it. Do you think it's the same gun he used on his sisters?"

Sticking the pencil in the trigger guard of the revolver, Fielding lifted the weapon carefully, peering at it as though hypnotized. "I wouldn't be a bit surprised," he said softly. "But we'll soon find out for sure."

I started to get up then, but he put out his arm to restrain me. "Look, Dez, I'm sorry I blew up at you today. I overreacted, I know. It's just that I can't stand the thought of that S.O.B. getting away with it." He favored me with a faint smile. "Now I owe you *two* lunches."

"You can leave it at one," I told him magnanimously. "This time, I deserved it."

"Yeah, you did—you do," he agreed, breaking into a full-fledged grin. But if this *is* the same gun, all is forgiven."

"Uh, Tim?"

"What?"

"Speaking of Bromley—"

"That was ten minutes ago. But, all right, what *about* Bromley?"

"Have you been able to reach her yet?"

"Jee-*sus*! You don't let up for a second!" he yelled, but this time it was in that mock-angry tone he'd been using with me ever since we first met. I felt comfortable then.

"Well ... uh ... have you?" I persisted—but cautiously.

"As a matter of fact, we've been trying her all morning and getting the same old taped message on the answering machine."

"Tim? One more thing ..."

"*Now* what?"

"You'll call as soon as the ballistics report comes in, won't you?"

"I guess I owe you *that*," my once again very good friend conceded.

Chapter 38

My four absolutely gorgeous veal chops remained in the freezer; I really wasn't up to preparing anything. Tonight, it would have to be dinner à la Ellen. In other words, Chinese takeout.

Since Ellen was coming over so late, I decided to order ahead of time, which I could do with no hesitation. The one thing in life I know with absolute certainty is my niece's favorite Chinese dishes.

She got to the apartment at a little after nine. "Something's wrong," she said as soon as she walked in.

Now, for the life of me, I still can't figure out how she arrived at that conclusion. I mean, all I did was open the damned door, for God's sake. And I'd seen to it that my hair was combed and then spritzed with its customary ton and a half of hair spray, and I'd spent at least fifteen minutes applying makeup. (After all, Ellen is a very sensitive person, and I didn't want to put her into trauma.) "What makes you say that?" I asked.

"I'm not exactly sure. You've got a kind of funny expression. Anyhow, I'm right, aren't I?"

"Well, I had some trouble last night, but I'm okay now." Just thinking about it made me queasy.

Ellen's skin immediately seemed to lose some of its pigment. "Tell me what happened," she demanded nervously.

"After we eat; otherwise I won't be able to swallow a bite. I'm really fine now," I assured her again.

She opened her mouth to protest, then changed her mind. And by the time she was out of her coat, the doorbell rang. Dinner was about to be served.

I can't tell you how much I enjoyed everything that night. The Peking spare ribs were almost burned to a cinder— just the way I like them. The egg rolls were crisp and greaseless. The fried rice was wonderfully tasty. The scal-

lops in black bean sauce were . . . well, "divine" might not
do them justice. And is there any higher praise I can give
the lemon chicken than to say it was the best I'd ever
eaten?

Ellen didn't seem quite as enamored of Ping Chow's fare
as I was. But it didn't even cross my mind at the time that
my perception of things might be directly related to my
recent near-fatal encounter. It stands to reason, though,
that food *would* taste a whole lot better if you'd just come
close to not being around to enjoy it ever again.

Anyway, once we'd finished our coffee and the Italian
pastries Ellen had brought (there's no law that says you
can't have coffee and Italian pastries with Chinese food,
you know), we went into the living room. And when we
were comfortably settled at either end of my newly reup-
holstered sofa, Ellen insisted on her explanation.

"I'll tell you about last night later; I have something else
to tell you first," I said almost offhandedly.

She looked at me questioningly.

"Eric Foster shot his sisters."

I'm never disappointed in Ellen's reaction to things; she
always gives you one hundred percent. "Nooo!" she
shrieked. "See? I knew you'd do it! How did you find out?"

"Well," I began, "let me preface everything by saying
that all along I was aware—just as you were, as I recall—
that the key to the crime was the bizarre way those poor
girls were shot. And I kept going through all these mental
gymnastics to try and make some sense out of it—including
coming up with the theory that Mary Ann played a prank
on the killer and pretended to be Meredith, which is the
kind of stuff the two of them used to pull as kids. Of
course, that was not only a real stretch but, from what I
know of the adult Mary Ann, not *her* at all. In other words,
I had my usual quota of dumb ideas."

"You always do that to yourself! Isn't it enough that you
came up with the truth *now*—before anyone else did?" my
loyal niece demanded hotly. Then, experiencing a brief moment of doubt, she said hesitantly, "You *were* the one to
solve it, weren't you?"

"Yes."

"I don't know why I asked that. Of course you were;
you *had* to be."

I forced myself to refrain from basking in the glow of

Ellen's admiration—at least for the time being. "At any rate," I went on, "the real reason for the disfigurement was a whole lot simpler. It was absolutely *essential* to Foster's motive. But, of course, I would never have pieced the whole thing together if I hadn't gone to the video store."

Ellen, as you can appreciate, looked hopelessly lost.

"Let me explain." I told her. . . .

"There wasn't anyone involved with this case who didn't lie to me for one reason or another," I said, approaching things more or less as I had with Fielding, but this time actually taking the pains to make sense. "Larry Shields lied about arguing with Meredith. And Lucille Collins lied to back him up. And Roger Hyer lied when he denied knowing Mary Ann was involved with someone else. Even my own client set himself up with a phony alibi. But Foster's lie was different from all the rest. *Because once it was uncovered, it put him directly at the scene of the crime.*"

I started clarifying the statement immediately. "Remember how I told you he seemed to know just which way to turn the day we both went up to the twins' apartment?"

"Of course," Ellen replied. "But that was because he'd gone there once before to surprise Mary Ann, wasn't it?"

I shook my head. "He never went to the apartment that time. It was a lie—and a lie that could only serve *one purpose:* to conceal when he'd *really* been up there before."

Ellen thought that over for a few seconds. "I see what you mean, Aunt Dez. But how did you find out he wasn't telling the truth?"

"Look, in October—when Foster claims to have made that visit of his—Meredith was in *Show Boat.* And she was playing *Julie.*" I emphasized the name to the point where I was almost shouting it. "But Foster said that when Meredith opened the door that night, he initially thought it was Mary Ann."

"So?"

"So, a while back, when I went to see Claire Jospehs—this childhood friend of the twins'—she talked about how dedicated an actress Meredith was. Even when she was a little girl playing *Annie,* Meredith refused to wear a wig; she dyed her hair and got a home perm. And then, not too long ago, when she was Joan of Arc—she *cut off* all her hair."

Ellen's face was completely blank.

"Evidently, you've never seen *Show Boat*."

"Once, when I was a kid, but I don't remember too much about it."

"Well, Julie was a *mulatto*."

"Ohhh, I get it. That means Meredith would have been a brunette at that time. Am I right?"

"It would have been totally out of character for her *not* to be."

"So Eric *couldn't* have mistaken her for Mary Ann."

"Not for a second."

"You are really something, you know?"

"Don't be too impressed," I protested modestly. "I didn't link up Foster's story and what Claire had told me for the longest time. And when I finally did, it was only because I came across *Raging Bull* in this video store."

"Raging Bull?"

"It was a movie, a biography, about this fighter—Jake LaMotta, his name is—and Robert De Niro gained I-don't-know-how-many pounds to play the part. And that's what made me remember about Meredith and how she approached her roles the same way."

Ellen nodded. Then, a minute or two later: "I have a question, though. Why would Foster even mention anything about Meredith being home that night?"

"That threw me in the beginning, too. But after I thought about it a while, I could see his reasoning. Mary Ann must have said something to him about Meredith's having to take a few days off from the show at that time. And by telling me she was home sick the night he supposedly went up there, he'd be lending credence to his story if I checked with anyone in the company. And, incidentally, I did—check, I mean. And he was right; it did make the lie more believable."

"A pretty fast thinker, wasn't he?"

"I'll give him that—although he evidently didn't think about that hair business. At any rate, once I realized Eric Foster had been lying through his teeth, I looked at everything a lot differently. And suddenly it all started to fall into place."

"You said a few minutes ago that it was *essential* for him to . . . uh . . . do that to their faces."

"That's right. You see, it has to do with Meredith's will. We haven't located it yet, but according to what Peter was told—and he does seem to be straight on this—Meredith left a will providing that if she died first, everything she had would go to her sister. But if Mary Ann predeceased her, Meredith's money would go to some AIDS foundation. I don't know if I mentioned this, but Meredith's husband—Garibaldi, his name was—died of AIDS."

"He died of *AIDS*?"

Ellen's tone immediately put me on the defensive. "I only found out about it recently myself, and then everything happened so fast these last few days." But Ellen's nose was definitely out of joint; I've accustomed her to expect to be filled in on these things. "I really *did* mean to tell you about it," I offered apologetically before hurrying on. "Anyway, since it doesn't look like Mary Ann made out a will, in the event of *her* death, her next of kin would inherit whatever it was she had."

"Eric," Ellen murmured.

"Eric. Or if Mary Ann died before her sister, Eric and Meredith. The thing is, though, Mary Ann didn't have a dime in her own right."

"I don't understand. I thought they were wealthy."

"*They* weren't wealthy; *Meredith* was wealthy. I assumed they both had money, because I somehow got the idea they'd inherited from their parents. The fact is, though, the parents died practically broke. The money came from Meredith's husband, who was an inventor. It seems he designed some kind of gadget and sold it for millions." Then, after a moment's pause—and sounding exactly like Peter—I added reluctantly, "I guess I didn't get around to telling you about that either, huh?"

"No, you *didn't*," Ellen responded, and the look she threw me did not warm my heart. But almost immediately her expression was more benign. (Unlike me, Ellen doesn't hold a grudge. But listen, she's a Libra.) "Go ahead," she urged, "continue."

"Well, Foster apparently wanted money badly. Very badly. And he must have known something about the terms of Meredith's will; he probably pumped Mary Ann like crazy. Anyhow, he realized that in order to get his greedy little paws on any of those Garibaldi bucks, Mary Ann would have to die—but *after* inheriting from her sister. In other words, he would have to get rid of Meredith first and then dispose of Mary Ann.

"So he goes to their apartment on a night when there's a good chance he can catch Meredith alone, and, a few hours later, have a shot at Mary Ann—literally. If you recall, Mary Ann had already told him she'd be meeting a friend for dinner and a movie that evening. But the way things worked out, at the last minute her appointment was canceled. So when Foster rings the doorbell, who opens the door? Mary Ann.

"I can take a few passes at what happened next. Mary Ann undoubtedly asks what he's doing there, and he thinks up something to satisfy her. Maybe he even tells her he's come hoping to make peace with Meredith. Whatever, they go into the living room; that much we're sure of. Now, I would guess that at this point Foster's intention is to wait until Meredith comes home, shoot her, and *then*—no doubt after keeping Mary Ann at gunpoint for a time—let her have it, too.

"Naturally, I don't know that for a fact—although it does seem to fit. But what I *do* know is that he can't postpone the murders. He has to make his move during this trip, because once Mary Ann gets married—and she's already engaged—he'll no longer be her next of kin. And this one night could be his only chance at both his sisters before he has to go back to England.

"But, at any rate, something forced his hand. And I'm willing to bet it was Chuck Springer. I—"

"Chuck Springer?" Ellen interjected.

"Their neighbor—the one who found them after they were shot. Maybe everything changed because Mary Ann mentioned that Springer had called and would be stopping by in a few minutes. Or maybe it was when Springer actually rang the doorbell. Either way, though, this Springer business tears it. It was bad enough finding the wrong sister home. But now there's this neighbor who wants to come in and maybe hang around for hours. Well, Foster certainly can't allow Mary Ann to let this guy into the apartment. So—"

"So he shoots her," Ellen finished for me in a voice barely above a whisper.

"That would be my guess. It's also possible, though, that he held a gun on her for a while, waiting for Meredith to show. But then she may have tried to make a break for it or something, and he had to do away with her ahead of schedule."

Ellen stuck out her hand. "Wait a minute. If Mary Ann had been shot at the time this neighbor guy was standing right outside the door, he would have heard something, wouldn't he?"

"Uh-uh. The building's soundproof. And for all I know, Foster could have used a silencer, besides."

"Okay. Sorry. You were saying?"

"Well, anyway, once he shoots Mary Ann, Foster's whole scheme is a shambles. But you were right before; this son of a bitch is a quick thinker. He comes up with what I think was a rather brilliant alternative." I paused to give the next words—which truly defined the strange circumstances of the tragedy—the impact they deserved:

"He's going to fix things so no one can *tell* who died first."

Ellen sat there stunned, her eyes widening in horror. Then she said softly, "So *that's* it. *That's* why they were both shot . . . the way they were."

"That's why. After he shot them initially, he very deliberately blasted them in the face so it would be impossible to figure out who was who."

"But did he really have to go through all that—disfiguring them, I mean?" Ellen wanted to know. "The medical examiner probably wouldn't have had any idea which of them was killed first, anyway. Every mystery book I've ever read says things like: 'The murder occurred between twelve and one' or 'between two and four.' "

"Well, we don't know just how far apart the shootings took place, of course, and there are a lot of different factors that come into play. But from what I've been told, a good pathologist can sometimes determine the time of death to within a half hour. Maybe Foster was aware of that. Or," I suggested in a lighter vein, "maybe he doesn't read murder mysteries."

For the first time since I'd been reconstructing the crime for her, something crossed Ellen's face that might have passed for a smile. It didn't last long. "I'm surprised he didn't examine them to make sure they were dead," she said with a little shiver.

"Obviously, the poor guy was too sensitive for that," I

responded caustically. "Or else he just made a mistake—two of them, in fact."

"I don't know *how* you figured everything out," Ellen enthused then.

"It was the only solution that tied in with all the facts. And," I admitted, "it really wasn't that hard to arrive at, once the *Showboat* thing sunk in and I started concentrating on Foster."

"That's what *you* say. Did I tell you before that I think you're a genius?" There was a kind of awe in Ellen's voice, and by all rights I should have felt uncomfortable. But I didn't. Even though her appraisal was completely out of whack with reality, it was still nice to hear—especially since I'd been having such frequent doubts about my ability lately.

"I don't think you ever used those exact words—not recently, anyhow," I responded, "so please feel free to rave on."

Ellen grinned. But in a few moments she was thoughtful again. "I was just wondering," she said. "Suppose Foster's plan—to confuse his sisters' identities, that is—had worked out the way he wanted it to. Would he have come into all of Meredith's money?"

"I was wondering the same thing. So, to satisfy my curiosity, I checked with Pat Sullivan—you know, one of the law partners in my office—to find out what he would legally have been entitled to. Pat says that under New York State law, if the twins were judged to have died simultaneously—which would be the case if no one could determined the order of their deaths—Foster would have inherited half of what they held as *joint tenants*. In other words, Mary Ann's share of the assets. And we know that the condo, at least, was in both names, so he would have gotten a nice little bundle when that was sold. Oh, I wish you could see that place, Ellen; it's really something," I gushed.

Ellen forced me to get back to business. "And the other half of the money from the apartment? That would have gone to an AIDS charity?"

"Uh-huh. According to this phantom will of Meredith's. But listen, Tim Fielding's been saying all along that those girls must have a lot of money around *somewhere*. And from what Peter told me last week about Garibaldi's success with his invention, I've got to believe that. Anyway, if it *does* turn out to be true, Mary Ann may be listed as a joint tenant on a lot of things. So Foster could actually have made a real killing." I was aware of my unfortunate choice of expression almost instantly. "Oh, geez," I muttered.

But Ellen was too caught up with finances to notice. "And if it was found that Mary Ann had actually died first, he wouldn't have gotten *anything*?

"Pat said that if any assets in both names stipulated the right of survivorship—which is very common—Meredith would automatically have inherited Mary Ann's share. So Foster would have been out of luck."

"What if the—what is it called—*wasn't* stipulated?"

"Right of survivorship. Well, I'm not positive, but I imagine, in that case, Foster would have had to split Mary Ann's share with Meredith's estate, since he and Meredith would both have been in line to inherit."

Ellen's forehead scrunched up, and she cocked her head to one side as though listening to her own thoughts. After a while, she asked, "Do you think Foster knew about all this stuff when he concocted the scheme to disfigure them?"

"Oh, I doubt it; I mean, why would he? It was a last-minute thing, remember? Most likely he was desperate after shooting Mary Ann, and he just figured it would be his best chance to glom onto at least a piece of those millions."

"Well, now we know the real reason the devoted brother wanted to hang around here; he was worried about his sister's regaining her memory."

"You'd better believe it," I said. "*And* he wanted the money. He probably couldn't wait to have another crack at her."

And that led right into my describing my own aborted scheme to catch Foster in the act.

And *that* led to my describing the terrifying fiasco that precluded it.

As I recounted the previous night's attack in every lurid detail, I watched the parade of expressions march across Ellen's face: surprise, apprehension, horror, and, ultimately, relief.

"I'm so glad you're all right," she said, close to tears when I finished. With that, she leaned across the sofa and grabbed me in a hug that was almost fatal. (Ellen, I discovered for the very first time, is a lot stronger than she looks.) "What made him follow you to that place, do you think?" she asked when she released me.

"Oh, I don't think he followed me at all," I replied as soon as I was breathing normally again. "I suppose he came to the same conclusion I did: that there was a good possibility Bromley was already back from her vacation. He must have heard she was a jewelry designer and that she might very likely have some knowledge about who owned the ring. Which means he had to get to her before she talked to the police."

"Do you think he actually went there to ... ?" It was left to me to fill in the rest.

"Look," I told her, "Foster had no idea whether that ring was found on the survivor or on the corpse. So he wasn't about to risk Bromley's giving out any information that could establish who it belonged to.

"Trust me, Ellen, if she'd been home last night and Foster had gotten in to see her, there's an excellent chance Charlotte Bromley would have been victim number three."

Chapter 39

"I'm sorry I didn't return your call yesterday," Peter was saying. "But I didn't check my machine all day. And then, after the hospital, I met one of the guys at the agency for a couple of drinks, and, well, it turned out to be more than a couple. I didn't get home until two."

I looked at the clock: six-thirty. No one seemed to give a damn about my beauty sleep.

"I didn't wake you, did I?"

"Don't worry about it," I answered, trying unsuccessfully to swallow a yawn.

"I guess I did," Peter murmured contritely. "I wouldn't have called so early, but your message said you had news and to get back to you as soon as I could."

That shook me awake. "We've got the killer."

There was a long pause. "Who was it?" Peter finally asked, his voice low and even. I could appreciate the effort it took to maintain that kind of control.

"Eric."

"That son of a bitch," he said in the same quiet tone. Another long pause. Then, his voice growing more forceful with every word, he demanded, "Why? Why did he do it?"

"Listen, it'll take a little while for me to explain. Why don't we get together later? I could meet you for lunch down by St. Catherine's."

"No, please. I'd like to hear now."

So for the next ten minutes I proceeded to give Peter an abbreviated version of the circumstances I'd laid out for Ellen the night before.

"Damn him to hell!" he growled when I was through. He had some questions after that, which he interspersed with a variety of impassioned, but minor-league, curses. Then we both fell silent. And when he spoke again, Peter's entire manner was changed. "Listen," he told me brightly, "you haven't heard *my* news yet. Mary Ann's doctors say she could have her first operation in maybe a couple of weeks."

"That's wonderful!" I responded.

He immediately proceeded to elaborate a bit on how pleased everyone was with the girl's progress. So, in spite of everything, the conversation ended on an upbeat note.

But I was only too conscious of the fact that my job wasn't done yet.

At a quarter of nine, and with almost zero optimism, I tried Charlotte Bromley. The recording still claimed she'd be back the day before. Then, on an impulse, I decided to stop off at her building before going to work that morning.

As soon as the taxi pulled up in front of the familiar yellow brick facade, I was reminded of my last visit here and my throat promptly closed up on me. And when I went to open the cab door, I was disgusted to note that my hand was shaking.

By the time I entered the vestibule, though, I'd succeeded in composing myself a little. Checking the directory, I found a listing that said R. SCHMIDT, SUPER and pressed the buzzer. There was no answer. I was trying to decide what to do next when I heard a slight commotion coming from the direction of the lobby. I turned to see a woman with a baby carriage struggling with the door. She was fighting to keep it from closing in her face, so I grabbed it while she maneuvered the carriage through. Then I let myself into the lobby.

If the super wasn't around, I could at least try talking to Bromley's neighbors.

Walking to the elevators, I had to pass the very spot where I'd so eloquently demonstrated the kind of mush I'm made of. And it came to me then that Sunday night was only the second time in my life I'd passed out like that, my first dead faint occurring during that earlier murder investigation of mine. And under not too dissimilar circumstances, too. Well, it looked like I was one of those women who swoon whenever things get really hairy. *And so what!* I thought defiantly.

The first thing I did when I got off on the seventh floor was to ring the bell to 7H—just in case. After satisfying myself that Bromley still wasn't home, I tried 7G, the apartment directly on the left. I had no luck there, either. So I pressed the buzzer to 7I.

"Who is it?" someone demanded even before I had a chance to take my finger from the bell. The voice sounded like it was coming from at least a million miles away.

"I'd like to ask you a couple of questions about your neighbor!" I shouted through the closed door.

"What?"

"I want to talk to you about Ms. Bromley!"

"Speak up!" The voice seemed a little closer.

"I'm Charlotte Bromley's cousin!" I yelled.

"Can't hear a damn thing through these damn doors," the voice muttered, and it was obvious that whoever it belonged to was now just on the other side of the door.

I heard five locks being turned then. A second or two later, the door opened a crack, and a man no taller than I am—most of him hidden from view—was peering out at me from behind a chain. "Oh, a redhead," he said in this frail, high-pitched voice, and I could feel him eying me up and down. "Always had a weakness for redheads. When they're natural, anyways. You natural?"

"Of course," I answered with a straight face.

"Yeah. Like I'm Ronald Colman," the man shot back, cackling. "Don't even mind if my redheads got a few extra pounds on 'em," he informed me magnanimously, removing the chain from the door and opening it wide.

Framed in the doorway was this wizened little fellow who must have been close to eighty and who was so thin that his bones jutted out. But he had a handsome thatch of pure white hair and the most mischievous gray-green eyes you've ever seen. "Now, who'd you say you was?" he asked. As soon as he spoke, I noticed he didn't have a tooth in his head.

"I'm Charlotte's cousin—Charlotte Bromley, your neighbor. She expected to be back from vacation yesterday, but she's still not home. I don't suppose you'd know anything about that."

He gave me this gummy, elfin grin. "Izzatso? Well, you don't suppose wrong, little girl." *Little girl?*

"Then you *do* know where she is?"

"Betcher life, I do. The super was up here fixin' my damn sink the other day, and he tells me she's gonna be stayin' at her sister's a little longer. She had to have her gallbladder taken out real sudden over there, and the doctors don't want her doin' no travelin' yet."

"Do you happen to have her sister's address?"

"Don't *you* have it? You're the one's the cousin; not me."

"Europe is all Charlotte told me," I answered, taking a clue from his using the words "over there." But the little man was looking at me skeptically. "I just got into town; I'm from the Midwest," I put in quickly. "And Charlotte didn't say too much to me on the phone—just that she was going to visit her sister." He still didn't appear to be satisfied, so I finished up with: "Uh . . . Myra moves around a lot." The name seemed to go pretty well with "Charlotte."

"Myra?"

"Her sister."

"Paris, France; that's where she is," he told me then, "but that's as much as I know."

"I don't imagine you'd have any idea when she's due home."

Another gleeful cackle. "Wrong again," the little man announced. "Super says she'll be comin' home next Monday—the twenty-third—if all's well. That's the day before my wife's birthday, may she rest in peace. She woulda been seventy-seven."

"Well, ummm, thank you very much, sir," I said, already moving away from the door. "I'll get in touch with her then."

"Leo," he said, stopping me in my tracks. "Name's Leo. What's yours, little girl?"

"Mary," I told him for no reason I can think of.

"Say, you got a husband, Mary?"

"I'm a widow."

"Listen, you like steak?" He didn't bother waiting for an answer. "My son—he's a butcher, see?—he brings me the best tenderloin you ever ate in your life. It's even worth puttin' in my damn dentures for; *that's* how good it is. You come up here one night, and I'll fix you a dinner'll bring tears to your eyes."

"I can't tell you how tempting that sounds, Leo. Only I'm afraid I just wouldn't be able to trust myself with you."

Moments later, when I was getting into the elevator, I could still hear Leo's merry cackle reverberating through the hall.

Chapter 40

"We nailed the bastard," the message from Fielding read.

"All *right*!" I exclaimed.

"Does that mean what I think it does?" Jackie asked, catching some of my excitement.

"You bet." I was grinning from ear to ear.

She jumped up from the chair and ran around her desk to give me a congratulatory hug. Like Ellen, Jackie turned out to be a hearty hugger. And since she's a pretty fair-sized woman, my nose ended up smashed against her shoulder somewhere, so I had a little trouble breathing. "I want to hear all about everything!" she informed me when she was (mercifully) done with displaying her enthusiasm.

"You will," I promised. "Just let me make a few phone calls."

I left Jackie and hurried down the hall, shrugging out of my coat along the way. As soon as I walked into my office, I dialed Fielding.

He was exuberant. "It's the same thirty-eight that was used on the twins, and it's got Foster's prints all over it!"

"Hallelujah! Has he been arraigned yet?"

"He certainly has. And he's being held without bail."

I was so hyped up by these latest developments, I couldn't wait to share them with Peter's machine, which took things in stride. After that, I phoned Ellen at Macy's, and she, of course, squealed in all the right places.

When I finally managed to calm down a little, I tried R. Schmidt, Charlotte Bromley's super. He was home now—and barely civil.

After quickly explaining who I was, I said how much I'd appreciate it if he could supply me with Bromley's Paris address.

"Listen, the police were here about the same thing yesterday. And I'll tell you what I tole them: I don't have no idea *where* she's stayin'."

"Wait!" I put in, just as he was—I know—about to hang up. "How did you hear she was operated on?"

"This friend a hers who dropped off the rent for her a couple weeks ago—four days late, a course—tole me about it. Not that it's any a your business." I was primed to ask another question, but R. Schmidt anticipated it. "And I don't know who this here friend is, how to get in touch with her, or even why I'm spendin' all this time yakkin' with you when I got so much work to do."

It was a little before five that afternoon when another piece of the puzzle fell into place.

I'd just been to the ladies' room prior to leaving for home, and when I got back to my desk, the message was sitting there. All that was written on it were the name Helen Ward and a phone number. For a minute or so, I drew a blank. Then I remembered: This was the girl Claire Josephs had suggested I get in touch with—that actress friend of Meredith's who'd been off shooting a movie in some jungle. I returned the call right away.

Helen Ward sounded very bright. And very concerned. She explained that she'd arrived home from Africa that day, and her roommate told her how anxious I was to talk to her. Ward, it seems, was every bit as anxious to talk to me. She'd just heard about the shootings, and she wanted to know how the survivor was and whether she'd been identified yet. I said the victim seemed to be improving but that so far we hadn't made any headway in establishing who she was.

"Well, I'm relieved that she's doing all right. My roommate saved yesterday's paper for me, but it didn't say too much about her condition."

"Yesterday's paper?" I hadn't looked at a newspaper in days.

"The *Post* had the story about the police picking Eric up at the airport Sunday night. I'm not surprised, you know—about Eric."

"You're not?"

"Not after what he pulled on Meredith's husband."

"Oh, you mean trying to buy him off."

"Who told you *that*?" Ward scoffed. "It was just the

opposite. Eric was after Gene, Meredith's husband—although he wasn't her husband at the time—to pay *him* off. Blackmail. Eric told Gene that if he didn't come across with twenty thousand pounds, he'd see to it he never married his sister."

I was completely thrown. "Are you *positive*?"

"Absolutely. Eric had some kind of connections with the police, and he found out Gene had been arrested for drug trafficking years back. Well, when Gene refused to fork over the money, Eric went ahead and tattled to the Fosters—which is what he'd been threatening to do—and the parents put Meredith under a lot of pressure to break off with the guy. It was really a terrible time for Meredith. Things were never the same between her and her parents after that, either. And then, of course, they died."

"That Eric is some piece of work, isn't he? You heard all this from Meredith herself?"

"That's right. It's not something she'd normally talk about, I'm sure, but one night I was crying to her about all this trouble I was having with my sister, who's the bitch of the Western world. Well, Meredith started commiserating with me about how awful it is when a sister or brother lets you down like that, and then she just opened up to me about Eric. I guess, in a way, my problems gave her an excuse for getting it off her chest."

Thanks to Helen Ward, things had suddenly become a lot clearer to me. I could certainly understand now why, even after all this time, Meredith would have nothing to do with her brother. But it *did* make me wonder about Mary Ann. After all, she'd given everyone—including her own fiancé—Eric's version of things.

It was almost as though Ward had been reading my thoughts. "From what Meredith told me," she said, "Mary Ann always refused to believe—on a conscious level, at any rate—that Eric could do anything like that. At first she tried convincing Meredith that Gene had lied to her about the blackmail, that drug addicts *always* lie. Then, after a while, she started insisting that it must have been some kind of misunderstanding, and she'd talk about how Eric was their only brother and how Meredith should at least let him have a chance to explain.

"But Meredith always felt that, deep down, Mary Ann *had* to realize there was no reason for Gene to make up a story like that. And besides, Eric's demanding money wasn't exactly out of character for him. When Meredith and Mary Ann were growing up, he used to hit their parents up for loans all the time. Loans that, of course, he never paid back. She—Meredith—was worried about how traumatized Mary Ann would be when one day she was forced to admit to herself what her brother was really like."

"Talk about misplaced loyalty, huh?" I remarked then.

"You said it. But tell me, what made him try to kill them, anyway?"

"It's sort of complicated, but he stood to come into a pretty nice inheritance if both his sisters died."

"*Naturally* it would be money. The man's a compulsive gambler—the horses, I think. Also, he's been living with some woman who has very expensive tastes."

This girl was full of information! It occurred to me at this point that there might be one more little piece where the rest had come from. I crossed my fingers. "Did you, by any chance, ever notice Meredith wearing a ring of some sort?"

"Uh-uh. Not that I can recall."

Well, I couldn't expect her to clear up *everything* for me, could I? Uncrossing my fingers, I thanked her for all her help.

"Shakira—my roommate—thought you'd probably want to see me."

"It won't be necessary," I responded, thanking her again. "You've already answered more questions than I'd ever have thought to ask."

Chapter 41

On the way home that night, I got to thinking about Meredith and Mary Ann—about everything, really. And all at once it dawned on me where the rest of Meredith's millions might be!

It was something that should have occurred to me long before, of course. And I tried to take some consolation from the fact that Fielding had been just as big a blockhead as I was. But it didn't help much.

Well, anyway, we were getting together tomorrow for that lunch he'd been promising me. I'd talk to him about my idea then.

Knowing that I love French food, Fielding had picked out this lovely—and quite pricey—French restaurant not far from my office. We'd both heard wonderful things about the place, and I was looking forward to a very special meal. Which, I guess you could say, is just what I got.

For starters, Tim ordered a bottle of cabernet sauvignon, and as soon as the waiter poured the wine and we made a little toast to ourselves, he leaned across the table. "I have some news for you, Dez."

"Good or bad?"

"I'd call it 'interesting.' I've been saving it for when I saw you."

"I have something to tell you, too," I informed him.

"Ladies first," he said with mock gallantry.

"Oh, no, after you; you're older."

"That's debatable," Fielding retorted. "But okay, I just thought you'd like to know that we've located Meredith's assets."

Well, how do you like that! I took a very large gulp of wine. "Where?"

"Of course, we were pretty slow-witted about this, I

admit," he digressed—and I could tell that he was going to milk this thing for all it was worth. "And by the way, when I say 'we,' Shapiro, you can feel free to include yourself." A protracted break in this little monologue to allow me to fully appreciate my own failings. "But anyway," he finally went on, "as soon as we found out Meredith was the only one with an inheritance, we started approaching the problem differently—concentrating on where *she* might have put the money instead of where *they* might have put it. Understand?" He sat back in his chair then, a smile on his face, and looked at me expectantly.

"I understand," I responded impatiently. "Go ahead."

"Garibaldi!" he proclaimed. "Meredith's *married* name was *Garibaldi*."

So I'd been right! Slow-witted—as Fielding had been kind enough to point out—but right. I could take at least a little satisfaction from that. "Everything was in Meredith's name alone?" I asked.

"Yup. More than two million dollars worth, in fact. Besides the condo, the only thing in both women's names was that checking account we came across earlier. Only, on that, Meredith used the name Foster like her sister—to keep things simpler, maybe."

"Congratulations, Tim. That was good work," I said graciously.

"What's important, though, is that we found the will," Fielding continued hurriedly, looking ill at ease. (He takes a lot better to insults than he does to compliments.) "That should help in prosecuting the slimeball."

"The will was made out under Garibaldi, too?"

"It was. And you were on the money—the woman used Leibowitz, Leibowitz and O'Donnell, just like you said. We ran into a little problem at first, though. She saw some pain-in-the-ass kid over there, and the pompous young jerk refused to talk to us. All we wanted him to do, for chrissakes, was verify what we already knew about the terms of the thing from Winters. But young Perry Mason was claiming privileged communication. Said if we gave him Meredith's death certificate he'd probate the will, and *then* we could find out what was in it. I came close to strangling the little puke!"

"Didn't you explain *why* you couldn't give him a death certificate?"

"What do *you* think? I finally told him he could . . . Well, forget what I told him. Anyhow, since we had probable cause, it wasn't too tough getting Judge Wilhelm to issue a search and seizure."

"What did you find out?"

"There were no surprises. It appears your client actually got something right, for a change."

I knew Fielding was riding me; nevertheless, I felt obligated to protest. "Wait just a damned minute—"

"Hey, I like Winters myself," he broke in, grinning. "But you gotta admit, he *is* kind of an airhead."

"He is not!" I responded heatedly. "He's very bright; it's just that he's been under so much strain with this thing."

Fielding put up his hand. "Okay, you win. But you mentioned before that *you* had something to tell *me*."

Now, my good friend was so pleased with himself for finally uncovering those missing assets that I didn't want to stomp on his ego by letting him know I'd reached the same conclusion he had (although he probably wouldn't have believed me, anyway). At any rate, I said I'd wait until after we ordered, since I figured that would buy me enough time to come up with some plausible substitute for the theory I'd intended discussing with him, which, of course, he'd already unknowingly confirmed. If you can follow that.

Fielding vetoed the postponement. "You might as well spill it now," he told me, scanning the room. "I don't see our waiter anywhere; I think the guy must have gone on sabbatical."

"It . . . uh . . . really wasn't anything important," I said, floundering for a moment. Then it occurred to me: *Helen Ward!* "But, on the other hand," I amended hastily, "it *was* kind of enlightening. . . ."

A few minutes after I quickly recapped what I'd learned from Ward, our waiter materialized and we ordered lunch.

It was a delightful meal. Although I did feel a *little* guilty enjoying it at Fielding's expense knowing that, once again, I planned to try and beat him to the punch with Bromley.

But, unwittingly, Fielding had his revenge.

Thanks to *his* damned restaurant, I woke up that night with a first-class case of food poisoning.

Chapter 42

I stayed home Thursday and Friday.

All of Thursday I remained within dashing distance of the bathroom. And except for a brief call to Jackie telling her I wouldn't be in (which I didn't *dare* forget to make), I avoided all human contact. The phone rang once late in the afternoon, but I couldn't even consider answering it, and the caller didn't leave a message. But who cared? I was too busy praying for death.

Friday was somewhat better. I made myself some tea and toast around eight, when I got up, and at a little after ten I heard from Peter.

He was jubilant. "Mary Ann remembered something last night! She said, 'The play; there was this play ...' That's all she said, but it's the first time she remembered *anything*. It's the proof you're always talking about, Desiree—the proof that she really *is* Mary Ann!"

I didn't know how to respond.

"Don't you *get* it? We *met* at a play! *That's* what she was referring to!"

What good would it have done to point out that those words could as easily have come from Meredith—more easily, in fact? I was sure the same thought had entered Peter's mind, too; only he'd shoved it right out again. And the thing is, I couldn't really blame him.

My next call, at a little before noon, was from Stuart. He'd tried me at the office just to say hello, he said, and Jackie told him about the food poisoning. "How are you feeling?" he asked solicitously.

I assured him that I was a lot better than yesterday.

"I've been meaning to call you, but I just haven't had a chance. I don't think I've ever been this busy in my life," he explained. "But listen, I've been thinking. Instead of going upstate to my brother's place when this madness is

over, it might not be a bad idea to take a week off and fly
down to Nassau or Bermuda—somewhere like that. What
do *you* think?"

I wasn't sure just how he meant that, so I answered cautiously. "Sounds good to me. And you'll certainly be able
to use a vacation after tax season."

"I wasn't just talking about me; I meant the two of us.
Hopefully, by that time you'll have everything wrapped up,
too. How's it coming, by the way?"

Knowing how busy he was, all I said was that things were
finally falling into place and I'd fill him in when I saw him.

He was apparently more than willing to settle for that.
"Well, how about it?" he asked then. "Think you could go
for a little R&R at some tropical island paradise?"

"I might be able to force myself."

He promised to pick up some travel folders as soon as
he could.

And I hung up happy.

Don't get me wrong. Stuart and I will never be more to
one another than good friends. But I'd been missing the
physical part of our relationship more and more lately—
slut that I am. Besides, think of all the calories I'd be burn-
ing off!

I fixed myself a light lunch after that. And a short while
later, inspired by thoughts of my liaison with Stuart, I decided to tackle this other matter I'd been meaning to see to.

Now, I don't know if I mentioned this before, but I'm
not really much of a telephone person. Sometimes I have
to psych myself up to make a normal business call. And
what I had in mind right then was a whole lot trickier.

You wouldn't believe how nervous I was just dialing that
number. The only thing that got me through it was the
almost certain conviction he wouldn't be home.

"Lynton," he announced, picking up on the first ring.

"This is Desiree Shapiro, Mike—the woman who spent
so much time at your feet last Sunday night, remember?"

That carefully rehearsed line brought the hoped-for response. "I remember," the young doctor answered,
chuckling.

I mentally rolled up my sleeves. For the past few days,
I'd really been agonizing over how to present my proposition without sounding like a terrible busybody. But I'd finally concluded that there was no way to *avoid* sounding

like a terrible busybody. So I just took a deep breath and said, "I hope you won't think I'm too forward, but ... uh ... I was wondering, do you have a girlfriend?" *There must have been a more tactful way to put that!*

A long pause. Then Lynton answered warily, "Well, I *do* see this one woman."

He really wasn't very convincing. And at that moment it occurred to me we might have a little glitch in communications here. "You don't think ... that is, I hope you realize I'm not asking for myself," I tittered.

"Oh, of course not," Lynton lied, an audible exhale betraying his relief.

With that clarified, I barreled ahead. "I have this lovely young niece," I told him, "and I just *know* you two would get along. Believe me, I wouldn't be making such a complete ass of myself if I weren't *positive* you'd hit it off."

"I'm sure your niece is great, but I never go out on blind dates." Then—in what was unmistakably a preface to terminating the call—he said quickly, "It was nice of you to think of me, though."

"But it doesn't have to be really blind," I said just as quickly. "I could send you a picture of Ellen. Ellen Kravitz is her name, by the way."

There was a smile in Lynton's voice now. "Thanks, but I'm really not—"

"A video?"

He laughed. "You don't give up, do you?"

"Look, what have you got to lose? Meet her for a drink or something. If you like each other, fine. If you don't, all you've wasted is about a half hour of your whole life."

A moment's hesitation. "I don't know. I—"

He never got a chance to finish what by now had withered to a halfhearted protest. I closed in for the kill. "Do you realize how many wonderful experiences you can miss out on by being overly cautious?"

"Well ..."

"She'll pay for her own drink. Hey, maybe I can even talk her into paying for yours."

"Okay, okay," he said laughing heartily at this point. "You can stop selling; I surrender. Let me have her number."

"You'll call her?"

"I'll call her. Scout's honor."

At nine-thirty that night I reached Ellen. I could hardly wait to fill her in on my coup.

She didn't exactly applaud my efforts. "You did *what*?" was how she put it. Then, on the very brink of tears: "I can just imagine what he thinks of me, having my aunt drum up dates for me that way! He's probably got me down as a total reject! What's next? Are you planning to stand on a street corner with a lasso?"

Now, while past experience wouldn't let me discount the possibility that Ellen might be a little embarrassed by my contacting Mike Lynton, past experience had also led me to believe she'd get over it in about three minutes. Apparently it was different this time. And what was worse, I had just accomplished the last thing in the world I'd intended: to further erode Ellen's already very eroded self-confidence.

I pointed out then that, if anything, Lynton might have the idea there was something weird about *me*—not her. After which I went on to rave about all of the young doctor's admirable qualities (and I did very well by him, too, considering our rather brief acquaintanceship).

"Look, he's not going to call; he said he would just to get rid of you. But even if he *does* call, I won't see him," my usually pliable niece stated firmly. "Not if I want to have any respect for myself at all."

That's pretty much how we left things. And afterward I spent a long time trying to justify my actions to myself.

There was nothing I wouldn't do for Ellen. I just wanted to see her meet someone she could care for; was that so wrong? Besides, I *had* to make up for Will Fitzgerald.

All right. So maybe I did get a little carried away, phoning someone I hardly knew like that. But my heart was certainly in the right place. The trouble was—I finally got around to conceding—my brains must have traveled south. Thanks to me, Ellen now felt like one of the ten most desperate women on the planet.

God! When would I learn to mind my own business?

I vowed then and there that I'd never *ever* meddle in her personal life again. Well, anyway, not for a long, long time.

Chapter 43

Ellen and I had never had words before—at least, not like this. And it was making me nuts. I considered giving her a call on Saturday morning, but I was afraid she's ream me out some more or even refuse to talk to me altogether—both of which, looking back, I realize would have been totally unlike her. But anyway, I took the cowardly route, persuading myself it would be better to wait a couple of days and give her a chance to cool off a little.

Pat Martucci phoned me late Saturday afternoon. Her latest, Peter Castle (yes, the guy with the *Crazy for You* tickets), was out of town for the day. And she wanted to know how I felt about dinner and a movie. I said I felt fine about it. I was getting pretty tired of staring at the four yellowing white walls.

When I got home from my night out with Pat, there was a message on the machine: "Aunt Dez? Please call me."

I checked my watch: twelve-fifteen. Damn! It was too late to get back to her tonight; I'd call first thing in the morning.

But on Sunday I wound up sleeping until after ten, and Ellen was already out of the apartment when I tried reaching her.

I wasn't able to get her that entire afternoon, and in the evening there was something else I had to give some thought to: Tomorrow was March 23.

Now, all along, I'd planned to check and see if Bromley came home on Sunday night—*tonight*—instead of on Monday the twenty-third, when she was actually scheduled to return. But suddenly I was having second thoughts. If I *did* find her in, there was a good chance—make that a near-certainty—Fielding would not take too kindly to it, particularly in view of last Sunday night's disaster. I could just picture his reaction if he and Corcoran showed up at the woman's apartment tomorrow and she said, "Oh, I just gave that information to this private detective, Desiree somebody-or-other." So, after making every effort to contact her this week, I was going to back off. Anyway, there really wasn't any need for me to talk to Bromley personally; I had no doubt Tim would relay whatever it was she had to say. Besides, I could always follow up myself if for some reason I felt I needed to.

Less than fifteen minutes after I'd become convinced of the wisdom of this decision, I picked up the phone and called her anyway. But her machine was still spewing out the same lie it had been repeating for more than a month now.

Well, I was getting a little hungry by then, so I whipped up one of my refrigerator omelets—this one with salami, scallions, mushrooms, green beans, and tomato. And after I'd finished eating, I gave Bromley another try.

"Hello," said the breathy, little-girl voice that had become so familiar to me by now. I couldn't believe it! Was this really Charlotte Bromley herself—in the flesh?

"Hello?" the voice said again.

"Ms. Bromley?" I finally got out.

"That's right; who's this?"

I proceeded carefully. It was possible that Charlotte Bromley, having been abroad for so long, might not even be aware of the tragedy. "My name is Desiree Shapiro," I told her. "I'm a private investigator, and I'd like to talk to you about the Foster twins. It would only take a few minutes."

"Mary Ann and Meredith? Why? Is something wrong?" she asked, uneasily.

"If I can just come over for a little while, I'll explain everything."

"Can't you tell me what it's about on the phone?"

"I don't think that would be a very good idea. Look, I wouldn't trouble you the day you got back from vacation if it wasn't important."

"All right," she agreed. "How soon can you get here?"

"In about an hour. Is that all right?"

"Okay, but please try to make it earlier if you can. I've had a long trip, and I haven't been feeling too well."

I promised to be there as quickly as I could.

I threw on my clothes, grabbed my wig, my hair spray,

and my cosmetic bag, and in fifteen minutes I was sitting in a taxi headed downtown.

Now, normally I would probably have been a basket case trying to anticipate what lay ahead in my meeting with Bromley. But not then. I was too busy struggling to put myself together under the kind of conditions you can't imagine—unless you've been in a New York City cab, that is.

Anyway, I had quite a ride that night. I don't think we missed one pothole between East Eighty-second and West Twentieth streets—and we were going at a clip worthy of the Indy 500. But even with my wig bouncing up and down in my lap, I somehow managed to make it look semipresentable. And then I cemented the results with the mandatory megadose of hair spray, which prompted the driver to turn almost completely around in his seat, narrowly missing a passing bus. "Hey, take it easy, lady," Moe Bittner admonished. "You trying to asphyxiate me? Didn't you ever hear of those aerosol pump things?"

I apologized meekly (in Bittner's hands, that taxi was an extremely dangerous weapon) and carefully adjusted the hairpiece to my head. Then I was ready to apply my makeup.

As soon as I started, Bittner took a corner on two wheels, and half a bottle of foundation spilled over into my lap. For my next trick, I managed to mascara my chin. (And to remove the stuff, I practically had to rub myself raw, too.) What's more, I never *did* get my lipstick on straight. I settled when some of it, at least, wound up below my nose.

On the positive side, though, we made good time—*unbelievably* good time, in fact.

When we stopped in front of Bromley's building, Moe Bittner swiveled around again, this time to critique my labors. "You need a little practice with that lipstick, lady. You should do like my wife does: Use a lip pencil for the outline, then take a brush and fill in the rest. You'll get a much neater result that way; you'll see."

A couple of minutes later, I was standing at the curb in a cloud of gas fumes. And that's when reality hit. It came to me in a rush that I might finally have the answer I'd been so anxious for.

And I was scared stiff.

*   *   *

Going up in the elevator, I finally acknowledged the one contingency I'd been banishing from my mind since I first heard about that amethyst ring: *Suppose the twin in the hospital had borrowed her sister's ring that day?*

Sisters did that sort of thing all the time, didn't they? What's more, if that was common practice with the twins, it would account for no one's being quite sure who the ring belonged to.

Stop it, I commanded myself. After all, it was highly unlikely Mary Ann would have put on her sister's ring when all she was doing was having dinner with a friend after work that night. Or that Meredith wore Mary Ann's ring just to go to rehearsal. And besides, the girls' tastes were really totally different.

By the time I rang Charlotte Bromley's doorbell, I'd managed, once again, to bury that extremely troublesome thought.

I estimated Bromley to be in her late thirties. Short and chunky, with long brown hair and a face like a full moon, she was dressed in a peasant-style blouse and a voluminous three-tiered cotton skirt that emphasized her far-from-svelte proportions. But the most noticeable thing about her was her accessories. I mean, the woman was a walking showcase of her handiwork. Decorating her person were a huge pair of triangular, shoulder-length earrings set with semiprecious stones, one very large silver pin, more than a half dozen rings, two armfuls of bangle bracelets in varying widths and styles, and three good-sized necklaces—one with a handsome bronze pendant that nestled between her ample breasts.

Bromley's artistic bent, however, did not extend to her living room, which was carelessly furnished with what looked like Salvation Army rejects. As soon as I'd settled myself into the almost springless sofa, she looked at me apprehensively. "You wanted to talk to me about Mary Ann and Meredith," she said in that breathy way of hers.

"Uh, yes. I'm afraid there's been a terrible tragedy, Ms. Bromley." She immediately sat up straighter, seeming to steel herself, as I proceeded to narrate, as delicately as I could, the events connected with the shootings that left one of her friends dead and the other critically wounded. By the time I was through, Charlotte Bromley's face was ashen and she was clutching at her chest. She opened her mouth as if struggling to say something, but no words came out. My first thought was that she was in the throes of a heart attack. But in a moment her hand was back in her lap and she was speaking normally—as normally as possible under the circumstances, that is.

"I was going to call Mary Ann in the morning and see if the three of us could have dinner one night next week," she told me in a hushed tone. "Oh, God, their own brother . . ." Her voice trailed off. "What kind of an animal *is* he?" she demanded softly an instant later, her eyes brimming with tears. "Mary Ann was always talking about him, too. And she wrote to him all the time. She even wrote to him about me—although what there was to tell, I have no idea. She said she wanted us to meet." Taking a tissue from the pocket of her skirt at this point, Bromley hastily dried her eyes. Then she seemed to remember something, and she looked at me, perplexed. "But just why did you want to see me?"

"There's a question I have to ask you. You were friendly with both sisters?"

"That's right. Although I met Mary Ann first, and I saw her a lot more often. She buys from me—for her shop; I design jewelry."

"That's why I'm here. I think you may be able to help us sort out their identities."

"Me? But how?"

"Did you ever notice either of them wearing a ring of any kind?"

"Oh, sure," Bromley answered promptly. "There's no way I could have *missed* it! Mary Ann had me design a ring for her a few months ago, and she used to wear it quite often."

At last! I was thrilled, *elated*! But, unfortunately, Bromley continued. "And Meredith liked the ring so much she had me make one up for her, too."

"Are you talking about *the same ring*?" There was now a definite possibility I might slash my wrists.

"That's right. Which was kind of unusual, I guess, because their tastes weren't at all alike. I suppose it was because the basic design was so simple that it worked for both of them."

God! Another dead end! I had never known such complete and utter frustration. No, it was more than frustration—*despair!*

And then Charlotte Bromley added one thing more:

"It was only the *stones* that were different. One had an amethyst and the other was set with a garnet."

"Which—"

But before I could put the question to her, the phone rang, and an apologetic Bromley jumped up and ran to the adjacent kitchen to answer it, assuring me she'd only be a minute. She was still talking many minutes later.

I was too edgy to just sit there. I got up and began pacing back and forth in front of the sofa. The kitchen was only a few yards away, so I could hear that little-girl voice quite clearly. And it was saying things like "I've got company, Ma; I'll call you back." And "We'll talk about it later." And about three times: "I've really gotta go now, Ma."

And then suddenly I didn't mind waiting for the call to end. In fact, the two of them could stay on that phone all year, for all I cared.

Because now I knew what Charlotte Bromley would be telling me.

Chapter 44

I was sitting on the sofa again by the time Bromley came back into the room. But by then I was no longer as confident as I'd been a few minutes earlier. I needed to hear her confirm my thoughts.

"I'm sorry, that was my mother," she murmured sheepishly, taking a seat. "And I haven't learned *yet* how to get her off the phone. You were just about to ask me which ring was which, weren't you?"

"I was, but I think I've already answered my own question. The garnet was Meredith's, wasn't it?"

"Why, yes, it was. How did you know?"

"I remember someone telling me that Meredith was actually born on January thirty-first—right before midnight. So, technically, the garnet would be her birthstone. While Mary Ann didn't come along until a few minutes later—on February first. And the birthstone for February is an amethyst." (The more trivial the fact, the more likely I am to know it.)

"That's *right*," Bromley said, impressed. "Meredith didn't care for amethysts. And since she once mentioned that she was really born in January, I suggested the garnet." And then the jeweler added poignantly, "Garnets are dark red, you know. And Meredith loved red."

I nodded, a picture of the girl's bedroom springing to mind.

"But just why are the rings so important?"

"Because the twin that's in St. Catherine's was wearing one of those rings the night she was brought in." I answered the question in Bromley's eyes. "The one with the amethyst; Mary Ann's the surviving sister." As soon as I said it, I asked to use the phone.

Peter had been waiting long enough to hear those words.

*   *   *

The instant I was back in my own apartment, I dialed Peter's number for the second time. (He hadn't been home when I tried him from Bromley's, and I hadn't left a message.)

When I heard the recorded "Hello, this is Peter ..." again, I wanted to scream. But, gritting my teeth in frustration, I said, "Peter, it's Desiree; call me the second you get in. I have news—the news you've been waiting for!"

I'd barely put down the receiver when I began to worry. Had I mentioned I had something *good* to tell him—something *wonderful,* really? I should have been clearer. So, neurotic that I am, I made another call. "It's me again, Peter. I don't think I told you; the news is *fantastic!*"

Waiting for Peter to get back to me, I put up some coffee I didn't really want. And because I hate to have just plain coffee, I paid a visit to the freezer for a little Macadamia Brittle to keep it company. Only a little, you understand; I was much too antsy to actually *enjoy* it. But it seemed to have a calming effect on me (at least, that's what I told myself), and I soon made a return trip to the freezer—this time, for a much more generous portion.

The telephone rang when the last spoonful of the Häagen-Dazs was en route to my mouth. I threw down the spoon. *Peter!* In my hurry to talk to him, I managed to trip over my own feet. Only the fortunate placement of the kitchen counter—which I grabbed on to just in time—kept me upright.

"Aunt Dez?" the hesitant voice said when I made it to the phone.

Ellen! I'd forgotten all about her! "Oh, Ellen, I'm so glad you called. I tried reaching you earlier."

"I just came in about a half hour ago. I spent the day in Great Neck at my friend Vickie's—this woman I work with. Listen, I feel just terrible about the way I acted Friday night."

"Why are *you* apologizing? I'm the one who was at fault. I can't tell you how sorry I am about embarrassing you like that."

"But you meant well. You only did it for me."

"I *did* mean well—you know I'd never hurt you intentionally. But I was really very stupid. If I promise to behave from now on, can we just forget it?"

"No, I'm afraid not."

"Why? What do you mean?"

Then came the giggle. "I just spoke to Mike Lynton."

"Oh?"

"He was very nice, too. We talked for about fifteen minutes, and I'm meeting him for drinks Wednesday night."

"Ellen!" I squealed. "I am *so* glad. I just *know* you're going to like each other."

"Well, even if we don't, it's worth a try."

"That's right. And listen, if it doesn't work out, I'll bet Peter knows some very—"

"Aunt Dez!"

"Not that I would ever approach him," I assured her hastily, "but if *he* should happen to say something to *me* . . ."

Things were certainly looking up, I decided after Ellen's news. She had a date with an absolutely darling young man, and you never knew where *that* could lead. (I caught myself picturing Mike Lynton's refrigerator filled to capacity with near-empty containers of Chinese food.) Even more important, Peter's fiancée was alive and, while not exactly well, hopefully on her way. As for me, I had that lovely vacation with Stuart to look forward to.

But I *did* wish I'd hear from Peter.

The call came at eleven-fifteen. "Peter!" I screeched. "It's Mary Ann! The girl in the hospital is Mary Ann!"

"Are you sure?" he asked cautiously.

"Absolutely! I saw Charlotte Bromley tonight. She told me Mary Ann was the one with the amethyst ring—the ring found on the survivor! And you can't get a better I.D. than that, since Bromley designed that ring for her in the first place!"

"Thank God!" And now he was so exuberant he could barely contain himself. "I really *did* know it all along," he told me, seeming to pick up speed with every word, "but sometimes I was afraid that maybe it was because I wanted it so badly. And then when Larry Shields was at the hospital yesterday, he acted like it was Meredith in that room. But maybe that's because *he* wanted it so badly. But anyhow, it's finally official. I can't even begin to thank you for all your help, Desiree."

All at once he started to sob—deep, wrenching sobs that expelled all the horror and fear he'd kept under rein for so long. A moment later, there I was, joining right in with him. (No one ever has to cry alone as long as I'm around.) I couldn't seem to stop myself, either. Even after Peter had pulled himself together, I was still at it.

I produced a fresh supply of tears when he reported that this morning Mary Ann remembered something about having tea in London when she was a child. And I kept right on going when he insisted he was taking me to the Four Seasons for dinner on Friday to celebrate. I didn't even let up when Peter apologized for making me cry in the first place.

"I really got you started, didn't I?" he said awkwardly. "I'm sorry I carried on like that. I guess it's because I've been keeping everything bottled up inside me and because I'm so happy it worked out the way it did."

"I know," I sniffled, finally managing to compose myself, "and *I've* been crying because I'm so happy for you. Anyway, I guess we'd both better go get some rest now."

"Good idea. I'll talk to you in the morning. And, well, thanks again, Desiree. For everything."

After we hung up, I sat there quietly for a while, thinking. And I found myself growing more and more depressed. Was it only minutes ago that I'd rejoiced with Peter over Mary Ann's survival? And just a couple of hours ago that I'd been feeling so good about *everything*? At that moment, it was hard to believe. Because, at that moment, I couldn't seem to shake from my mind the tragedy that was Meredith Foster.

And then I started blubbering all over again. But those tears had nothing to do with joy.

I recalled how Meredith had nursed her husband during his losing battle with AIDS. And how she'd always looked after her sister. And I reminded myself of her talent and her dedication to her craft. What sad irony that just when her career seemed to be taking off and there was a caring new man in her life, *this* had to happen to her.

And that's when, to my mortification, I became aware that I was actually angry with Mary Ann—and furious with myself for feeling that way. I mean, how dared I, when the poor thing was virtually shackled to a hospital bed, going through such hell!

Really, though, it blew my mind that she'd remained neutral in this feud between her sister and brother. How could she *not* have sided with Meredith, for God's sake!

But what was the matter with me, anyway? After all, things turned out just the way I'd wanted them to, hadn't they? Besides, from everything I'd been told, Mary Ann was a sweet, warm, friendly girl. And just look how ecstatic Peter was now!

Still, I couldn't help wondering—and not for the first time—if, in real life, there was any such thing as a truly happy ending.

Here's a preview of the
next exciting Desiree Shapiro
mystery novel,
*Murder Can Stunt
Your Growth*

I've never really been sure what a private investigator is supposed to look like. I mean, I realize that when most people think of a P.I., they picture some seedy character in a trench coat with a cigarette dangling from his mouth. Still, even when someone comes into my office *knowing* they'll be meeting with a woman, for some reason they never expect the woman to look like me.

It might have something to do with my lack of stature, since I never made it past the five-foot-two-inch mark on my mother's kitchen wall. Or maybe they're thrown by the glorious red hair (a product of Egyptian henna). Then again, it could be my weight that's getting me those open-mouthed stares. I have to admit to being just the other side of pleasingly plump (all right, *way* the other side). But what that—or any of these things—has to do with my being a bona fide, practicing member of my profession completely escapes me.

At any rate, as soon as my eleven a.m. appointment walked in that Thursday, she developed the same slack jaw I've been encountering since I first took out my investigator's license more than twenty years ago—when I was practically still teething, of course.

My elderly visitor was tiny—I doubt if she was even five feet tall—and elegantly turned out. Her salt-and-pepper hair was pulled back into a beautifully groomed chignon, and her carefully made up olive skin was almost devoid of lines. But what really struck me were her eyes; the woman had maybe the brightest blue eyes I'd ever seen. The one discordant note was that she had to rely on a cane—although a fairly decorative one—to make it the few feet from the doorway to my desk.

It was almost impossible to get a real fix on the woman's age. Taking a stab at it, though, I'd have put her at close to seventy, in spite of her youthful appearance. But that was mostly because of the cane and the fact that her hair had quite a bit more salt than pepper in it—neither of which, of course, really proves a thing. Anyway, I found out later, to my complete astonishment, that she was well over eighty.

I stood up quickly as she hooked the cane to the back of my desk, and then I hurried over to greet her.

"Mrs. Shapiro?" she asked tentatively, looking like she'd feel a lot more comfortable if I responded in the negative.

"Call me Desiree," I told her, extending my hand.

If she was disappointed, I had to give the woman credit, she hid it well. "Mrs. Corwin, Desiree. Mrs. Evelyn Corwin," she said softly, briefly grasping my outstretched hand with her own. Her icy touch jarred me.

"Let me have your coat," I offered.

As she undid the buttons of her expensive-looking navy cashmere reefer, I saw that her fingers were trembling badly.

I disposed of the coat on a hanger behind the door. Then I resumed my seat as she took the chair alongside my desk—the only other seating accommodation in my cigar box of an office. I noted that she was restricting herself to the very edge of the chair, as though poised for flight.

"What was it you wanted to see me about?" I asked gently, as she sat there nervously, hands fidgeting in the lap of her smart navy and green tweed suit. But even after an audible intake of breath and a few flicks of the tongue over her lower lip, the woman didn't seem able to find the words. I waited a minute or so before quietly prodding her again. "How can I help you, Mrs. Corwin?"

"I . . . uh . . . it's about my granddaughter who . . ." That was as much as she managed before choking up, the bright blue eyes overflowing with tears.

Now, after so many years of dealing with the anguish generated by philandering husbands, runaway kids, and missing cats and dogs (and even an errant pet boa constrictor one Christmas Eve)—to say nothing of the grief I encountered on my more recent forays into murder—you'd think I'd know how to handle that sort of thing, wouldn't you? Well, as it happens, I don't. And by this time, I have to assume there's very little hope I ever will. "Uh . . . can

I get you something?" I ventured awkwardly, as my elderly visitor, the tears streaming down her cheeks, rummaged around in her handbag, finally extracting a delicate lace handkerchief, which she immediately pressed into service. "Uh ... a glass of water?"

"Please," she whispered without lifting her head.

I rushed out of the office and hurried down the hall to the water fountain, grateful for the opportunity to leave the woman's unhappiness behind me, however briefly. When I returned, she was dabbing at her eyes. She all but grabbed the paper cup I handed her, quickly disposing of its contents.

"Thank you," she said when I held out my hand again for the empty cup. "I'm sorry. I was hoping I could get through this without losing control, but—" She broke off, embarrassed.

"It's okay; please don't apologize. Just take your time."

"I'm all right now."

"Just take your time," I repeated.

She looked at me gratefully. Then, flicking her tongue over her lower lip again, she said softly, "Mark Valentine advised me to talk to you. He thinks you might be able to help me."

Well, how do you like that! Valentine was an attorney I'd done a little work for on a child custody case years back. I was surprised he even remembered me, much less sent me a client. But you never know, do you? Of course, it really wasn't that long ago that I'd been involved with those two murder cases of mine, the first of which made all the papers here. (My picture even showed up on the third page of the New York *Post.*) Maybe those fifteen minutes of semi-fame were what had brought me to mind.

"I lost my granddaughter three weeks ago," Evelyn Corwin was telling me now in this hushed, faltering voice. "She died exactly a week before—before her tenth birthday."

"I'm so sorry," I responded gently. I mean, what can you say in the face of a tragedy like that?

"Yes, well, I guess that—that losing Catherine will get easier eventually. Anyhow, that's what they tell me. But the thing I can't live with is knowing that Catherine didn't just *die,* she was murdered. And I—"

"Murdered?" I blurted out before I could stop myself.

"It's true," Mrs. Corwin responded angrily. "And what's

particularly terrible is that no one believes me. But while I'm still around, I'm going to prove it. To all of them!" Her mouth began to quiver, and it looked very much as if she was about to have herself another cry.

"You've talked to the police, I suppose," I put in quickly.

"And talked. And talked some more. But according to them, Catherine's death was due to respiratory failure. *Acute* respiratory failure, they said it was. She had a bad case of asthma, you see, along with a congenital lung problem that I'd never even heard of until—until my poor Catherine had the misfortune to be born with it."

I looked at her questioningly.

"Something called alpha 1 anti-trypsin deficiency."

I shook my head to convey that I'd never heard of it, either. (And if I had, I probably wouldn't have been able to say it.)

She locked her eyes with my own then. "Look, Desiree, it's a known fact that my granddaughter's health wasn't the best. But that doesn't preclude her having been murdered, you know."

She did have a point there. But then again . . . Well, there was no avoiding it; I'd have to ask.

I had no idea how to phrase the question delicately, so I hemmed and hawed a lot, and it still sounded a lot harsher to my ears than I'd intended. "Your granddaughter— she wasn't— her condition wasn't— her illness, that is—I gather it wasn't considered terminal?"

There was a long pause before Mrs. Corwin replied, and when she did, she seemed to be choosing her words with care. "The doctor said that Catherine's life expectancy wasn't a long one. But, of course, she might still have had *years* ahead of her. And someone robbed her of those years. Besides"—and her voice was almost belligerent now—"with all that medical science can accomplish these days, they might even have been able to cure her eventually." I didn't respond immediately, so she challenged with: "Well, you never know, do you?"

I admitted that, no, you never did. Then I said, "I assume, though, that in light of her prognosis, you have a pretty good reason for believing Catherine's death wasn't the result of her illness."

Once again, Mrs. Corwin appeared to have difficulty responding. She looked down at her hands, which for the past few minutes had been more or less stationary in her lap. I followed her gaze. She was now viciously digging the beautifully manicured nails of her right hand into the soft, tender palm of her left. "I have a very good reason," she said finally, without raising her eyes. "It was the *second* attempt on Catherine's life. She herself told me just two weeks before her death that someone had deliberately tried to run her over. I didn't believe her then, just as no one believes *me* now. What is it they say: 'What goes around comes around'? At any rate, I kept insisting to her that the car must have been out of control—after all, who could possibly want to do something like that *deliberately*?—but Catherine was sure the driver was aiming straight at her." Evelyn Corwin shook her head slowly from side to side. "God! If only I'd listened. If only . . ."

With that, a fresh supply of tears came in a deluge, and hard-boiled P.I. that I am, I could feel my own eyes begin to sting. I warned myself I would kill me if I didn't manage to get a grip on my emotions.

"Would you like some more water? Or how about some coffee?" I suggested, feeling totally useless.

Unable to reply, the woman rejected both offers with a wave of her hand. It must have been at least three or four minutes before the final trickle of tears was wiped away.

"Do you feel up to continuing?" I asked then.

"I'd better be," she answered, with a game attempt at a smile.

"Good. Mrs. Corwin, can you think of any reason at all that someone might have wanted to harm your granddaughter?"

"It's completely beyond me," she admitted. Then she looked me full in the face, and her voice took on an authority that hadn't been there before. "But the fact is, someone *did* harm her, didn't they?"

"And you have no idea who it was."

"None at all," she confirmed.

"And Catherine? She didn't get a look at the person who almost ran her over?"

She shook her head. "It all happened so fast."

"What can you tell me about it?"

Mrs. Corwin sat back in her chair, evidently making up her mind at last that she'd be staying a while. "It was a Saturday morning, about eleven-thirty," she began. "Catherine and Terry—she was my granddaughter's nanny—were walking over to Central Park, which is only a few blocks from the house. They didn't get very far. As soon as they came to the corner—it happened." She shivered almost imperceptibly before going on. "Catherine had hold of Terry's hand. The light was in their favor, and they were just about to cross the street. Catherine stepped off the curb first, and suddenly, this car came barreling around the corner, heading straight for her. Terry just froze. But my granddaughter saved her *own* life—she jumped back just in time." There was a momentary look of pride on Evelyn Corwin's face. Then it was gone, and the face was blank. "The car kept right on going," she finished bitterly.

"I don't suppose your granddaughter told you the make of the car? Or the color?"

"I'm afraid not. Catherine doesn't—*didn't*—really know anything about cars. All she said was that it was a dark color—black, she thought—and that it was big. But I have no idea what she would have considered big. And I didn't bother to press her at the time, because I was so sure she was mistaken—about the thing being deliberate, I mean."

"How about the nanny?"

"Terry? She wasn't able to tell us any more than Catherine did. She just kept repeating over and over that a car almost ran Catherine down, and that she—Terry, that is—didn't even react. She was very hard on herself about that."

"But Terry didn't get the idea that it was on purpose?"

"Oh, no! She thought maybe the driver was drunk or on drugs or something. It never occurred to her that it might have been anything intentional." And then, sighing, "It never occurred to any of us. Donna attributed Catherine's version of what happened to the fact that she spent so much time watching all those crime programs on television."

"Donna is . . . ?"

"My daughter-in-law. Catherine's mother. Silly of me," she added sheepishly. "I should have mentioned that, shouldn't I?"

"And your son—what did he think?"

"My son died of a heart attack six months ago," Mrs. Corwin answered evenly. *Well, this woman had certainly had her share!* I opened my mouth to commiserate, but before I had a chance, she murmured, "I keep wondering if things would have been different if Clark were still with us. Maybe *he* wouldn't have doubted her. Maybe he— Oh, I don't know."

"Did anyone report the incident to the police?"

Mrs. Corwin shook her head slowly. Then, in a voice thick with regret: "I wish we had. I *did* consider it at the time. But there was really no harm done, you see, so I— so *we* just decided to forget it.

"Let me ask you this. How many people were aware that Catherine would be going to the park that day?"

"Everybody who knew her well, I suppose. She and Terry always walked over to Central Park on Saturday when the weather was nice. If Catherine was feeling up to it, that is. And then they'd go out and have lunch somewhere like Rumpelmayer's. Catherine *loved* Rumpelmayer's."

I smiled. What kid didn't love Rumpelmayer's? (And some of us older kids don't exactly have an aversion to those sinful ice cream concoctions of theirs, either.)

"Unfortunately," Mrs. Corwin said then, "the day Catherine died, it was nasty out. The weather report predicted rain—incorrectly, of course—but, anyway, Donna thought it would be best if Catherine stayed at home. Particularly since she'd had a little upset stomach the night before."

"Tell me about that day. What exactly happened?"

"The housekeeper found my granddaughter dead on the library floor; *that's* what happened."

"This was two weeks after the incident with the car?"

"Exactly two weeks."

"I'd like you to fill me in on what took place before the housekeeper discovered your granddaughter's—before the housekeeper discovered your granddaughter. Whatever you can tell me."

The dark, carefully penciled eyebrows shot up, wrinkling the smooth forehead. "Let's see.... Catherine had been in her room all morning, reading or maybe watching some television. Then at a little after twelve, she came downstairs. Luisa—she's the housekeeper—was just about to start cleaning the library when Catherine walked in and said she was hungry. Well, Luisa was so happy to hear it, she went right into the kitchen to prepare lunch. My granddaughter was not the world's best eater," the old woman explained with a poignant smile.

"Catherine didn't go to the kitchen with the house-keeper?"

"No. She went into the library to read."

"What happened then?"

"Well, as soon as Luisa opened up the refrigerator, she saw that, since breakfast, someone had finished up the last of the milk. So she had to run out to the store to pick up another carton. She was back in fifteen or twenty minutes, and then as soon as she had lunch on the table, she went to call Catherine into the kitchen. She found her on the library floor, and it was—and she was—" Mrs. Corwin stopped and took a deep breath. A moment later she resumed her narrative in a surprisingly level voice. (I noticed, though, that her nails were digging into her palm again.) "Luisa dialed 9-1-1, and the emergency people were there within minutes. But it was too late. It was probably already too late when she—when she found the body."

"And the police say your granddaughter died of acute respiratory failure; is that right?"

"That's what they *say*."

"Let me ask you this. Aside from that business about the car, do you have any other reason to believe that Catherine was murdered?"

"I certainly do. For one thing, one of the chairs was overturned. And a lamp was broken, too. It certainly looked as if a struggle had taken place in that room."

"What did the police have to say about that?"

"They believe that Catherine had this asthma attack, and they think the furniture must have been knocked over when she was trying to get to the telephone to summon help. There's a phone on one of the end tables in the room; it has a buzzer system that connects to various parts of the house." A shake of the head. "They *believe*, they *think*," Evelyn Corwin reiterated with disgust. "Very scientific, isn't it?" She looked at me piercingly then. "All right. Now, tell me. What do *you* think?"

I tried hard to be diplomatic. "Look, Mrs. Corwin," I said, "I can see why, because of that near miss with the car, you might have come to the conclusion that there was something sinister about your granddaughter's death. And I can understand your feeling guilty about having doubted her. But honestly, from what you've told me, this whole thing was just a terrible coincidence. There's absolutely no reason to believe Catherine died of anything but her illness."

"Oh, yes there is," Evelyn Corwin insisted, her small chin jutting out stubbornly, the bright blue eyes glaring at me defiantly.

"I really don't—"

"Catherine kept *saying* that someone tried to kill her, and two weeks later she was dead. I wouldn't call that a coincidence." She leaned toward me, and the words came out slowly, emphatically: *"I'd call it murder."*